The Final Dream

The
Final
Dream

Wendy Pulford

Matador
9 Priory Business Park,
Wistow Road, Kibworth Beauchamp,
Leicestershire. LE8 0RX
Tel: 0116 279 2299
Email: books@troubador.co.uk
Web: www.troubador.co.uk/matador
Twitter: @matadorbooks

ISBN 978 1800465 039

British Library Cataloguing in Publication Data.
A catalogue record for this book is available from the British Library.

Printed and bound in Great Britain by 4edge Limited
Typeset in 11pt Adobe Caslon Pro by Troubador Publishing Ltd, Leicester, UK

Matador is an imprint of Troubador Publishing Ltd

My thanks once again to all family and friends who have supported me throughout this latest endeavour.

Chapter One

Haiti – March 2010

Rose McKenna pushed back the strands of long dark hair threatening to escape from the tight knot at the nape of her neck. It was hot and humid inside the small dispensary and she longed for the chance of a breath of fresh air. However, ignoring the discomfort, she continued to restock the plastic containers with the appropriate drugs from the boxes stored on shelves around her. Glancing at the fob watch pinned to her disposable apron, she noted her scheduled relief was overdue, and managed a smile. Gwenny lived in a world where time was an unnecessary nuisance, except in dire circumstances, and Rose considered it might soon prove to be one of those. If Gwenny delayed their handover any longer she might miss her flight out tonight... and she couldn't wait to escape.

At that moment her friend bounced into the room. 'Yes, I know I'm late Rosie, but I couldn't find my glasses.' Almost helpless without them for any close work, it didn't stop Gwenny from misplacing this vital tool on an almost hourly basis. 'Oh, you sweetie, you needn't have started restocking, that should be my job. You've just done your shift, and you'll be missing your plane if you're not careful.'

Rose stepped away from the table, stripping off her disposable gloves and apron. 'It's all yours, Gwenny. I just thought it might be wise to be ready if any emergency cropped up.'

Running a hand through her mop of blonde curls the new arrival pointed outside. 'It looks as if we might be busy tonight.'

Glancing out through the open door, Rose saw a line of mainly women, children and the elderly already forming up outside. Many of them had that lost and dazed look, with which she was only too familiar from her experiences in other parts of this war-torn and environmentally damaged world.

'However much we do, it never gets any better, does it. I feel bad about leaving you all but...'

Her eye was caught by a pleasant-looking man of medium height with light brown hair, who was in animated discussion with one of the local Haitian representatives. She was overwhelmed by a seesaw of emotion; attraction and remembered intimacy fading into anger, the depth of which she still could not fathom.

Gwenny touched her arm. 'He'll be gone in a month. You could always stay on. MSF needs someone like you too badly.'

Rose turned away, her dark eyes shadowed, and reached for her jacket. 'No Gwenny, it's for the best. The sooner I get away from Dr Max Stevens the better I'll like it.'

'One thing's for sure, Rosie, I'll make his last month here as awkward as I can, the louse!'

Her face breaking into a fond smile, Rose wrapped her arms around this amazing new friend. 'It would almost be worth staying to watch. Thanks, Gwenny, for everything. You've been a brick.'

Seeing that the two men had now moved away, Rose stepped outside into the comparatively fresher air. Gwenny's voice came floating after her. 'Go find yourself a rich, handsome, sexy man, and have a ball; then break his heart for a change.'

*

As her flight gained its cruising height Rose relaxed back into the seat, trying to turn her thoughts away from the ravaged country below. After the earthquake struck, the humanitarian effort had been enormous. A fluent French speaker, she had been working at a clinic in Paris but, as many times before, had offered her services to Médecins sans Frontières, who were only too glad to make use of her experience.

Max had been among the other members of her group. He was a thirty-two-year-old South African. They soon came to admire their respective professional skills and began to coincide any off-duty time, where possible, and found their mutual respect turning into something warmer, leading, even in their difficult surroundings, to a physical relationship. They spoke together about plans for the future, and it seemed so right, both of them combining their medical expertise in a new venture. Then one day she had been in his office and an errant breeze had blown papers onto the floor. Picking them up, she noticed a handwritten letter in an obviously feminine hand, with the signature 'Diane' surrounded by kisses. Max had spoken of his lack of family and she began to have a bad feeling. She was so transfixed by the signature the letter was still in her hand when he came through the door. Even now, she could feel the hurt slicing through her as he haltingly explained that Diane was the reason why he had left South Africa. She had been a long-time girlfriend since college, but they had both decided on a break to make sure of their feelings. The letter had made it plain that Diane was waiting for him to return and he now realised that it was the same for him. His words about valuing their time together under difficult circumstances and never meaning to hurt her passed through her mind without registering – until later, when the tears came, and Gwenny found her.

Was there something wrong with her to have relationships ending this way? She was an intelligent, grown woman, and had been told she had inherited her ancestral dark Irish beauty. Paulo had called her his "dark princess". He had been an Italian diplomat at the embassy in Paris when she first met him at an MSF fundraising evening. They had been a couple for nearly six months when he took her to Italy to visit his home and she immediately became aware of a problem. He came from an aristocratic Italian family, and it was obvious that his formidable grandmother took an instant dislike to her, making it plain that her grandson would make a better marriage with her own choice. Speaking to Paulo about it, expecting him to dismiss the matter out of hand as not important, she noticed he evaded any answer, and although they remained together for another month or so she knew there would be no future for them. His posting back to Rome, hastened she was sure by his grandmother's influence, assisted in a civilised end to their association.

Tearfully explaining the situation to her mother on a visit back to Ireland, she had received merely a philosophical shrug and general words of comfort. Maureen McKenna's pragmatic viewpoint, however, was probably based on the situation with her own husband. When Patrick McKenna had ended his career as an oil tanker captain, he announced his wish to settle in Australia and spend time tracing the families of McKenna ancestors who had also settled in that country; not all of them at their own choosing. Maureen had travelled the world with him during his career but now preferred to settle in the old family house in Ireland and expand her love of gardening. It was an amicable, if unconventional situation, but it seemed to work.

Rose often wondered if she had inherited a restless streak from her father, as, when qualified, she had sought nursing work in many parts of the world. Now, with her thirtieth birthday and two failed love affairs behind her she needed to reassess what she wanted out of life. For a start, she had decided to terminate her association with MSF. The clinic in Paris had left her theatre sister position open for her, but she would work her notice and leave. Returning to Ireland immediately was not an option. She could almost see her mother rolling her eyes heavenwards, lamenting yet again her daughter's poor choices. No, she would

4

go to London and see Aunt Moira, her mother's twin sister. It was possible Uncle Henry might have a temporary job for her in his plush clinic. A little bit of pampering for once in easier working conditions might be just what she needed.

*

England – June 2010

The shrill note of fear in the young voice finally broke through Simon Deveraux's mind-numbing tiredness.

'Daddy! Daddy!'

Struggling to raise himself on one elbow, Simon forced his eyes open, and attempted to focus on the small shape outlined in the pale wash of light from the open bedroom door.

'Joanna, how many times have I told you not to burst into my bedroom without permission. What on earth is wrong!' At that moment, a bright flash of lightning lit up the room, sharp enough to penetrate the closed blinds, followed by a loud clap of thunder. Another cry from the child confirmed why he had been awakened. His voice, harsh with frustration, cut through the outside noises. 'For goodness sake, I've explained to you about thunderstorms. Now go back to your room and go to sleep.'

'Please Daddy, can't I stay with you?'

'No!' His reply was instant and emphatic. 'Go back to your own room.' Then he sighed, and added, 'I'll... I'll be along there in a moment.'

As he watched the small shape retreat into the corridor he slumped back on the bed and groaned, annoyed at being woken, but even more so at his thoughtless reaction to the child's obvious distress. Everyone in the household knew of Joanna's fear of thunderstorms and always did what they could to allay those fears. On this occasion, however, he was just too tired – tiredness brought on by weeks of exhausting worldwide travel and meetings.

Struggling out of bed, he padded through into his bathroom to retrieve a towelling robe. Wrapping it around his naked body, he walked back through the bedroom and out onto the curved galleried landing which overlooked the wide hallway. Another flash of lightning illuminated the staircase and area below, chasing away the dark shadows lingering in the corners, but only for a moment, and then darkness descended again. Further along the landing the door to Joanna's bedroom stood wide open, with muted light spilling out onto the deep red carpet, thick enough to muffle any footsteps, especially his bare feet. He stood in the doorway for a moment. Joanna was sitting on her bed, fingers in ears and eyes screwed shut. Even allowing for the fraught situation, he found the sight faintly amusing.

He looked around the room, wincing as his eyes took in the sea of pink, now mandatory for young girls, he'd been assured. This was the first time he had seen the new decorations, a penance extracted from him for missing her sixth birthday, fog-bound in Europe.

Crossing over to the window he made sure the curtains were fully closed. 'Time for you to be back in bed, young lady. The storm's passing and you'll be asleep again in no time.' Turning back, he saw she had heard and obeyed him, her dark hair standing out against the pink bedclothes.

'Why didn't you go to Mrs Horton? She was closer than me, and how did you know I was back anyway?'

'I heard Mr Gilmore talking about you, and don't you remember, Daddy, Mrs Horton is still not well.'

He did remember then. Margaret Horton had looked after Joanna since she was a baby, but she had now run into health problems. As a gesture of his appreciation for her years of diligent service he had paid for private health care, but recovery from her necessary operation was not going well. He could see a potential problem looming – likewise the house. Woodhayes was old and becoming difficult to run in this modern age. It was, however, near Joanna's school and within an acceptable commute to the City.

'Daddy, please read me a story.'

Before, in similar situations, he had calmed her to sleep by reading to her – but not every time, and this was one of them.

'No story Joanna. It's time for sleep. Now close your eyes. I'll stay here for a while.'

He sat down on the twin single bed, a recent installation after the redecoration, having been informed, with dire warning, that sleepovers were the next inevitable milestone in the life of a young girl. He felt something uncomfortable beneath him and found he was sitting on a rather moth-eaten rabbit with long floppy ears.

'I see you left Mr Floppy to fend for himself during the storm. That wasn't very nice.'

'Oh Daddy…' a yawn punctuated the words, muffled by the covers, 'I'm getting too old for him now.'

Those few words hit home. Yes, she was growing up, and he knew that in so doing, further complications would arise. He looked over at the now sleeping child and his mind replayed a vivid flashback of the last argument between his father and himself on the subject. He remembered only too well his father's final warning.

'Simon, you're a fool, storing up trouble for yourself the like of which you cannot imagine, and you might come to regret your decision.'

*

He still failed to understand just how badly his instinct, normally sharp and intuitive, had let him down all those years ago. From the start, his fledgling financial business had thrived, exceeding even his expectations. He considered this success had vindicated his decision to study economics and not law and join his father's firm as expected; a decision which had not been well received. He found he enjoyed the finely judged cut and thrust of big business finance, albeit at times taking risks which could have collapsed his whole enterprise. At first this had been the fun of it for him, but with the growth of Orion Investments there had come a responsibility for those who worked for him worldwide. To that end, although still remaining in total charge, he now employed legal and financial managers, who were a backstop to rein in his, sometimes, impetuous nature.

Had that been the problem? Had Olivia been the one impetuous decision that went wrong? At the time it had seemed such a perfect idea.

He had first met Olivia Sanchez at one of those obligatory cocktail parties on the opening of... something or other. She was beautiful and stylish, a former model, but now working for one of the top fashion magazines. It was inevitable that their association became more personal, and soon after they became lovers, he proposed marriage, considering that she would be an asset in the necessary social side of his business. She was bright company, always part of a crowd, although, he now recalled, this was something he had later come to resent. She had demanded that she keep on working, despite his assurances that it was not necessary. Their city-centre apartment became either a party base for all the socially aspiring jet set or covered in tissue-filled boxes containing the next season's "must haves", which Olivia assured him in her position were paramount.

She was never keen on accompanying him on his business trips abroad, unless it was within a stone's throw of Paris or Milan, places she frequented often anyway; therefore, their interaction became limited. As time went on, he began to think they ought to consider starting a family with a proper house somewhere, rather than in the continual smart set party base of the London flat. Although the subject had never been discussed between them at any time, he had assumed this was the normal evolution of a marriage. However, when he had suggested the idea during one rare holiday together in the South of France, it was rebuffed with a ferocity he had not expected.

So life had returned to their normal sporadic meetings, until the day, a month or two later, when Olivia had confessed to him that she was pregnant. He could remember his feeling of amazement and then pleasure at this news. Her subsequent statement, therefore, that she would be seeking a termination, had shocked him. He could not understand her contemplating this course of action and attempted to reason with her, until he finally lost his temper.

'For God's sake, Olivia, you can't do something like this, as long as there are no health risks. I have a part in this decision as well, you know, and I won't let you do this to our child.'

She had then become hysterical and begged him to agree. She said she had never wanted a child and all that went with it. She loved her job and her way of life. She became so distraught he began to worry about her state of health and when she was calmer suggested they both saw a physician to discuss the matter. In the end there was no termination – but the pregnancy frustrated her every day and the relationship between them became worse. After Joanna arrived, he thought matters might improve, but Olivia was emphatic in informing him that, as she had done her part, it was now up to him to employ someone to care for the child – and so Margaret Horton came into the household.

Then a few months later the first of a succession of blows rocked his world... and now each day was a constant reminder, continuing to fuel the anger still inside him.

Chapter Two

Late down for breakfast the next morning, he found Joanna already seated at the table, neat in her school uniform. The recommendation of Carlton House School came from the principal of Joanna's day nursery and, after making his own enquiries, Simon had sought an interview with the headmistress, Harriet Freeman. She had impressed him, not only with her views on the role of teaching within the framework of preparing young girls for life's challenges ahead, but also with her own personal degree of integrity. He immediately made the decision to be honest with her about his confidential circumstances. At first, he had sensed wariness in her attitude, but finally she asked for time to consider the matter, promising to get back to him within a day or two. Her final agreement was a relief, and led him to confirm his purchase of Woodhayes, and the employment of household staff.

So far everything appeared to be working out well and, after a shaky start, Joanna's schoolwork had improved enormously over the last few months. Spying the occupant of one of the chairs at the table, he commented, 'I see Mr Floppy is back in your good books.'

Joanna glanced up at him from her cereal bowl and, in a voice older than her six years, informed him, 'Miss Watson says we should always value good friends.'

'Ah, I see. Miss Watson again.' With a slight smile he helped himself to some toast. 'That lady seems to be a paragon of virtue.'

Interested now, Joanna put down her spoon and looked at him, her head on one side. 'What's a para...thingy... of... whatever you said?'

'It's PARAGON.' He spelt out each letter. 'A paragon of virtue is a – well, I tell you what, why don't you find out for yourself what it means.' He'd used this idea several times before as a way to increase her vocabulary. He wrote the words down on a scrap of paper torn from a newspaper lying on the table, and in a dry tone added, 'I'm sure Miss Watson would approve.'

This Miss Watson and her comments had peppered Joanna's conversation for several weeks now. He had formed the impression she was a new employee, assisting the existing Year One/Two teacher who was still recovering from a bout of illness. Whatever the circumstances, Joanna's schoolwork had certainly shown a marked improvement.

'I look forward to meeting this good lady at the Parents Evening on Friday.'

'Oh no! Do you really have to go, Daddy?'

'It seems I'm free and I need to discuss some matters with Miss Freeman anyway. Now, if you're ready I must get moving. I've an early meeting today.'

*

The summer shower rattled against his office windows, but the sun was already coming out from behind the clouds as Simon watched the mist of rain sweep away to the west.

His companion was collecting together the pile of papers on the table in front of him and glanced up. 'Well, I think Brandt will fold. There's no way they are ready to play with the partners they seem interested in.'

'I'm not so sure, Charles. There's steel – literally – behind some of the ideas they have.'

'They could also decide to try their luck elsewhere if they consider your terms are too harsh.'

Simon turned away from the window and studied his chief legal adviser. Charles McDonald was nearly fifteen years older and had been with him from the early days when he had sought independent legal advice. They worked well together, and Simon had come to trust his usually sound reasoning. However, he erred on the side of caution, which sometimes sat at odds with Simon's own inclinations. But, after all, that was exactly why he held the position he did.

'Dieter has some good figures buried under a lot of uncertainties. I'm sure he can do better, and I want to give him the chance to flesh the whole concept out a bit more and then we'll have another look at it. Give him a call at the hotel Charles, will you and tell him that. I need to see some improvement and then I'm happy to talk some more. If he seems a bit frosty, perhaps we could suggest we go over to Germany and see him.'

'OK, but I'll need a lot more persuading about them.'

Simon turned back from his desk and grinned at him. 'You usually do!'

At the other end of the room the door opened, and a blonde head appeared.

'Your guardian dragon's missing, showing out your visitors, so I thought I'd sneak in. That woman's worse than a crocodile with toothache.'

The Australian twang was very evident, but the other men knew it was only put on for effect and for those who didn't know better. It disguised a university education and military career of excellence, and a very sharp mind. But, as Charles McDonald had once made the tongue-in-cheek remark, 'it was a pity that all of the effort had taken place in the back of beyond'. This good-natured jibe had been met by its intended recipient with the unperturbed serene countenance of one used to such remarks.

'As you appear to have summoned up the courage to make

a frontal attack, we'd better do the decent thing and offer you sanctuary – so come in.'

Simon liked Jack Fletcher but also admitted to looking upon him as a necessary evil. He was his security adviser, both from an IT perspective and also with regard to the company's dedicated connections in various parts of the world, some of them in what could be volatile places.

'Thought I'd drop in and see if you'd read my Rio report. After that little bit of trouble, I've been looking into other potential associates.' Fletcher lowered himself into a seat opposite McDonald and eyed the whisky decanter on the table between them. 'Oiling the wheels of commerce, I see,' and promptly helped himself to a small glass.

McDonald glanced up at Simon and then shook his head and leant back in his chair. 'I suppose it's because you think we're frightened of your macho muscle that you think you can get away with that.'

'No way mate, that one over there has had my backside on the floor before now.' Fletcher waved his glass towards Simon. 'Got to teach him how to look after himself somehow if he wants to parade around naked.'

With an impatient sigh Simon turned and sat down at his desk. 'If that's all you've come to see me about, apart from sampling my whisky, save your breath. You know my views on protection heavies. I just don't want all that extra clutter. What would anyone think they can get from me anyway? I hardly know my own bank account numbers, let alone anything to do with clients. You made sure of that with all your encryption ideas.' He looked over at his security chief with an impatient blue gaze.

Fletcher wasn't backing down.

'The size of your bank account might give someone an interest in any female companion – and by that, I mean Miss Joanna.' His face bore a decidedly wide smirk as he glanced at McDonald, who finally caught on to his meaning, and suppressed his own smile.

Simon cast a dark glare at them.

'I've told you before, Jack, the security in place at the school looks OK to me, and otherwise, if Joanna's not at Woodhayes she's out with either Frank Gilmore, my father or myself. It's one reason why I don't parade around all the society hotspots if I can help it.'

'Not saying you don't do what I suggested to you, but it's still a risk. Some parts of the world have a long reach these days. Why don't you let me have a look at the situation again and we can have another chinwag?'

'Fine, fine – if it will get you out of my office and away from my whisky.' A tiny smile curved Simon's mouth. 'Anyway, you'd better go before Susan returns.'

A look of horror crossed Fletcher's face and he leapt to his feet and downed the rest of his whisky. 'Christ, I'd forgotten about her.' He moved to the door and peered out, then let out a sigh of relief. 'OK, I'm off. Read the Rio report and let me know, and I'll be back to you on the other situation.' He disappeared.

Simon looked over at McDonald, the slight smile still evident. 'I forgot to mention to him Susan's in HR for a while, interviewing a new staff member.' He then stood and picked up his briefcase, selecting one or two files and placing them inside. 'Right, I'm off, too. I have the joy of a Parents Evening at Joanna's school to face tonight. I'll take these files and see if I get any time to go through them. I want to have another look at that Colombian matter. Susan says Grainger's been on to her a couple of times about it.'

'After all that nonsense with de Santos, I'd have thought you would want to stay away from South America, at the moment.'

Simon made his way over to the door. 'I'm not keen, but I haven't made up my mind yet, Charles. Don't forget to ring Dieter.'

*

The two men sitting at the corner table of a bistro on the other side of town were like chalk and cheese. One was dark and swarthy, middle-aged but not overweight, and in fact the business suit only just concealed a highly developed muscular frame. The fact that it did conceal something which most businessmen did not normally carry with them was not lost on his companion. He was younger, mid-thirties, as fair as the other man was dark.

'So, you have no further news for us, Mr Grainger.' The voice was as dark as the expression.

Mark Grainger ran a hand through his blonde hair and tried to control any tremor.

'It's as I told you. I've been pressing for a decision, but nothing so far. He's been abroad and he's now busy catching up, according to his secretary. That's why he's one of the best around, everyone wants to do business with him. Miguel, if you want a quick decision choose someone with more time. I can find someone else for you.'

Grainger's companion eyed him without expression. 'It is as I explained to you, my employer insists on business with Orion Investments, and no-one else. You assured us that you would arrange it.'

'I'm doing my best, aren't I?' Grainger tried to sound more forceful than he felt.

'I would like to think that what you say is correct, Mr Grainger.' Finishing off the rest of his drink, the man stood and looked down at his younger companion. 'We will meet here again in one week. I suggest that you have better news for me.'

As Grainger himself left the bar to return to his office, he regretted ever coming in contact with Miguel Hernandez and his anonymous employer.

A young couple, obviously tourists, also finished their drinks and strolled off down the street, busy snapping away with a camera, but not always in the direction of London's landmarks.

*

Amy Watson was in a panic. Today, of all days, her hairdryer had chosen not to work, and her hair was still wet. She hoped the evening sunshine would dry out the loose copper cloud flying behind her as she cycled along, but it would be a nightmare to get back under control. It was fortunate she had taken the opportunity of a lift to school yesterday to bring in her change of clothes for tonight. She had wanted to look as smart as she could and not let Miss Freeman down.

She knew she owed her a lot. It could not have been easy for her to convince others to give an unqualified person such an important role, and she had gone out of her way to be worthy of that opportunity.

She still could not believe how lucky she was to be working in this prestigious girls' school. She had noticed the advert in someone else's newspaper as she travelled on the bus into work one day, and for some strange reason she couldn't get it out of her mind. It had led her to purchase her own copy of the paper and once again read the full content of the advert in detail, which indicated that, due to teaching staff illness, assistance was required during the last part of the school year for a few hours a week. Previous experience with young children would be an advantage.

Well, she certainly had that, she thought to herself. Her current job was in a toy store, and she had also worked for a while in a church crèche for working mothers. Her other experiences were still painful enough to consign to the back of her mind, but in this case, they might also be of use.

She had applied, and then, with some surprise, attended the subsequent interview. Miss Freeman, the headmistress, had been friendly and encouraging, and before long she found herself explaining her past life to this complete stranger, something she had never wanted to do before. The air of sympathy and understanding she encountered nearly reduced her to tears, and she left the interview sure that she must have given the impression of being neurotic, and that would be the last she would hear. The unimagined offer of the temporary position had elated her, and she had put her heart and soul into everything she had been asked to do.

Mrs Kitching was the Year One/Two teacher, but a recurring back problem hampered her mobility, especially where young active pupils were concerned. Under direction Amy was allowed to assist with scheduled reading sessions and supervising transit around the extensive school buildings when required. Her willingness to do anything else won her popularity with the other teachers and it was soon apparent that her few hours were turning into a full-time position. It became impractical for her to travel from her present accommodation everyday and she was allocated rooms in the local village.

Amy soon found herself enjoying the rapport between herself and the young minds around her and sensed that they responded to her as someone a little nearer their own age. She was given more and more responsibility and thrived on it. On numerous occasions she was so wrapped up in her tasks that she failed to see Miss Freeman quietly observing from the far corner of a room. The music teacher, Anne Francis, in particular became grateful for her assistance, and obvious musical knowledge. They had, in fact, between them achieved a triumph at the recent Open Day, devising a dance routine set to "Dance Macabre" with the Year One youngsters cavorting around dressed in skeleton costumes.

As the time went by Amy found herself so engrossed in her duties that it came as a shock when she noticed that the term was passing. She had begun to see the school and its inhabitants as part of a family and dare not let her mind dwell on what might happen to her when the summer holidays began. She tried to concentrate all her efforts on her young charges. By now she had come to know them as individuals, and one in particular, Joanna Deveraux, had made an impression on her from the beginning. It appeared her mother had died in some sort of accident and her father, an important businessman, not unlike most of the other children's fathers at the school, was often away on business. Somehow Amy had formed an impression that there was not as close a bond between father and daughter as there might be. Joanna had made odd comments from time to time, and there was sometimes a strange wistfulness about the child which discomfited her.

One day she was reading with her. The story was about a family, and suddenly the girl looked up, dark eyes filled with tears, and said, 'I wish I had my mummy. No-one ever likes me to talk about her. Alice has a locket with a picture of her mummy and daddy in it, but I don't. I talk to Mr Floppy about it sometimes, but he can't help.'

For a moment Amy didn't know quite what to say. Finally, she said, 'You have a daddy, and some little girls don't even have that.'

'I know, but he's always away or busy. Sophie's daddy took her to the zoo last weekend. It was such fun, she said. Mrs Horton used to take me out, but now she's not well enough. Daddy won't even sit on my bed at night anymore and read me a story. He says I can read it for myself now I'm bigger. When Grandpa comes it's better; we do things together, but he doesn't come very often.'

Amy's heart ached for the child, and her words evoked reminders of her own past. In an effort to give some sort of comfort, she said, 'Perhaps with the summer holidays coming up you could ask your father if he could take you on holiday somewhere. You could be together then, and perhaps he would like it too.'

She saw the young face brighten. 'Do you think he might?'

'Well, why don't you ask him and see? Now, let's get back to this story. We have to finish it today.'

Later in her room that night Amy thought again about Joanna's comments. From her own background she knew how important a secure home life was to a child. Perhaps the father could be made aware of his daughter's feelings somehow. Then again, she considered, he should have recognised them himself; and an unconscious sense of dislike for this man began to form inside her.

*

Simon stood in the hallway, rooted to the spot. He'd been ready to leave for the school when Joanna had made her parting comment.

'You told her what!' He looked down into the apprehensive young face. 'What on earth possessed you; it was just a bit of homework to do on your own, not cheat and ask someone. It was something private anyway, not to be discussed, particularly with the person involved.'

He watched Joanna's head go down, and she began drawing circles in the hall carpet with one toe. 'That's what Miss Watson said. Private comments about others… should… should not be discussed…I think she said I might have some more reading homework to do.' The last statement was said in a resigned tone.

'Well, good for Miss Watson, that's all I can say. What will happen when I meet her tonight, I don't know.' With one further look of frustration at the child he turned and left the house.

Of all the stupid… he fumed as he drove along. Still, he comforted himself, perhaps this woman had it coming to her. All these pious ideas of behaviour were bordering on Victorian principles rather than a modern way of life. She must be someone brought back from retirement for a temporary posting. Whatever it was, he thought, tonight was going to be a trial – in more ways than one. There would shortly be a vacancy for a new governor at the school, and his name had been suggested. He was undecided whether to take it on. There appeared to be much more to it than first impressions would suggest when he had gone into the paperwork involved with McDonald. He didn't know if he had the spare time anyway. He surmised ruefully that tonight would be an exercise in vetting, on both sides – and now he would have to start with a grovelling apology. Damn!

He swung the silver Mercedes into a space in the parking area at the front of the large 18th century house. Climbing out, he unconsciously straightened his tie, and marched up the steps to the front hall.

Chapter Three

Amy stood in the teachers' cloakroom battling with her wayward hairstyle. She was wearing her best grey dress and black high-heeled sandals. She didn't possess much jewellery, only small silver studs for her ears and a matching necklace, and they would have to suffice. With a sigh she finally dragged her copper curls back into a knot just as Anne Francis burst into the room.

'There you are. I've been searching for you. I didn't see you come.'

'I hope nobody else did, the sight I looked when I arrived,' she said, and went on to describe her disaster.

Anne swept her with a glance. 'Never mind, you're fine now, but then you always are.' She turned to a mirror. 'I mean just look at me, there's nothing you can do with this, is there!' She picked up a strand of straight black hair.

Amy fiddled with a recalcitrant curl and then gave up. She looked at her watch. 'I suppose we'd better be going.'

Anne led the way out into the corridor. As they walked along the wood-panelled hall Amy thought how she had come to love this old building. The rich patina of the surfaces spoke volumes about the history within the walls. She knew it had been built by a rich merchant whose family had lived here until after the First World War. They had then fallen on hard times and it had been sold to a succession of owners until taken over as a hospital during the Second World War. It was then used as a boarding school, finally being converted into the current day school, more modern additions at the rear blending in sympathetically with the original.

'I wonder why Miss Freeman asked me to come tonight? I know Mrs Kitching said she wouldn't be able to make it, but this isn't something I should be involved with, surely?'

'I don't know why you think that. You know as much about our little charges as Marion Kitching by now, if not more. You seem to deal with them as individuals and can probably discuss their needs with the parents better than she could. Anyway, you won't miss the treat of seeing Simon Deveraux in person. He's supposed to be coming and everyone's in a twitter about it.'

'I don't see why he's more important than any other parent, even if he does have more money, and I doubt that. Don't forget we have the daughter of a sheikh as a pupil, and she told me he would be here tonight.'

As they approached the large wooden doors to the assembly hall, Anne turned to her with a quizzical look. 'It's about time you knew that it's not the pollen alone which attracts the bee to a flower, and if the society gossip is right, this one has more than his fair share of everything.' She grinned at Amy's shocked expression and pushed open the door.

*

It was becoming an effort for Simon to conceal the boredom he was feeling. Colonel Bedfield, the retiring governor, had been extolling the importance of the duties imposed by the role for the last twenty minutes. Simon was well aware of its importance, but this man had elevated it to the level of the Holy Grail. Then, more charitably, he thought that perhaps the man might have nothing else worthwhile in his life and tried to listen more closely. His eye was caught by a sudden flash of fire and he turned his head towards it. A ray of watery sunshine had fallen across one area of the large room, catching the copper hair of a young woman standing there, turning it to brilliant gold. He felt himself mesmerised by it. She was possibly an older sister of a pupil, or, more likely, he thought cynically, the young wife of one of the older businessmen he had already met. As if sensing some scrutiny, the girl started to turn her head in his direction, but then she was swallowed up by another group of people. With difficulty he turned his attention back to the Colonel. After a few more irritating moments, when he contemplated excusing himself and renewing his convivial and productive conversation with Sheikh Asif, Miss Freeman appeared at his side.

'I'm sorry, Colonel, but I need to introduce Mr Deveraux to a member of staff.'

With relief Simon moved with her to the other side of the room. He was startled when Harriet Freeman stopped in front of the young copper-haired girl and, turning to him, announced, 'Mr Deveraux, I'd like you to meet Miss Amelia Watson, who joined us only recently as a temporary non-qualified assistant for Mrs Kitching. As you know she's had some problems...' Her voice receded into the background as his mind registered her first few words with disbelief. This young creature was unqualified but had been allowed to interact with Joanna! She had also been spouting all those lifestyle commandments as if she was the fount of all wisdom, and God, she was hardly older than the pupils. What the hell did she know of life – and he'd been about to grovel an apology to her – as if that would happen! He realised Harriet Freeman was still talking and forced himself to concentrate.'... and I think you would agree from what I have seen of Joanna's work lately there has been a marked improvement. Perhaps I could leave you both to discuss it in more detail.'

With that she moved to another group of parents and Simon, still trying to take in what he had just heard, looked down at the girl. Even in her high-heeled sandals she only came up to his shoulder and was now staring up at him with something like alarm registering in smoky grey eyes set in a pale face. He noticed that the mass of copper hair appeared too heavy for the slender neck and was already breaking loose from its confines. However, it softened the more severe lines of her plain grey dress, which would otherwise have seemed drab, and he reluctantly admitted to himself that she was attractive in an innocent kind of way. Still wondering, why the hell he should have been left to discuss important matters with this…this child, he felt compelled to say something.

'So, you are the Miss Watson I have heard so much about.' The scathing tone was deliberate, and he saw the small chin lift.

'Yes, Mr Deveraux, I am the "paragon of virtue" you discussed with Joanna.'

Damnation, what the hell did he do now? He caught just a glint of triumph in the grey eyes as if she fully expected his meek apology. OK – she was in for a big surprise!

'Having now been made aware of your youth and lack of qualifications, Miss Watson, I am more than ever surprised by your "words of wisdom"– or have you perhaps been quoting from some eminent educationalist to enhance your position here?'

He noticed his remark had registered by the set of her slim shoulders, but the voice was quiet. 'I am simply passing on the lessons I myself was taught, which I consider totally suitable for instructing young minds…' she paused for a moment and then a slight smile curved her pink mouth, '… or sometimes rather older minds too.'

This little minx was getting under his skin, but he tried to hold onto his rising temper. Casting about for some sort of polite reply, he saw a determined look cross the pale face and, taking advantage of the momentary silence between them, she launched into what he judged was a prepared speech.

'As you will be aware, Mr Deveraux, your daughter's schoolwork has shown great improvement of late, but I feel she has problems in other, more personal areas. It appears that your business affairs do not allow the sort of time she would wish for proper contact with you on a personal level as father and daughter. Mr Deveraux, as Joanna grows, she will have questions about many things which may trouble her and she will need the comfort of knowing that, without a mother, you are the one she can turn to for answers and who will be there to give her the time and support she needs. From things she has confided to me it is obvious she misses the presence of a mother, about whom I gather she has been told very little, with not even the comfort of a photograph. Things like this can be detrimental to a child's emotional growth. I understand with your other commitments it must be difficult for you to prioritise your time, but Joanna is not a sterile business deal, she is a child with obvious emotional needs. Don't you think—'

Simon nearly exploded with the rage he felt inside him. He had given Joanna everything she could possibly require since she had been born. This young woman now had the barefaced nerve to stand there and castigate him for his supposed failings, insinuating he had not done his duty. Well, enough was enough! He stopped her in full flow.

'Miss Watson, what I *think* will be passed on in private to Miss Freeman. However, I can tell you now that I shall make it clear to her that I have reservations as to whether this is the correct establishment for Joanna's further education, especially with exposure to untrained staff who nevertheless feel justified in arriving at ill-informed conclusions.' He looked down with satisfaction at the sudden look of anxiety in the grey eyes, and, with a curt nod and 'Good evening, Miss Watson,' turned away from her.

He heard her call after him, 'Oh, but… but, Mr Deveraux…' However, he continued walking, and left the room, heading for his car, cold anger consuming every part of his being.

*

With a frown Harriet Freeman looked again at the two sheets of handwritten paper in front of her.

She still considered her judgment had been sound in employing Amelia Watson against the advice of others, and so far, things had worked out better than she had hoped. The girl had all the attributes necessary for a good teacher and, in her view, should be supported in obtaining official qualification. Anne Francis had enthused about Amelia's obvious musical ability and this was probably the best avenue for her to pursue.

Now, however, with the content of a letter received from Simon Deveraux and the receipt this morning of Amelia's resignation, together with a full description as to why she had taken this step, matters were becoming complicated. If Deveraux, as threatened, took Joanna away from the school, this would send out a message to other existing or potential parents that there might be perceived failings with the school. For Joanna's sake she hoped this action would not be taken, as it would undoubtedly unsettle the child. She would stress this fact in any interview with Deveraux, suggesting that in Joanna's special circumstances this was more than ever critical.

On the other hand, she felt in some ways that Amelia's reasoning had been sound. She had obviously found a rapport with the child, if Joanna had been able to open up to her so readily about her inner thoughts. The only fault had been not to have brought up the matter with herself first rather than with Deveraux. Despite the problem a smile touched her mouth at the thought of a man like Simon Deveraux being told some home truths by what he considered to be "an inexperienced girl". The exchange would have been worth hearing. Amelia's youthful bravado must have been a shock to a man used to getting his own way.

Now she had to decide on her next course of action.

*

Simon moved the last of the folders across his desk.

'If you can deal with those by tonight, I'd appreciate it, Susan.'

The middle-aged woman looked up from her notepad, nodded, and smiled at him. 'And the other six I'm already working on!'

Simon looked up and returned the smile. Every day he thanked his good luck he had employed Susan Peters. She had been one of those rare finds; intelligent, capable and, more importantly, unflappable. Over the last ten years her role had evolved to that of an immoveable buffer between him, the clients and staff, so his time could be channelled more productively. Between them they had cultivated the illusion which had earned her the nickname of "dragon" but, as he well knew, in reality she was a humorous, mild-mannered person. Four years ago, she had come to him announcing her forthcoming marriage, and he found himself faced with the prospect of someone new working for him. However, this had not happened as, shortly afterwards, with some embarrassment she had informed him that the engagement had been broken. He sensed she had taken the matter hard, and he made it clear to her that he would value her continuing employment. After a month's thought she agreed, and he had felt a sense of relief that matters could return to normal.

His smile still in place, he remarked, 'We do seem to be pretty busy at the moment, thank God! How did the interviewing go?'

'I have my eye on one particular candidate. I would like to call her back for a second interview, if that's all right?'

'Yes, fine. I'll see her too if you like, although as I said, this is primarily a post as your assistant, and you must be happy with the choice.'

'I'll organise something as soon as possible.' She stood and picked up her files and papers. 'Oh, by the way, Carlton House rang to say that Miss Freeman will see you at any time tonight.'

Simon leant back in his chair. 'I bet she will.' It was almost a remark to himself, but Susan caught the tone of voice and stopped as she was leaving.

'I hope there's nothing wrong with Joanna.'

'A little minor difficulty, but nothing that can't be sorted out.' He suddenly found himself picturing the red-gold hair and smoky grey eyes, and once more felt his anger rising.

Turning to leave the room Susan commented, 'Perhaps she just needs the long summer break. Incidentally, do you want me to keep any time clear for you during those weeks?'

Simon looked up, and the germ of an idea started to form in his mind. 'Thanks for reminding me, Susan. I'll let you know. Get back to Carlton House will you, please, and say I'll be there about seven o'clock.'

*

Looking up from her papers, Harriet Freeman's stern gaze settled on him. 'I appreciate the points you have raised, Mr Deveraux, but I hope you can see that, in observing any problems with our pupils from their emotional standpoint, we are also fulfilling one of the criteria of how we wish the school to be managed.'

Simon relaxed back in his chair. The interview was evolving into the pattern he had expected. Harriet Freeman would fight to protect her school and staff, and he couldn't blame her. He also knew he would have to appear magnanimous in defeat if he was to put his newly formed plan into action, but he wouldn't give in too meekly. 'I still maintain that someone as young and inexperienced as Miss Watson cannot possibly diagnose the true nature of family difficulties, let alone comment with any certainty on them.' He looked up as a sudden thought occurred to him. 'I hope she has not been made aware of my, er, special circumstances?'

'No, Mr Deveraux, she has not. Your confidence has been maintained. By the same token I feel that Miss Watson herself has been able to bring a certain personal insight into this matter, for confidential reasons of her own.'

The comment intrigued him, but he decided not to push her on the matter.

'Am I to understand from your remarks that Miss Watson will be employed again in the autumn?'

'I am not sure yet, Mr Deveraux. I have to give it further consideration. It might be that she moves on to achieve her qualifications, but I can assure you that she will be missed. I have asked her to stay in the locality during the holidays in case she can be of assistance, but she may find it necessary to obtain other employment.

Can I ask, Mr Deveraux, now that you know more about Joanna's feelings, whether you had any thoughts on managing her future relationship with you?'

He could now tell that Harriet Freeman felt on more certain ground. Her comment did not surprise him and was the convenient opening he required. He ran one hand through his dark hair. 'I have to admit, Miss... Harriet... if I may?' – he raised an eyebrow in query and produced the smile he knew would achieve the result, and sure enough she gestured her agreement to this change of formality – 'I have been giving it some thought. I am rearranging my schedule to allow more spare time, but even so my problem still appears to be Margaret Horton's inability to assist for several more weeks. I have, therefore, come to a conclusion, about which I would welcome your comments. You may think it strange in the circumstances but, looking at it from Joanna's standpoint, I think it might be the answer, especially in view of your last remarks.' He paused for a moment, as if giving the matter some further thought. 'I wondered whether I might employ Miss Watson as company for Joanna during the school holiday.' He hesitated for a moment. 'It might have a beneficial result all round.' He gave Harriet Freeman a wry smile just to confirm his capitulation, and went on, 'Needless to say, I would require Miss Watson to live in, but I intend she would also receive remuneration. If her services became vital at any time for your purposes, I am sure an arrangement could be made.'

He could see that his suggestion had been totally unexpected and for a moment his companion appeared to be lost for words.

'Well, er, Simon, I can see the arrangement would have its advantages, but I am not sure Miss Watson would be amenable.

Are you suggesting I should approach her on the matter?'

'I feel that would be the best course initially, although I would be happy to speak with her should she wish. I am sure she would agree that a period of being employed by me would look well on her CV.'

He could see that Harriet Freeman had grasped the truth of his statement and he smiled to himself. She was now certain to encourage her, no doubt, rather more reluctant employee that this opportunity should be seized. So far, so good.

Chapter Four

As the black SUV turned into the sweeping gravel drive at Woodhayes and Amy saw the house for the first time, she felt daunted by the prospect of living in such grand surroundings. The property was a large nineteen-fifties red-brick dwelling under a tiled roof with leaded windows. The garden appeared to extend on all sides, itself surrounded by tall trees.

Frank Gilmore pulled up in front of a sizeable double garage with storeroom attached. Built above the garage, in the same style as the main house, was what appeared to be further accommodation. Mr Gilmore had told her that he and his wife lived at the property and Amy wondered if this might be their quarters. She would have felt much happier to be lodged with them rather than in the main house. The prospect of being in close company with Simon Deveraux in his home still filled her with unease.

When Miss Freeman had first spoken to her about the arrangement, she dismissed the idea as ridiculous. There was no way that Simon Deveraux would want her anywhere near him, or his daughter. However, Harriet Freeman had persisted, suggesting that this arrangement might benefit Joanna's interaction with her father, and would personally be useful to her own employment in the future.

An awkward meeting between herself and Simon Deveraux had followed, at which he seemed polite and grateful for her assistance, but she sensed the same air of arrogance about him.

She would never admit that she had tried, and failed, to forget her immediate reaction on that night when they had first been introduced. He was the most attractive man she had ever met, and the sensations created by the sheer force of his personality had been an experience completely new to her. However, she considered that the anger and ferocity of his comments and attitude that night, still seemed out of all proportion to her remarks, and had left her with the feeling there had been something rather more behind his show of displeasure.

He suggested that as she was still employed by the school, as agreed with Miss Freeman, she would receive any further monies through the usual channel and he would reimburse Carlton House. The amount of salary offered by him was amazing, but when she demurred, he had smiled slightly and indicated that she might be required to act as a chaperon in public. As his eyes had wandered up and down her serviceable green skirt and white blouse, she had felt plain and dowdy. No doubt his intention, she had thought. It was this look which had made up her mind. She might not be in the same league as any females he normally associated with, but she would make sure he would have no cause for complaint.

'I'll get your things from the back, Miss Watson.'

Frank Gilmore had just begun to unload her bags when the large wooden front door opened, and Joanna Deveraux came racing out to them.

'I thought you'd never get here. I've been waiting ages.' Her excitement was obvious, and she was almost hopping from one foot to the other.

As Mr Gilmore was within earshot Amy felt she had to start in the right way.

'Good morning, Joanna. I hope you are well.'

The young girl picked up on her tone of voice and immediately stood still, belatedly remembering her manners. 'Good morning, Miss Watson. It's so nice to have you here.'

Amy smiled in reply, and then, nodding towards the assembled luggage said, 'Perhaps we could assist Mr Gilmore with my things.' She handed the girl a small soft bag, and, picking up a case, followed him towards the front door. Just as they entered the house, he turned to grin at her, and muttered, 'Been up since six this morning. Her father's not best pleased.'

Amy's heart sank on hearing this. So, it was already a bad start.

*

The hallway of the house was impressive and reminded her of Carlton House with its oak floor and panelling but it seemed lighter inside than she had expected. The largest rug she had ever seen covered most of the floor and glowed deep red, matched by a vase of roses on a table at the foot of the staircase. Various recessed doors led off the hallway and she would, no doubt, find out in due course what lay behind them. A woman in her fifties was coming down the stairs. She smiled and held out a hand in greeting.

'Good morning, Miss Watson. I'm Helen Gilmore. Welcome to Woodhayes. Mr Deveraux is in town until later today so we have time to get you settled in.'

It was a relief to Amy, knowing that she would not have to contend with Simon Deveraux immediately on her arrival.

Mrs Gilmore turned to follow her husband up the stairs. 'Would you like to come up and see your room?'

'Thank you, yes I would.'

So far Mr and Mrs Gilmore seemed very pleasant, and she followed them up the red carpeted staircase to the gallery above, eager to see more of the house.

Invisible from the front, the property curved outwards at the rear and the landing opened into a wide semi-circle. Pointing to her right, Mrs Gilmore indicated, 'Mr Deveraux's rooms are at that side, with the corresponding left wing reserved for other visitors.' She stopped in front of a row of four doors in the middle of the landing. 'This next room is kept for Mrs Horton, with a connecting bathroom in between her room and Joanna's.' She moved along to the fourth door. 'This will be yours. I hope you will be comfortable.' She opened a door and ushered Amy inside.

The size of the room appeared palatial to Amy and she was almost lost for words. The understated elegance of the green and cream furnishings glowed in the sunlight flooding in from the large window. She found herself only able to comment, 'It's a beautiful room, thank you. I'm sure I will be very comfortable.'

'I hope you won't mind sharing a bathroom with Joanna. It's not ideal, I know, but…'

Amy turned and saw the anxious look. She smiled at the other woman, 'No, of course not. It won't be a problem. After all, I'm only here for a short while.'

Appearing relieved, Helen Gilmore indicated the luggage. 'We'll leave you to get settled in. Lunch is at twelve-thirty. I'll send Joanna to show you the way.'

'Can't I stay and help to unpack?' The young girl sounded disappointed, already tipping out the contents of the bag she had carried.

'I'm sure Miss Watson would like some time on her own to do that, Joanna. You can help me with lunch if you like.' Turning at the door as they left, she gave a wink.

It was obvious Mrs Gilmore knew how to cope with Joanna, and Amy hoped over these next few weeks she would be able to do the same, to the satisfaction of her father.

*

After a light lunch in the dining room with views over the garden, Amy spent the rest of the afternoon being shown around Joanna's room. No little girl could have wanted anything better, she thought, but then it didn't seem that it had necessarily made Joanna completely happy. She noticed that there was no sign of any technology in the room by way of a television or computer. She knew from discussions with some of the other girls in the First Year that they were accustomed to these as normality at home and decided to question Joanna on the point.

'Daddy says that he would rather I read a book than watch television in my bedroom. If I want to see anything I have to do it downstairs. He also has a laptop, which if I need to use it to find any information for homework, there has to be another grown-up with me, in case I get in a muddle, he says. He told me I can have a phone when I'm older, but I know Sophie has one already because she's showed me.'

Amy thought about all this. Her own phone was a basic model, more for emergency purposes than any other use, but technology these days was becoming the norm. However, Miss Freeman had taken the view that for the First to Third Years no girls were allowed mobile phones in school. A designated room had been equipped with computers plus a television for limited use under supervision, but this was not accessible to the First Year. As far as her doctrine was concerned, a young brain should be encouraged to work for itself without any outside aids. It appeared that Joanna's father also favoured this approach, and, she reflected, was also a display of considered safe parental control for the young girl which could not be faulted.

Admiring all the clothes hanging in a large cupboard, it was hard not to feel envious comparing it with her own circumstances. She noticed a soft toy rabbit with long ears lying on one of the beds. It looked worn; obviously something well-loved.

'Is this the Mr Floppy you've told me about?'

'Oh yes, he's my best friend. Daddy brought him home from abroad when I was only little, so Mrs Horton said. He always listens and I tell him lots. I think Daddy likes him too and we sometimes have conversations at mealtimes.'

Amy wondered just what the rabbit had been hearing over

the years, and wished she knew. Simon Deveraux was obviously providing for his daughter in every material way, within strict limits, but on hearing about his interaction with this much loved "friend", was she now seeing a softer side to him?

*

It was late in the afternoon before Amy was aware that Simon Deveraux had returned home. Mrs Gilmore popped her head around the door with the news. Amy felt her stomach muscles tightening and told herself not to be so ridiculous. She had already made up her mind that if there was a problem, she wouldn't continue with the arrangement, however disappointed Joanna might be.

She was, however, concerned to notice that Joanna did not seem keen to seek her father out, as she felt any normal child might when a parent returned home – but then, neither had Simon Deveraux come to find his daughter.

'If you want to go and see your father, Joanna, I have things to do.'

'It's all right, Miss Watson, Daddy sometimes brings work with him which he does before we have dinner. He doesn't like to be interrupted.'

This arrangement still seemed wrong to Amy. For Simon Deveraux to take just a few moments to greet his daughter was surely not much to ask. She gave a sigh. Was it just her own wishful thinking – to have someone who cared enough about you to be interested in your day?

*

As it transpired, Amy had to wait even longer for any meeting with Simon Deveraux. Through Helen Gilmore, he conveyed his apologies that he would be detained in his study on business and might not be able to join them for dinner. Joanna seemed unconcerned by this, but Amy considered that a personal apology would have been more acceptable. She felt her dislike for the man growing even stronger.

After a delicious meal, with still no sign of Joanna's father, Amy suggested that they have some reading practice before bedtime. As she was about to accompany Joanna upstairs Mrs Gilmore came to tell her that Mr Deveraux had requested her presence in his study at eight o'clock that evening and pointed out the appropriate doorway. Looking at her watch, Amy saw that it gave her nearly an hour in which to compose herself for the forthcoming meeting.

*

Promptly at eight o'clock Amy knocked on the door and was told to enter. This room too, as with all those she had seen so far, was of considerable size with a large window framed in dark blue curtains overlooking the front of the house. She noted bookcases on two walls and a large desk in the centre of the room standing on yet another enormous rug, its dark blue colour taken up by two upholstered chairs.

As she advanced into the room Simon Deveraux stood from his position on a large, blue leather Chesterfield set under the window, tossing a sheaf of papers on the seat beside him as he did so.

'Good evening, Miss Watson. Welcome to Woodhayes. I am sorry not to have been able to greet you before now – business pressures, I'm afraid.'

She noticed that he made no attempt to shake hands, and neither was she quite sure of the genuine nature of the apology.

'I have no problem with waiting, Mr Deveraux, and perhaps there might still be time for you to see Joanna before she goes to sleep – should you wish.'

She wondered if she had gone too far with her remark when she noticed the cool gaze and tightening of the jaw, sensing again that this man was quick to anger and not one to cross lightly. To her relief he turned away and moved over to his desk. He was still wearing his business suit, but the jacket was unbuttoned, and his tie loosened. As he leant back against the desk, the action stretched the material of his trousers over muscular thighs and Amy was conscious that, although he must be about forty, Simon Deveraux was obviously not desk-bound and kept himself fit.

Although he could not fail to have understood the meaning of her remark, it appeared he had chosen not to make any immediate response. Instead, indicating one of the chairs in front of his desk, he merely said, 'Perhaps you would care to take a seat, Miss Watson.'

As she walked towards him, she was conscious of his eyes moving over her. However, with the knowledge of her increase in salary, Amy had spent more money on clothes in the last few days than she had ever done in her life before, and she was sure that even he would not be able to find fault with her lime green dress and matching jacket.

'I hope you have settled into your accommodation. I regret the bathroom arrangements are perhaps not ideal for you, but Mrs Horton still has some of her belongings in her room and —'

Amy quickly forestalled any further apology. 'I wouldn't dream of imposing on anyone else's privacy considering the short time I will be here. I am sure there will be no problem.'

He inclined his head and gave half a smile. 'Very obliging of you, I'm sure.'

The remark, to her ears, sounded condescending, and she had the sudden desire to storm out. Things were no better between them than they had been that night at the school, and there was no way she could stand this attitude for several more weeks. However, almost as though he sensed her thoughts, he stood up straight and moved to sit behind his desk.

'I think we need to clarify your duties, Miss Watson. As this is supposed to be a holiday for Joanna, I have no wish for her to see you as a governess; therefore, I suggest, with your agreement, we should keep school formality to a minimum.'

His mood now appeared brisk and businesslike. For her part Amy felt it safer to keep things on this footing and, adopting the same tone, commented, 'I have discussed the situation with Miss Freeman, and she considered that if I make sure that already set homework is completed, plus certain reading goals, and perhaps incorporate something educational in any outings, she would consider it sufficient. Would that be acceptable to you?'

She watched as he leant back in his chair and pinned her with a level blue gaze. 'Yes Miss Watson, I'm quite happy with that, but I do wish to reassure you that you will have some free time to yourself. There is only one important thing I need to point out. Joanna does not leave this property unless in company with either myself, Mr Gilmore or any other adult I personally have sanctioned. I hope you will understand my reasons for this request.'

Here was another example of his strong parental concerns, she thought, which were, after all, consistent with the security arrangements in place at Carlton House. Amy nodded. 'I quite understand, Mr Deveraux.'

With the obvious intent of bringing the interview to an end he stood and said, 'If you would care to liaise with Helen Gilmore, she will inform you of the usual household routine. I intend to try and arrange my schedule over these next few weeks so that I can spend as much time here as possible.' A slight smile then played around his mouth as he went on, 'I would also mention that I will be taking Joanna out tomorrow. I understand she requires a tennis racquet for next year and it would be better to deal with this now rather than leave it too late in the holiday. I hope this will make up for my obvious shortcomings this evening.' Before Amy could make any comment, he crossed the room and opened the door. 'I have also been informed that my father will be coming to stay shortly, so Joanna will have plenty of company.'

Amy was now a little bewildered. If all this had been arranged, why then was she here? Appearing to read her mind once more, as she moved past him to leave the room, he said quietly, 'Please be assured, Miss Watson, your presence is still required.'

She looked up into the dark blue eyes and for some reason her heart skipped a beat at the warmth of the look, matching the soft tone. As the door closed behind her she felt as if she had made some sort of escape.

Chapter Five

Simon returned to his desk and sat down, staring at the closed door, allowing the tension to ebb away. Somehow, he had managed to control his temper in response to the girl's veiled inference about his absence tonight, but it had been a near thing. She seemed to have the ability to prick at his conscience with little apparent effort. However, over these next weeks she would learn first-hand that his business life never worked to a regular timetable and learn other things too.

For the purposes of his plan, it was a bonus that she was an attractive young woman, and had, he judged, already been spending some of her extra salary to good effect. He was interested to note that although she still appeared to disapprove of him, he sensed in her reactions to him tonight that she was not immune to masculine charm – and this was something to work with.

The ringing of the telephone broke into his thoughts, and he answered without checking the caller.

'Deveraux…Oh, good evening, Arthur…Don't worry, it's not that late…Sunday lunch…er… well I'm not sure. It's just with the school holidays starting…I see, if you consider it that important, yes, all right then. I'll be with you at say twelve o'clock… Thank you, Arthur.'

Damn, this was the last thing he wanted – his strategy for Amelia Watson required as little time away as possible, but it would have been difficult to refuse, and the request had sounded important.

*

After breakfast the next morning, when an excited Joanna had left with her father, Amy made her bed and tidied the bathroom and then made her way down to the kitchen.

Mrs Gilmore greeted her with a smile. 'Would you like another cup of coffee before I start upstairs?'

'Yes, thank you. Oh, by the way, I've dealt with my room and the bathroom.' Sitting down at the kitchen table Amy now felt a bit diffident about mentioning this. Perhaps the other woman might consider it as interfering.

Helen Gilmore turned round, surprise showing on her face. 'My dear girl, you needn't have done that, although it's very nice of you.'

'I just thought that you had enough to do already, and I'm not exactly a guest.'

Placing the mugs on the table Mrs Gilmore sat down beside her. 'I rather inferred from how Mr Deveraux spoke to me that he did consider you in that light.'

It was Amy's turn to look surprised. 'I can't imagine why. He's paying me to look after Joanna for a few weeks, that's all.'

'He seemed adamant in his instructions that you join him and Joanna for meals. Over all the years the nanny, Margaret Horton, has never been asked to do so.'

Amy thought about this but could find no explanation. 'Mr Deveraux said that I should ask you about how the house is usually run so that I can sort out a routine with Joanna.'

'It very much depends on his movements. At weekends and holidays breakfast is, as today, at eight to eight-fifteen, lunch at twelve-thirty with the evening meal at about six o'clock. If Mr Deveraux is going to be away on business or staying in town he tries to let me know as soon as possible, and either Frank and I, or Margaret Horton, deal with Joanna. With Margaret's unfortunate absence of late I've been sleeping in the house if Mr Deveraux has had to be away.'

Amy didn't want to appear to be asking questions but, she told herself, if she was to make any progress in his relationship with his daughter, she had to know a bit more about him.

'So does Mr Deveraux also have a house in London?'

'It's only an apartment, but he does use it, quite often. I've been there once. It overlooks the Thames. Apart from Mr Deveraux's father there have been no other guests here at Woodhayes, so perhaps the apartment comes in... handy at times.'

She winked at Amy over the rim of her coffee cup, and when she finally understood the meaning of her words, Amy felt a flush of colour in her cheeks. It confirmed her opinion that it would have been strange if a man like Simon Deveraux had spent the last few years without female company. He had obviously decided to keep these activities separate from his home life with Joanna. It then dawned on her that at night, apart from a child, she herself was alone in the house with him. Remembering last night in the study and her reactions to the look in his blue eyes and the strange feelings inside her, she told herself she must concentrate on Joanna; this was why she was here, and for no other reason. As Anne Francis had said, Simon Deveraux must be an experienced man as far as women were concerned, and perhaps thought he would have some amusement in playing a little game with her. Well, he wouldn't get it all his own way, she would make that very plain.

'I believe Joanna's grandfather is coming to stay shortly.'

Mrs Gilmore rose and took the mugs to the sink. 'Yes, in about a week, I understand. He usually comes later in August. Joanna is very fond of him and gets really excited when she knows he's coming.'

'How often does he come?'

'Oh, once in the summer and again just before Christmas.'

Amy was puzzled. 'That's not much during a whole year.'

Mrs Gilmore turned and regarded her. 'He lives in Canada. It's rather a long way for a quick visit.'

'Canada! I didn't know that. Joanna has never said anything.'

'Mr Deveraux Senior owns a large law firm in Montreal.'

'That means, if he was born there, Simon Deveraux is Canadian too, although I would never have guessed.'

'Frank says he has spent a lot of his time in the UK and Europe.' She hesitated for a moment. 'I should perhaps warn you that Mr Deveraux and his father have a somewhat strained relationship, but nothing, I'm sure, that Joanna has noticed.'

Did this at last explain why Simon Deveraux had an awkward relationship with his own child? thought Amy. Perhaps she would be able to judge when she saw them together.

*

Simon had been to the London home of Sir Arthur Dunne on two previous occasions. Lady Pamela Dunne had always struck him, not only as a considerate host, but an astute woman who must have been a great asset to her husband over the years in his senior post at the Treasury. It was she who greeted him when he was shown into the drawing room on arriving at the Chelsea house.

'Simon, my dear, it's so good of you to come at such short notice. I warned Arthur that it might be difficult for you to leave your daughter, but he did seem to think it important.'

'It's always nice to see you, Pamela, and Arthur made it all sound very intriguing.'

Pamela Dunne motioned him to take a seat on the plush settee opposite. 'I've been given strict instructions to offer you a lighter than normal lunch, after which I understand another visitor will arrive for some sort of discussion. Arthur is just making a few phone calls. He'll be here in a moment.'

Simon smiled. 'My curiosity is growing by the minute.' Inside he was beginning to wonder just what this was all about. He cast around in his mind for a broad view of the UK's financial circumstances at the present time. The worldwide financial markets were still rattled by the recent problems, but after certain regulatory measures had been taken in the USA and other financial centres things were no longer in a critical state. It would take a while for full confidence to return, if ever, but practical considerations made the attempt a necessity, and there was optimism in this regard. He had been requested in the past to join think tanks and various other committees but the approach to him had always been made on a more formal basis. He would just have to be patient and wait to be told what this was all about.

Over lunch there was only social small talk. Sir Arthur was obviously not prepared to say too much in front of his wife.

As they drank their coffee, Pamela Dunne commented, 'I assume Joanna is looking forward to her long holiday, Simon. How old is she now, about six?'

'Yes, Pamela, six going on seven – going on a young lady! She's just finished her first year at proper school.'

'Oh, I can remember Richard at that age – they just race away from you. Do you still have someone looking after her? I believe you mentioned to me that there was a problem in that respect.'

Simon carefully replaced his coffee cup, and considered his reply. 'Long-term there might still be a problem, but a short-term solution was to employ one of her schoolteachers to assist during the holiday.'

'Oh dear, that sounds rather formal for a holiday. Why don't you come to town for a few days and bring them with you, and I'll get Richard's terrible two to come and stay and we can have a children's party or something. In any case I asked Cook to prepare a little treat to take home with you that Joanna might like, as you've had to leave her.'

Simon was not sure about the London visit, but there was no doubting the sincerity with which the offer had been made. 'That is immensely kind of you, Pamela. Can you give me some time to consider your idea?'

At that point, the butler entered and indicated that the other guest had arrived. Leading the way out of the room, Sir Arthur turned to him. 'Come on, Simon, before Pamela organises your whole life for you.'

Simon followed Sir Arthur across the hall and into his study. As they entered, another man about his own age rose from his seat, stepped forward and took Sir Arthur's outstretched hand.

'Good to see you again, Sir Arthur.'

'Likewise, Mr Reynolds. Can I introduce Simon Deveraux? Simon, this is Mr Daniel Reynolds from the American Embassy.'

As the two shook hands the introduction explained Simon's immediate noting of the American accent.

'You could almost call us neighbouring cousins, Mr Deveraux.' Reynolds' reference to his Canadian roots was accompanied by a broad smile, but Simon sensed there was an element of assessment behind the pleasantries, much like his own. Reynolds was playing the brash American but, observing a certain watchful look in his eyes, Simon judged that this man should not be taken at face value.

When they were all seated Sir Arthur glanced over at Simon. 'If you have no objection, Mr Reynolds would like to ask you a few questions, with the ultimate hope that you will be able to assist in a... certain matter.'

Even more mystified as to what this was all about, Simon turned to Reynolds. 'I'd be interested to know just what I can assist you with.'

Reynolds gave him a direct look. 'If our reading of a situation is correct, we're wondering whether we might put a proposal to you in a matter which would ultimately benefit a number of countries, albeit in different ways. I am empowered to speak for my superiors, and Sir Arthur, I understand, the same, on behalf of any British involvement. I don't wish to call into question your confidentiality credentials but, just for the moment, I am reluctant to give full disclosure to you. Sorry.'

Simon had a sudden urge to tell them both to go to blazes. They either trusted him and wanted his help, or they didn't, but he was curious to find out what was going on, so he just shrugged and settled back in his seat. 'Carry on with your questions, Mr Reynolds.'

Reynolds glanced over at Sir Arthur, who nodded and motioned him to continue. 'I believe you have dealt with business factions in South America from time to time.'

'Yes, that is so.'

'One recent venture ran into some problems, I believe. Could you tell us about these problems?'

Reynolds looked at him with a polite query in his eyes, but Simon had the immediate idea that this man already knew all the details. 'Mr Reynolds, I have a feeling this isn't really necessary.' He wanted the man to know that he was just as astute, but he could hear his voice sounded edgy.

Sir Arthur leant forward with a slight smile. 'I assure you, Simon, this is an informal off the record discussion and we are not intending to pry into your business dealings. I have, in fact, already taken the liberty of suggesting that I felt you would be prepared to assist us.'

For a moment Simon resented this casual assumption, but he still wanted to know what was going on. He made himself relax and began to marshal his thoughts. 'Several months ago, I was approached through my Rio contact for financial assistance to a consortium in the building of a new refinery. Planning was well advanced, as was some initial construction, but not all the finance required was in place, hence my involvement. I started looking into the details of the scheme and those already on board, plus the financial shortfall. The companies involved seemed legitimate, but my Rio contact made me aware of rumours about possible unofficial backhanders and undue pressure, one name being mentioned several times.'

'Luis de Santos.'

It came as no surprise to Simon that Reynolds knew this much already. 'Exactly. I started to pay particular attention to this gentleman, and we took a highly detailed look at him personally and some of his other projects. There was a little too much doubt surrounding the financing and conduct of some of his past deals for my personal ease, and I cancelled my involvement with the project. It wasn't particularly well received. I can only assume, because I failed to come through, the deal faltered and, as matters were well advanced with some monies already paid over, de Santos lost a considerable amount. Things became so heated I finally threatened to submit a report on my findings to the local Rio authorities. After that, the matter went quiet, and I took no further action. On reflection, perhaps I should have.'

'I believe your Rio office suffered a recent burglary.'

Simon looked at Reynolds with a frown. 'As you seem to know so much, why do you ask?' He then controlled himself with an effort. 'Yes, as you say, about two months ago. Apart from a small amount of cash nothing appeared to have been taken. We have a security encryption method on our files, making it difficult for sensitive data to be collected. The local police were informed.'

Reynolds continued to regard him with a steady gaze. 'I understand your Rio contact met with a fatal road accident a week or two later.'

'Yes, as a probable consequence of a heavy rainstorm, Jose Ramos' car went off the road and hit a tree. A pity, he was a diligent worker. His wife said she'd been worried as he was very late home. Perhaps if he'd left at his usual time, he'd have missed the rain. He was a good man and I'm finding him hard to replace.'

Reynolds spoke very quietly, 'Mr Deveraux, would it surprise you to know that he did leave work at the proper time, but he didn't leave on his own?'

Simon stared at him in surprise. 'What on earth do you mean?'

'Perhaps I could suggest to you that, because of your security, when the burglary proved fruitless, other methods were employed to find the exact nature of any information which could have been detrimental to certain persons. I believe it possible an attempt was made to um…persuade…your contact to reveal that information and then an accident was arranged.'

Simon voiced his astonishment. 'That's just nonsense. What sort of proof is there for that sort of idea?' He pierced Reynolds with a narrowed gaze. 'Do I take it that some sort of surveillance has been in place? If the authorities felt there was any suspicion of foul play, why wasn't I informed?'

'Only partial surveillance was being kept, and not by the local authorities. Your contact left the premises that night in company with someone of... interest... and another man. It looked like an after-work drive by friends but unfortunately, due, as you say, to the adverse weather conditions, the target was lost. After receiving news of the accident, it was concluded, in retrospect, that things might not have been as they appeared.'

Simon remembered Maria's ravaged face and the bewilderment of the two small children when he had attended the funeral. Even though he had made immediate arrangements for the family's financial security, it would never bring back a husband or a father. 'I still say the authorities should have informed me of all this.'

'Mr Deveraux, as I said, the local authorities are not aware of all the facts.'

It was obvious from Reynolds' statement that something more serious was involved, and Simon came to a decision. He was not prepared to play any more cat and mouse games with these men. He wanted all the facts, or he would just get up and walk away.

'I want to know what's going on, Reynolds, or I'll leave here and find out myself. If what you say is true, then this thing's personal now.'

Chapter Six

Reynolds lent forward in his chair, glancing across at Sir Arthur, who, once more, just nodded. 'Mr Deveraux, certain international agencies have been interested in the dealings of Luis de Santos for some time, but so far authorities have been reluctant to take any action against him because of a lack of sufficient hard evidence. They have also been swayed by the benefits of important infrastructure developments which his financial involvement has brought about. However, with the recent severe financial situation, politicians are insisting, more than ever, that any business deals appear watertight and free from any undue influence or corruption. As you are no doubt aware, Colombia is one of the major trading partners with the USA and we have obvious mutual benefits in this continuing. Recently, at the request of certain selected Colombian officials, we have been investigating information brought to their attention by an informer about a particular project in that country for the development of a nickel mine.'

Simon now understood all the questioning. 'You appear to be aware that I have been approached in this project to find extra funding, but if you're after de Santos I've seen no evidence of his involvement here. If he's got any brains at all he would know I would give it a wide berth if I had any such suspicions. Jose

Ramos was detailed to do an assessment of the site involved, but with his death that's now shelved. The approach came through a small financial broker here in the UK, who, I have no doubt, is hoping this deal will widen his business contacts. It appears that a consortium of two new companies has been put together with the aim of having enough clout to take on something like this, but they require a more experienced financial partner. I am not averse to assisting in start-up enterprises; after all; I've been through it myself, however, I'm not certain at the moment if I do want to be involved. With new companies there is no proven track record, and this is always a gamble as to viability. I have taken gambles before, but as you say, with the financial meltdown we've just experienced, I think I've made up my mind to steer clear for once.'

Sir Arthur spoke for the first time. 'You will be aware that these companies are Brazilian and American in origin. Why then do you suppose a small British financial firm was employed to approach your company for assistance. Why didn't they come to you direct in the first place or go elsewhere closer to home?'

Simon gave a shrug. 'Perhaps they judged they didn't have the expertise themselves to put together a good enough-looking package to interest a financial partner and found a cheap firm to help them set it out.'

'Has there been any sign that they've approached anyone else?'

Simon sensed there was something more behind Sir Arthur's question. 'Mark Grainger, their broker, has given the impression that Orion was the first choice, but that's not unusual. It's an attitude I've worked hard to achieve in the marketplace.' He decided to bring out into the open his growing feeling of where all this was leading. 'Are you suggesting that de Santos is behind this mine project and for some reason he wants to get me on board with it? Arthur, he's in business himself, so he knows the unwritten pitfalls about becoming involved with new unproven companies. He knows very well they can pick up the money they want in certain other places in the world without a lot of regulatory constraints. He would know I'm aware of this too, so why would he imagine I'd be interested?'

Reynolds spoke again. 'He has obviously judged your character and is banking on your being prepared to assist and take a chance in a new venture. Mr Deveraux, you remember the surveillance in Rio I mentioned to you? This was again in response to a request from our Colombian partners. They, and in fact we, have a shared interest in a certain Colombian national who has come to our notice through our own covert surveillance on known drug cartel figures. Because of this, he was nearly apprehended re-entering the States over the Mexican border but, unfortunately, was warned off in time. He then evaded us, probably by using false papers, but we suspect he was instrumental in the exposure and… elimination of our operative. After several weeks, he was flagged up entering the UK. For some reason he felt secure enough to use his original name. He is at this moment living in London and has been seen in company with Mark Grainger, who has in turn now been linked to you. The Colombian is known to have had close contact with de Santos for some while.'

Simon stared back at Reynolds for a moment while his mind absorbed this news. 'If that's the case I'm definitely wiping my hands of the whole deal.'

Reynolds fixed him with a hard stare. 'Mr Deveraux, we are asking you to do exactly the opposite. The Brazilians, the Colombians, my bosses and Sir Arthur's here all want de Santos rolled up, and we want you to help. He cultivates the veneer of a respectable businessman but, as you have no doubt found out, he is prepared to be involved in anything which makes him money: drugs, human trafficking, money laundering, fraud, bribery and much more. We believe this whole mine project is fictitious, because in our view de Santos is after you. He wants to embroil you in a deal which will go sour in a bad way, and will cost you big – not just money, but, as you said a moment ago, the good name of your company. We need you to agree to go ahead and put funds into this deal to keep it live, to give us time to put pressure on the Brazilian authorities for them to take action. However, until they can show their hand, things could be a bit awkward for you when doubts are raised as to the legitimacy of this deal. Whilst enquiries are made there might be whisperings in various quarters. It's a big ask, I know.'

Simon let out a soundless whistle. 'You can say that again. Have you any idea of the damage it could do? No-one would trust me again.'

'We must take this chance of getting people like de Santos out of the running. For our part, our administration intends to crack down on companies created in America and used for illegal purposes, particularly, as in this case, where it could be to our detriment and loss of trust with our trading partners. We must inspire confidence in our financial circles and law enforcement. By setting up this deal solely to get even with you de Santos is now making a fatal mistake, giving us a chance to pin something on him. Having lost one of our own people, we have a vested interest in this, and,' he relaxed back in his chair like a man who knew he had a winning hand, 'I feel sure you would also like to get justice for Jose Ramos.'

Simon nearly opened his mouth to make an immediate confirmation of the point, but then realised that what he was being asked to do was far bigger than justice for Jose. If this went wrong, it could be the end of Orion and the livelihood of all those who worked for him.

'I need to think about what you want from me. It's a major decision. What time frame is there before you can get the Brazilians to respond, Arthur? How long do I have to hang out for?'

'I cannot say for certain, but we will move as fast as we can to minimise your involvement.' He looked a little apologetic. 'I need your answer within the next day or two. Simon, one thing we must stress; no-one else can know the truth of anything to do with this until it's all wrapped up, therefore decisions you might have to make will seem unusual or out of character to others around you. It could make things difficult, but you must stand your ground.'

Simon needed to think – on his own. He stood and turned to Reynolds. 'I can't promise anything, but you will have my answer by Monday night. I'll leave you now. I'll be in touch, Arthur.'

'That's fine, Simon. You know where to find me. Don't forget to pick up Pamela's little treat for your daughter on your way out.'

As the door closed, Reynolds looked over at Sir Arthur. 'Do you think he'll agree to help? It's going to be rough. He might need some propping up at the end, and as he says, some mud might continue to stick.'

Sir Arthur rose from his chair, picked a decanter and two glasses off a side table and offered one to his companion.

'If I've read him right over the years, he has a fair sense of duty, and loves a challenge. I think he'll play.' He raised an eyebrow at Reynolds. 'I'm sure my people and yours can smooth his path in some way in the future.'

*

As there was still no sign of Joanna's father during the afternoon, and rain showers had driven them in from the garden, Amy agreed to Joanna's request to watch some DVDs in the TV room next to the study.

Looking around the room she noted the bookcases, soft settees and media area with a large TV and hi-fi...and then she saw it – standing near the window at the far end of the large room – a baby grand, the same make, even the same colour. The coincidences were so strong she was overwhelmed by memories and found it difficult to bring herself back to the present. Joanna had never mentioned a piano or having lessons, and she looked down at the child.

'Does Miss Francis know you have a piano at home, Joanna? Are you taking lessons?'

The look she received from under dark lashes was one Amy was beginning to know well.

'No, I didn't tell Miss Francis, and I don't really want to have boring lessons with scales and things.'

'But if the piano has been bought for you, perhaps you ought to try.'

Joanna walked over to the instrument and lifted the lid. She struck a few discordant notes. 'Grandpa had this sent over from Canada. It belonged to Grandma before she died. I suppose he thought I might like to play it,' she turned and looked at Amy with a somewhat defiant stare, 'but no-one asked me first.'

Walking across the room to join her, Amy wondered just how much expense had been incurred in shipping the instrument all that way... for nothing.

'Practice doesn't have to be boring, and you might find you like to play. Pianos should be used and enjoyed.'

'You play, don't you? Will you play something for me, Miss Watson?'

There was nothing Amy wanted to do more, but the instrument didn't belong to her. 'We ought to ask your father's permission first, Joanna.'

'Well, he's not here, and you won't hurt it, will you?'

Faced with that logic Amy sat herself on the stool and rested her fingers on the keys. Without any conscious thought her hands instinctively remembered the notes of her favourite piece: "Clair De Lune". She was soon lost in the melody, transported back to those days that had been happy. Only as she finished did she notice that Mrs Gilmore had come into the room. She felt embarrassed and was on the point of apologising, when the now smiling woman broke into a round of applause.

'I knew it couldn't be Joanna playing, it sounded too much in tune.' She smiled down at the child standing beside her. 'I think we'd like to hear some more, don't you think, Joanna?'

'Oh, yes please, Miss Watson. Can I come close and watch?'

Amy looked over the small dark head at Mrs Gilmore, who gave an encouraging nod.

'All right,' she said, 'come and sit on the seat beside me and I'll play it again slowly so you can see how I make the notes.'

After a second run-through of the same piece, Amy was encouraging Joanna to play one or two notes herself, giggling together at the resulting lack of harmony, when a loud voice from behind made them both start.

'What on earth is all this noise about!'

Simon Deveraux was standing in the doorway, looking far from pleased.

Joanna reacted first and called out to him. 'Come and see, Daddy, Miss Watson is teaching me to play.'

'I've no time for that now. I've had a busy day and a long drive. I need some peace and quiet, and this is the last thing I want to be greeted with. Kindly keep the noise down... both of you.' His cool glance moved between them.

Still vulnerable to the emotions of the last hour, with tears very near, Amy carefully closed the piano lid and stood, taking Joanna's hand. 'We'll go upstairs, Joanna, and do some more of that puzzle we started.'

As they left the room she glanced up at Simon Deveraux, wanting to make a retort of some kind, but decided it was better not to. They had started up the stairs together when he called out, 'Oh, Joanna, I nearly forgot. Lady Pamela Dunne asked me to give this to you.' He held out a small package and Joanna went back to him to retrieve it. 'I gather it's something edible, so you'd better have a look at it now.'

With a subdued, 'Thank you, Daddy,' the small figure raced away up the stairs, leaving Amy looking down on her father.

'I'll be working tonight. Perhaps you would be kind enough to ask Mrs Gilmore to bring me a sandwich later. I'll be in town again tomorrow.' He then turned away to his study before she could make any sort of reply.

*

Simon spent the next few hours putting various thoughts down on paper. He could have stayed in the London flat tonight and saved the return journey in the morning, but during the drive home he had redefined his initial decision. He had worked out ways to minimise any fallout should things go badly wrong, but McDonald would still think he was off his head. Simon contemplated letting him in on the whole scheme but considered it would not be advisable. Charles would make the obvious comment that it was a knee-jerk reaction to Jose Ramos' death – and now Simon knew all the probable facts, in truth it was, but he also agreed with Reynolds that countries needed to regain stability and trust if they were to fully recover from the last few years and they could do without the likes of de Santos.

As the world financial problems had escalated, he'd kept an eye on the situation, and tried to second guess where the blows would fall first. He'd made some adjustments to his own and clients' finances and these had proven beneficial. There had been losses, but not as bad as some, and he was now working to claw them back. He had watched with concern as Northern Rock and then Lehmans sank into trouble. It became a case of holding your nerve – and that is what he had to do now. However, despite what Reynolds or Sir Arthur might say, he'd decided he was going to play this game not with Orion money, but his own.

He began putting the papers away in his briefcase, only then becoming aware that it was after one o'clock in the morning. He felt like a stiff drink but decided a glass of water might be better. As he entered the kitchen he noticed, with annoyance, that the light was still on, but then saw the slim figure near the fridge. She turned as he crossed towards her. She was wearing a cream dressing gown and her long copper hair was loosely tied back. He didn't miss the instinctive move to tighten the sash of her gown around her slim waist and smiled to himself. It was a nuisance all this other business had come at an inconvenient time, and he must not lose sight of his original goal. After all, he only had a few weeks.

'Having a midnight feast, Miss Watson?'

'Just a glass of milk, Mr Deveraux, if that is allowed.'

There she was again; pricking his conscience, but in all truth, he had been rude earlier tonight and she deserved an apology. As she had led Joanna away it had surprised him to see the sheen of tears in her eyes. It had been totally unexpected and made him feel uncomfortable.

'That's quite all right, Miss Watson. In fact, I was of the same mind, but water for me, I think.'

He picked up a glass from the counter and filled it from the tap. Turning, he found she was standing regarding him, with grey eyes solemn and troubled.

'Have you been working until this hour?'

'I'm afraid so, but I'm finished now.'

'It's not a very healthy lifestyle.'

'I tend to agree with you, but at times things are out of your control. Anyway, I'm off to bed now.' He watched as colour flooded into her cheeks. He cleared his throat. 'I feel I should apologise for my attitude earlier. I appreciate you were doing what you were employed to do – entertaining Joanna.'

'Perhaps you might say something of the kind to your daughter. She was rather upset. She had been enjoying herself.'

'I rather thought you both were when I came in.' Despite himself he remembered his feeling at seeing the two heads close together over the piano, laughing: the sound of a home. 'I hope I'll be in a position to make up for it soon. Incidentally, what was the present?'

She had turned away and was moving out of the room but looked back over her shoulder at him. 'A gingerbread man – all consumed in five minutes. I think it rather saved the day. There's a thank you note on the hall table if you would please see it's delivered. Goodnight.'

He drained his glass, switched off the light and followed her upstairs, turning away to his own room with a strange feeling of reluctance. The relaxation of someone to have a normal conversation with for a while would have been welcome.

Chapter Seven

So far, the day was going as Simon had predicted. He had arranged for Frank Gilmore to drive him into town, a wise precaution because of his lack of sleep, and he had already been working for an hour when Susan walked into his office, surprised at seeing him there. He handed her his list of instructions; cancellation of all appointments for the day, an urgent meeting to be arranged that morning with Charles McDonald and Stuart Mannion, his chief financial manager, and a meeting with Mark Grainger in the afternoon.

'Tell him I want him here at two o'clock sharp, Susan. No arguments or excuses. From the look of my diary, I have the next two days clear. Keep them that way. I'll work from home. Thursday and Friday try and reorganise things scheduled for today. Next week isn't looking too bad but refer to me before you book anything else in.'

As she made to leave the room to follow his instructions, he halted her. 'Er, Susan, you might find the next few weeks a bit awkward, even rough…but I'd appreciate it as a personal favour if you'd stick with me.'

She hesitated for a moment but then gave him an amused look and said, 'So what's different!' raising the only smile of the day for him.

He was now sitting at his desk, watching the astonishment and disbelief forming on the two faces opposite.

'You've really lost it now, boy, if you're thinking of doing something as stupid as this!' McDonald was almost red in the face.

'Sorry Charles, but I'm going ahead with the Colombian project. I know there are risks, which is why I've decided to use my own money rather than involve Orion. I'm seeing Mark Grainger this afternoon to let him know. However, I'm only putting up three-quarters of the funds to start with. I'll negotiate an option for the rest once the project has moved on.' He looked at them both. 'I can't see too much of a problem liquidating the funds I need. I will, however, have to pull out of the Azerbaijan deal.'

'That will cost you, Simon,' warned Stuart Mannion, looking extremely uncomfortable.

'I'm aware of that, Stuart. I'll have a word with Dimitri personally. See what sort of bargain I can strike.'

'I still don't understand why you now want in on Grainger's project. I thought you had reservations about it. I certainly have. New unproven companies, development sight unseen...' A look began to come on McDonald's face. 'This isn't some sort of crazy philanthropic idea for helping South American countries, a sort of memorial to young Ramos?'

Simon shifted in his chair. This was now getting difficult, and he had to shut it down as soon as possible. 'Whatever it is, Charles, it's what I want done and I expect both of you to do your best to achieve it as soon as possible.'

He saw the look pass between the two men, and then McDonald gave a shrug. 'OK, if you want it that badly, we'll get it organised.'

'Thanks, Charles. There was one other thing. I want you to move my Turner painting, currently on loan to the Tate, into Joanna's Trust Fund. Susan will give you the details. Can you also do a check on the Fund generally, making quite sure that it's properly in place and totally independent from my personal finances and Orion's. I know we set it up that way, but just make sure for me.'

After another quick glance between the two men, they rose and left the room in silence. Simon ran a hand over his face. He had felt the hostility and disapproval and had an urge to tell them what it was all about, but knew he had to maintain his silence. He looked up and saw McDonald standing in the doorway.

'You OK, Simon? Nothing wrong? I hope you would feel after all this time together you could talk about it.'

Simon was touched by the genuine concern, but made himself say, 'I'm fine, Charles. No problems. Just a bit tired. I've got a couple of days at home this week which will be good.'

McDonald just nodded and left the room.

*

Simon had come to the conclusion that he disliked Mark Grainger. He had arrived punctually at two o'clock, with the obligatory smart suit and official-looking briefcase. However, Simon judged his air of slick confidence hid an inadequate grasp of the intricacies of his subject, and Simon considered his company would not be around for very long.

He wondered just how much the man was aware of the factors surrounding this particular deal. It was quite possible he knew very little, and regarded it only as a money-making opportunity. Outlining his conditions for entering into the agreement Simon saw Grainger's instant lack of confidence in judging whether to accept them.

'You understand that we had anticipated Orion itself would be involved and you are only offering three-quarters of the sum required?'

Trying to hold on to his temper, Simon fixed him with a cool stare. 'I have certain best practice reservations about the deal, but I am prepared to make this offer, and as it is the only one I will make, I suggest you have a clear choice to either accept... or not.'

He pointedly looked at his watch. He could tell Grainger was thinking desperately and then he appeared to come to a decision.

'All right, I will accept your offer on behalf of my clients in the terms as stated. Three-quarter funding now with an option for the rest when the project is more advanced.'

'That is exactly right, Mr Grainger. My legal department will liaise with you regarding the paperwork,' he came to his feet and held out his hand, 'and, if you will excuse me, I'm afraid I am already late for my next appointment. I squeezed you in as you had been wanting an urgent reply. Good day, Mr Grainger.'

They shook hands and the younger man left the room in a hurry.

*

Outside on the pavement Grainger took a long steadying breath. Well, he'd got a sort of deal. Surely it would be enough for Hernandez's client? All right, it was going to be Deveraux's money and not Orion's, but that was near enough, wasn't it? He'd better get back to his office and make a call. He started to feel better. If this went through, he could make a tidy sum, and in a few years he would give the likes of that pompous Deveraux a run for his money.

*

The deep tones and thick accent of Dimitri Orloff came clearly over the telephone line. 'Nice to speak with you again, my friend.'

'When you hear what I have to say, Dimitri, you may not think so.'

Simon had not looked forward to this telephone call. He'd first been introduced to Orloff at a private dinner party when stopping off in Instanbul during a six-week business tour some five years before. Orloff, having left Russia more than twenty years previously, had become the "go-to man" in the region for funding and deal-

61

making, particularly by oil companies. He was fair but tough as old boots. Simon liked the man and trusted his judgment, and, out of courtesy, a personal explanation had been necessary.

'Ah well, there is not much more left of the day to spoil, so go ahead.'

'I'm afraid I'm pulling out of our deal. There is a situation at this end I must address first, and I need the funds.'

He heard a chuckle at the other end.

'Have you been paying your mistress too much… or too little? You have to keep them sweet, you know; I thought I'd taught you that.'

Although much older, Dimitri's prowess with the opposite sex was legendary, and Simon had first-hand experience of his lifestyle.

'Sorry to disappoint you, but I seem to have neither the time nor the inclination just lately.'

'Well, you must come over here soon and I'll help you revive it.' Another chuckle, but then Simon could tell the conversation was now serious. 'You realise that to pull out will cost you money? The penalties are quite specific.'

'Yes, I know, but despite that, as I've worked it out there will still be enough left. Perhaps when I get this other matter sorted in a month or two, I can renegotiate.'

The reply was instantaneous. 'Simon, you and I go back a long way. You have enjoyed hospitality at my home on many occasions, and I have always trusted you. You can have your money, and I will put the penalties on hold for two months. If you are able to come back afterwards, then we say no more about it. If not, I'll take you for every dollar you have.'

Simon was in no doubt that he would. This man could eat people like Mark Grainger for breakfast and still be hungry. 'Thank you, Dimitri. I appreciate the gesture.'

'Simon, my young friend, you are not in trouble in any way? I hope you would come to me if you were. This is nothing to do with Joanna?'

Simon had often wondered whether, during some of their more…lively evenings, he had at any time unwittingly revealed his personal circumstances. The problem was that he couldn't remember! There had been other times when odd remarks had been made by this man which had left him wondering. However, touched by the sentiments, and trying to make his voice light and casual, he said, 'It's just a project in South America and nothing for major concern, Dimitri, but I won't forget this.'

As the call finished Orloff sat for a moment, eyes closed, then he picked up the phone once more.

*

Slumped in the front seat of the Mercedes as Frank Gilmore drove him home, Simon felt totally drained. However, he knew this was only the start and things would get considerably worse from now on.

He needed the peace and quiet of Woodhayes, but even there, it wouldn't be straightforward. His father was arriving later this week, and there was still Amelia Watson to deal with. Idly watching the countryside from the car window he suddenly pictured her grey eyes and mass of copper hair.

*

Joanna's grandfather was due later in the day, and Mrs Gilmore appeared busy. Amy offered to help, but this was refused with a smile. In an effort to calm an excited Joanna, she suggested it would be a nice idea if she tidied her own room. After a less than enthusiastic start Joanna warmed to the task and it soon became a full-scale spring clean. At one point Amy regretted making the suggestion, and noticed she had the bruises to prove it, but by late afternoon order had been restored.

Simon Deveraux arrived home only minutes before his father, Frank Gilmore having been dispatched to meet him at the airport. On hearing voices, Joanna raced into the hall and flung her arms around the distinguished-looking grey-haired man just entering through the front door. Standing in the doorway to the lounge Amy considered Emile Deveraux must be in his early sixties. She immediately noticed the family likeness and was instantly warmed by his interaction with Joanna as he wrapped her in a huge hug.

'Oh, Grandpa, it's so lovely to have you here! You'll never guess what I've been doing today. Miss Watson and I have been tidying my room, and it was such fun.'

Amy glanced over at Simon Deveraux and found him regarding her with one eyebrow raised in query. Well, if he didn't like what they'd been doing it was just too bad, she thought. However, saying nothing he turned to the older man and they shook hands. Amy was curious that there was no more affectionate greeting between them, and then remembered Mrs Gilmore's recent comments.

'Good to have you here again, Father. You came in from Paris, I understand.'

Emile Deveraux passed over the remark with a wave of his hand. 'I'll explain later.' His eyes moved over to Amy and with a polite smile he enquired, 'Should I be introduced to this young lady?'

'Oh, Grandpa, this is Miss Watson. She's staying here for the summer.'

Amy noticed him give a quick glance at his son before she stepped forward, holding out her hand.

'Good evening, Mr Deveraux. I'm Amelia Watson and I'm very pleased to meet you. Joanna has been looking forward to your visit.'

She felt herself examined by eyes of a slightly less intense blue than his son's, but she judged there was the same astute mind behind them. There was also a sense of warmth, and as he smiled and took her hand, she knew she would like this man.

However, at dinner that evening Amy could sense Emile Deveraux's surprise that she was joining them; she would have felt extremely uncomfortable had he not obviously recognised this and made a point of including her in the conversation. She sensed again the warmth in him and felt relaxed in his presence, unlike in that of his son. The conversation anyway was dominated by Joanna's endless excited chattering, trying to bring her grandfather up to date on all her activities since she had last seen him. He appeared to have no problem in indulging her, but a sharp retort from her father finally silenced the girl. Joanna seemed suddenly deflated and remained so for the rest of the meal, eyes on her plate as she studiously ate her food. When coffee was brought through Amy felt it wise to encourage Joanna to return to her room, using the excuse of finishing the last bit of tidying up before bedtime. Emile Deveraux stood as they both rose from the table and he patted Joanna's head. 'I look forward to hearing some more of your exciting adventures tomorrow, but after my travelling I think I too will have an early night.' He smiled at Amy and she had a shrewd idea he had understood the reason for her action. 'Goodnight, Miss Watson. We will meet again tomorrow.'

Taking the hand of a rather reluctant Joanna she led the way upstairs and, looking down, saw both men walk into the study and the door close.

Chapter Eight

Emile Deveraux looked over at his son and spoke in French.

'I see nothing changes in your relationship with Joanna. Or has it? Who exactly is this Miss Watson?'

Simon sat down on the Chesterfield and regarded his father, then replied in the same language. 'She's a teaching assistant from Carlton House. I've employed her as company for Joanna during the school holidays. Margaret Horton is still unable to return.'

'She's very young. What do you know about her?'

'She's twenty-something, I suppose. I never enquired. Harriet Freeman employed her, and seems to think highly of her efforts, and as she indicated that she had kept my personal details confidential, it seemed convenient for me, in the circumstances. Joanna appears to like her, and it will be useful, if we are out, to have a female chaperon.'

'Exactly. That's one of the things I warned you about. I see you are including Miss Watson at mealtimes too, not something I remember with Mrs Horton.'

'I thought it seemed a good idea.'

'Did you consider the fact that at night she is alone in the house with just you, even though, of course, with Joanna? It's not an ideal scenario, Simon, or did that seem a "good idea" too? She's a pretty girl.'

'It was just the same with Margaret Horton.'

'If I remember correctly, Mrs Horton was already in her forties when she first came to work for you. This is something slightly different. I assume the current "arrangement" has no... other purpose?'

Simon stood and moved over to his desk.

'There's no need for your concern, Father. Now, you said earlier you would explain your travel arrangements, as if I couldn't guess. How is Madame Moreau?'

Emile gave a shrug, aware that the topic of conversation was being diverted. 'She is very well, thank you for asking. I shall be able to see her more often now I'm living in Paris.'

'Living in Paris!' Simon turned to his father, amazement showing on his face.

'Yes, I've decided it's time for me to take things easy. I've just sold the firm and I intend to make my home in France.'

Simon appeared completely lost for words. 'I've not seen anything in the press. Major changes at a big law firm like Deveraux's would cause a ripple or two.'

'It's not common knowledge yet; probably the end of the month. It's an "in house" sale. I gave them first refusal; thought it only right. I'm staying with Justine in Paris until I find something to buy: more convenient for Joanna, too. I can see her more often. Whatever the circumstances, I feel I have a duty to stand by her. I take it you have no objection? Perhaps she can come to visit,' he gave a small chuckle, 'we might even try Disneyland.'

'Father, I've always appreciated your consideration for her, but for God's sake don't mention anything about a visit. I'll never control her.'

'I'm sorry you think I would consider doing something like that without your knowledge.' The reproach came through in the tone of voice. Simon ran a hand through his hair and closed his eyes for a moment. Watching him, his father went on in a more conciliatory tone, 'You could do with slowing down a bit too, Simon. You look worn out.'

'It's just busy at the moment. Something important I'm working on... but once I'm through that I might take a break. Anyway, I intend to work from home as often as I can during these next few weeks.'

'Glad to hear it. Perhaps we can all spend some quality time together for a change.'

*

Over the next few days, true to his word, Amy noted that Simon Deveraux spent more time at Woodhayes, working part of the day and then spending time either with Joanna on her own, or in company also with his father. On one occasion Amy was asked to join them on an outing, and although she tried to avoid it, for some reason her presence was considered necessary. In any case, she couldn't resist Joanna's beaming face. During lunch, on finding it difficult to address both father and son as 'Mr Deveraux', a smiling Emile Deveraux was adamant he would not be called 'Deveraux Senior'.

'My given names are Henri Emile, but somehow I became known as just Emile. I have no objection to the use of this name, and would I think be a good idea all round. It is holiday time, after all.'

Amy was sure Simon Deveraux would object but to her surprise he agreed. Although she could not envisage having the courage to call him Simon at any time, she felt it would seem stupid to make an issue about it. Then with a polite smile, he enquired, 'Should we call you Amelia or are you used to the derivative Amy, by any chance?'

'Umm... Amy would be fine,' she managed to assure him.

Joanna then piped up, 'Can I call everyone by their names too?'

'You may call Amy by her Christian name, if she has no objection, but,' Simon raised one finger at her in warning, 'this is just for the holidays, and there is no allowance for a different form of address for myself or your grandfather. When you're older it might be a different thing.'

She gave him a mutinous stare for a moment. 'It's not fair. Everyone keeps talking about the things I can do "when I get older", but I never do.' Taking out her frustration on the crust of her apple pie, she missed the smothered amusement around her.

*

A day or two later, on a particularly hot afternoon, at his request, Amy sat with Emile on the terrace overlooking the garden. Joanna was out to tea with a school friend and her father was still in town.

Emile had been talking about his decision to retire and move to France. Amy sensed a strong link to his past heritage and queried him on the origins of the Deveraux name.

'It's Norman French, with perhaps a bit of Irish too,' he smiled at her. 'I now intend to spend some of my free time seeing if I can trace any ancestors. I've always felt the connection with France, but it seems Simon has done his best to anglicise himself as much as possible. He tells me it's better for modern day business, but I'm not convinced it's made any difference. I've never had any doubt as to my son's abilities. I think he would have succeeded in anything he turned his mind to. I will admit I was initially disappointed that he would not follow me into the firm and keep it in the family, but that's the way of life. It doesn't always work out the way you expect. I know Helene would have been proud of him.' He looked over at her. 'It's so nice to hear the piano in use again, my dear. My wife loved to play. She passed away after a long illness when Simon was in his early teens, and he was no musician. Joanna hadn't appeared interested either, until now. She's always been adamant that she didn't want to learn. Of late I've thought of suggesting to Simon he give the instrument away to a needy cause, rather than have it just standing idle.'

'That's what I told Joanna. A piano should be used. It was the idea of boring scales she disliked, although whether she has real interest, I'm not sure at the moment. I'm just trying to get her to pick out a few tunes with me, so she finds enjoyment in it.'

'I have noticed your rapport with Joanna, my dear. I've seen other changes in her – all for the better.'

'It's natural that she will change more as she gets older, Emile. I don't think it's so much down to me. I just wish…' she broke off, not knowing if she should say more.

'Go on, my dear. I won't betray a confidence if that's what you're worried about.'

Amy took a deep breath, thinking back to that dreadful evening at Carlton House. 'I just wish Joanna had more close contact with her father. He obviously looks after her, but there is a sense of detachment sometimes in his attitude. She seems more natural with you. She's confused about not doing some of the things with her father that her friends appear to do with theirs. She also confided in me that she misses a mother and doesn't understand why she knows nothing about her. I spoke to your son at a Parents Evening recently and told him of my feelings. He made it clear he didn't like what I said, and quite frankly I was surprised at being offered this position.' She looked over at her companion and saw the closed expression on his face. 'I'm sorry. I didn't mean to criticise. I know it's not really very professional, but I must admit to having grown quite fond of Joanna.'

'Don't apologise, Amy. I'm glad she is being looked after by someone who genuinely cares. By that I don't mean that my son, Margaret Horton or the Gilmores haven't cared for her, but you seem to have found an extra emotional attachment to her. I think that this is because of some experience in your own life?'

Amy looked down the length of the immaculate lawn, listening to the rustle of the trees surrounding them, and the muted bird calls in the fading heat of the day. She didn't want to reveal personal details to the Deveraux family. After observing their lifestyle first-hand she could see more than ever that she was not in their class, and after these few weeks she would return to living her normal life. She was startled when she felt her hand being squeezed.

'My dear, I have no wish to pry into your personal situation. I would just say that others also have circumstances thrust upon them, not of their making, with which they have to deal as best they can. Some handle it better than others. I regret to say that Simon sometimes tends to make impulsive decisions, and this can lead to problems and misunderstandings, but then again what family doesn't have them?' he smiled ruefully. 'But whatever the case, we must still help as much as we can.'

Amy felt tears pricking at the back of her eyes. She had never felt as close to a man since Uncle George. They both talked in the same fashion. She knew that she had been told something in confidence, not in detail, but just enough to understand that there was a problem and allowances had to be made.

'I understand, Emile, and I'll do anything I can to help.'

*

Miguel Hernandez listened intently to the voice at the other end of the phone.

'Yes, Senor de Santos, this is the information as I have been told. The Grainger person has today informed me that documents have already been received and the deal, as agreed, is progressing. Deveraux is obviously prepared personally to accept the inherent risks.' His face now showed a frown as he listened further. 'I will tell him, senor, but he will complain that this is not part of his professional services. I'm not sure that he is the best person to compile any personal information on Deveraux, he does not have the skill, and it was agreed that I am better placed to —' He stopped abruptly at the interruption on the other end of the line. 'But, of course, if you wish it. I agree with you that we can apply pressure. We can make him aware of our knowledge of some other deals he has made; after all that is why we chose him. Senor, there is, however, always the possible risk that *he* decides to inform the authorities and they start to make investigations. Therefore, I feel it would be as well if I make sure he is… dissuaded from this course of action.' A smile then crossed his dark features. 'Thank you, senor. I will deal with the matter as you say.'

*

Stuart Mannion closed the door behind him and seated himself in front of Charles McDonald, worry evident on his face.

'What do you make of all this, Charles? I've just been with him. He's going ahead with this Colombian thing, the money's just come in from Orloff. I've seen him sail close to the wind before, but as far as scale of risk this is way out there. I know it's his own money, but it still comes down to judgment. If it all goes pear-shaped, private money or not, and the word gets out, it might make people think, especially now.'

'I know what you mean, Stu. I had a quiet word with Susan this morning, trying to pump her for anything that might be wrong. Didn't get me far, she's too loyal. You know what really worried me was when he asked about checking Joanna's Trust Fund. Right from when the Fund was set up, just before she was born, he's always accepted that the trust managers we appointed knew their stuff and we weren't to interfere. It's almost as if he's expecting trouble. However, I have thought of something we might try.'

'Well, come on then, let's hear it. I'm damned if I'm going to sit here and do nothing. I've worked my backside off for Deveraux, but so far I've been glad to do it. He's one of the best at the game, but if, for some reason, he's losing his edge, I want to be in a position to try and do damage limitation.'

McDonald picked up his phone. 'I want to know what Fletcher's doing at the moment.' The number rang out and after a moment or two the call was answered. 'Jack? Where are you, boy? Good… where did you say again? Right, get the beers in, Stuart

72

and I will be right over… Yes that's what I said. See you shortly.'
He stood up, rummaged in his briefcase, removed some papers, and headed for the door. 'Fancy a drink?'

Mystified, Mannion followed him out of the room.

By the time they reached the nearby bar, Jack Fletcher had indeed placed the order.

'Well, I must say, this is a surprise. Are we all playing hooky on a Friday afternoon or something?' He grinned at the other two, but this faded when he took in their solemn faces. 'Trouble?'

'I hope not, Jack, but I want you to do something. Are you in a position to get off immediately to South America? To be precise, Colombia, but I suggest make it via Rio first. We want you to have a sniff around a piece of real estate. Simon was going to get Jose to do it… but of course that's not possible now.'

'Yeah, shame about that.' Fletcher took a long pull on his beer, studying McDonald over the rim of his glass. 'Why do I get the idea that Simon doesn't know anything about this?'

Mannion spoke next. 'Jack, he wants to do a deal, a personal deal, and Charles and I are seriously worried about it. From every viewpoint it's risky. Sure, he's taken risks before but nothing like this. We want to know what it looks like from on the ground, literally. Charles here has some papers detailing what's proposed, and where. Can you make an excuse of dealing with the new Rio office to get yourself down there and have a look for us, without him knowing?'

Fletcher looked from one to the other. 'This seems a bit underhand, boys, don't you think? If he finds out he could kick my arse… hard.'

'And ours too, don't forget.' McDonald looked at Fletcher long and hard. 'Jack, we all like the guy, and I for one don't want to see him get burned.'

Fletcher knocked back the rest of his beer and placed the glass down on the table. 'OK, mates. I'll be on the next available flight.'

*

After her grandfather returned to France, Joanna's attitude became moody and difficult, earning her several reprimands from her father. Even Amy was beginning to feel her temper stretched to the limits. It was still a surprise, however, when one evening Simon Deveraux suggested she join him in the sitting room once Joanna had gone to bed. Since Emile had left, she had felt diffident about remaining downstairs in the evening and usually stayed in her room.

On entering the sitting room with its comfortable sofas and chairs and magnificent view of the terrace and garden from the curved full-length window, she was immediately conscious of the figure standing near the large red brick fireplace. Although she had seen more of him over these last weeks it had not diminished the aura of power and wealth that she sensed about this man. Father and son were in many ways alike, both physically and in their success in business, but Emile had given her the impression of approachability and warmth. His son's attitude appeared harder, and she sensed it would be dangerous for anyone to anger or cross him. Standing just inside the door she was uncertain what to do next.

'Would you care for a drink, Amy?' She found herself greeted by a rare warm smile, and a gesture for her to sit on one of the sofas.

She had on other evenings accepted an after-dinner drink but felt disinclined to do so on this occasion. 'Umm...no, thank you.' Then to her surprise he came and sat next to her.

'I wondered what had become of you these last few evenings. There is really no need for you to retreat to your room after dinner. Both my father... and I... are quite happy with your company.'

She recognised his meaning but would never admit to him that she still found it difficult to be alone with him. 'I've had things to do, and assumed you were the same, Mr Deveraux.'

The fact that he did not believe her excuse was evident from the amused look in his eyes. Flecks of light danced in the deep blue and despite herself she wondered what it would be like for a

woman to have this handsome man look at her with affection…
and more.

His amusement still evident, he shook his head. 'Tut, tut, I
thought we had dispensed with formalities. I see no reason for
it not to continue even though my father is no longer present.'
Before she could make any reply, he went on, 'There is a matter
I wished to speak to you about, Amy.' He stood and returned to
his position by the fireplace. 'What on earth are we going to do
about Joanna? Since my father left, she's become impossible. To
be frank, I need your assistance and some ideas.'

Now that he was no longer in such close proximity to her, and
she knew the topic of discussion, Amy relaxed.

'I know what you mean. I'm finding difficulties myself. She
seems to have lost interest in everything. I've come upon her on
several occasions deep in conversation with her rabbit, but she
stops as soon as I approach and although I've questioned her
about it, she never tells me the subject of these conversations.'

'I sometimes wish I'd never brought that thing back with me.
An associate of mine in Turkey purchased it as a present for her,
and she seems to have forged a strong link with it. I have even
found myself joining in with the pretend game. I wonder now
if it's healthy for her to have this connection with an inanimate
object.'

'I'm sure it's quite normal Mr… er…Simon. I know of a
situation where the "friend" was entirely imaginary, and that
would worry me more. At least she can see and touch the rabbit,
and young girls in particular talk to their dolls, sometimes telling
them little secrets.' She knew from personal experience the
comfort it gave. 'Imaginary play is an aid to increasing confidence
in vocabulary. Dolls can't answer back, telling you there is no
such word, or it's mispronounced. Young children can also treat a
family pet in the same way.'

'This all sounds very profound for someone so young.'

The superior look on the handsome face infuriated her. His
attitude to her had obviously not changed and probably never

would. He had admitted there was a problem, and had asked for her help, but if he wasn't prepared at least to consider what she had to say in a serious fashion, the whole exercise was pointless. She rose to her feet, about to announce the fact that she wished to terminate her employment, when he came to stand beside her.

'I'm sorry, Amy. I seem to have a knack of upsetting you.'

Before she was aware of the fact, he had drawn her down onto the sofa beside him. His thigh was close to hers and she could feel the warmth of his body and smell the subtle lemony tang of aftershave. His face was the picture of sincerity and despite herself she felt her anger draining away.

'Do you think Joanna has a secret that's worrying her? Does it involve my father?'

Trying to gather her thoughts again, which seemed strangely difficult, Amy commented, 'I just wonder if she thinks that without her grandfather, she might not be going on any more outings with you. I'm sure she has seen that lately you have spent a considerable time working, albeit from home, and fears life might revert back to a lack of time spent with you. Perhaps you could take it as a compliment that she enjoys your company and wants more of it.' She wondered how he would take her remarks and studied his face for a sign of anger, but found none, and in fact he seemed quite impassive.

'So you're saying all this moodiness is because she wants me to take her out?'

Hearing the frustration in his voice she knew she had misjudged his reaction.

'I don't know anything for sure, but it's a possibility.'

'I'm a busy man with other responsibilities. She can't expect to be entertained the whole time. Financially I'm able to indulge her in all things, but I have resisted this as not being in her best interests. I don't want her turning into a spoilt little brat. She needs to understand the meaning of money and treats.'

Amy knew only too well the advantages of Joanna's lifestyle, but it didn't account for everything.

'May I make a suggestion?' She refrained from using a Christian name, but from his quick look she judged he had noticed her omission.

'Of course, that's why I'm asking.'

'If I'm right, and she needs the comfort of knowing that outings are still intended, why don't you ask her what she herself would be interested in doing. We could make a list or something.'

He looked at her with no apparent reaction for a moment, and she expected a firm denial of the idea, but with a slight smile he then said, 'I shudder to think what ideas she might come up with – but perhaps it's a start. Ask her to give it some thought and you can see me tomorrow night with the answer.'

Chapter Nine

Trying to keep the amusement from showing on her face Amy sat on the sofa and watched as Simon Deveraux glanced once more at the paper in his hand. On speaking to Joanna after breakfast, she appeared immediately energised by the task in hand of compiling her list, and Amy felt it vindicated her take on the situation.

'Oh, my God, it's worse than I imagined. Legoland! The cinema to see...*How to Train your*... what? *Dragons*? McDonalds! Over my dead body!'

Trying to keep the laughter out of her voice Amy felt she had to make some comment. 'It's what someone of her age would want to do, even if it doesn't appeal to you.'

The blue gaze settled on her. 'I'll agree to some sort of compromises, the first being that I will pick and choose, and the second is that you will accompany us, as it was your idea in the first place – always providing you can refrain from enjoying yourself too much at my expense.'

Before she could utter a word, his smile broadened until he was actually laughing. It was such an unexpected show of genuine amusement its impact took her breath away. To her amazement he came and collapsed onto the sofa beside her, still chuckling to himself.

'I think we'd better get Legoland out of the way first before I change my mind. Maybe tie it in with a fast-food snack. Frank

Gilmore might be able to give us some ideas on that side, if you would ask him. I think I've Wednesday and Thursday free next week. If the weather looks suitable, we'll fix it for then. OK?'

The smile was still in his eyes and, as she nodded her agreement, she felt herself slipping under the spell of this attractive male.

*

Mark Grainger stood in a doorway out of the rain, feeling out of his depth. What did he know about spying on people; and more to the point, he ought to be working in his office. However, the bottom line was that Miguel Hernandez had frightened the life out of him at their last "discussion". He had no idea that anyone knew about his siphoning off money from two of his past deals. The threat of exposure had at first angered him, but he realised very quickly that he could be in much more trouble from the thinly veiled threats if he opened his mouth to the authorities about anything at all.

Why information on Deveraux was needed he had no idea. As far as he knew there had been no whiff of scandal in his private life. In fact, not a great deal was known about him anyway. Since his wife had died Deveraux appeared to have led a fairly quiet life, as far as the press was aware anyway. In his business deals he was regarded as trustworthy with no hint of anything improper. He smiled to himself at that. Perhaps the authorities just hadn't caught him. Now there was an idea. Was that at the bottom of all this cloak and dagger nonsense? Did Miguel's client know something? The prospect of tripping up someone like Deveraux had now become an interesting exercise. He'd been watching the comings and goings at Orion's offices all day, but perhaps he ought to keep an eye on his home near Windsor. It was more private and out of the way – ideal for certain meetings?

*

Dan Reynolds finished his call and made some notes. Why was Grainger staking out Deveraux's office? His recent meeting with Hernandez had been observed and noted as one of the few occasions on which their target had been seen leaving his accommodation. It was possible Grainger had been given some instructions, but why use such a novice? He'd stood out like a sore thumb, much to the amusement of Reynold's colleagues. Should he warn Deveraux? At this point he decided against it. What worried him more was he'd also been told that Deveraux's security man had flown to Rio yesterday. Surely Deveraux hadn't been stupid enough to ask him to take a look at the Colombian site. If news got out in the wrong quarters that might start alarm bells ringing with de Santos. He would need to give this matter some urgent attention.

*

Amy was amazed that the visit to Legoland worked out better than expected. Once the decision had been made, she sensed that Simon Deveraux had decided to enter fully into the spirit of the outing. He was dressed more casually than she had ever seen him, in a short-sleeved shirt and slacks which, in her opinion, made him look younger. She herself had opted for the practicality of trousers and a lace-trimmed blouse and had decided to dress Joanna in bright red shorts with a red and white striped top and red sunhat, so she would be easily visible.

As they wandered around the attractions Simon didn't give any impression of impatience or boredom. For one moment she wondered if he was secretly enjoying it, but, of course, she would never have the courage to actually ask him.

In some of the more crowded areas she noticed him take hold of Joanna's hand, and at one point much to her amazement felt him grasp her own; his only comment when she glanced up at him was, 'We don't want to lose you either.' The feel of his hand and the smile in his eyes left her silent and confused.

Late in the afternoon they finally persuaded Joanna to leave, after promising a return visit with her grandfather. Amy gave directions, obtained from a surprised Frank Gilmore, as to the best place to eat, which proved to be a McDonalds where they could purchase their food at the Drive Thru and then eat it at a more secluded picnic area nearby. This was approved by Simon, who adamantly refused to eat inside the establishment surrounded by 'hordes of screaming children'. Although the air was still warm, with not a breath of wind, they found themselves virtually on their own at the picnic area and ate in peace and quiet. While Joanna was out of earshot feeding scraps of bun to a flock of birds, Amy looked over at the man opposite and, noting his relaxed appearance, dared to comment, 'I don't suppose you have often eaten a meal this way?'

He turned away from watching the feeding display and a cool blue gaze settled on her. 'I haven't always dined in fine restaurants with white tablecloths and sparking cutlery, Amy. When I was young my father and I used to go camping in some fairly remote spots, catching our own food most of the time. During college I went on various treks to some out of the way places where the usual offices were, to say the least, rudimentary.' He then smiled at her. 'Much as I am sure you would like to think otherwise, I do know what it's like, as with most students, to work at various jobs to earn extra money. I have actually slaved over a hot griddle in the past, even cleaning up after closing time. My upbringing might have been quite affluent, but I was taught the value of money, and as I've said to you before, I want Joanna to appreciate this for herself.'

Again, it was an attitude she could not fault, and gave her yet another insight into this enigmatic man.

Looking up at the sky, he commented, 'It looks as if we're in for some rain, so we'd better head home I think.' He called out, 'Joanna, time to go. If you feed those birds any more they'll be too fat to fly.'

As they drove home the sky turned a livid yellow, and dark storm clouds rose over the horizon. The first drops of rain started to fall as they turned down the lane towards Woodhayes. Simon suddenly muttered an oath under his breath and swung the wheel of the Mercedes sharply. They were passing a shallow cut out in the dense undergrowth on their side of the road and a small blue Peugeot car was parked there. The male driver turned his head as they passed. All Amy noticed was some sort of hat and dark glasses. Suddenly, for some unaccountable reason, she had a sense of foreboding and felt shivers running through her. As if from a long way away she registered Simon's comment.

'Stupid place to park, especially in this weather.'

The odd feeling within her had reawakened memories from the past she would rather forget, and, still in a dream, Amy helped Joanna from the car and ran inside, out of the deluge now falling.

Following them into the house, Simon observed, 'Looks as if we're in for a wet evening. It's a good job we left when we did.'

Joanna turned to him, and actually grabbed his hand. 'There won't be a thunderstorm, will there, Daddy?'

'With it raining like this it will probably pass over. Don't worry about it.' He looked over at Amy. 'Joanna doesn't find thunderstorms particularly pleasant, I'm afraid.'

'Neither do I.' With that statement, Amy comforted herself that this was the possible reason for her unease, of a moment ago, and felt herself relaxing.

Simon shook his dark head. 'So, it seems as if I may have two damsels in distress to look after.'

Amy took hold of Joanna's hand and led her to the stairs. 'I'm sure neither of us will be any bother to you. I think we'd better get out of these damp clothes, Joanna, but first of all perhaps we should say thank you for a lovely day?'

To her surprise Joanna pulled away and ran back to her father and gave him a hug. 'Thank you, Daddy, for a lovely, lovely time today.' She then turned and raced away up the stairs.

Amy watched as various emotions crossed Simon's face and then without a further word he turned and disappeared into his study.

Mark Grainger noted the Mercedes pass. It was going to be difficult to keep a watch on the house. There was no safe parking for a car, and he was not prepared to skulk about in bushes, especially in weather like this. The rain was much harder now and he could hardly see a thing. When the car had passed it was lighter and he was able to glimpse the occupants. The daughter was in the back, and he saw a woman in the passenger seat. For a moment, the red copper hair reminded him of someone else, someone from the past, but that would be crazy. It was surely just a coincidence.

*

The storm didn't pass but broke with a vengeance several hours later. Just lightly asleep Amy woke with a start after one brilliant flash of lightning and sat up in bed. She always felt safer awake and dressed at these times, so she climbed out of bed and found her dressing gown, slipping it on over her nightdress. Pushing her long hair out of her face she crossed to the window and pulled the curtains closed. She then remembered about Joanna. Should she go and take a look at her? With her bare feet muffled by the thick carpet and drowned by the outside noises, she moved soundlessly towards Joanna's door. She heard the crying almost immediately and found the little girl curled up at the foot of her bed, sobbing. She looked so small and alone with her fear that Amy forgot her own and crossed to her. Kneeling on the floor beside her she cradled the distraught child in her arms, rocking her back and forth, but not able to contain her own gasp as yet another vicious streak of lightning crossed the sky.

She didn't hear Simon come into the room, until strong arms picked her off the floor. For a moment she was held close to his chest and smelt again the lemony fragrance on his skin, then he gently moved her towards a soft armchair and sat her down, murmuring, 'Curl up there for a moment while I deal with Joanna.'

He pulled the curtains fully closed and shut the bedroom door. The room was now very dark. He picked up the still crying girl and placed her back in bed, pulling the covers up to her chin. He retrieved the toy rabbit and then sat on the bed beside her. 'It seems after all as if I do have two females to look after.' He tucked the rabbit under the covers and pulled them more firmly around the child. 'Mr Floppy's here to keep you company and Amy and I will stay with you, so close your eyes, and you'll soon be asleep.'

From her position in the chair Amy saw him move away from Joanna and sit on the spare bed. He looked across at her as thunder growled close by and she flinched. 'Are you all right?'

She could only nod in reply. His presence was raising conflicting emotions within her. There was comfort in his calm attitude, but inside she felt anything but calm. He, like her, was wearing a robe but she had the vague notion that he was naked beneath it. Even with a now-sleeping child present, in this dark room it felt very intimate to be with him, dressed in this fashion. She uncurled herself from the chair and moved softly towards the door. She knew he had followed her but was still surprised when he took her elbow and walked the few paces to her own room. Just as she turned to thank him, another, louder, rumble of thunder echoed around the trees. She nearly cried out but found herself pulled tight against him with her head buried in his chest. As he gently stroked her hair and her agitated trembling began to fade away, he whispered, 'It's all right, you're quite safe.'

Memories of years ago crowded into her mind. There had been a thunderstorm the first night *he* had come into her bedroom. After that, each time he had stayed at the house she could remember the wild beating of her heart whenever she heard footsteps stop outside her room. She also remembered the false smile when he had said those same words as he bent over her, the smile growing even broader as he recognised her fear. He would just stroke her face and neck… and then leave, but it had always taken a long while before she could relax enough to return to sleep. For some time now the memories had not been so vivid. Perhaps it was tonight's thunderstorm and feeling the fear in the small figure curled at the foot of the bed. However, at the back of her mind she also knew the sensations she had experienced as they neared Woodhayes tonight were still preying on her mind.

She vaguely realised that Simon was now holding her away from him, looking down into her face with concern in his eyes. 'It's really frightened you, hasn't it? I thought Joanna was bad but…if you want, I'll stay with you for a while.'

Embarrassed, she pulled away from him. 'It's quite all right. I'm just tired, I suppose. Thank you for your trouble. I'll check on Joanna and then go back to bed.'

'I'll deal with Joanna on my way past, although she'll be dead to the world now, even if there was another storm. It's always the same. Get some sleep yourself… but if you want me, you know where I am.' He gave her a searching look. 'I mean it.' He then left, closing the door behind him.

Amy sat on her bed, the odd shiver still running through her from time to time. She would have liked him to stay, to tuck her up in bed and feel his reassuring presence. Held in his arms tonight she had felt safe and secure. She had nearly told him about her memories, but they would have seemed childlike to a man of his experience. No, it was better to say nothing, wasn't it?

Chapter Ten

In his own room, Simon was finding it hard to sleep. Joanna's spontaneous gesture earlier had unsettled him; a polite thank you was her normal response to any treat. He admitted that he, too, had rather enjoyed today, watching the interaction between Amy and Joanna. It was like seeing two sisters sparring with each other, but with Amy subtly steering the younger girl into the correct choices. Observing their shared reaction to the storm tonight, he'd felt an immense duty of protection toward them both. Amy, in particular, had surprised him. Her depth of fear had seemed out of all proportion and he sensed that the storm had triggered other memories. He had felt the emotion in the slim body, held close in his arms, and wondered about the cause. However, people's lives were private unless they wished to disclose them, as he well knew.

He turned over and eventually drifted off to sleep.

*

Jack Fletcher lay back on the bed in his Rio hotel room, looking again at the papers Charles had handed to him. Since arriving, he'd spent a day or two reassessing his suggestions for the new office. It would at least give credence to his visit if Simon were to enquire. His flight to Colombia was booked for the next day, and it was obvious he would then have to hire a robust vehicle as the area in question appeared to be totally off the beaten track.

After purchasing some maps of the general area he'd gone for a drink in the hotel bar and with pleasant surprise had encountered an old friend. Brian 'Bonzo' Thompson was an ex-army acquaintance who had gone on to work all over the world in the civil engineering business. He had now decided to retire and, liking the look of the girls in the area, he'd decided on Rio, or so he said. Knowing better, Jack rather thought it was the ease with which certain "deals" could be done which had attracted him more. Bonzo was by no means a crook, but he did enjoy widening the horizons somewhat.

Without going into too much detail Jack spoke about his intended visit and described the rough area of his investigations. When mention was made of possible mining exploration with excellent projected returns, Bonzo had grinned broadly.

'Well, they can save themselves the trouble; they'll find nothing there. It's not the right geology in that part. Farming, yes, and that's what it is at the moment. I thought I heard on the grapevine that some money had been poured into the area to assist the local people to do just that. Seems odd if permission has been given to rip it all out again. Someone's on a bum steer there, Jacko my boy. If you want, I can take you to some better areas your contacts might be interested in.'

Fletcher had thanked him, but declined the offer, and they had parted, promising to get together again for another drink before he left the country.

Jack himself was now beginning to worry. He knew that McDonald and Mannion didn't frighten easily. As with Simon, they were too used to multi-million-pound deals hanging on a knife edge, waiting for someone to be the first to blink. He had, however, been concerned at their high level of anxiety, even before he set foot in South America, and he was now sure there was definitely something wrong. Should he make a call to them?

He heard a loud knock on his door. He looked at the time;

ten-thirty. Could be Bonzo, of course, but a bit late for a social call. Upon opening the door, he was confronted by two men, one in the uniform of a senior police officer. He immediately went into security mode and half shut the door with his weight braced against it.

The uniformed officer spoke in English. 'I assure you that this is an unofficial visit, Mr Fletcher.'

'Unofficial or not, it's a bit late in the day, don't you think? I was just about to go to bed. My papers are all in order.'

The other man spoke then, and Jack noted the American accent. 'We are aware of that, Mr Fletcher. We would just like a few moments of your time, if we may.'

Reluctantly Jack let them into his room, first giving a glance out into the corridor, which appeared to be empty. 'What can I do for you then, gents, but make it quick; as I said it's late and I have a flight to catch in the morning.'

The American spoke again. 'We are also aware of that, Mr Fletcher, and this is the reason for our visit. We would be most grateful if you would cancel your intended trip and return to the UK.'

Jack looked from one to the other. 'Just what makes you think you've any right to tell me when and where I can or cannot go?'

With a slight smile, the American produced some identification and gestured for the police officer to do the same. He then handed them both to Jack. 'This, I think, will confirm our authority, Mr Fletcher. I am here to inform you that there are several interested parties who would have genuine concerns if you completed your intended visit. It could upset the delicate balance of certain investigations which are ongoing. If successful, they might even bring about a prosecution in relation to the unfortunate recent event which befell Jose Ramos.'

At the mention of this name Jack looked up from his contemplation of the two sets of identification. The Brazilian police officer appeared to be very senior indeed, and the other was a Jonathan Grover, apparently attached to the American

Embassy. Jack was bright enough to know just what position Grover probably did hold – but what was that remark about Ramos? Was there more to his death than appeared to be the case? Then a name popped into his head – de Santos! Were the authorities after him for something? He then asked himself, did Simon know more than he was letting on about this matter? Charles and Stuart had certainly been worried by his actions – but how far was Simon mixed up in it? If Bonzo was right, this whole deal looked a bit suspect, but was Simon being led down a path not of his own making?

He returned the appropriate identification to the two men, and appeared to give the matter some thought, although he had already made up his mind. 'Well, if my journey upsets you so much that you have to make a late-night visit, perhaps I can postpone it for a while.'

The Brazilian police officer looked relieved and informed him, 'You will find that your Colombian ticket has been transferred to the ten forty-five BA flight to London tomorrow. The new ticket can be picked up from their desk at the airport. Thank you for your co-operation, Mr Fletcher.'

He made to leave but stopped as Jack took hold of Grover's arm. 'Will your masters be equally happy, Mr Grover? I actually visited Langley once, several years ago. Quite an interesting place.'

Grover smiled and gently disengaged his arm. 'You know bosses, Mr Fletcher, they are never really happy. Goodnight.'

Jack locked the door behind them. There was something big going on if it shook people like that out of the trees. He reaffirmed to himself the decision he had made. He needed to get back to London and speak to Simon and get to the bottom of this, whether he liked it or not.

*

As the London flight took off, a call was put through from the airport to an office in Turkey.

'Thompson here, sir. As I reported to you, after keeping a watch on all arrivals and spotting a name I recognised, I made contact at the hotel with the person who turns out to be Deveraux's security man, so your information was correct. It looks like a deal in Colombia, but in my estimation, from what little he told me, the supposed area involved is a lost leader. Interestingly, he then had a late-night visit from important local security and has just hot-footed it back to London. I'll bet it was a "Keep off the Grass" warning... Right, I'll keep my ear to the ground.'

*

The suggestion of a picnic in the country came out of the blue to an astonished Joanna and Amy during breakfast one morning. It was over a week since the Legoland trip and Simon had been in London for most of that time.

Looking at their faces, and the silence, he smiled ruefully. 'Not such a good idea after all, eh?'

Joanna was the first to speak. 'Oh no, Daddy, that would be marvellous, wouldn't it, Amy? Oh, please say yes!'

Amy looked into blue eyes and saw amusement lurking in their depths. He knew she couldn't refuse and upset Joanna, as she had clearly been included in the invitation.

'I'm sure that would be very nice. Thank you.'

'Good. We could all do with some fresh air and exercise. I spoke to Mrs Gilmore earlier this morning, so she's been busy. I suggest we leave in about an hour?'

The weather was ideal and the countryside resplendent under a clear blue sky. Amy was glad she had remembered to pack some sunscreen, both for herself and Joanna. Simon appeared to be heading for the Sussex Downs, but after a while he stopped off at a local public house for a comfort break and sat outside with them for coffee and biscuits. When they resumed their journey, it was obvious he knew the area and, after negotiating some narrow lanes, came out at a parking area with wonderful panoramic views over the undulating countryside. In the distance the sunlight was sparkling on a small stream curving around a tree, bent over by years of exposure to the prevailing wind.

'We'll have a walk first and then see what Mrs Gilmore has prepared for us.' He watched as Amy produced her suncream. 'A good idea. With your fair skin you could burn.' He moved closer and smoothed a smear of the cream into her bare arm. His touch did strange things to her insides, and she had to turn away, pretending to make sure that Joanna was also well protected. When she turned back and glanced up at him, she could see from the amused look in his eyes that he had interpreted her actions correctly.

They walked for some while, not encountering another person. As Joanna skipped on ahead, on one steeper slope Amy found herself skidding on loose stones and a strong arm came round her waist. She extricated herself from his grip, and heard a soft chuckle as his hand reached for her own and held on tight. 'I don't want to administer to a sprained ankle,' he murmured. 'If you're getting tired, cheer up, we're almost back full circle and we can have our picnic.'

'How did you know about this spot?' Amy was curious, as it was obvious Joanna had not remembered being here before, but now part of her was strangely reluctant to hear his answer.

'Oh, I used to see a... friend in Chichester on occasions and discovered it on my journeys.'

This could have meant anything, but somehow Amy guessed who his "friend" might have been, and she felt uncomfortable.

Simon settled her into a hollow overlooking the shallow stream, and, ignoring her protests, he and Joanna went back the short distance to the car. Mrs Gilmore had even thought of a blanket, and Amy felt herself in the lap of luxury when the picnic hamper disgorged its mouth-watering surprises, all tastefully packed with proper cutlery. There was even a half-bottle of wine, cooled in its own container, with orange juice for Joanna.

The next hour was probably the happiest she had ever

experienced in her life, and she forgot all about her earlier reactions. The conversation was easygoing, full of humour, and the food was delicious. From time to time, other voices could be heard in the distance, but tucked away in their hollow no-one was visible, and, apart from the occasional birdsong, no other noises intruded. Joanna asked if she could go down to the stream, and although Amy was nervous about this, Simon agreed, with the dire warning, 'Don't try and paddle though, or you won't sit down for a week.'

Amy sat upright, watching the small figure until she felt his gaze on her. 'Relax, I can see her. She needs occasions when she chooses her own risks or she'll become too cautious, and, in case you're worried, I don't subscribe to corporal punishment.' He placed his hand on her shoulder and gently pushed her down onto the rug. 'Have a rest for once. You do far more for Joanna than I ever intended. You're so slender, at times you seem almost frail.'

Amy didn't know how to reply to this statement, so just lay back in the afternoon sun. After a while she closed her eyes, feeling completely relaxed and half-asleep, helped by the wine, no doubt. The touch of his lips was unexpected, and she should have pushed him away, but they were soft and warm, and she wanted the sensation to continue … perhaps for just a little while longer. His arms folded around her and held her close, and his kiss became deeper and more urgent. Her brain began to register that this should not be happening. Anyone could come along, and perhaps Joanna was on her way back. She struggled slightly. 'It's all right, there's no-one about and Joanna is still by the stream.' His breath was warm against her throat. 'You're so sweet, anyone would be tempted.'

She enjoyed his caresses for a few more moments but her conscience was telling her this was wrong. She opened her eyes and stared up into a smiling face and half-closed dark blue eyes. 'It's all right, I'm not going to hurt you.' His words broke the spell and catapulted her back to those awful nights when *he* had said the same.

'No! No, please!' She struggled out of his grasp and sat up. 'Joanna is just coming.' She gasped with relief on seeing the small figure trudging up the slope.

'There's no need to sound so relieved. What did you imagine was going to happen, Amy? It was just a summer kiss after a pleasant day. Anyway, your Victorian attitude is at odds with how you appeared to be feeling a moment ago.' His voice now sounded cool and distant.

She couldn't look at him, as she knew he was right, and her face flamed at the thought. This man was so experienced with women and she felt completely out of her depth. There had been such pleasure at his touch, and his kiss had sent waves of sensation she had never known before coursing through her.

Joanna gave her a searching look when she joined them. 'You've turned pink, Amy. Hasn't she, Daddy?'

Simon stood and started repacking the picnic basket. 'Probably too much sun. We need to tidy up now and get moving. We have a long way to go.'

During the drive home he hardly spoke and even Joanna ceased chattering after a time. The day had been spoilt and Amy felt guilty for causing this by her overreaction to something that could be regarded as harmless fun. However, in her heart she was beginning to sense that it would be easy to slip into further closeness with this man and catastrophic consequences might result.

As they approached Woodhayes, she became aware of a vaguely familiar blue Peugeot heading towards them down the lane, and noticed Simon looking in his rear-view mirror several times after they passed. Turning into the drive she heard him mutter under his breath, 'Now what!' as he parked next to a red sports car.

Joanna scrambled out and headed towards the house. 'It's Uncle Jack, Daddy.'

'Yes, I'm aware of that.' Helping Simon with the contents of the boot, Amy sensed a tone of resignation in his voice, and guessed the day had taken an even worse turn. She felt dreadful and cast about for something to lighten his mood, but, unable to think of anything, followed him into the house in silence.

*

It had been a conscious decision to make an unannounced visit to Simon at his home rather than the office. Jack wanted to see a spontaneous reaction to his questions. Now, it seemed it would have to wait after all. Frank Gilmore had informed him that Simon had been out all day with his daughter and wasn't sure when they would return. Just about to head out to his car, Jack heard a vehicle in the drive. After a moment or two the front door burst open, and a slightly dishevelled young girl hurled herself at him.

'Hello, Uncle Jack. Have you come to take me swimming?'

Before Jack could reply Simon came through the door and deposited a hamper on the floor. He was followed by a young woman carrying a blanket. He estimated she was in her early twenties with gorgeous red hair.

Hearing the remark Simon raised his voice. 'Joanna, you've just been taken out for the day. The whole world does not revolve around entertaining you.'

Jack noted the tone of voice, cold and sharp, and judged that his unexpected appearance was to blame. He patted the dark head. 'Sorry, Princess, perhaps not today, but we'll make it another time, eh?'

'I suppose so.' The small face was glum, but then brightened. 'Can Amy come too?'

He pretended to be mystified and looked around. 'What's an "Amy" and where is it?'

Joanna was now giggling and pulled him over toward the young woman. 'Don't be silly. This is Amy. She's here for the holiday, and we're having such a lovely time.'

Noting the soft grey eyes and pretty, delicate face surrounded by that burnished halo Jack could only say the truth, 'I can understand why. I might have had a good time too.' He extended his hand. 'Jack Fletcher, Miss…?'

A sweet smile came to the young face as she took his hand. 'Amelia Watson, Mr Fletcher. I'm pleased to meet you.'

He held onto her hand and would have said something further, but a harsh voice intervened.

'Jack, I suppose you did come to see me?'

The smile disappeared from her face as he watched her turn to Joanna. 'I think it's time you had a bath and then bed. We've had a long day.' She looked back for a moment to the figure leaning against the study door. 'Goodnight.' Then her glance returned to him. 'Goodbye, Mr Fletcher.'

Not to be browbeaten, Jack decided to up the ante. 'I would prefer 'Au revoir', Miss Watson.'

With another glance at the still silent figure, and a hastily remembered, 'Goodnight Daddy, goodbye Uncle Jack,' from Joanna, he watched as the two figures climbed up the stairs.

Chapter Eleven

Ushering him into the study Simon slammed the door shut behind them.

'Why all the urgency for this visit, Jack?'

'Sorry to barge in on your… arrangements. Very nice, too, I might add.' Jack was well used to Simon's moods and for the most part ignored them.

'Miss Watson is standing in for Mrs Horton during the summer holidays… and that's it. Got the message?'

'You should have run it by me, Simon. A stranger in your house, this close in. Not good.'

Simon flung himself down into the chair behind his desk. 'She works at Carlton House. The headmistress has vouched for her, and Joanna thinks the sun shines out of her. She's happy; I'm happy.'

Jack wondered about the level of 'happiness' for a moment longer and then dismissed it. He'd make some enquiries of his own in due course, but there were more pressing issues.

'I understand you're moving into a deal in Colombia.' He sat down on the Chesterfield. Simon, he noted, had started drawing aimless circles on his blotter and was no longer looking at him directly, and he felt a moment's disquiet. 'I was in Rio having another look at the office potential there when I heard, so thought I might take a peek, as I was near.'

Simon's head shot up and he leant forward in his chair. 'You did what? You stupid bastard! Who gave you permission to do that?' He then subsided. 'As if I didn't know.'

'Two very worried men, Simon, and after my experience you can make that three.'

'What experience? Did you actually go to the site?'

'Didn't get that far. I virtually got thrown out of Brazil for even thinking about it, and by some pretty heavyweight government bouncers. If they had to do that then this is something big, and something not good, and what are you doing getting mixed up in it, mate?'

'What the hell are you talking about?'

'I was booked on a flight to Colombia, and I had a late-night knock from Brazilian police and, unless I'm very much mistaken, a representative from the CIA, no less, indicating my intended trip was not "in the best interests of certain parties". It was even indicated that it might be counter-productive to investigations into that lad Ramos' death. Now that really made me take notice. Simon, what are you getting into here? The word is, despite the projected figures, the site proposed for the nickel mine is good for farming, and that's all. The only beans you might make out of it will be coffee. More importantly, I have a hunch de Santos is mixed up in this somehow.' He noticed a slight reaction to this remark from the man sitting behind the desk. Yes, he was on the right track here, but he knew Simon prided himself on his integrity and would never countenance mixing with people like that.

There was silence in the room, apart from the soft ticking of an ornate clock on the mantelpiece behind the desk.

'Jack, I have my reasons for doing this deal, and that's all I can say. You've been warned off once, just leave it at that.'

Rising from his seat, Jack leant his hands on the desk and looked directly into the blue eyes, noting the worry lurking there.

'For God's sake Simon, does someone – de Santos – have a hold over you? I have warned you about this, and it could affect

Orion, or even Joanna. If I know what it is you're into, I'll be better placed to give you advice. You have friends, Simon, let them help you for once.'

'I'm sorry, Jack. For the last time, just leave it, will you?'

With a heavy sigh, Jack straightened up. 'OK, if that's the way you want it. The company can look after itself, but don't come sobbing to me if Joanna ends up in any danger, cos I warn you now, if you do, you won't know what's hit you.'

Anger coursing through him, Jack had turned to leave the room when the question came in a quiet voice.

'Did you see a blue Peugeot in the vicinity when you arrived?'

Looking back at the figure still sitting at the desk, Jack's anger slowly turned to curiosity. 'Certainly did, the stupid idiot was parked in that little cut-out just down the road. Nearly ran into him. What of it?'

'It's been here once or twice over the past few days. It passed us as we came in tonight. I tried to catch the number, but it was too late.'

Jack walked back over to the desk. 'For the love of God, Simon, please tell me what's going on.'

He saw indecision plain on Simon's face, then he heard a sigh. 'Take a seat, Jack.'

*

With Joanna bathed and sound asleep in bed, Amy too felt tired. This was not an unusual feeling, and something to which she had become accustomed over recent years. However, tonight she also felt restless. She would have loved to go downstairs and play the piano, but with Simon's visitor still here, that wasn't possible. She had a bath, and curled up on her bed with a book, but found it difficult to concentrate. Her thoughts kept returning to the events of this afternoon. She had been kissed once before, but it had been nothing like today. Although she knew that the incident must never happen again, and Simon had just been having some fun with her, she found herself wishing that things were different. Since the night of the storm, she had begun to feel more comfortable and secure in his presence, sure that he had some concern for her welfare.

It was late, but she decided she needed a drink before going to bed. As she left her room and walked along the gallery, Simon's study door opened, and he ushered out his visitor. As the car drove away, he secured the front door and she sensed weariness in his actions. She had an overwhelming desire to help him in some way and started down the stairs. Turning, he came up towards her.

'I was going to make a drink; can I get something for you?'

Now he was closer she saw her assumption had been correct. He did look tired, but he smiled at her. 'That would be very welcome. I'll be in my room.'

Bringing the drinks upstairs on a tray, Amy hesitated at the top of the stairs. She hadn't ever gone near his room and was now a little nervous. He answered her tentative knock and held the door wide for her to enter but did not close it behind her, she noted with relief. She looked around for somewhere to place her tray. Her first impression was of another large room. In fact, it reminded her of the plush hotel suites she had sometimes seen in magazines. There was a small lounge area with a low table and two armchairs near the window, and beyond the large bed she could see a door through to a small corridor, off which she could see two more doors: probably the bathroom and a dressing room. The décor in shades of pale grey and cream had a subtle restfulness about it.

'I've made some chocolate, it's what I normally have, but if you don't...'

He took the tray from her and placed it on the small table. 'I'm sure I'll find it delicious, and if you would stay and share it with me,' he pointed to one of the comfy chairs, 'perhaps you can have an instant report.'

She felt embarrassed by the situation but decided not to make the same mistake as earlier in the day.

'It's another late night for you,' she commented. 'Your visitors must keep some strange hours.'

Simon came and sat on the chair opposite. 'Jack Fletcher is my IT security chief and has just come back from South America. He wanted to discuss something important with me. It went on longer than we both thought.' He looked at his wristwatch. 'I must admit I hadn't realised exactly what the time was. You're right, it is late, and you must be tired.'

'Joanna was. She nearly went to sleep in the bath, and I almost did too.'

She watched a strange look cross his face and sensed again that sudden change of mood. He stood and placed his mug back on the tray, which must be a hint for her to leave, she thought, but she still had to make some apology.

'I'm sorry for my overreaction today, and if it offended you. It really was one of the most pleasant days I have ever spent. Thank you.'

He considered her for a moment and inclined his head slightly. 'I enjoyed it too, some parts more than others.' He smiled then and the blue eyes were full of warmth. The room seemed suddenly too small, and she stood, collected the tray and started for the door. Gentle hands on her shoulders turned her round and before she was aware his mouth was on hers. Holding the tray, she was powerless to do anything, even if she wanted to. He raised his head and whispered, 'Goodnight, sweet Amy,' and she found herself outside on the landing, the door closing quietly behind her.

*

Jack sat at his desk, pen in hand, but so far, the sheet of paper was still blank. During the drive back to his London flat, he had kept his eyes peeled for anything untoward but had detected nothing out of the ordinary. Now, intent on compiling his list of enquiries, his mind was still reeling from tonight's unexpected revelations.

He had never known Simon to be so forthcoming, especially about his private life, and felt privileged to be included in the small number of people who knew the truth. What would he have done, faced with the same circumstances? He had so far avoided marriage, by the skin of his teeth on one occasion, and perhaps he still had some regrets. She had been a nice girl, but wanted her own career, and after hearing tonight of Simon's experiences, maybe it had been for the best.

He began to write. There would have to be some tighter security, whether Simon liked it or not. He needed to organise some overview of all movements and if he used the right people, they would be invisible to amateur and professional alike – and he knew where he could find people like that. Extra security at the house would be a problem. He would have preferred someone on the inside, but Simon was adamant this would not happen. Outside surveillance would be tricky, as the occupant of the blue Peugeot had probably found out, but he would work on that one. Had any security cameras in the vicinity captured this vehicle, he wondered? He'd pestered Simon to have this facility himself, but he'd never been keen. Perhaps he'd regret his attitude now.

Once any news broke about the difficulties Simon anticipated, there would be reporters, not only at the office, but some would eagerly attempt candid pictures at Woodhayes. He could have more visible security in place if that happened.

He also needed to find out what he could about those named as officers in the Brazilian and American companies involved in the mine deal. Even more imperative was to establish the identity of the Colombian who had ties with de Santos and Grainger. As he was supposed to be out of the loop, he could hardly ask this Reynolds bloke for any information. Simon's comment about how much Grainger himself knew about the deal was interesting, and this too would need some thought. With reluctance he ought perhaps to make some enquiries about that enticing little Miss Watson. Simon must be made of stone if he had been able to ignore her youthful charms over these past weeks.

He gave a yawn. Well, he'd made a start for tomorrow. It was late and perhaps daylight would bring some other ideas.

*

The swarthy face broke into the semblance of a smile.

'Yes, senor, this is what he told me. He was able to get a good look at her as they passed, and he recognised her... No, no he assured me she would not have suspected a thing. He said he had used some sort of disguise. I thought he seemed a little shocked about the discovery but also, I sensed in him an element of pleasure, that he had found her so close in with Deveraux, and I feel he will make use of the knowledge for his own benefit. He gave me the impression that he had some sort of hold over her from years ago. I thought you might consider it an advantage for us also.' His smile broadened even more as he listened to his instructions. 'Yes, senor, I will make him understand the position. Unknown to him I am also continuing my own observations as we agreed.' He listened further. 'Yes, the letters have been delivered to me and I will see that they are directed to the correct recipients when you give the order.' More instructions followed, then, 'I will do as you say, senor, as always.'

Hernandez closed the call and looked at the two letters on his desk; one was addressed to the Serious Fraud Office, the other to his favourite English newspaper. Tomorrow he would leave his pre-booked rented room – but, as on many other occasions, by the back entrance. It made sure that certain of his movements were unobserved, always a wise precaution. He would again retrieve the black Audi saloon, a second vehicle he had rented under another name, then deal with delivery of the letters... and other business too. The BMW, rented at the airport, would remain stationary outside his lodgings, keeping any possible watchers guessing.

*

Joanna burst into Amy's bedroom after lunch a few days later; the beaming smile heralding some good news, she thought. She had been lying on her bed taking a rest as Simon had driven Joanna into the village with him on an errand.

'Daddy's arranged for Sophie and me to go and see that film I put on my list tomorrow afternoon, and then out to tea. Sophie's mummy and daddy will take us, he says.'

'That sounds lovely.' Amy swung her legs to the floor, relieved for once that she wasn't being asked to accompany them. She then noted the excitement fading from the small face and wondered about the reason. Joanna came and sat next to her, and to Amy's surprise she slipped a small hand into hers.

'Daddy also says that next weekend we're going to Uncle Henry's clinic in London. We do this every year. I don't like going; they stick needles in your arm, and it hurts. Can you come with me?'

Amy had to think quickly. 'Well, if you go every year, you must know what they are going to do, so it won't be a surprise, will it? I'm sure you'll soon feel all right again. They might even give you a sweet if you're good.'

'Maybe... anyway Daddy said to ask you to go down and see him in his study. He wants to talk to you, he said.'

Amy sighed as she brushed her hair and made sure her dress wasn't creased, then ushered Joanna out of the room. 'Have you finished reading the book we started yesterday?' It was obvious from the sheepish look she received that the answer was in the negative. 'I suggest while I'm seeing your father that you carry on with it, and we'll talk about it later... and Joanna, you really must learn not to burst into other people's rooms without knocking first, it's not very polite.'

She carried on down the stairs, wondering why she had been sharper than normal with the child, but put it down to the slight headache she was experiencing. She knocked on the study door and heard his response. He was working at his desk in a short-sleeved shirt, his jacket and tie thrown over one of the chairs.

Looking up from the papers he was studying, he threw them down on his desk with an angry gesture.

'I suppose that child immediately tore straight up to you with her news, disturbing your private time. I didn't mean I wanted to see you right now but... well, as you're here.' He stood and motioned her over to the Chesterfield. He sat down beside her and studied her for a moment. 'Did she burst in and wake you? If so, I may cancel tomorrow. It's time she learnt not to be so impetuous and rude.'

Amy didn't like to say that she had already administered a warning and therefore have the treat spoilt, so she told a white lie. 'No, it's all right, we met on the landing.'

For a moment longer he studied her, and she felt he was about to make a comment, but then changed his mind.

'I gather you know about tomorrow. David and Freda have been kind enough to agree to act as chaperons and I'm picking up the bill. That absolves both of us from any encounter with dragons!' He smiled at her then and she felt compelled to respond.

'It is rather warm to be in full armour.'

The study window was open wide, but only a light breeze was stirring the curtains and the room was warm. Her dress was low-cut thin cotton and she felt his eyes moving over her. He reached out a finger and moved some tendrils of hair from her forehead. His gaze sharpened. 'In future, lock your door and that will stop unwanted visitors.' She knew then he had guessed she had not spoken the truth, but his words also had another meaning, and she felt her face growing warm.

He leant back, away from her, his mood changing again. 'Next weekend we will be in London; by that I mean the three of us.' Before she could make any sort of comment, he went on, 'I make a habit of a complete annual health check for Joanna and myself. It's at a private clinic run by Henry Carlisle, a physician I've known for years. Joanna refers to him as Uncle Henry. She doesn't enjoy the process but I'm going to sweeten the pill, as it were, by tying in with it other more enjoyable things over the weekend. On the Sunday afternoon we have been invited by Sir Arthur and Lady Dunne to their house. I gather their son and his two boys will be present so Joanna will have someone of her own age to play with.'

Amy eventually found her voice. 'I'm sure my presence is not necessary.'

'Things are a little different this year, and *I am* requesting your presence.'

He stood and returned to his desk. 'We'll leave on Friday afternoon and stay at the London flat.' He looked at her. 'To answer your obvious question, there are two bedrooms, each containing two single beds. The accommodation is sometimes used by visiting clients or overseas staff. I suggest we keep these arrangements to ourselves until Thursday or Joanna's excitement will go right off the scale. All right?'

There was nothing really Amy could say, so she just nodded and left the room, part of her as excited as she knew Joanna would be.

Chapter Twelve

The long-running discussion as to whether Mr Floppy remained at Woodhayes or was treated to a weekend in London was only settled when Simon, through gritted teeth, announced that if the rabbit did accompany them, at the first opportunity he would open the car window and pitch the creature out onto the motorway. Joanna's shrieks of horror were only stilled by a grave-faced Frank Gilmore promising to guard the unfortunate animal with his life until she returned. With a set face, Simon then headed the Mercedes in the direction of the capital, far later than intended. Music had immediately filled the saloon, which he quickly reached out to switch off.

Amy had recognised the music and decided to ask a question. 'Does Bach make your commute more pleasurable? You must do a lot of driving.'

Her query elicited the terse comment, 'I find I do enjoy it whilst driving, and it's relaxing.' Then, giving her a quick glance from behind dark glasses, Simon went on, 'If I like something, I enjoy listening to it. Other than that, there is no intellectual reasoning for my choices, and I don't always drive. Jack Fletcher warned me some time ago about routine, so I mix it; sometimes staying in town, if I have late meetings or if I've arranged a squash game, or asking Gilmore to drive me, or using the train. I even did the journey by helicopter once. I find the travelling time useful as a buffer between work and home.'

After that Amy remained quiet, not wanting to disturb him while negotiating the busy weekend traffic. Several times his car phone came to life, and, although not taking the calls but just glancing at each notified caller, she heard him swear under his breath. At this rate, she thought, it was going to be a difficult weekend.

They stopped for a meal, at a small restaurant just outside the city centre, before Simon finally drove into the entrance of an underground car park situated between two large buildings. With the business of parking and retrieving their luggage no notice was taken of a man watching them from the shadows.

A lift took them up to the tenth floor where Simon unlocked an imposing polished wooden door and ushered them into a small hallway. Joanna appeared to know her way; obviously she had been here before, and she dashed into a room off a corridor at the rear of a large lounge. Simon shrugged his shoulders. 'I think your bedroom has just been chosen.' He pointed out a kitchen area and then the second bedroom and bathroom. 'Everything should be here for us. It's serviced daily and they were aware it would be occupied this weekend. However, there is a twenty-four-hour concierge if you find you do need anything.'

Without thinking Amy commented, 'All that sounds frightfully expensive. The owners must charge a high rent.'

'The management company merely charges the going rate,' was the matter-of-fact reply.

Amy looked up at him, understanding finally coming to her. 'You own the management company?'

'Orion, on behalf of investors, owns this whole building and its counterpart next door.'

Once more she was reminded of the realms of immense wealth this man moved in, and how it was so far removed from her previously known world. There was no more she could say so she picked up her small case and followed Joanna into the bedroom.

Over a drink Simon informed them of the weekend timetable. 'Joanna, we're due at the clinic at ten o'clock. Amy, you can have a morning to yourself and we'll be back for lunch.'

He was interrupted by Joanna declaring that she refused to attend unless Amy went with her. To forestall any further wrangling between father and daughter Amy immediately agreed, and stared determinedly back into blue eyes, dark with exasperation. 'All right, all right, I can tell when I'm outnumbered. In fact, it will work out better as we can stay in the same area all day. We'll grab some lunch, after which I have some work to do, but meanwhile, as befitting young ladies, I have arranged for both of you to spend the afternoon in a beauty salon which has been recommended to me. Within reason, have anything you like. Joanna, you will be guided by Amy as to what this may consist of, do you understand?'

Amy was in a state of shock. She wanted to query the arrangements, but Simon looked at her in such a way she knew he was adamant in his wishes. A small part of her was also intrigued by the whole idea.

'On Sunday morning I suggest we spend a few quiet hours doing something educational – I think this was intended at some time, Amy?' Not waiting for an answer, he went on, 'We can go to the Tate in Millbank and absorb some culture, before we have a light lunch and then go on to Chelsea. I think it sounds like a good plan.'

There seemed little point in anyone arguing with him, so no comment was made. Simon then turned his gaze on Joanna and spoke in a stern voice, 'As you can see, the sleeping arrangements here are different to those at home. I will endeavour to be up first and clear the bathroom for you both, but Joanna, if you wake up and find that Amy is still asleep, on no account are you to make a noise which might wake her. If I hear differently, I will be very displeased. Do you understand?'

Amy watched as the young girl, after giving her a sideways glance, mutely nodded her head.

'Fine. I think with any luck we should all have a good weekend, and we might as well start with an early night.'

Appearing satisfied that his list of instructions had now been conveyed, Simon stood and, collecting up the mugs, took them over to the kitchen. Assuming this was the signal to leave, Amy nodded her head to Joanna and they both stood and wished him goodnight. He turned and smiled at them; Amy caught the glint of amusement deep in the blue eyes and knew that he had been in his element at issuing commands with which she, in particular, would not be able to argue. He had, no doubt, anticipated her annoyance but she wouldn't give him the satisfaction of making any comment.

*

The morning routine worked with military precision and shortly before ten o'clock Simon turned his car into a street lined with Georgian terraced properties, most of one side appearing to comprise the clinic. On entering the main foyer Amy was immediately aware of the plush surroundings and smartly dressed reception staff. Within minutes they were whisked to an upper floor, where they were met by a distinguished, well-dressed man in his late sixties, presumably Dr Carlisle, and a very attractive dark-haired nurse, smart in a white uniform trimmed with a deep blue belt. The man warmly greeted both Simon and Joanna.

'Welcome to you both. My goodness, Joanna, haven't you grown since last year.' His eyes moved to Amy and Simon made the introductions.

She was then totally shocked when Simon went on, 'If there's the time, Henry, I suggest Amy might benefit from some checks herself.' She was about to protest, until a stern glance silenced her, and she knew she would have to go through with it.

'I'm sure it will be no trouble, Simon. I'll deal with the ladies, and perhaps you would go with Sister.' He took hold of Joanna's hand and moved away along the corridor. Amy looked round and watched the other couple walk back towards the lift. She saw Simon glance at his companion and had no doubt that as a man he would be appreciating her undoubted good looks. A strange feeling of sadness possessed her which she didn't understand, but then, hearing Joanna calling her name, she turned and hurried off in the opposite direction.

*

As the lift descended Simon studied his escort. She had not introduced herself further and seemed reluctant to meet his gaze, although he was sure she was aware of it. She must be about thirty, he considered, and incredibly striking with her dark hair and eyes. When they emerged on the designated floor she conducted him to a small room, and he knew very well that the first job would be to have a blood test. Before she could say anything, he had removed his jacket and was in the process of rolling up a sleeve of his shirt, when she turned back to him. A small smile played around her mouth as she realised he had guessed the routine.

'Dr Page will be here shortly, Mr Deveraux, but we'll get this out of the way first.'

She really was quite beautiful, and he tried to place the accent he had noticed in her speech. Was it a slight Irish lilt?

In a competent and brisk manner, she began the procedure, but he also noted gentleness in her handling, which to him indicated sympathetic consideration for the patient. With her head bent over his arm he could see the sheen of her hair and felt a sudden desire to reach out and touch it. At that moment she raised her eyes to his and their liquid darkness seemed to flow through him. In that moment, he experienced a feeling so powerful it almost shocked him, and he sensed in her an immediate response. He wanted her fingers to stay against his skin, and he was sure that he had been about to speak, when the door opened and a man in a doctor's white coat entered. She immediately completed her task and turned away.

'Good morning, Mr Deveraux, I'm Dr Ralph Page, and I'll be responsible for your tests today. Is that the bloods done, Sister? Get them along to the lab if you will, so we can get the results back as soon as possible.'

Without another look she picked up her packages and left the room, leaving him almost in a daze, wondering what on earth had just happened.

*

Over the next hour or two both Amy and Joanna were subjected to various procedures. Amy sensed Joanna's nervousness at some of these, but her presence appeared to be of some comfort, much to the relief of one technician who must have experienced difficulties before. At one point she noted Dr Carlisle had returned and was consulting some notes handed to him by another doctor. He then came over to her and asked if she would accompany him for one further test. This meant leaving Joanna, but the nurse she had seen before arrived and Dr Carlisle assured her that Joanna would now be reunited with her father. After a further test she was allowed to dress once more in her own clothes and was then taken to an office and asked to wait. Amy began to fret about the time. Simon would be annoyed if he was kept waiting but after all, she considered, he'd been the one to have put her through all this. Finally, the door opened, and Dr Carlisle came into the room.

'I'm sorry to keep you, Miss Watson, but I think it important to go through the detail of some of your results.'

*

For Amy the lunch passed in a blur, her mind still dwelling on the conversation with Dr Carlisle. It had been hard to take in what he had told her, but perhaps in his seriousness he was just being extra diligent with his interpretation and resulting diagnosis.

Conscious of Simon giving her one or two searching glances from time to time, she finally made an effort to concentrate. After a short walk, Simon ushered them both through large glass doors into a bustling perfumed salon with sofas, low tables and flower arrangements dotted around. A smart middle-aged lady, dressed in severe black, came over to them, and Simon, for once looking slightly out of his depth, murmured, 'I believe Mrs Charles McDonald has arranged an appointment for my daughter and... friend.' The young woman smiled. 'Yes, of course, it's Mr Deveraux, is it not? Mrs McDonald was with us this morning and confirmed the booking. If the young ladies would like to follow me.' As she turned away Simon took hold of Amy's arm. 'I'll be back for you at four-thirty. If you're ready before then, don't go anywhere else. Stay here and wait.' She nodded her understanding, then he smiled slightly. 'Have a good time and indulge yourself for once.' She watched as he walked back out into the street.

As well as the automatic choice of hair styling, after much pleading, Amy agreed to a pedicure and manicure for them both. With mischief written all over her face Joanna then went into a huddle with the assistant and after a conspiratorial discussion it was announced that Amy would benefit from a massage. After initially being rather dubious, Amy found that the sensation of the treatment was in fact very pleasant and relaxing. Later, she listened while a male stylist suggested slight modifications to Joanna's hair. Amy considered none of this would displease Simon, nor breach school protocol, so gave the go-ahead. When it came to herself, she was amazed at the stylist's radical ideas but as he seemed so certain of his suggestions Amy's initial diffidence melted away. The final result amazed her, and during the rest of their beauty procedures from time to time she couldn't help glancing up at her reflection in the mirror. Joanna was in raptures, assuring her that her father would like it. Amy hoped so, as she judged the afternoon must have been horrendously expensive.

They were both ready and waiting as, on the dot of four-thirty, she saw Simon come striding into the salon. She noticed the other women gave him several glances and knew that they too sensed the commanding presence he radiated, accentuated by his good looks. She was warmed by the feeling of pleasure that he was there for them and they looked part of his world. To Amy's surprise, he merely glanced at them both and commented, 'Very nice,' before moving off to settle the bill. She had the immediate impression that he was preoccupied by something and his mind was elsewhere.

They went straight back to the flat, where a meal had been prepared and it was only later, after they had eaten, that he seemed more relaxed. Joanna must have sensed this too as she began to describe their experiences. He confirmed his approval of her new hair style and was shown the pale pink nail varnish on her hands and feet. His eyes glanced over at Amy and he took one small hand and inspected her choice of a pale coffee colour. 'Much nicer than bright red,' he commented. He also studied her short copper curls, now free from any restraining clips. 'An inspired choice, well worth the money.'

Amy felt awkward under such close scrutiny, and murmured a small, 'Thankyou.' She wanted to comment on his financial outlay, but she was still unable to fully understand this man. Although he must be immensely wealthy, as far as she could judge, his personal lifestyle was not overtly ostentatious. In the end she decided she should not spoil his gesture by reducing it to mercenary details, and she could see by his expression that he had guessed her dilemma and approved her restraint. He squeezed her hand for a moment and then let it go.

Joanna piped up with the tale of Amy's "special" treatment. 'They allowed me to sit in a corner of the room, Daddy. Amy had to lie on her tummy and a lady put warm stones all down her back. She said it felt lovely.'

'I'm sure it did. I would have liked to see that.'

Something about Simon's tone of voice made Amy glance up, and she was surprised at the expression lurking deep in his eyes, something dangerous and elemental. It took her breath away and she was relieved when, with one of his quick changes of mood, he suddenly stood and suggested Joanna should get ready for bed.

'For once I think you're big enough to cope with that on your own, while Amy and I clear the dishes. She can come through in a few minutes to tuck you in.'

When Joanna had left, he looked over at her. 'I think it's high time she was encouraged to do things like that. If she was at boarding school, she would be dealing with it. We just need to keep a handle on the situation.'

Putting the dishes away in the dishwasher Amy knew he was right. Her own experiences told her this. 'Yes, I agree with you. She will feel really grown up.'

He smiled at her. 'Perhaps… until the novelty wears off. Go and check on her, then why don't you come back, and we can spend a quiet evening together.'

The prospect of this raised all sorts of strange emotions within her, and it was with mixed feelings that, after seeing Joanna into bed, she returned to the lounge. Simon was over in the kitchen area, so she crossed to the large window and sat on the window seat, looking out over darkening London with the river glistening below.

'I've made some coffee if you want some.' Simon placed a tray on the small table and then came and sat beside her. 'You seem fascinated by this view. I've watched you sitting here several times since we arrived.'

Amy considered her reply and said, 'At the moment the skyline seems familiar, but when it's dark and the lights come on, it will turn into a strange magical wonderland. Of course, it's an illusion, there is no such thing. In reality, it's populated with difficulties and dangers, just like life.'

'That's a very sobering thought for one so young. Children believe in fairy tales, and you seem to have an empathy with them.'

Amy bristled with indignation. He was treating her like a child again. 'Yes, I may have believed once,' she snapped, 'but that was a long time ago, and illusions can be spoilt.' She wanted to tell him these should never be shattered at any age, as had happened to her. Even now she remembered the unfeeling remarks and rejection, and the need to speak to someone about it. Uncle George had been there for her in the beginning, but even he had changed in the end. Now, in some ways, this man sitting beside her was taking his place. Despite his challenging remarks, and his recent unsettling actions, she had begun to feel she might be able to talk to him about her past and Dr. Carlisle's unexpected news today, thoughts of which she had managed to keep at bay for the afternoon. His display of assurance and caring on the night of the storm had affected her deeply and she now believed he was someone she could trust. The trouble was she had no idea how to start explaining but, slowly, words started to form in her mind.

At that moment Simon caught her arm and pointed out at the night sky. 'See it, Amy, a shooting star! You must have a wish.' So she did, but somehow she doubted it would come true. He went on, 'If we were back on the Downs the sky would be filled with things to see, but there's too much light here. Do you know any of the constellations? Father taught me when we were on camping trips.' He moved closer to her and pointed in one direction. 'Do you see that grouping of stars just above the church steeple? That's Orion, the hunter.'

She turned her head to look at him, not realising he was so close. She had to think of something to say. 'Why did you choose it for your company name?'

'For that very reason – the hunter. I was hunting down money to be used in various situations to make other money. I found I derived a far greater kick from that sort of unpredictable chase than I ever would have done practising law. It upset my father, but I had my own life to live. I've worked hard and it's paid off, both for those who work for me and clients alike... so far.'

Being so close to him Amy noticed the change, a sudden tenseness in his body. In an intuitive moment she remembered his reactions of late, to the blue Peugeot, the visit from Jack

Fletcher and the telephone calls in the car. Somehow, she knew they were connected, and guessed it was linked with his earlier preoccupation. For a moment she felt again that strange premonition of something about to happen.

'Simon, is anything wrong?'

He turned his head and looked at her for a long moment, then smiled. 'It's just business, Amy. Thank you.' He lowered his head and placed his mouth over hers, gentle at first but then with more urgency. She needed to feel his arms around her, strong and sure, to dispel her sudden fears. Without any thought she reached up and wound her own arms around his neck and ran her fingers through his dark hair. She was drawn tightly against him, and time stood still before he finally released her. His fingers threaded into her soft curls as he turned her face up to his. In the muted light of the room, it was difficult to read his expression, but his hand, as it stroked her neck and cheek, was gentle.

'You seem to be a fast learner, Miss Watson.'

She heard the smile in his voice, but instinctively knew that this time he wasn't making fun of her. More than ever, she wanted to unburden herself to him and hear the words she needed. Then, somewhere out in the darkness, the strident notes of an emergency vehicle's siren intruded into the quiet room. She felt him stir and then he stood. He pulled her to her feet and slid his arms around her waist.

'I think now is the right time for each of us to retire to our respective rooms.' He bent and kissed her again. 'Goodnight, Amy. Sleep well.' Bending down he picked up the unused coffee tray and moved into the kitchen.

Feeling bereft and bemused, all she could do was wish him goodnight and walk through into the corridor to her room.

*

Simon lay for hours just staring up at the ceiling, unable to sleep. He was conscious of her only a few yards away in the other room. She was beginning to confuse him with inappropriate feelings he had not anticipated. With her better clothes, and new hairstyle, she was even more attractive, and he was certain this would increase as age and experience lent her more confidence. Her response tonight had surprised him, and, if the spell had not been broken, could have evolved further as she had seemed willing. However, this only confirmed his initial judgment that her attitude to him would change – with the right approach.

He was annoyed with himself that, in spite of her sometimes abrasive attitude, he was finding pleasure in her company. Also, by following her lead, he was acting more naturally with Joanna. Her questioning remark tonight had demonstrated an obviously caring nature and it would be easy to lose sight of his goal. The days were going by and the holiday would be ending soon. He needed to use all that remaining time to maximum effect.

Then he found his mind retracing the events of the morning, trying to convince himself it was with reluctance, but he knew this was untrue. Once again, he felt the same sensations as on the first encounter with the dark-haired nurse. Sister Rose McKenna, as he now understood her name to be, had returned Joanna to him while Amy had been kept back somewhere and she had sat for a while talking to the child. Her attention had been focused on Joanna and she had barely glanced at him, but, again, he knew she was very aware of him. Joanna seemed quite taken with her and even more so when a sweet was produced in recognition of her good behaviour.

He found himself comparing the two women. They were so different, and not only in age and colouring. Amy still had the sweet inexperience of youth and for that very reason a protective feeling would combine with any attraction, as it had with himself, he admitted. Rose McKenna was a fascinatingly beautiful woman, appearing in control both of herself and her life, but looking into her eyes he had sensed vulnerability. She had been hurt and he felt an unreasoning anger against who, or what, had caused it.

117

He turned over and slammed his fist into his pillow. If he went on this way, he'd drive himself mad. He had other things to think about. Despite sensing that Amy had wanted to talk to him about something tonight, he hadn't been in the mood to hear other people's troubles – he had enough of his own.

This afternoon he'd returned the telephone call from Dan Reynolds. The game had started and was now very real – and for once he had no idea of the outcome.

Chapter Thirteen

The door to the private hospital room opened and Rose turned to see her uncle entering.

'Everything ready for our young guest today, Rose?'

'Yes, Uncle Henry. I understand he'll be arriving later this morning. I thought I'd come in early to make the room a little less like a hospital. After what will have been a nerve-racking first flight and no family with him, he's bound to be apprehensive.'

Her uncle came over to where she had just placed a handwritten sign next to a soft toy. 'What does this say?'

'It means 'Welcome' in his language, and then his name.'

He patted her shoulder. 'I'm glad we have you here, Rose. Your experience is invaluable. Even with one good eye I'm sure the little chap will appreciate it. By the time Clifford has finished I hope he'll have two again. He's coming to see the boy this afternoon and might even operate tonight. Will you be involved?'

'Sister Anderson will be on duty and is better with ophthalmics. I'll be around for when he wakes up.'

'OK. So, what did you make of Simon Deveraux yesterday?'

Rose carefully took time straightening the already pristine bedclothes. 'He has all the trappings of a rich and successful man. He seemed pleasant enough.' She remembered the sudden feeling of excitement when she first encountered the man her uncle had told her so much about, but she had attempted to remain detached. Then, touching his skin, she had sensed his increased pulse rate. Looking up into deep blue eyes she had been overwhelmed by something so powerful in their depths it had taken her breath away, leaving her weak and confused. She was sure he'd been about to speak when they were interrupted. Those same feelings came back to her as she remembered the fleeting few seconds of connection, which she had struggled to dismiss ever since, and her annoyance at the unprofessionalism of the moment. Bringing her mind back to her uncle's question, she tried to reply. 'Joanna seems a nice child. Remembering what you told me about the situation I spent some time with her. She seemed intelligent and articulate, all things considered.'

'Don't forget she knows nothing of the true circumstances. If she ever did, I'm not sure how she would react.'

'Like everything else, I assume Mr Deveraux would just throw some money at it and sort it out.' Rose realised her tone sounded scathing and noticed her uncle giving her a sharp look.

'Don't forget, my girl, if it weren't for people like Simon Deveraux, we might not have some of the equipment we have here at our disposal nor could we afford to give free medical services to unfortunate people like our young patient. There have been many others over the years, thanks to his generosity. I'm sure it doesn't stop there either, but he keeps quiet about it.'

'Yes, I suppose you're right, Uncle.' She had to ask the question which had been in her head for hours. 'Who was the young girl? Joanna seemed quite attached to her.'

'I gather Miss Watson has acted as a companion for the school holidays.'

Might she also have been a companion for someone else, too, wondered Rose. 'At least she is nearer the girl's age, and not a grey-haired elderly governess.'

Her uncle turned to go but commented, 'Yes, and what we found out makes it even more of a shame. I did consider having a word with Simon, but she seemed adamant that nothing should be said. I hope she does as I urged and contacts her own doctor as soon as possible.'

Rose studied him. 'What's wrong, Uncle?'

Henry Carlisle sighed. 'One of those things which, for some reason, has gone unnoticed for too long and it might now be too late. A pity.'

*

Amy opened her eyes as early morning sunlight poured into the room. Carefully she turned her head to see if Joanna was still asleep, only to find herself being regarded by wary dark eyes.

'Are you awake, Amy?'

Trying to hide her amusement, she sat up and glanced at the alarm clock on the bedside cabinet between them. It was only six o'clock.

'Yes, I'm awake but it's a bit early to get up yet.'

'Amy, you know this afternoon, will they be wearing long robes and tiaras, and will we have to curtsey?'

Sensing the question had been asked in all seriousness, Amy gave an equally serious answer. 'They aren't lords and ladies, and even if they were, clothes like that are not worn when you invite people to afternoon tea. Sir Arthur and Lady Pamela will seem quite normal, and they certainly won't expect any special treatment like a curtsey. Just be well-mannered and pleasant, as I know you can be. It will be nice for you to meet their grandsons.'

Joanna wrinkled her nose at that. 'I wish they were girls, but you'll be there, won't you?'

'Yes, of course, I will, and you might find you enjoy it more than you think. You'll be able to impress your father with how grown up you can be in company.'

'Did you know that it's his birthday next weekend?'

'No, I didn't. Do you get him a card?'

'He says he doesn't celebrate his birthday, so I just wish him

Happy Birthday. He doesn't have a cake or anything – but I do think he should have a card. Will you come with me to buy one?'

Amy had a sudden idea. 'You could always make one for him. We could do it together next week. I'm sure he'd like that much better. Perhaps we could ask Mrs Gilmore to make one of his favourite meals on the day.'

Joanna clapped her hands. 'Oh, that would be lovely. We could have balloons.'

At this point Amy decided that it might be better to warn Simon of the impending celebrations, rather than risk any adverse comments from him which would upset his daughter, who now seemed to be deriving as much pleasure from his birthday as if it were her own.

They then heard a light tap on their door, and Joanna's face was a picture of consternation. Amy climbed out of bed, put on her robe and opened the door, expecting to face stern words, but amused blue eyes regarded her.

'As we all seem to be awake, suppose we start the day early. We can take our time for once. I'll let you know when the bathroom's clear.'

Deciding it might be wise to wait until after breakfast before she and Joanna dressed properly, Amy watched with some relief as Joanna retrieved a spot of marmalade from her cotton top. Simon glanced at her, raised his eyes heavenward and commented, 'I think you made the right choice.' His smile was warm, and Amy wondered if, like her, he was remembering the events of last night. Being here, just the three of them, the same as any other family starting the day, Amy felt a longing inside her for something that always seemed out of reach.

Joanna had demanded to wear a pretty dress, but Amy managed to coax her into a pair of smart green cropped trousers, more suitable, she judged, if games with boys might be the order of the day. She did give in and allow a pretty blouse, but carefully folded a cream jumper away in her bag, just in case. She herself had decided to wear a light summer dress with a white and green leaf pattern, the small white belt emphasising her slender waist. Thinking she would probably be involved with the children she decided not to wear high heels but chose more serviceable footwear. Her new hairstyle lived up to expectations when a quick brush restored order to her curls.

Simon had warned them that, as they would not be returning to the flat, they must make sure they took all their belongings with them. She had just finished packing when he appeared in the doorway. 'All ready to go?' She turned to face him and watched as his eyes travelled over her. He stepped forward and slid his hands round her waist. 'You look wonderful. I wish we were having a day to ourselves.' He lowered his head and placed a light kiss on her lips. He released her and bent to pick up the cases. 'I'll take these down to the car. Have another look around, just to make sure.' Amy stood there for a moment before checking cupboards and drawers, glad of the time to allow her pulse to calm down. She acknowledged she would have enjoyed spending the day with him, too. She was falling under the spell of this man and the situation was becoming difficult. There was only one more week of the holiday left and after that she still wasn't sure if she would be returning to her job at the school. Her mind told her there was no realistic prospect of any relationship with Simon continuing, but somewhere inside her she held onto a faint hope that it would.

With a small sigh, and a last look around the flat, she walked out to join the others.

*

Never having been to the Tate before, Amy found herself overwhelmed by the enormity of being so close to priceless works of art. She would have loved to linger and soak up the beauty of the things she was seeing, but Simon appeared to have a goal he wished to reach, and, although not hurrying, kept them moving along. Joanna, for the most part, appeared unenthusiastic, not surprising for one so young, Amy considered. She tried to make comments about various paintings or artists to keep the child interested, but it was only water colour landscapes which provoked any real reaction. Although appreciating all forms of artwork and the technical expertise involved, Amy found herself in agreement, at least as far as the subject matter was concerned. At one point Simon was approached by a smartly dressed older man, who, she sensed was someone in authority within the gallery. They obviously knew each other and stood talking together. Even dressed casually in beige trousers, pale blue open-necked shirt and navy jacket, Amy was again forced to admit that Simon fitted so well into these surroundings and with these people.

She then began to have the feeling she was being watched. The sensation was unpleasant, and a small shiver of fear ran through her. She looked around, but everyone seemed to be acting normally. She noticed a dark, swarthy man about six feet away, studying his catalogue, then he looked up and stared straight at her. For no reason her fear increased, and she gazed around in desperation for Simon. She was startled by his voice close by and, swinging round to find him standing behind her, without any thought she clutched at his arm.

'I'm sorry, Amy, I was waylaid by one of the officials here. Did you think we'd lost you? Don't worry, I could see where you and Joanna were all the time.' He sounded amused but then his gaze narrowed, and he put two fingers under her chin and tipped up her face. 'You really were frightened, weren't you, silly girl? At least it now gives me a valid reason to hold your hand. Come along, there's something I want you to see, and then we can have some lunch before Joanna dies of boredom.'

Amy shook off the feelings of a few moments ago. She now felt ridiculous, but it was comforting to have the warmth of his strong hand around hers. Simon led them into another area where the paintings were those of JMW Turner.

'You were talking about fairytale London after dark; I've always considered Turner's painting style sometimes has an ethereal quality about it. What do you think?' He released her hand and allowed her to move from painting to painting. 'Well, what do you think?'

She turned back to him, sure that the pleasure she found in each one must be reflected in her face. 'They are truly beautiful. Thank you for showing them to me. I think this last one is my favourite.'

Joanna tugged on her father's arm. 'Which painting is yours, Daddy?'

Simon looked down at her. 'It seems Amy and I have made the same choice.'

Amy turned to the painting again and then looked back at Simon, a terrible dread forming inside her. 'You mean you own this original painting?' She could hardly form the words.

'I do. It's here on loan at the moment. I have another original at home by a lesser known, although increasingly popular artist. You might have noticed it in the sittingroom.'

Amy felt as if she needed to sit down. 'I did notice it, but I thought it was a... copy. They must be worth a fortune.'

Simon turned around and led them away towards a café area. 'Works of art, jewellery, classic cars have long been used as another form of currency. Hedgefund managers sometimes prefer them to stocks and shares; less volatile.'

'But they *are* works of art, to be looked at and admired, not figures on a balance sheet. That isn't why the artist created them. They themselves often received a mere pittance, and now someone else becomes rich on the back of their talent.'

'Meaning me, I suppose.' They were now seated at a small table, and Joanna was looking from one to the other, sensing a problem. 'If, over the years, people like myself hadn't acquired examples of all forms of creative art with the object of preserving them, then others, such as yourself, might never have had the chance to experience the pleasure of seeing them. I paid the current market price for both paintings, but fashions can change, and values can go down as well as up. I'm taking that risk. Now shall we order?'

His voice was clipped and cold, and Amy wished she had remained silent. The rest of the day was now going to be awkward.

*

As they were ushered into the main hall at the Chelsea house Simon was still smarting from Amy's comments. Once again, her remarks had needled him. She had made him sound as if he was buying and hoarding treasure for his own financial purposes. He no longer had any interest in living an inflated lifestyle – he had already experienced that in the early days with Olivia! Now, having come out on the other side, he could see it for what it really was. With this in mind, he had joined the ranks of others like him, who were endeavouring to ensure the preservation of priceless artifacts of all kinds. He had contributed heavily over the years to fundraising efforts of one kind or another to make sure important pieces would remain available for the benefit of all and not lost forever. He had, for the most part, attempted to remain anonymous in this, only lending his name where he felt it could do some good for the cause.

From a personal standpoint, he freely admitted he derived pleasure from having the work of craftspeople in his home, with the chance to enjoy this daily. After all, he'd worked hard for the privilege, but, as with the Turner, he was also ensuring that Joanna's future was secure. Once more, in his view, discharging his duty towards her…and yet again, this girl was admonishing him. He neither knew, nor cared, about her personal circumstances, but it was evident she was nervous about money. Yet she appeared to have no qualms about taking a job in a school geared for daughters of wealthy parents and had obviously been keen enough to spend the generous salary he was giving her. He found it difficult to rationalise her, sometimes, waspish attitude with her sympathetic nature in other respects. Well soon, very soon, she would be learning some hard lessons.

'Good afternoon, Simon. It's nice to have you here again.'

126

Pamela Dunne came towards him from a back room, and he bent to kiss the proffered cheek, trying to bring his mind back to order.

'Hello, Pamela. This is Joanna.' He turned to where she was standing very close to Amy and saw they were actually holding hands. There must have been some silent communication between them as Joanna stepped forward, holding out her hand, and said in a quiet voice, 'Good afternoon, Lady Dunne. Thank you for inviting us here today and thank you for the delicious gingerbread man.' It was obviously a well-rehearsed speech and his eyes moved to Amy, but she studiously avoided his gaze.

'I'm delighted to have you here, Joanna, and we'll meet the boys shortly. Perhaps you would like to introduce me to your companion.' Pamela Dunne kept hold of the small hand and smiled over at Amy, who for a moment seemed rooted to the spot.

Simon was about to make the introduction when she finally stepped forward. 'Good afternoon, Lady Dunne. I'm Amelia Watson. Joanna and I are very pleased to be with you today.'

He noted Pamela taking a long look at the younger woman and then, seemingly satisfied, took her arm and turned them towards the garden. 'Oh, Simon, would you go along and see Arthur in his study? I believe he wanted a word with you. Meanwhile we'll go and find Richard and the boys.'

Taking a deep breath, Simon turned away just as Sir Arthur put his head out of his study door.

'Thought I heard you come. I'll get round to introductions later, but we need to have a word.'

Once they were both seated Sir Arthur passed over a sheet of paper. 'I gather you've spoken to Reynolds. This is a note of the official statement by the Colombians.'

Simon glanced at the few typed lines. 'It confirms what he told me, that a minor official has admitted to accepting bribes to rubber stamp a fictitious licence for mining, in order to draw in foreign backing, some of which, he says, will miraculously disappear when the project founders. The appropriate authorities are making other detailed enquiries.' He looked up. 'It might yet take a while for things to filter through over here.'

He saw Sir Arthur shake his head. 'I fully expect some sort of deliberate leak of the matter. Don't forget, it's you de Santos is after. I have a suspicion that when the Colombians dig a little deeper the bribed official will somehow be linked to you, and the two virgin companies will complain that they followed your "wise counsel" in this matter which encouraged them to follow through on the deal. They'll want their day in court too.'

Simon shifted in his chair. 'When someone comes knocking on my door, do I plead innocence and throw open my bank account for their inspection?'

'They have to prove the guilt, so say nothing for now. After all, de Santos would be quite happy if his little scheme produced nothing more than a dent in your hitherto spotless reputation. If asked, say the usual 'No comment' and 'It's in the hands of my solicitors.'

Simon grimaced. 'Which always makes you look as guilty as hell. McDonald's going to love this. He'll want to light a fire under them.'

'We don't want him to do anything. Let it brew and simmer for a while. We need the time. This has to be watertight.'

'It's going to cause some media interest, Arthur. I don't want Joanna caught up in this. Whether you like it or not, I'm going to have a word with my security people.'

Sir Arthur gave him a steady look. 'I rather think your man Fletcher knows something anyway, don't you? Reynolds had to get him out of Brazil in a hurry, I understand.'

Simon was not prepared to divulge just how much Jack did know, even to Sir Arthur. He shrugged. 'As I suspected, my senior office managers were worried enough about the deal to give him instructions to have a sniff around. He was in Rio anyway on company business. He told me about it when he got back. I made it sound as if the deal was hush-hush with money sloshing around from various governments. I think he had a laugh about it in the end. First time he's been thrown out of anywhere!'

This answer seemed to satisfy Sir Arthur. 'Well, my advice is don't ramp up the security until you get the press banging on your door, otherwise it will look as if you expect trouble.'

Sounds of a commotion could be heard somewhere in the house. 'I think it's time we joined the rest. Just keep cool, Simon, that's my best advice.'

As he prepared to leave the study, Simon considered that, as good advice as it was, it wouldn't be easy to implement.

*

After an awkward few moments upon Joanna first being introduced to Robert and Andrew Dunne, the initial stilted conversation gave way to the inevitable jostling for supremacy, and Amy was pleased to see Joanna fighting her corner. Robert was one year older and already had the stereotype view of females as totally useless, whereas Andrew, the same age as Joanna, couldn't care less. He was more interested in the earthbound contents of the flower borders, and soon found he had a new willing helper. Richard Dunne, after being introduced, vanished somewhere back into the house, to spend endless hours on his mobile phone, according to his mother, who then excused herself to go and supervise the catering.

As suspected, Amy was left with the children, and after a deal of persuasion encouraged them to play a game together, with herself making up the foursome. After a while she began to feel hot and tired and in need of a drink. Robert suddenly emerged from the shrubbery and chased after Joanna, who screamed loudly and raced indoors. Amy hurried after her, wondering what on earth had happened. She found the child in the hallway, shaking at her blouse and nearly in tears. 'He put a worm down my back, Amy. I hate him.' On investigation all Amy could find was a wet leaf. 'If it was a worm, I imagine it was more upset than you. Boys think it's fun to frighten girls like this, Joanna. If you show you're not afraid they get bored. Go back outside and tell him not to be so silly. I'll be out there again in a moment.'

Watching the child run back outside she then turned to see she had an audience of four adults. The man she took to be Sir Arthur Dunne stepped forward, and, with a beaming smile, held out his hand. 'By God, I wish I'd had a teacher like you at my school. I'd have been prepared to do any amount of detention. Well handled, my dear. Richard, I think you need to take charge of your brood again.'

As Richard left, Sir Arthur said he needed to tend to the barbecue and suggested Simon could either join him or the children. As Simon moved past her, slipping off his jacket, Amy felt her arm taken. 'You need to have a rest; you look tired out.' Before she could make a reply, Amy heard Pamela Dunne call to her from the conservatory. 'Come through here, my dear, we can have five minutes of peace and a talk.'

The food was delicious and plentiful and resulted in the children feeling less energetic. An impromptu quiz was suggested, compèred by Sir Arthur, and won by the surprisingly amicable partnership of Robert and Joanna. Drinks and cake followed and then it was time to set out for home.

Amy was touched by the genuine warmth of the Dunne family in acknowledging her contribution in making the afternoon such a success. Joanna appeared even more so when Robert, in a bashful fashion, thrust a flower, roughly picked from his grandparents' garden, into her hand. Five pairs of adult eyes looked at each other and anywhere else apart from the two children, smiles hidden behind solemn faces.

As the car left the city Simon could see Joanna in his rear-view mirror, fast asleep strapped into her seat, but still clutching her first female trophy. With a smile he turned to look at Amy sitting beside him, only to find her also asleep. She had been an invaluable help over this weekend, again showing her prowess in dealing with children. With his left hand he smoothed some strands of hair off her pale cheek. Turning his gaze back to the road he modified his speed a little and increased his concentration. Paying extra attention to his driving, he took no notice of a black Audi following him all the way.

*

Amy woke with a start. She didn't remember dealing with the bedtime rituals of either Joanna or herself last night, she had felt so tired. Dr Carlisle's words came back to her again, but she pushed them to the back of her mind and glanced at the bedroom clock. She saw she had overslept and was late for breakfast.

Hurrying into the dining room she found Joanna still at the table.

'Daddy's in his study. He said we were to let you sleep.'

Feeling highly embarrassed, Amy watched, as Mrs Gilmore brought in some fresh toast and coffee, and was even more surprised when an envelope was laid down next to her, with the words, 'This came for you on Saturday, my dear. I forgot to give it to you last night.'

Amy looked over at Joanna and decided to wait until she was in her room before she read it.

'We had a lovely weekend, didn't we, Amy? I'd like to tell Grandpa all about it. Do you think Daddy would let me speak to him on the telephone?'

Remembering she had to see Simon at some time about his, as yet, unknown birthday celebrations, she said, 'When I've had breakfast, I can ask him. Don't forget we have to deal with your father's birthday card. When we go back upstairs you can find some paper and start thinking of some ideas.'

Finally, alone in her room, she turned the envelope over in her hands, unwilling for the moment to open it. Somewhere inside her she sensed it would not be good news, and it proved to be the case. Harriet Freeman regretted having to inform her that Mrs Kitching had tendered her resignation. Through an existing member of staff, a replacement had been found who wished to put her own stamp on the organisation of the new intake pupils and there would no longer be a position at the school for her. She expressed her personal thanks and that of the governors for her valuable contribution during the last term. She did, however, suggest that Amy should make an urgent appointment for an informal discussion on her career prospects in the future, which was something. It was also a relief to read that as her accommodation was paid for to the end of September there was no immediate need for her to move out. Even allowing for this, a move would be inevitable, and it made Dr Carlisle's advice difficult to implement.

If she was honest, Miss Freeman's news was hardly a surprise, but how on earth would she tell Joanna! She decided to say nothing until she had spoken to Simon. She needed to speak to him now, about so many things.

*

Matters were really beginning to escalate, Simon thought, as he reread the email from Dan Reynolds. It was considered likely that he would soon receive a visit or some form of communication from the Colombians. Only a select few officials knew the true nature of the situation and as far as the rest were concerned Simon would be required to answer some questions. The whistleblower had, as anticipated, been found to have possible past connections with him, all fabricated, and he now needed to consider his next actions. To make matters worse, Susan had just contacted him to say that a request had been made for an interview by a member of the Serious Fraud Office about Mark Grainger. This had been unexpected, and worrying, but he'd given her the go-ahead, making a mental note that he would have to speak with Sir Arthur prior to any appointment. He was anxious about lying to them and it might even be the case that they would have to be informed of the true situation.

There was a knock on his door. He didn't really want any interruptions, but it was probably Mrs Gilmore with fresh coffee. He was surprised when Amy came into the room.

'I'm sorry to intrude, but...'

Her fresh, bright appearance distracted him from his worrying thoughts, and he rose from his seat and walked round to the front of his desk. 'It's quite all right. Come and take a seat.'

At that moment Mrs Gilmore did appear with his fresh coffee and, he noticed, a second cup.

'Did you want some coffee, Amy?'

'No, thank you. I've just had breakfast. I'm sorry I was late.'

His eyes skimmed over her face. She still looked pale but more rested than she had last night. 'It doesn't matter. It was a busy weekend, but I hope you enjoyed it. I certainly did.'

'Yes, I did, it was very pleasant. Joanna thought so too; in fact, that's why I'm here. She is keen to tell her grandfather about it and wondered if you would give her permission to ring him.'

'I think, in the circumstances, we'll allow that.' He moved back around his desk and opened a drawer. 'You might as well use this,' and passed her a mobile phone. 'Mrs Gilmore keeps this spare charged up.' He found a piece of paper, consulted his own phone, jotted down some figures, and handed it to her. 'This is my father's number. Just don't let her talk for hours! OK?'

She appeared to hesitate. 'There was something else. Joanna tells me it's your birthday on Saturday. She seems very keen to mark the occasion with not just a card but...'

Simon closed his eyes for a moment and counted ten. This was all he needed. 'But what?'

He watched as the small pink mouth broke into a tiny smile. 'Perhaps a cake, and Mrs Gilmore could cook something you liked? Joanna is keen on balloons, but I think that might be too much.'

His eyes were still on her mouth, and he remembered the feel of her in the quiet room in London: soft and innocent. 'Tell me, Amy, when's your birthday?'

The smile disappeared and she looked down at her hands. 'Umm...'

He turned her face up to him again. 'I'll be forty-one on Saturday, so now you know my secret, it seems only fair to tell me yours.'

After a moment he heard her whisper, 'I was twenty the day we went for the picnic on the Downs.'

He was shocked. God, so young! She was still a child! 'Why didn't you tell us?'

'You don't like celebrating yours.' Her voice was defiant.

Her youth and bravado now irritated him and his plan, which he had begun to reject, came back to him again. He studied her for a moment longer and made up his mind. 'We will have a cake, with blue and pink icing, but no words. Two balloons only, one blue, one pink. If anyone asks the reason the secret will be ours.' He watched the grey eyes widen. Now for the important part. 'On Saturday evening I've been invited to a local music recital, held each year for charitable purposes. I was considering giving it a miss, but I think in the circumstances a joint celebration is required. I would be delighted if you would join me. It's rather formal, I'm afraid; do you have a suitable dress?'

The eyes were impossibly wide now. 'I really couldn't...'

She wasn't going to be allowed to back out of this now. 'Of course you can, and the matter is closed.' He removed some notes from his wallet and passed them to her. 'Get Frank to take you somewhere where you can purchase anything you need. We've appeased Joanna and now it's time for us to enjoy our own celebration.'

His phone began to ring, and he turned to pick it up. She rose from her seat, but he was aware of her, still hovering. 'There was something else I wanted to...'

He noted the caller's name, Tony Broadbent, the only financial journalist he had any time for. So the news was really out now. He turned back to the girl. 'I'm sorry, I have to take this call.'

He saw her looking down at the paper in her hand and for

a moment imagined that her face had turned even paler than usual, almost registering shock, but she just mumbled, 'Yes. Yes, of course. I'm sorry.'

As she turned for the door he felt a moment of concern, but the insistent sound of the phone distracted him once more, and when he turned his head again, she was gone.

Chapter Fourteen

After they had worked out how to use the phone, it being a far more complicated model than her own, Amy had watched as Joanna carefully entered the number. As the child proceeded to chatter excitedly to a no doubt astonished grandparent, she turned away and sat on one of the sofas. Her mind was still trying to come to terms with seeing that name – Mark Grainger – a name she had tried so hard to forget. Why was his name written on a piece of paper in Simon's study? Was it the same person? It could, of course, just be a coincidence, but something inside told her it was unlikely. How had he found her again, and what had he told Simon?

As she gazed around the sittingroom, with Joanna's voice fading into the background, she felt her world shifting again. She had been unprepared for the depth of feeling at the knowledge she would have to leave Carlton House. It was more difficult than she had imagined to accept the fact she would no longer be among the surroundings and people which, in such a short time, had become so familiar. However, if she was honest, it was knowing she must leave the Deveraux household which affected her the most. Joanna had become part of her life, as if an invisible bond had formed between them over these last weeks. If she had to leave both Woodhayes and the school, how would Joanna react?

As her eyes lingered on what she now knew to be an original painting, her fingers touched the bank notes in her skirt pocket; money which had been so casually thrust into her hand. For all her own blossoming hopes, there was no way she could stay in touch. Inevitable questions would be asked about her past, and once they knew, why would they want a nobody like her involved with their lifestyle. Perhaps Mark Grainger intended telling them, or had already done so, but something told her that no-one knew anything yet. She would have to move on again; another "family" she would have to leave. She decided the best thing was to casually mention the Carlton House situation at breakfast on Sunday, and Simon's attitude to her of late gave her the courage to face the prospect… somehow. She tried to make herself smile as she heard Joanna's animated chatter continuing, 'and, Grandpa, she said all the nurses wore different-coloured belts to show how important they were and… Oh, yes Grandpa she is…All right then… Amy, Grandpa would like to speak to you.' Taking a deep breath, she tried to focus her mind as she was handed the phone. 'Good morning, Emile.'

'Good morning to you, my dear. From the kaleidoscope of impressions that I have just been given, I suspect this holiday is surpassing all others. No doubt a good deal of this is down to you, although Simon seems to have been involved a fair amount. I'm even hearing about birthday celebrations.'

'Yes, that's right.' She again fingered the notes hidden in her pocket. She wouldn't tell him of the extent of those celebrations. 'It's all been very pleasant.'

'But I have a feeling school is looming closer.'

'Yes, on Monday.' She wouldn't say any more.

'I might come over for a day or two. Perhaps my presence might help to smooth over any withdrawal symptoms.'

Knowing the changes about to occur, Amy couldn't stop the break in her voice. 'Oh Emile, it would be wonderful if you could.' Simon's father had been so kind and considerate to her, a virtual stranger, he was certain to ease the situation with Joanna.

'I'll see what I can do.' There was a moments pause and then he said, 'Is everything all right, Amy?'

She wanted to say, 'No, please let me talk to you,' but there was no way she would drag this family any further into her affairs.

'Yes, everything's fine, Emile. We'd better finish this call. Simon said not to run up too high a bill.'

'I suspect he might be able to afford it, Amy.' The dry tone wasn't lost on her, but at least the awkward moment had been averted.

She placed the phone back on the table and turned to Joanna. 'We'd better give some more thought to that card, and also see about pressing Robert's flower, if you want to keep it.'

She led the way back upstairs, and an hour later there was a loud tap on Joanna's door. When she opened it, Simon stood on the landing, a bag on the floor beside him.

'I'm afraid I have to be in London for a few days, and I'm leaving now. I just thought I'd tell you.'

At first taken aback by the fact that he had come in person to tell them of his movements, she remembered she still needed to speak to him. 'Oh, but…'

He smiled at her, for once incorrectly reading her thoughts. 'Don't worry, I'll be back on Friday. Make sure you behave, Joanna.' He picked up his bag and a few minutes later they heard the sound of the Mercedes driving away.

*

Mark Grainger had thought it wise to keep Hernandez fully informed. The visit from the Serious Fraud Office had been totally unexpected. How had they found out about his 'imaginative book-keeping'? Had someone finally worked it out and made a complaint? Various papers had been taken away and he had been informed they would be interviewing others connected to him. He would also be called in to make an official statement.

'I have no idea how they found out. Same as you did, I

suppose. It was nothing to make a fuss about really. If the clients had gone to a larger firm, they'd have paid those amounts in fees, anyway. The thing is they might now connect me with Deveraux, so I thought I'd better inform you.'

He had no idea that at the other end of the phone Miguel Hernandez was wearing a smug smile of satisfaction. 'Yes, I quite understand, Grainger. It's a pity, but we must deal with it. I would suggest that you now make use of the girl. Find some way to get in contact with her and see what she knows about Deveraux's affairs. Put some pressure on her. We might even have to take some sort of direct action. How closely is Deveraux's daughter watched? They were all in London last weekend. I followed them around and saw no obvious security. They did, however, visit a Sir Arthur Dunne at his private home. He is some sort of top Treasury official. I wonder what was talked about. I need you to find out.'

'I'll do what I can, Miguel. She might not know anything.'

'Then I would suggest that you… um… encourage her to find out. It would be to your advantage.'

Suddenly Grainger liked the idea. If he could extricate himself somehow from his current difficulties, the last thing he wanted was for this girl spoiling things just when he might be on to something advantageous. It was time to see what he could do about her, for good. He'd attempted to get his own back before, but in the end, she had slipped through his fingers. Not this time!

'It will be a pleasure, Miguel.'

*

Jack Fletcher was satisfied with his endeavours so far, although it had taken longer to set everything up than he would have wished. However, as from Sunday night there would be covert surveillance outside Woodhayes and the London office. Both Simon's Mercedes and the SUV would be followed, at all times, and this should take care of Joanna's movements as well. His enquiries into the two companies had already proved useful.

His sources had obtained details of the company officers in the American firm, and one had been found to have past links through employment with de Santos. He had every expectation of finding the same information coming from Brazil, but here he had to move more carefully. It would be a disaster if de Santos caught wind of any investigations. To this end, needing someone he could trust, he had managed to contact Bonzo Thompson and asked him to make some casual enquiries. He himself had, so far, drawn a blank on finding Reynolds' Colombian, but, with full surveillance, information might yet turn up. Simon would be in town for much of this week and he would bring him up to date. Perhaps Simon himself would have some further news.

*

Thompson consulted his notes again. 'Yes, those are the details I was asked to obtain, Mr Orloff. I was also encouraged to proceed with caution. I have an idea, like you, that there is someone's particular mark over this whole matter.'

He listened for a moment to the voice at the other end of the phone. He then commented, 'It is, of course, possible Deveraux isn't as trustworthy and diligent as you think,' only to wince as this remark was met by an angry outburst. 'Then perhaps, sir, we have to think that others are asking him to venture down this risky road. If his name becomes tainted by any perceived wrongdoing it would be very bad for his company.'

Once more he listened. 'There is that thought, sir. Shall I see what I can find out about any past connections between the two? Yes, sir, I'll get on to it immediately. I agree with you, time could be critical.'

*

Simon was beginning to lose patience in attempting to remove an irate Charles McDonald from his office. The interview with the

Serious Fraud Office was scheduled for ten-thirty. It was already ten o'clock and he needed time to collect his thoughts.

After receiving a seven-page dossier of questions via the Colombian Embassy he had felt obliged to let Charles view this and his intended answers. One or two points had been discussed but basically it was merely an affirmation of the facts which were known at present or noncommittal answers. Considering it a total waste of time, McDonald suggested they should refuse to answer, but Simon, knowing the need to play for time, had to insist the matter was dealt with as required. Equally McDonald had been adamant that Simon should have legal representation during the SFO interview, despite Simon's refusal.

'I still say I should be present, Simon. This whole matter might turn into something serious, both for you and the company. I've already had John Harding on the phone after he read Broadbent's column and the inferences it contained. He wants some assurances, gilt-edged ones, or I formed the impression he might move his business elsewhere. If he goes, it could cause a landslide.'

Simon felt his hackles rising. If these people wouldn't trust him, after all the time they had dealt with him – and made money – then they shouldn't be questioning him now, especially without any concrete proof. If they wanted to try somewhere else, then good riddance – but he knew it wasn't as simple as that. The money world was always volatile and suspicious and once trust was lost, it took a lot of effort to win it back, if ever.

On briefing a concerned Sir Arthur, he'd been advised to appear polite but noncommittal at the SFO interview. If it was only Grainger they were interested in, so much the better. The man had obviously committed some misdemeanour, and it could be possible that de Santos knew of this. Perhaps it was why Grainger had been chosen.

'Look Charles, if I think there should be a legal representative present then I'll call you through. I don't know what it's about myself yet.'

Rising from his chair McDonald half mumbled to himself, 'It's a pity you got mixed up with Grainger in the first place. I won't say I warned you but…'

'Then don't say anything, Charles.' Simon realised his voice sounded cool, and this was borne out by the equally icy glare McDonald gave him as he left. Simon knew he had to be careful; he needed people like Charles McDonald in his corner at the moment. Without staunch people on his side, he could very soon find himself exposed and vulnerable. Now was the time, he thought, when he would really find out who his friends were.

A knock on his door announced Susan ushering in a small man of about fifty, and Simon found his first impression a little disappointing. It was only as the man approached that Simon saw the intelligence in the sharp features.

'Good morning, Mr Deveraux. I'm Inspector Christopher Grant.' He proffered his identification.

Trying to maintain as friendly an atmosphere as possible, Simon gave it a cursory glance, and with a smile ushered his guest over to the comfortable chairs. 'Can I offer you some refreshment?' Once they were both seated, with his offer declined, Simon decided to open the interview himself. 'What can I do for you, Inspector?'

'I'm making enquiries into the business practices of a Mark Grainger. I have reason to believe you are involved in a business deal with him.'

'He is acting for clients with whom I have a private matter ongoing.' Simon could see that his subtle correction of the nuances of the facts was not lost on the other man.

'Quite. May I ask if this is the first time you have had any dealings with Grainger?'

'Yes, it is. He came to me in response to a request made by his clients for my assistance in a particular matter.'

'So, just to clarify matters, this is the first time you have had any contact with him.'

Simon nodded his affirmation of the statement.

'Do you have procedures in place for checking the credentials of any party you do business with?'

'Indeed, both I and my company operate this as a matter of routine. Grainger appears to have been working as a self-employed outfit for a number of years, albeit in a small way, and is fully accredited to all necessary professional bodies. This current deal could be said to be slightly larger than his normal involvement, but everyone needs a helping hand at some time to grow their business. In this case I decided to take a personal interest rather than involve Orion.'

Grant fixed him with a steady look. 'Would you care to tell me exactly why that was, Mr Deveraux?'

Simon wondered how to phrase his reply. 'Logistically, as I appeared to be dealing with two foreign companies already, one Brazilian and one American, I decided not to complicate matters by bringing in a third company. I considered I might have a better rapport with the other officials on a more personal level. It's not the first time I've used that approach, and it seems to work. Although the two companies will deal with the practical on-the-ground considerations, they are newly formed, and it is not impossible that there could always be unforeseen problems. I decided to relieve Orion of the possibility of becoming bogged down in long-running headaches and take on the matter personally.' He now wanted the discussion to change focus. 'Am I to understand from your questions that there is some potential problem connected with Grainger?'

Again he was subjected to a long hard stare. This man had seen through his tactics. 'Certain information has come our way. It appears that there may have to be investigation of some past irregularities, and, of course, this has a knock-on effect on current associations. I have to warn you, Mr Deveraux, that this matter will no doubt come to the notice of the Financial Conduct Authority, and you may find them taking some interest in your own dealings.'

Simon returned the look. 'I have no problem with that,

Inspector.' Damn Grainger, he thought. What had he been involved in? Was this anything to do with de Santos in the past, or, as Sir Arthur had surmised, had he somehow been found out and used as a pawn in a bigger game? Now with SFO as well as possible FCA involvement this would make things even more awkward.

'Mr Deveraux, I am aware of certain "problems" arising in your South American venture. As I understand the matter, there is a suggestion that the two companies represented by Grainger have been drawn into a bogus scheme and that you have been reported as having knowledge of certain of these proposals. Now that Grainger has been found to have acted unprofessionally in the past, it is unfortunate, and, one might say, something of a coincidence, that you were particularly singled out by him in this matter. I would suggest, Mr Deveraux, if you have any information which you feel might assist, it would be wise to inform us immediately.'

Simon looked at the other man and read in his face and manner that he suspected there was more going on than he had been told.

'I quite understand, Inspector, and if I am able to help you any further, I will be in touch.'

Grant stood and moved over to the door. He paused halfway and looked back. 'At the moment you are well thought of in financial circles, Mr Deveraux. If I may offer a word of advice, it would be a pity to jeopardise that. I would not find it pleasant to have to return in my professional capacity. Good morning.'

Simon let out a long slow breath. Grant was right, but he had the feeling it was too late to do anything about that now.

*

During the last few days, surprisingly, Simon had rung to speak to Joanna and had also exchanged a few words with herself, but Amy had sensed that he was again preoccupied by something.

She had also thought that Frank and Helen Gilmore appeared worried; at one point coming across them quietly talking together but stopping when she entered the room. Something was wrong but she had no idea what and perhaps things would become clearer when Simon returned. Her time was largely taken up by preparation for school, the following week, and trying to maintain a sense of proportion with Joanna's insistence on being allowed to organise the birthday celebrations. Bubbling with excitement, she had been taken out with Frank and Helen Gilmore to purchase blue and pink decorations for the cake and table after Amy had, apparently on the spur of the moment, suggested that this colour scheme could then be for both Joanna and her father. The child had accepted that idea, but Amy pretended not to notice the curious look from Helen Gilmore. Joanna had also insisted on being involved in the making of the cake, and after one fraught, messy afternoon in the kitchen, appeared happy with the rather lop-sided offering as it emerged from the oven. The icing was to go on today and Joanna had demanded that the outcome should be a surprise for everyone, except Mrs Gilmore, to whose presence she had reluctantly agreed. Amy had the feeling that there would be a second edition of the cake tucked away somewhere if a disaster threatened.

On the Friday morning Amy remembered she had done nothing about purchasing an outfit for Saturday night, but Frank Gilmore said he was quite willing to give her a lift to enable her to shop that afternoon. After Frank dropped her off to deal with some errands of his own, Amy searched for a suitable dress, but nothing really took her eye, and they were all so expensive. She thought about the sum of money she had been given to spend and the imminent change in her circumstances. Knowing full well she would need funds to tide her over until she found other employment, it seemed a waste to fritter away so much on a dress she would probably never wear again. She was also sure Simon was not expecting her to return any unused portion of the money. Eventually she found herself in front of a shop catering for the sale of new or nearly new designer clothes. Here she found the ideal thing; a simple straight-skirted dress with delicate lace-trimmed bodice and short sleeves in a beautiful shade of blue. The proprietor insisted that both the teal blue and style suited her slender build and colouring. On the spur of the moment, she also purchased some silver sandals and a small silver handbag and left the shop, happy with her purchases.

Glancing at her watch she decided to wait for Frank Gilmore's return in a café on the other side of the road. Ordering tea and a piece of cake, the waitress had just moved away when she was conscious of someone slipping into the seat opposite. She looked up, straight into a familiar face bearing that smile she knew so well. As her heart began to pound, she wanted to run, but found she was rooted to her chair.

Chapter Fifteen

Since receiving his latest instructions, Mark Grainger had wondered how to carry them out. For a brief moment, he had even considered ignoring them. Things were becoming awkward. He had been asked in for a formal police interview, which he was trying to avoid. He knew his business would now be finished, but it might just help his case if he mentioned to the authorities what little he knew of the Deveraux matter. But what did he know? He could put them on to Hernandez, but he knew nothing about who was controlling him. Then he thought again about the implied threats made to him if he even considered such a course of action, and his moment of bravado died there and then. In any case, he was now on to the girl again, and she was unfinished business.

Without any particular plan he had decided to leave London and come down to the Windsor area to try and work out how he might make contact – and then, not believing his luck, there she was, walking along the street just ahead of him. He watched her go into a tea shop and followed.

He ordered a tea and slipped into a seat opposite her, hoping this was a good idea. He was banking on the fact that she was less likely to create a fuss in a public area.

'Hello! This is a nice surprise.'

He watched a look of astonishment and then something

like despair cross her small face. He remembered her as a pale child with carrot-coloured hair, but now she was older and there was a delicate beauty to her features which would be a definite attraction to some men. Someone like Deveraux?

'What are you doing here?' Her words were almost a whisper.

'I could ask you the same thing. I'm in the area on business and decided to stop off for some refreshment…and here you are.' It was near enough the truth for her to believe him. He thought he would try something else. 'You know, I had an idea I saw someone like you in London last weekend, in the Chelsea area, with a man and a little girl, but decided I must have been mistaken. I knew the man because I'm doing business with him on behalf of clients.' He noticed a reaction to his comments and then a slight relaxing of her body. 'It couldn't have been you with Simon Deveraux, could it?'

He watched her as the waitress brought their orders and judged she was undecided whether to be truthful or not. He somehow knew she would be.

'Yes, it was. I've been working for him during the school holidays, looking after his daughter.'

'My goodness me, how did you land a job like that?'

'I had temporary employment at her school, and I was… available.'

He eyed her over his teacup. Had she also been "available" to Deveraux himself for the summer?

'I would imagine a lot of females would be very envious of you, living closely in his household like that. He's a handsome, wealthy man. I'm sure he hasn't been celibate since his wife died.' He eyed her shopping bags. 'Treating you to some nice clothes, is he? Trips to Chelsea.'

'It's nothing like that.'

The retort was adamant and almost defiant. It was obvious she had guessed his meaning and had reacted in the same way she used to when he had goaded her as a child. Then her momentary anger passed.

'I've just bought something for a special occasion and the Chelsea trip was an invitation for his daughter to a children's party.'

Well, he'd learnt something for Hernandez, but did she know anything about the current financial troubles? He recollected his name hadn't appeared to mean anything to Deveraux, so perhaps she'd never spoken about her past, and it would be better to keep it that way. 'In the circumstances it might be a good idea if you didn't mention to anyone that we know each other. Financial circles can be funny that way. It might look a bit odd – both of us involved with Deveraux. Undue influence, that sort of thing. But then if you're living at his house, you would know all about some of his clients.'

'He doesn't have people to the house, not at least since I've been there and now the holiday's over, I doubt I'll be needed anymore.'

'But you'll still be working at the school?'

He noticed she turned her head away and looked out of the window. 'That's finished too, although the headmistress is going to see if she can help me get into a college course.' She turned her head back to him and he saw the accusing look in her grey eyes. 'I thought I was going to do that once before.'

He had to be careful; now was not the time for her to find out what had gone on all those years ago. 'Yes, it was unfortunate about the funds as I told you at the time, and then you disappeared. But now things are different, and I may be able to help again.' He passed over a business card. 'Ring me and we'll see what we can sort out. I'm around for a day or two more, perhaps we could meet up.' Her indecision was plain but eventually she picked up the card and then looked at her watch.

'I'm due to be collected at any moment. I have to go.'

'Don't forget, this meeting is just between us.'

She nodded and he watched her leave. Outside he saw a black SUV pull up and she climbed in without a backward glance.

Well, that had gone better than he could have hoped. He'd better ring Hernandez tonight.

*

Amy found the chance meeting with Mark had unsettled her, and she couldn't sleep. Simon had not returned home before bedtime and she had been forced to exert some stern control over Joanna, whose excitement was at fever pitch. Finally, she heard the car in the drive. She looked at her bedside clock and it showed eleven-thirty; another late night for him. She was tempted to go downstairs and offer him a drink after his long drive but decided against it.

Her mind went back to the meeting in the café. It was a strange coincidence for Mark to be doing business with Simon. This explained the noting down of his name, but, as Mark had said, it might be better not to mention her knowledge of him.

When she was fourteen and had first arrived at the vicarage, Mark had been away at college. From the outset, every time he returned home she formed the increasing impression that he disliked her. His parents, however, were always kind to her, and his father, Reverend George Grainger, had taken a great deal of interest in her even when she was in the children's home. He had been the one to sit down with her and tell her about her circumstances; that no-one had been able to trace her parents, and that she had been given her name and birth date by the various authorities involved. She had remained in care until he had apparently suggested that her senior schooling would be better served in a home environment, with extra tuition from him. Over the years she had seen other children leave permanently or go to temporary foster homes, but she, for some reason, was never chosen. Perhaps she was too useful helping with the remaining children, was one thought which had come to her, but she had clung onto the hope of one day being part of a proper family. The Graingers had come close to that. Uncle George, true to his word, gave her extra tuition. He was a well-read man and introduced her mind to all manner of wonderful things. Violet Grainger also made her welcome, but as she suffered from bouts of ill health, regularly retired to her room. Amy willingly helped the part-time housekeeper in her duties, and Uncle George in his work for the church, particularly the Sunday School. When her musical ability was discovered, Mr Sessions, the choirmaster and organist, took her under his wing. He was a retired professional musician and had played all over the world with some important orchestras. Some of her fondest memories were of playing the baby grand in his comfortable front room with Uncle George sitting nearby, listening, puffing away at his pipe. Talk was made of her going on to college to further a career in music and Uncle George hinted that some funds had been put away for that purpose. All this, however, didn't mean much to her at the time.

After turning sixteen everything seemed to change. Whenever Mark was at home he would spend a lot of time with his now increasingly bedridden mother, and Amy found Violet's attitude altering towards her. She didn't understand why. Then Mark started the habit of coming into her room late at night. He would smile at her, always knowing she was afraid of what he might do, but then leave. There was no lock on her bedroom door, and she didn't want to put something heavy in front of it, in case it would wake everyone and there would be a fuss. Even when she knew he was away she found it hard to sleep, her nerves on edge, just waiting to hear the footsteps on the landing. As the Graingers had been so kind in welcoming her into their house, she felt diffident about mentioning Mark's behaviour to them, and never did. Somehow, she knew that he guessed this too.

The worst time came when Uncle George began behaving differently to her, almost as if she had disappointed him in some way. Eventually, one day she was told that she would be going to another school in Bristol until she was old enough to leave care. It was Mark who drove her there, and on the way he told her that due to some unfortunate investments by his father, against his advice, the monies which had been set aside for her had been lost. However, when the time came, he was prepared to see what he could do to help her. She should have been grateful, but the smug look on his face frightened her rather than acting as a comfort. She knew that she would do anything she could rather than rely on his goodwill.

The time at the school was the worst she had ever experienced. Nothing was ever said but she felt that she was there as some sort of punishment. The other girls freely talked about their own problems, and she never felt as if she belonged. Even worse, she was cut off from all her music. She wrote to Uncle George on a number of occasions, but never received a reply. She wasn't sure her letters were ever sent. One of the other girls had said that they were opened and read.

Knowing that she would soon be on her own to fend for herself she worked hard at all her exams and received good marks. During her final week she was told that Mark would be coming to collect her on the last day. Sensing that to allow him any control over her affairs would be the worst thing that could happen, she made elaborate plans to avoid him at all costs. She managed to get into the town without anyone suspecting but it was clear she must move as far away as possible. To her this meant somewhere in a big city and, with trepidation and fear of the unknown, she boarded a coach for London.

Arriving with no work or even accommodation she had no idea of what to do or even where to go. Drawn by the sound of music outside the coach station she encountered a group of Salvation Army band members and this was her good fortune. After telling them part of her story, they were able to suggest some temporary accommodation which led to the possibility of a job in a church crèche for working mothers. Several short-term jobs followed until she eventually obtained the position in the toy shop and began to find a settled rhythm to her new life. She contemplated writing to Uncle George to tell him that she was safe and well, but as no-one had appeared to make any effort to trace her, the fear of Mark finding out her whereabouts made her reluctant to do so. She needed to concentrate on her future. With the goal of still trying to attain her musical qualifications she had started to make tentative enquiries, but it was then she saw the Carlton House advert. Amy knew she would always have fond memories of her time at the school. Now her life seemed to have come full circle. Mark's business must be doing well if he was dealing with Orion and perhaps over the years he had changed and now did want to help her – but part of her was still wary of him.

With the house now quiet, she turned over and tried to sleep. She would need all her stamina for the birthday celebrations tomorrow.

*

At breakfast Joanna had declared herself too excited to eat, until Amy had threatened to remove the birthday card sitting beside the empty place and make her wait until lunchtime.

When Simon finally arrived, he had to endure a full version of "Happy Birthday" sung slightly off-key by his daughter. With a swift look at Amy, he then folded back the tissue paper surrounding the card next to his plate. Joanna had worked hard on the masterpiece, and Simon appeared suitably impressed, and quite moved.

'It's wonderful, much better than something shop-bought. Thank you very much.'

When lunchtime arrived Mrs Gilmore had surpassed herself. The table was laid with blue and pink serviettes, plus the requisite balloons. Amy didn't dare look at Simon as he took his seat but wondered what he was thinking. She noticed there was a bottle of wine on the table and three glasses. Amy was amazed when Simon not only poured a glass for them both but then put a small amount in the third glass and handed it to Joanna. 'I thought it appropriate as this is a special occasion.' He raised his glass. 'Here's to all birthdays.' He looked across at her and Amy knew he was including her birthday as well. He then transferred his gaze to Joanna who, after taking a tentative sip, wrinkled her nose in obvious distaste. The blue eyes were again turned back to her and Amy saw there was warm laughter in the depths. 'In twenty years, I'm sure she'll think otherwise.' Amy could only smile back at his infectious amusement and once again acknowledged her growing feelings for this man.

The meal of pan-fried sole, followed by raspberries and cream, was pronounced delicious, but then it was time for the grand moment as Mrs Gilmore brought in the cake. Amy could see that it was Joanna's original, warts and all, and silently praised Helen Gilmore's sensitivity to the young girl's feelings.

'My goodness, I'm really being spoilt today. I hope this tastes as good as it looks. Someone's been to a great effort.' Trying vainly to keep a straight face, Simon deftly cut into the confectionery offering and pronounced it magnificent. Joanna looked as proud as punch, and Amy's heart warmed for her.

After lunch Simon asked Amy to join him in his study, and she followed him through, leaving Joanna to help Mrs Gilmore clear away.

'Thank you for being so understanding today. It's meant a lot to Joanna.'

He turned to face her after closing the door behind him. 'I must admit I've enjoyed it, particularly the wine tasting! And you? Don't forget it's your celebration as well.'

Feeling slightly confused, she murmured, 'Yes, the meal was splendid.'

He came closer and placed his hands on her shoulders. 'Now we've done our duty, tonight will be just for us.' She watched as his head lowered and felt his mouth against hers, warm and soft.

He released her and walked to his desk, then looked back, his mood changed. 'Are you all set for tonight? Do you have everything you need?'

She could only nod in reply.

'I'll leave about six-thirty, if that's all right. I must do some work now.'

Amy found her way out of the room, confused emotions coursing through her.

Simon turned away from the window, his knuckles white as he gripped the phone. 'It's as I said, Charles, if they want to go, then let them.'

'For God's sake, Simon, that's two big accounts gone. Can't you even say something to them?'

'I'm not going to beg, Charles. If they can't trust me after all this time, then I don't want to have their business.'

He heard a sigh at the other end. 'All right, boy, have it your way. If you want to commit professional suicide, then it's up to you. I can only tell you that I'm worried. There's a bit more in the press today. Have you seen it?'

'No, Charles. I've had other things to deal with.'

'Sounds as if it's creating a bit of interest. What did that SFO Inspector say?'

'We had a very civil and courteous conversation. I answered the questions he asked and said I would be pleased to answer any more.'

'And that's it! I'll tell you something, Simon, don't be surprised if the FCA start getting interested. They're bound to be nosing around Grainger now.'

'Well, we'll deal with it as it arises, Charles.'

'I must say you seem to be taking all this fairly calmly, but I don't like the outlook for the future if it goes on like this. We'd better have another talk, and start setting the record straight.'

'I'll be in the office on Monday.'

Closing the call, Simon felt touched that Charles hadn't questioned him further about the basis of the accusations and was obviously still prepared to speak out for him. Then his phone rang again. 'Yes, Jack?'

'I just wanted to let you know that the extra security I mentioned to you will be in place from Sunday night, not that you'll notice anything. Has Grainger been in touch with you? It seems he's gone walkabout, and the SFO want to pull him in.'

'I've heard nothing, Jack. I'll let you know if I do.'

'I thought I might mooch around outside your place myself tonight, you never know.'

'Thanks, Jack, but don't bother. I'm out tonight anyway until late. The Gilmores will both be here with Joanna.'

'Fair enough but tell them to stay alert. I should be getting some information on the Brazilian company coming through any day and I'll be in touch.'

Simon sank down on the Chesterfield and rubbed his temples. He was feeling tired and tense, with a headache hovering in the background. Perhaps the evening out would help – then he would be able to play his master stroke at last. Part of him had to admit, however, that it now seemed less important.

*

Amy was dressed and ready before six-thirty, trying to suppress the butterflies. She was sure there would be a lot of important people at tonight's event, a good proportion of whom would already know Simon, or want to know him – and she would be there by his side. At least she was happy with her appearance, sure that in this she would not let him down. Having promised Joanna that she would see her before they left, she made her way down to the lounge, careful of her long skirt on the stairs.

Joanna was dancing around her, clapping her hands in excitement when they heard the door open. Amy glanced behind her to see Simon standing in the doorway. He looked even more suave and handsome in his dinner jacket.

'Doesn't Amy look pretty, Daddy?'

Without acknowledging his daughter Simon came further into the room. Amy saw his eyes run her up and down and then focus on her face. For a moment something blazed in his eyes, and then it was gone.

'I would say that was an understatement. Are you ready? We ought to go.'

Amy retrieved her small silver handbag. 'Yes, I'm quite ready, thank you. Goodnight, Joanna.'

Simon stood aside as she left the room, but she heard him speaking to Joanna, thanking her for making his birthday so special but warning her to behave in their absence. As he joined her at the front door she heard him murmur, 'That child is far too excited for her own good.'

Amy felt that this could also apply to her. Dressed as she was, and with this undeniably handsome man at her side, what girl wouldn't be?

*

After driving towards London for about thirty minutes, Simon turned the Mercedes through two large gates and joined other cars moving down a long driveway towards a house which, in the gathering dusk, appeared to Amy far larger than Carlton House.

'The property belongs to Christos Anoglou and his wife Julia. I've known them both for some time. He's a self-made man. He started off as a deckhand on a clapped-out cargo boat in the Aegean, saved enough to buy it and began to make a profit. He went on to own a whole shipping line before selling it. Late in life he met and married Julia. She used to be an international violinist. I've been to one or two of these annual gatherings. I think you'll enjoy it. They've had a proper acoustic building erected in the grounds and Julia still gives the odd recital, but mainly she offers private lessons. This event is always for charity – a different one each year.'

Seeing the number of people milling around, Amy's nerves were stretched to the limit and she wondered if she would in fact be able to enjoy the evening. As Simon helped her out of the car, he held onto her arm for a moment. 'I can feel you shaking. Don't worry, Christos and Julia are nice people and I'm with you. Just enjoy the experience. By the way, perhaps I should have told you that I think you look beautiful.' He bent his head, and his lips brushed her forehead. 'Come on now, let's have a wonderful evening.'

Amy felt herself drawn along with the other well-dressed guests and Simon was soon spotted by their hosts. A lady in her fifties in a wonderful full-skirted black gown came towards them, followed by a much older short, rotund man.

'Simon, I thought I spotted you. How nice to have you here again.'

She allowed Simon to place a kiss on her cheek, but her eyes were on Amy, who, deciding she wasn't going to let Simon down, straightened her back and pinned a smile on her face. 'Won't you introduce us?'

Simon took Amy's arm and held her to his side. 'This is Amy Watson, a music lover and a birthday celebrant, just like me.'

The woman clapped her hands in a theatrical, but in Amy's view, genuine gesture of delight.

'How wonderful! Christos, guess what, Simon and his guest are celebrating birthdays so we must make tonight special.'

To Amy's surprise the small man took her hand and gallantly kissed it. 'If you become at all tired of your present company, my dear, feel free to seek me out.' There was a twinkle in his dark eyes and Amy instinctively knew that he had sensed her nervousness and had attempted to put her at ease. The couple moved on to greet other guests and Simon led her through a large ornate hall and then a small passage until they came out into the brilliantly lit concert area. A small orchestra was setting up in the middle and rows of chairs were placed around in a circle. As Simon ushered her towards some spare seats, Amy saw one or two people acknowledge his presence but, as he had promised, he stayed with her.

After about another ten minutes, as the hall filled to capacity and their hosts took their own seats, the lights were dimmed slightly, and the recital began. The printed programme announced a selection of Mozart, Vivaldi and Bach and there were to be piano and violin solos. Amy was soon in a world of her own. To her, sitting there listening to beautiful music in an even more beautiful setting was almost magical. During the interval Simon accompanied her back into the entrance hall where light refreshments were now offered. At one point she excused herself and found the ladies cloakroom. On exiting, she looked around for a moment, anxious to find Simon again, and was startled when hands reached round her waist and a swift kiss was placed on her bare shoulder. 'Don't worry, you haven't lost me.' She turned around under his hands and looked up into the smiling blue gaze. 'Are you having a good time?' She could only nod, the slowly building emotions of the evening robbing her of speech. During the second half Simon moved his chair slightly closer to her, took hold of her hand and placed it on his knee. She could feel the warmth of his body through the material, and at first, she felt nervous but then began to relax.

At the end of the evening, after the orchestra and soloists had taken their bows amidst rapturous applause from the audience, Christos Anoglou gave a short speech, thanking his wife for organising such a marvellous evening and reminding his guests of the main purpose of the event.

As they were leaving the concert hall Simon approached his hosts and removed an envelope from his inside pocket. 'I nearly forgot to give this to you.'

A voice from close behind commented, 'You'd better bank that quickly, my friend. You never can tell these days.'

Amy turned round to see a man standing close by. She felt Simon's body stiffen and was sure he was about to reply when Christos Anoglou spoke sternly to the other man. 'This is neither the time nor the place for such a comment, Joshua. Let us hear no more about it.' The man shrugged and wandered off. Julia placed her hand on Simon's arm. 'I'm sorry for that, Simon. It was uncalled for. Christos and I are happy to see you here at any time.'

Simon silently shook hands with them, and then Amy felt his touch on her elbow as he guided her out to the car. She didn't know what to make of the exchange, but something warned her not to make any comment. During the journey home Simon tuned into a radio station playing soft late-night jazz and she felt herself slowly relaxing again. As Frank Gilmore let them into Woodhayes Simon finally spoke. 'Would you like a drink, Amy?'

'Umm…nothing alcoholic, thank you, but I'll make you some coffee or chocolate if you want.'

He smiled at her. 'I think it's my turn tonight. Go on up to my room and I'll be there in a few minutes.'

Feeling strangely excited, she entered his room and sat at the little table. A short time later he entered with a tray, leaving the door slightly ajar behind him. Discarding his bow tie and dinner jacket, he picked up a small remote and the room was filled with the same soft jazz sounds as in the car. While Amy sipped at her drink, he stood in silence by the window, looking out into the dark. She felt she ought to make some sort of remark about tonight.

'It was a wonderful evening, thank you so much for taking me.' She hesitated. 'I'm sorry if that man spoilt…'

Turning to her, she now sensed something like anger in him. 'It's of no consequence.'

Without warning she found herself pulled to her feet and into his arms. She felt his body, lean and hard, wrapped around her and after a moment or two involuntarily laid her head against his shoulder. He moved one hand across her back, holding her even closer to him, and the other began to caress the bare skin of her shoulder and neck. His touch sent delicious waves of sensation through her and she wanted to feel his lips on her skin. As if sensing her need, he bent his head and began to kiss her face, but not letting their lips meet. After a few moments she needed still more contact and lifted her face to him. His kiss was nothing like the times before; it was deep and urgent, demanding the same response from her. One hand wound into her hair, holding her face to his as he deepened the kiss even further. When she was almost gasping for air, he trailed his lips down the side of her neck and onto her shoulder. She felt a strange ache beginning in her body. He turned her round in his arms and held her close to him, the arm around her waist moving higher. She then felt his fingers at the zip of her dress. Placing small kisses on the nape of her neck, he whispered, 'You like this, don't you? You want to stay with me tonight. Tell me you do, Amy.'

His voice was soft and caressing. With a multitude of sensations pulsing through her, there was no way she could resist the inevitable, something she now longed for. 'Yes, please let me stay.'

No sooner were the words uttered than she found herself thrust away from him. She turned in confusion. He was standing, watching her, his arms folded.

'I am sorry to disappoint you, Miss Watson, but in fact, contrary to your belief, I have no interest in your youthful charms.'

Amy tried to shake herself free from the spell he had cast over her. 'I… I don't understand.'

'I brought you here to this house with the express purpose of teaching you a lesson. All these weeks and especially tonight have been meticulously planned.'

Amy could not believe what she was hearing. All his attentiveness to her had been false? 'You deliberately let me think…how could you behave like that? Why?'

He took a step closer to her again. 'What's the matter, did you believe it was all true? You should have been more careful; made sure of the situation,' he took hold of her shoulders, his fingers digging into her flesh, 'just as you should have done before your little tirade at the Parents Evening.' His eyes stared into hers, like shards of blue ice. 'Perhaps now you need to be made aware of certain facts.' With his face pale and tight he announced, 'Joanna is not my child.'

For a split second there was silence in the room until he spoke again, his harsh, cold voice sounding loud in the quiet house. 'The child is the result of an affair between my wife and…her lover. She was leaving me. They were both killed in an accident abroad. It was only by a coincidence some short while later that I discovered I was not Joanna's biological father.'

Although reeling from the shock of his words, Amy looked at the open door. 'Please, Joanna might hear.'

'I've told you before, she'll be sound asleep.' He smiled slightly, but it was without mirth. 'You always seem to be so concerned about her, Miss Watson, but what about me? How do you think I felt, when I found out that the child I had believed for months was mine, was nothing of the kind?' As his anger came pouring out his voice became louder. 'I could have washed my hands of her, as everyone else did, but I decided to look after her to the best of my ability, until you, an inexperienced girl, came along, pointing out the supposed error of my ways without finding out or understanding the true circumstances.' He stepped back from her. 'So perhaps, Miss Watson, you need to look upon tonight as a lesson in life, to be remembered. Learn to be more careful before you make assumptions.'

The shock of Simon's revelations had rendered Amy incapable of movement, and she could only watch, transfixed, as he stepped closer again, a strange look on his face. He reached out a hand and stroked her bare shoulder. 'It could, of course, also be the time to teach you another lesson. Maybe tonight we should, after all, take matters to a conclusion. You seemed to be enjoying the experience a moment ago.'

Finally summoning the strength to back away from his touch, with tears running down her face, Amy blindly turned for the door. Stumbling along the landing, she eventually found the sanctuary of her own room.

Halfway up the dark staircase, unseen and unheard, a small figure detached itself from the shadows, slipped back into bed and hugged the rabbit close in comfort.

Chapter Sixteen

After a few hours of fitful sleep, Simon walked into the dining room, expecting to find he was the last in for breakfast. To his surprise the table was empty and, more importantly, looking as if it had not yet been used.

Helen Gilmore appeared with a pot of coffee, her face troubled.

'Good morning, Mr Deveraux.'

'Good morning, Helen. Where is everyone?'

'Joanna came down earlier, saying she didn't feel well, and has gone back to bed. She looked rather pale. I'll go up to see her later.'

Simon sighed. 'Considering the state of excitement she's been in for the last few days, it's perhaps not surprising. There's also the spectre of school tomorrow. No doubt Amy will look in on her.'

'We haven't seen her yet this morning.'

Simon averted his gaze and concentrated on pouring a cup of coffee. 'It was a late night, last night. Let her sleep.'

'Actually, Frank asked if he could have a word with you as soon as possible this morning.'

Simon glanced up, wondering what was troubling her. 'Tell him I'll be in my study in a few moments, and he can come and see me.'

After only one cup of coffee and a few mouthfuls of toast Simon decided work might be the best thing to keep away the unsettling thoughts filling his mind. Sitting down at his desk he saw the envelope tucked into his blotter. Ripping it open he cast his eyes over the few lines it contained. 'Christ!' He leapt to his feet and raced out of the room, nearly colliding with Frank Gilmore. Taking the stairs two at a time he flung open Amy's bedroom door. The room was empty. He looked in the cupboards and drawers, but all he could find was the dress she had worn last night, with bag and shoes neatly placed underneath. The gesture was obvious – she wanted no reminders. He heard a noise behind him and turned to find Gilmore in the doorway.

'That's what I wanted to see you about, sir. When I came back with the newspapers this morning, I found the kitchen door unlocked. I know it was secure before I left. I can't see that anything is missing. Do you want me to contact the police or Mr Fletcher?'

'Police! No no, of course not. Amy left me a note to say she was leaving today. I just… just… thought she meant later.'

He turned out of the room. 'Thanks for telling me, but leave it, Frank, will you?' He hesitated on the landing outside Joanna's room, and then quietly opened the door. All he could see was part of a dark head on the pillow with the covers drawn up around it. If she was asleep, he didn't want to wake her. He closed the door and moved away into his own room.

This wasn't what he'd expected. He'd expected Amy to be fired with anger this morning, hurling a withering onslaught against his behaviour. He'd intended smoothing it over, thanking her for the excellent service she had given him during the summer, promising her a sizeable bonus and dropping her back to her lodgings later in the day. She had obviously taken the whole matter to heart, enough to leave without seeing Joanna, and how did she even manage it on her own with all her luggage? What would he say to Joanna, a child already unwell! He shook his head.

Last night he had wondered whether it was even worth going through with the whole idea, but then she had reminded him of the snide remark made at the concert and it had once again fuelled his anger. People were behaving like baying hounds after a fox, making accusations before they heard the truth – just as she had – and so he'd made his decision.

He left his room again and went down to the study to start work. Whatever he told Joanna about Amy leaving, perhaps after seeing her at school tomorrow it would sort itself out.

*

Amy turned away from Mark Grainger and looked around the hotel room, luggage at her feet.

'Why have you brought me here? I asked you to take me to my lodgings.'

'After waking me up at some ridiculous hour begging for a lift, I think you owe me some sort of explanation.'

'I… I just needed to get away.'

'What's the matter, Deveraux coming on a bit strong? I thought there was more to this little "arrangement" than you were letting on.'

Amy ignored him; she didn't want to be drawn any further on the subject. Reaching for her handbag she pulled out her phone. 'I'll ring for a taxi to take me home.'

To her surprise Mark shot out a hand and took the phone from her. 'Not likely. We thought it was handy having you in thick with Deveraux, but now you've spoilt it all, as usual. I'm keeping you here until we find out if you can still be useful.'

Amy tried to snatch the phone back, but he pushed her roughly down onto a chair. She looked up into his face and felt sudden fear. 'What do you mean, 'we', and how can I be useful to you?'

'I'm telling you nothing yet until I've spoken with someone else.' He turned away and picked up his own phone. After a moment or two it was answered. 'Yes...yes, I know, Miguel, but I have a situation here. The girl's split from Deveraux. She called me for a lift early this morning in a panic... Yes, she's here at the hotel...All right.'

Amy watched as he came and sat down opposite her, that familiar smile on his face. 'We'll just wait until my associate arrives. He'll decide what we do next.'

'Mark, please let me go. I don't know what's going on, but I'm sure I can't possibly help.'

'Not on your life, sweetie, you slipped through my clutches once before, but it won't happen again. I'll make sure of that.'

Something about his tone of voice made Amy certain that in contacting him she had made a dreadful mistake. Last night, after reaching her room and finally staunching the tears, she had thought about all she had been told and her own foolish unattainable dreams. Lying on her bed, staring at the ceiling for hours, it had seemed imperative to get away from Woodhayes as soon as possible; there was no way she could face Simon Deveraux again. But how? At only just after five o'clock on a Sunday morning it might be too early to call for a taxi, and anyway she didn't want to risk the sound of it pulling into the drive. Her only other option was to call Mark. As she packed her things, she had put off the decision for as long as possible. She also hated the thought of leaving without seeing Joanna, but she just didn't know what to say to the child. It might be better to leave some sort of note, so she wrote a few lines which she would leave in Simon's study when she left. She knew that Frank Gilmore went for the newspapers between six-thirty and seven o'clock. She could hardly ask him for a lift but at least no-one should be about until he returned. She would ask Mark to collect her during that time slot. He sounded angry when she made her request, but eventually agreed. He said he would wait for her in the lane. After disarming the door lock, she had struggled away from the house without looking back, trying to hold the tears at bay. Now they were threatening again, and she wished she had been brave enough to stay. Woodhayes now seemed a safe haven.

Several long hours later Mark ushered in an older man, dark and swarthy. They spoke together in quiet tones and, after studying the newcomer, Amy recognised him as the man she had seen in the Tate. As he looked at her, she felt once more as she had that day – something bad was about to happen.

They both came over to where she was sitting, and the dark man spoke. 'You have caused us some trouble by your actions, and plans will have to be advanced. From now on you will do as we say.'

Trying to appear braver than she felt, Amy looked back at him. 'I have no idea what you are talking about, neither do I have any intention of remaining here, nor of taking orders from you.'

Unbelievably she found herself face to face with a small handgun. She felt sick with fear but tried to control the shaking in her limbs.

'I imagine you have now changed your mind somewhat.' The smile was unpleasant, and the eyes cold and dark. 'Now, who takes Deveraux's child to school and then collects her?'

What was he talking about? Then a terrible thought struck her. 'Leave Joanna alone. She's done nothing to hurt you, or anyone.'

Mark Grainger lent down and grabbed her upper arm, squeezing it hard until she cried out. 'Answer the question.'

She knew she would have no option. 'It depends, sometimes it's her f…father, other times it's Mr Gilmore. He usually collects her.'

The two men looked at each other. 'We will make it a collection, Grainger. I will leave now and deal with some arrangements. We need to hire an SUV of the same kind as you have described to me. I will return on Tuesday and we will take our chance that afternoon.' He looked again at Amy. 'Because you left in a rush, will Deveraux check up on you?'

'I left him a note to say I was leaving. I doubt he will bother.'

Not realising that her feelings came through so clearly, she jumped as Mark stroked her cheek and grinned. 'Never mind, we can get to know each other now. You may even like me better.'

She shrank back and the dark man brandished the gun in front of Mark's face. 'Do nothing like that, my friend, or attract attention in any way. Do you understand? It is possible the police might now be looking for you.'

'Yeah, sure, sure, Miguel, don't worry. Just having a bit of fun, that's all.'

They both left the room but after a moment Mark returned alone. Amy knew she had to try once more.

'Mark, please tell me what this is all about. Why is Joanna involved and what did that man mean about you being involved with the police? In any case I'm not staying here with you until Tuesday.'

'You heard Miguel. You're staying here. As far as the hotel is concerned you are my dear wife, returned after a trip abroad.' A broad grin spread over his face when he saw her reaction. 'I'll be with you all the time so don't try anything.' He flung himself down in a chair opposite and stared at her. 'You have no idea what's going on with Deveraux, do you? Don't you read the newspapers?'

Her mind still full of how to resolve her situation, Amy could only shake her head.

'Miguel works for a client with a grudge against Deveraux and they have enlisted my help in getting him mixed up in a dodgy deal, which has now been exposed to the authorities, and he's in big trouble. It could be the end of his little empire. They now want to turn the screw a bit more by snatching his daughter for a ransom.'

Amy gasped, shocked to think of that man and his gun anywhere near Joanna. There must be something she could do!

'I'm not going to stay here with you and allow that awful man to frighten Joanna. In any case, you can't just collect her. The school won't allow her to go with a stranger.'

Grainger sat forward in his chair. 'That's where you come in, sweetie. You'll do it for us.'

Amy jumped up and ran for the door, but he was too quick, and she found herself pinned to the wall in seconds. 'You are going to do exactly what we say. There's money in it for me. I need it to get me out of the country and this time you're going to help me. I'm not letting you interfere with my life again, spoiling things.'

She looked up into his angry face. 'How have I ever spoiled things for you?'

He turned away; his hands balled into fists. 'You never understood. My parents brought you into their home without even consulting me. *Me*, their own son! Oh no, Dad was so wrapped up with you. After you were dumped in his church, he considered it his Christian duty to look after you. He even told me he was putting money aside to help with your further education.' He turned back to her and shouted, 'He never did that for me. I had to work for my extra money to see me through college. I wasn't standing for that, so I saw to it they changed their minds about you. When Mum was in bed, I sat with her and told her you were being a nuisance in the house, pestering Dad when he was busy, and coming on to me. I said I would deal with it, so she needn't bother.' He grinned at her expression. 'I came into your room to make it look good. I knew you were frightened of me, and you wouldn't say anything. Even better, when Dad took you to those piano lessons you used to rave on about, I found the petty cash for the Sunday School and helped myself to small amounts, then, with regret, admitted to Dad that I had seen *you* take it. Yeah, that one really hurt the old fool.'

Amy felt her legs giving way and she collapsed on the nearest chair. 'How could you do such a thing? They gave me a home. I worshipped them, and never did understand the reason for their change in attitude toward me. No-one said a word. Why did you do it, Mark? Why?'

He came and stood in front of her. 'I told you. They were

my parents, it was *my* home. Any spare money should have been for *me*. In the end I couldn't risk them asking any questions, so I had to get you moved away. That school you went to was for girls in their last months of care who needed to be kept an eye on. Your circumstances were explained to them, but Dad didn't want to make a fuss about the money. I had to make sure you didn't get in touch, so I left instructions for mail to be intercepted. You didn't know Mum passed away not long after you left, and I took over Dad's affairs. I made sure what funds he had earmarked for you were controlled by me. I intended to collect you that last day and arrange it so that the money was handed over to me. I needed it for my new business, but then they told me you'd gone, disappeared. I couldn't let on to Dad, so I made him believe I was in touch, and you were OK. I couldn't afford a big hue and cry. In the end I still worked out a way to use the money.'

'I'll go to Uncle George and tell him the truth.' Amy tried to sound defiant.

'It won't get you far. He's in a home with dementia. He won't even recognise you.'

This was too much for Amy. The thought of that kind, gentle man being reduced to such circumstances was more than she could bear, plus it was obvious that he would not even have the comfort of a genuine loving son to care for him. There would also be no chance for her to tell him the truth about the lies he had been told. This thought finally broke the dam of tears welling up inside her. She put her head in her hands and sobbed.

'For God's sake, shut up, girl. If you do what we want, there might even be a bit of money in it for you. I'm getting out of the UK. The authorities have caught on to a little bit of "iffy" business I did in the past, so I'm finished here. Miguel is going to organise getting me away with a new passport so I can start again with a share of the ransom money. You could do well if you come in with me. You've turned into quite a pretty little thing. I can see why Deveraux was interested.'

Amy wiped her tears away. 'I have no wish to go anywhere with you, Mark, and I don't want any of your money.'

'OK, suit yourself, but just remember you do as we say. Understand?'

Should she tell him the truth about Joanna? Would it make any difference, or make things even worse? She just didn't know, and all she could do was nod. One thing was certain; although in the past she had been lonely and afraid, it had never felt as desperate as it did at this moment. However, she must not think of herself but focus on what she could do to protect Joanna.

*

In a temporary hotel room Hernandez discussed the changed circumstances with his employer.

'Yes, of course, senor, it can still be carried out; just quicker than we planned. Now we have the assistance of this woman, it will actually be easier to snatch the child. She will be made to understand her part and what might happen if she fails to comply. Grainger still expects assistance with a new start, and I will tell him nothing of our true plan. It will, as you say, also be the final blow for Deveraux. With your permission, I will deal with the matter as we have now agreed. Everything else is in place. On Tuesday evening I will instruct Grainger to make the first contact with Deveraux. It would be better to give him a short time span to accomplish our request and I will make sure he understands the urgency. When I have confirmation that Deveraux has complied with our financial instructions, do I have your authorisation to then finish the matter as agreed?' It was obvious the answer came in the affirmative, and a satisfied smile appeared on his face. 'I have my escape route arranged, and will be away before anyone realises, leaving both the woman and Grainger fully implicated by their actions. Yes, senor, when convenient I will contact you.'

*

Things were now starting to look bad for Orion. There was no way Simon could deny the fact. Increasing press interest had led to a haemorrhaging of clients, and, in two cases, members of staff also. The SFO wanted to inspect his Colombian file and the FCA had indicated they required information about his financial affairs.

The only good news had come from Jack. As expected, his contact in Brazil had reported that yet again one of the company officials was linked some while ago with de Santos, and better still there were rumours that the Brazilian authorities were, at last, considering investigating de Santos himself.

There had also been a call from Reynolds asking if he had heard anything from Grainger, confessing they had lost contact with their Colombian. His BMW car had been stationary outside his accommodation for over two days now, and no answer had been forthcoming from a cold call at the premises. It was, therefore, considered quite likely he had slipped the net, and possible that both he and Grainger were together somewhere. Simon suggested that they might have left the country, but Reynolds thought this wasn't the case.

There was nothing Simon could do about any of it, and he was more distracted by other thoughts.

Joanna had stayed in her room all day on Sunday but as far as Helen Gilmore could tell, there was nothing actually ailing her. He had taken it upon himself to explain Amy's absence. She had accepted the news quietly enough – a little too quietly maybe – and never once looked directly at him.

She had eaten her breakfast this morning but again in total silence. At the school she left the car without saying goodbye. He was going to call her back to explain her rudeness but decided against it. He also thought about Amy. She had obviously taken the whole matter badly and he ought to apologise. She had looked particularly attractive on Saturday night, tempting enough for any man, and she deserved to be assured of that. He considered leaving early to collect Joanna and maybe seeing Amy then, but that would be the second time he had gone to Carlton House with the idea of giving her a grovelling apology. He would perhaps wait to see Joanna's reaction tonight and possibly see Amy at her lodgings. If Joanna still showed any sign of a problem, he would ask Carlisle to check her over at the weekend. Unbidden, he felt that strong feeling stirring inside him once more – he might even see *her* again.

'Simon! Are you at all interested in this discussion?'

Charles's angry tone broke into his thoughts.

'Sorry, Charles. I was trying to come up with some suggestions.'

Charles McDonald gave him a piercing look. 'I think we're fast running out of those... unless, of course, you tell me what's really going on. I'm not a fool, Simon; neither are you. How did you get yourself mixed up in something like this?'

Simon looked up at the older man. Over the years he had given sound advice and had worked hard for the company. He deserved credit for this, and Simon knew he had to give him the courtesy of being told the truth.

'All right, Charles. I'll ask Susan to get Stuart in here, and then I'll brief you both.'

McDonald sat back in his chair. 'Now we're getting somewhere.'

*

After his senior managers had left, with McDonald's vitriolic epithets still ringing in his ears for even agreeing to be involved in such a hair-brained scheme, Simon stood looking out of his window. He appreciated their frustration as, for the time being, they knew they could do very little. The door opened behind him and he turned, as Susan came into the room.

'I thought you ought to know that Frank Gilmore has just rung to say that Joanna has been sent home from school and is back at Woodhayes.'

He sighed. Perhaps, after all, she was ill with something. He'd leave early and see if he could get to the bottom of it.

Nearing home an hour or two later he allowed himself a slight smile. This sudden change of movements would keep Jack's watchers on their toes, not that he'd seen a sign of anyone.

As he entered the house, he almost tripped over a school satchel lying in the hall. How many times had he told Joanna to tidy her things! Frank Gilmore came in from the kitchen, and Simon sensed trouble.

'I'm sorry to tell you, Mr Deveraux, but the school rang just after lunch, asking someone to fetch Joanna. She had apparently been causing some sort of disturbance and they thought it better if she came home. Miss Freeman will be ringing you later tonight.'

'Disturbance? I assumed it was because she was unwell.'

'I can't say, sir. She seemed very emotional when I collected her. She went straight up to her room.'

Simon ran a hand through his hair. 'I'd better go up and see if I can find out what's going on.'

He entered her room without knocking. She was lying on her bed, holding the rabbit. He placed her satchel on the other bed. 'I've told you before about leaving your things all over the place, and what's this I hear about you being sent home from school?'

There was silence. He could feel his temper rising, but he had to remember that it was just possible she might be unwell. 'Joanna, it's polite to answer a question.'

'I don't have to do anything you say. You're not my daddy.'

Chapter Seventeen

For a moment Simon wondered if he had heard correctly. Then it dawned on him. Oh my God, as Amy had feared, they had been overheard! He was stunned and his mind went blank. He always knew he would need to have this conversation with her at some time, but not now, not like this! His mind searched for the right words. 'Joanna, there are things which I have to tell you, but not right now. Perhaps when you are older and can better understand them. For the moment I want you to know that nothing will change, so there's no need to feel worried or frightened.'

She looked up at him. 'You're always telling me that things will happen when I'm older. I want to know now. I want to know why you shouted at Amy and made her cry. I want to know where she is. She's not at school. I tried to find her, but no-one would tell me anything and I was sent home. I want to be with her. I don't like it here anymore. You're never here with me, and you always tell me off.'

What could he say! 'I'm speaking with Miss Freeman tonight and I'll ask her about Amy. I'll come and tell you later but remember, there is nothing for you to worry about.' There was no response, and he didn't know what to do next. 'If you like I'll ask Mrs Gilmore to bring you up something to eat.' There was still silence, and all he could think of was to leave the room.

He went down to his study and shut the door behind him. He could feel his heart racing, almost like a panic attack. How was he going to deal with this? Why wasn't Amy at the school? Had they not employed her again? But if so, why hadn't she mentioned it to him? Then he remembered she had been trying to speak to him about something, and he hadn't stopped to listen. He ran a hand over his face. Perhaps he would know more when Harriet rang him. He sat down at his desk and noticed the letter. He recognised the handwriting – Margaret Horton. Opening the envelope, he read the contents. It was effectively her resignation due to ill health. She felt it was fairer on him to make a decision about her future once and for all. He dropped it on his blotter. One more problem to add to the pile, he thought.

*

Standing in his study, looking out of the window, Simon wasn't really seeing anything, just listening to Harriet Freeman's voice as they discussed the situation.

'I agree, Simon, it's not the ideal scenario, but now this has happened we have to deal with matters as they are.'

Easy for Harriet to say, thought Simon, she isn't faced with a silent, mutinous child.

'We must try and restore a familiar routine as soon as possible. I'm going to suggest that I call for Joanna tomorrow morning and after a little talk encourage her to return to school. Meanwhile I will have a word with my staff to make some allowances.'

'I was thinking more of keeping her away for a day or two, but if you consider your approach is the best, I'll go along with it. I gather you haven't been able to employ Miss Watson this term.'

'Unfortunately, it was out of my control. I wrote to her explaining the whole situation but asked if she might care to come and see me about her future career. Her lodgings were paid for until the end of the month, so I suggested she remain there for the moment. I must say I'm a little surprised not to have heard from her already.'

'Perhaps she's gone home to her family.'

'Simon, you will be unaware of the fact, but Miss Watson has no family. She was abandoned at birth and brought up in care. If you remember I mentioned to you that she had confidential issues as well as yourself.'

The news came as a shock to him, but it perhaps explained the unconscious rapport Amy had formed with Joanna and the origin of some of her other attitudes. Now, with Margaret Horton's news, depending on Amy's own wishes for the future, it might be that he could assist her with further employment, solving their mutual dilemma.

'As you say, I had no idea about this, Harriet. I find I need to speak with her myself. Perhaps you could inform her of that when you see her.'

'Yes, I will, but Joanna is my first concern. I should be with you at about eight-thirty. You can tell Joanna this, but I think it might be better if you were absent, so that we can talk more calmly.'

After speaking with Jack Fletcher and making him aware of the arrangements for Tuesday morning but deciding not to give him any reason, Simon went back upstairs, hoping his next conversation with Joanna would be easier, but he doubted it. He felt as if his whole world was spinning out of control.

*

On Tuesday morning, after two almost sleepless nights, Amy was tired – and also hungry. Although since Sunday night food had been brought up to their hotel room, she had eaten little, and had flatly refused to make use of the bedroom. She ignored the broad grin on Mark's face when the subject was discussed but took some comfort from the fact that he, too, was forced to attempt to doze on the only seating available. He had moved one chair in front of the door to block any attempt at escape and had placed himself next to the hotel phone. Amy had no idea what he had done with the two mobiles, but suspected they were on his person. This morning he had demanded that she smarten herself up by changing her clothing. She would be seen at the school, he said, and ought to appear presentable. He had done likewise. She had again tried to talk him out of the whole idea, but had only succeeded in making him angry. After this she felt it better to try and humour him, in the hope that there would be something she could do.

In the early afternoon the man called Miguel joined them. He looked them over and nodded his approval.

'I have everything arranged. Both of you pack your bags and take them when we leave. Grainger, you will settle the hotel bill while I take our friend to my vehicle. You will follow in your car and I will show you where this can be left, whereupon you will join us.' He looked over at Amy. 'What time is the child usually collected?'

'Between three-thirty and four o'clock.'

'I assume this is always the case?' He fixed his dark gaze on her. Knowing she would have to answer she nodded in the affirmative. He went on, 'I think we will arrive just before three-thirty. I have seen a place where I can park, half-hidden by shrubs. I know there is a person on duty at the door, as I called yesterday with the excuse of asking directions to another establishment. There was no obvious sign of any other security. Do you know of any?'

Amy now saw a chance of giving false information – if she dared. There had been talk that in the summer holiday trial CCTV surveillance cameras were to be installed, but she had no idea where the cameras were or even if this had been done. Was this man testing her? She had to say something. 'I don't know of anything else.' He stared at her for a moment, and she held her breath. He then turned away to Mark. 'You will both go and collect the girl. Sit in the rear of the vehicle with them in case we encounter a problem. Now get yourself organised and we will leave.'

*

As they entered the Carlton House grounds everything seemed so familiar to Amy that she could hardly believe the circumstances which now brought her back.

With shaking limbs, she climbed out of the SUV and walked up to the entrance. There were two other cars parked in the vicinity and young girls were already moving towards them. Mark draped his arm around her shoulders and whispered in her ear, 'Don't get any ideas. Miguel is watching and he has his gun. You wouldn't want anyone to get hurt, would you?'

In the entrance they encountered Mr Griffin, one of the maintenance staff, who smiled when he saw her. 'Well, hello Miss Watson. Nice to see you back.'

Amy tried to smile. 'I've come for Joanna Deveraux.' She saw him glance out into the car park and then at her companion.

Mark held out his hand. 'Hi there, I'm Amy's step-brother, Mark, on a surprise visit. We're taking Joanna out for tea.'

'She'll enjoy that, I'm sure. She's seemed a little down—'

His comments were drowned out by a sudden noisy rush of young girls and above it all, a cry which Amy recognised.

'Amy! Oh, Amy, I knew you'd come.'

Nearly knocked off her feet, Amy found herself enveloped in flying limbs and heavy satchel. For a moment she held the small form tight against her, frantic thoughts of screaming out loud stilled by the knowledge of the man with the gun.

Mark took the child's arm and picked up her satchel. 'Hi, I'm Mark. The car's waiting, let's go, shall we?'

In one last desperate attempt Amy looked over her shoulder. 'Mr Griffin, would you tell Miss Freeman that I am not able to come and see her just at the moment?' He nodded in reply. Perhaps, thought Amy, this comment might make some sense as events unfolded. She felt her arm squeezed, and a harsh whisper close to her face. 'What was that all about?'

She turned her head to the man beside her. 'I'm supposed to see the headmistress and if I don't turn up someone might make enquiries. I'm sure you don't want that.' She tensed and held her breath, then heard a grunt of agreement.

Joanna was skipping along beside them as they made their way down to the SUV and Amy nearly cried at her display of innocent enthusiasm. Mark quickly hustled them into the rear seat, and they drove away. Other vehicles passed them, entering the grounds, but none of them Frank Gilmore, and by the time they had turned out onto the main road there was still no sign of him.

Joanna was glancing at the driver and turned to look up at her. 'Amy, is Mr Gilmore unwell? Is that why you've come for me?'

Amy was about to speak but the voice from the front was sharp and cold. 'We're going for a little drive, so just shut up.'

Joanna's young voice echoed in the silence. 'I don't like you. You're rude. I want to go home.'

Afraid of what might happen, Amy patted her arm and motioned for her to be quiet. With obvious reluctance she was obeyed and there was silence again. Amy was looking at road signs and noticed they appeared to be heading via country roads in the direction of Reading. After a while, in the gathering gloom, they turned off down a rutted track and came to a stop in a clearing outside a single-storey building. It looked disused, with ivy and other vegetation growing around the outside. They were hustled through a small door at one end, Joanna grimly holding onto her satchel. It was dark inside with the only light coming from a small window covered in grime, halfway up the far wall. Mark was instructed to light an oil lamp which was standing on what appeared to be machinery at the back of the room. The whole place felt cold and damp. Mark's companion indicated Amy was to sit down on some sacking on the floor and motioned for Joanna to join her. She now saw fear in the small face, with tears threatening.

'I don't like it here. I'm afraid, Amy. Please take me home.'

Before Amy could reply, Mark came over and stood looking down at them. 'Well now, that all depends on your daddy, doesn't it?' As he turned away, he took Amy's phone from his coat pocket. 'Time to make the call, Miguel?'

*

For Simon the days at the office were getting harder.

Sir Arthur had rung first thing to tell him that, despite discreet checking, there had been no further word from Brazil on the intended action against de Santos, but he doubted the authorities there would be prepared to divulge their intentions anyway. It was just a question of waiting.

Charles McDonald had then joined him during a lengthy meeting with FCA representatives and was now assisting in organising retrieval of the information they required. It had appeared important for them to have assurances as to any monetary payments made in the South American deal and they seemed satisfied when informed that Simon's initial input of agreed funds was residing on deposit in a designated account known to the two other companies involved but, they were assured, not yet released. Stuart Mannion was also providing them with the relevant confirmation in this respect.

Media interest in Orion was growing and the press was becoming a nuisance. He had earlier asked for security to intervene as members of staff were being approached when entering or leaving the building. Charles was sending a letter to all employees trying to diffuse the situation and allay any worries, but he knew that if things went on much longer, he would run the risk of losing some more good people, as well as clients. In fact, the situation was worse than he had thought possible at the outset, and he was faced with the prospect of having to inject more of his private finance to make sure of continued liquidity. He had considered that his name and track record would stand him in good stead through the worst, but it seemed that the financial world was even more fickle than he thought. Although fending off several requests for press interviews, he had given a few brief words to Tony Broadbent who, once again confirming Simon's regard for his intelligence, hinted that he sensed something more was behind this whole matter and wanted to give Simon the chance of a fair hearing. Knowing he could not tell the whole truth yet, if ever, Simon had to stall him, but the angry part of him wanted to blow the whole thing apart.

He was now being forced to calm another client and was speaking with Dieter Brandt in Germany, trying to diffuse his concerns about the situation. 'I quite understand, Dieter, but I am sure by the time you get back to me with the revised figures as you've just outlined, everything will have sorted itself out... Yes, yes, of course, as I said, I quite understand, but don't make any decision just yet. Work out your figures and come back to me, I'll be waiting to hear from you... Yes, thank you, Dieter.'

Simon rose from his desk and walked over to the large glass window. He rubbed a hand over his eyes; they felt gritty and sore. He'd had very little sleep last night and it was now catching up with him. Overriding all other considerations was his concern as to how to deal with Joanna. There had been no word from Harriet of any problem at school today, so perhaps this was some good news, but he still had to find a way, and the right words, to try and explain to Joanna that... he felt a hand on his arm and turned with a start, to find Susan beside him, a look of concern on her face. He had been so deep in his thoughts he hadn't heard her approach.

'Mr Deveraux, I have Mark Grainger on the phone, insisting on speaking to you.'

'Mark Grainger! What the devil does he want? Tell him to get lost... no, wait a moment, perhaps I should speak to him.' If he could get an idea of where the man was, they could perhaps pass it on to Inspector Grant. He strode back over to his desk. 'Put him through, Susan.' He heard the click as the call was transferred.

'Good afternoon, Deveraux. Surprised to hear from me again? I hope the authorities are not keeping you too busy?'

Simon immediately became aware of the change in Grainger's attitude. Gone was the deferential tone from their previous meetings, and he even sensed insolence behind the words. Almost without conscious thought his hand reached out to the button on his desk console which set in motion the recorder, a useful aid in complicated discussions.

'The same could be said for you, apparently. What do you want, Grainger?'

'Well, a little more civility for a start.'

Trying to hold onto his temper, Simon bit back a harsh retort, as something warned him to stay silent.

'Have you by any chance heard from your daughter's school?' Grainger's voice now had a mocking tone to it, as if he was enjoying himself. Simon began to feel the first faint stirrings of genuine alarm. Grainger went on, 'Perhaps it's too early yet, but I'm sure you will… very soon.'

With coldness entering his stomach, Simon now suspected the reason for the call. Keeping the fear from his voice, he attempted to sound casual but impatient. 'Get on with it, Grainger.'

'Very well. I have your daughter here with me, Deveraux. She will, of course, be returned to you but, no doubt as you have anticipated, we need to speak about the conditions for that.'

Simon took a deep breath. 'I don't believe a word of what you're saying. Let me talk to her.'

'I'll perhaps let you talk to someone else who will confirm the matter.'

Simon heard muffled sounds in the background, then a voice came on the line; someone he had never expected to hear in these circumstances.

'Simon?'

In his mind he pictured her face as he had last seen it, white

183

and pinched with shock; tears threatening in the depths of grey eyes. He thought he heard tears in her voice now. 'Amy? What's going on?'

'Joanna is with us, but she is fine. I'm sorry I had—'

Her voice disappeared. He thought he heard what sounded like a second male voice, somewhat deeper than Grainger's, but then Grainger came back on the line. 'No doubt you'll believe what your girlfriend has said, so now we get down to business.'

Out of the corner of his eye Simon glimpsed Susan ushering a man through the door to his office. He half rose from his seat, but with gestures, the stranger made it apparent he was not to react to his presence. From Susan's demeanour he judged this person was not part of the same, or yet another threat.

'Did you hear what I said, Deveraux?'

Simon tried to concentrate again. 'I assume it is money you're after? How much, Grainger?'

'I want two million US dollars deposited in a Swiss bank account within the next eighteen hours. I will ring you again later tonight when I trust you can confirm to me the funds are available, at which time I will give you the appropriate account details for transfer. On confirmation of its arrival, we can then arrange collection of your "package". You know, she really is a sweet little girl, and I'm sure you wouldn't want anything to happen to her, so, of course, you understand that contacting the police will not be an option.'

Simon's voice, even to his own ears, sounded raw with emotion. 'You harm her in any way, Grainger—'

A sound, rather like a snigger, interrupted him. 'For once I don't think you're in any position to dictate terms, Deveraux.' The man was obviously relishing the situation. 'You must think that life really is going wrong for you at the moment.'

Simon thought for a second. 'Contact me on my mobile in future.' He gave the number and before he could say anything else the line went dead.

He looked up at the stranger. 'Who the hell are you?'

Chapter Eighteen

The young man standing in front of him did not appear intimidated by the sharp tone of address. 'I'm Andy Sinclair, one of Fletcher's people detailed to follow you. Gilmore contacted us when he found problems at the school.'

Simon stared at him. 'How in God's name did all this happen? What went wrong with their security?'

Sinclair just shrugged. 'Fletcher's given instructions that I'm to drive you to Woodhayes immediately. He wants you close at hand. I gather that was someone on the line dictating terms?'

Still not really believing the situation could be true, Simon rubbed a hand over his face, and nodded. He looked over at Susan, hovering near the door. 'Is Mannion still tied up? I need to speak to him urgently.' He watched as she left the room, then he reached out for his phone. 'I don't care what Grainger's threats are, we must tell the police.'

Sinclair held up his hand. 'No, Mr Deveraux, Fletcher doesn't want you to involve anyone else just yet.'

'I don't care what he wants, we've—'

Susan put her head back round the door. 'I'm sorry, Mr Deveraux, but Mr Mannion is still with the FCA people.'

Irritated by enforced inactivity Simon rose from his seat. 'OK,

OK, we'll play it Fletcher's way for now. Susan, I'm going to my car. Tell Mannion to ring me immediately he's free.'

Although younger, Sinclair had a presence about him, and he now stood barring Simon's way. 'Mr Deveraux, my instructions are to drive you home.'

Simon looked at him, his own gaze hard and determined. 'I don't know why Fletcher wants me at Woodhayes when I really need to be here to sort out the ransom money. *My* instructions from *Grainger* are to tell no-one about all this. If I'm being watched, and they see me with a stranger, it might make them suspicious. They might construe I have informed the police. I'll therefore drive myself.'

Sinclair gave a sigh and stood aside. 'Your secretary tells me that you record some of your calls. Did you do so in this case?'

Simon turned back at the door. 'Yes, I did. Susan will deal with anything you need. For the moment, Sinclair, I promise you I will refrain from making any contact with the police until I see Fletcher, but then I need some answers as to how we got into this mess.'

*

Despite a smooth journey home Simon had deliberately kept a rein on his thoughts and concentrated on his driving. When he turned into the drive at Woodhayes he was surprised at the number of cars and a motorbike parked there, as well as his black SUV. He saw one man at the gate and as he approached the front door it was opened by a second. Frank Gilmore came towards him, concern, and even fear, showing on his face. Simon didn't want to talk to him at the moment but looked around for Fletcher. He saw him waiting in the doorway to the study and acknowledged he had never seen him looking quite so angry. Well, that made two of them!

In a clipped tone of voice Jack outlined to him the series of events. 'Gilmore's admitted to being a little late in the timing of his school run, but felt safe in the knowledge that Joanna would be held to await his arrival. It was a shock to everyone when the exact circumstances were revealed. Gilmore said he immediately rang the given telephone number for his "shadow" operative, who then took over. Fortunately, newly installed CCTV has recorded what happened and I have already been to the school and viewed it myself. A copy is being provided for your benefit. The existence of the second black SUV suggests to me that the whole matter had been planned in advance, although the timing was lucky. If Gilmore had been on schedule the vehicles might have coincided, which, to me, indicates some element of last-minute chance alteration in the plan. The description of the man who arrived sounds like Mark Grainger, and as you will see, your little Miss Watson was also a participant in Joanna's removal.'

For Simon, Amy's involvement in the whole matter still continued to be unbelievable.

Jack stood in front of Simon's desk, hands on hips, anger still evident in every line of his body. 'I warned you, Simon, and now it's actually happened. I was unhappy about you employing that girl in your household without any proper checks and perhaps you should now consider your own bad decisions. This whole scenario must have been thought out. I'll admit she was pretty, I thought so too, but, boy, you really fell for it. Joanna gets besotted with her, and they know she will follow her anywhere. For some reason the headmistress seems to be in denial of the fact that Watson was complicit, and she insists on coming along later to speak with you.'

Simon looked up into a face full of frustration and anger. His own anger had abated, leaving just… nothing.

'However it happened, that can wait; we must concentrate on what we have to do now. I must speak to Mannion and sort out the money, and we must involve the police, particularly Inspector Grant, as it appears to involve Grainger.'

'I'm not having police clumping all over this until I get a handle on what Grainger's really up to. He knows he's in trouble and perhaps needs funds to get clear, but if he's asking for two million US dollars, that's a puny amount compared to what he could ask for. It smells to me more of a precursor of something else. I've got a strange feeling about all this. It's bigger than we suspect.'

Simon stood up. 'Well, while you're dealing with your 'strange feelings' I'm at least going to deal with the very real matter of finding two million dollars.'

*

There were, to Amy's relief, proper toilet facilities available, although only cold running water. She guessed that the building must be some sort of maintenance facility, possibly to do with the canal, which she had glimpsed through a bank of trees as they approached. However, it had the air of disuse about it so she felt no comfort from the fact that come daylight they might be discovered. Joanna was becoming fretful, complaining that she was hungry and cold. No food had been provided for them, so Amy tried her best to keep the child's attention elsewhere.

'I'm sorry Miss Freeman could no longer employ me at the school. I enjoyed being with you all, and I did intend to contact you somehow. Do you like your new teacher?'

Joanna sniffed, and rubbed her nose with the back of her hand. Amy decided to refrain from making any comment. 'She's better than Mrs Kitching, but we all think it would be much nicer to have you with us again.' Even in the poor light Amy noticed the uncertainty in the young face now turned to her. 'Why did he make you cry?'

Not understanding the question, she replied with her own. 'Who do you mean?'

'*Him.* I heard what he said; that he's not my daddy.'

Horror rendered Amy speechless for a moment. As she had feared, Joanna had overheard Simon's words. Did he know, and if so, how had he dealt with it? She had to say something, explain somehow. 'Sometimes mummies and daddies no longer want to be together, and they find someone else to be with. Your mummy must have felt that way, and then you came along. When she died in the accident you still needed to be cared for. Your daddy took on the responsibility and has looked after you all this time. He's cared for you as if you were his daughter, and you should be very grateful to him. Some poor children never have anyone to look after them, or even have dreadful parents and are ill-treated.' She decided to be honest. 'Joanna, I never knew my parents, I grew up in a care home.' She glanced down at the girl. 'You have been lucky to know your family and your daddy has cared for you and will continue to do so. I know it's difficult to understand at the moment, but you will as time goes on. What I don't want to hear from you is any bad words or feelings about someone who has tried their best for you and will go on doing so. Do you understand what I mean?'

'I suppose so.' The voice was small and uncertain.

'He must be very worried about you and will do everything he can to make this all right again.'

'He still made you cry. I'd been waiting for you to come home so I could ask you what other lovely dresses you had seen. I went downstairs for a drink. I saw you run to your room. I wanted to come to you, but I didn't know what to do about *him*.'

In her concern at the thoughts which must have been going on in that young mind, Amy spoke more sharply than she intended. 'Joanna, you will stop referring to your father as *him*. I will not stand for it.'

She then noticed the two men looking her way and with trepidation watched as they both came over to where she was sitting.

Mark grabbed her shoulder. 'Can't you keep quiet? Any more noise and I'll put the brat in the vehicle outside… and why does she have to keep dragging that satchel around. What's she got in there?'

The dark man made a lunge for it, and Joanna let out a cry. 'I only have an apple. There's nothing in there. Tell him, Amy.'

Not really understanding Joanna's concern, but worried the situation was getting out of control, Amy struggled to her feet and snatched the satchel back. Lowering her voice she murmured, 'The girls have to take a change of underwear with them... in case of accidents if they get over-excited...you know what I mean. She's embarrassed about you seeing her things, that's all.'

The man called Miguel moved away and Mark glared at her. 'Keep the noise down. Go to sleep or something.'

Amy returned to her position on the sacking. Opening the satchel, she saw the apple and took it out, handing it to the still apprehensive-looking young girl. 'You might as well eat this now before it spoils.'

As Joanna took it from her, she leaned in closer. 'Thank you, Amy. I was afraid he would see it.'

'See what? What's in there, Joanna?'

'It's a big secret, Amy.'

*

Sinclair and Harriet Freeman arrived at Woodhayes almost together. Harriet had with her a laptop on which they viewed the CCTV recorded that afternoon. Simon watched, transfixed, as it played through. He recognised Mark Grainger, who seemed quite familiar with Amy. He noted the arm around her shoulder, but on closer study formed the impression she seemed a little tense. The interaction between her and Joanna was the most painful to observe. Seeing the child's obvious pleasure at being with her was at odds with his own recent experiences, and, deep inside him, something hurt.

Jack turned to Simon. 'Miss Freeman confirmed that Mr Griffin said he observed the SUV parked at the bottom end of the car park, and assumed it was Gilmore as usual. He admitted later he did not see who, if anyone at all, remained in the vehicle nor check its number plate.'

Harriet interrupted. 'He didn't notice anything awkward about

Amelia and the man seemed friendly enough. As I mentioned to Mr Fletcher, I am not sure if this is of significance but apparently a motorist appeared a day or two ago asking directions. Because the system was not running until the following day we have no record of him, but he was described as dark, almost swarthy, with a foreign accent, albeit pleasant and polite enough.'

Jack looked hard at Simon. 'I think we know who that might be, but can we confirm the man with Miss Watson was Grainger?'

Simon nodded. 'Yes, that's Mark Grainger.'

'Excuse me, Simon, but did you say Mark Grainger?' Harriet's voice sounded sharp.

'Yes Harriet, I did. Why do you ask?'

Appearing slightly bewildered, she looked at both the men sitting opposite her. 'I would be very surprised if Amelia Watson would want anything to do with Mark Grainger.' She went on to describe the content of Amy's confidences told to her at the job interview.

As Simon tried to assimilate this new information, Jack's harsh laugh rang out in the quiet room. 'By God, it looks as though they just about took everyone in. Trot out a sob story like that and they've got entry into the school, access to Joanna and, if they played it right, obviously her father, too. I understand from Gilmore that the girl packed up and sneaked away from here early Sunday morning without any warning. Now you can't tell me that's normal.'

Simon remained silent. He looked over at Harriet and saw she was regarding Jack with an expression he had encountered himself.

'Young man, I appreciate you might know your profession very well, but I know mine. I am used to dealing with people, and I still maintain that Amelia Watson would never be a willing party to what is happening here. As you can see on the film, she turned back and asked Griffin to pass on a message to me that she was unable to see me at the moment. Consider this; it could have been some form of warning that she wasn't a free agent.'

'It's possible, I grant you, but it doesn't help us much right now.' Jack beckoned Sinclair over. 'Andy, let's have a listen to this phone call.'

Harriet stood and moved closer to Simon. 'I can't tell you how sorry I am about this. I feel the school has let you down. If there is anything I can do, just call me. I have asked Mr Fletcher to review our whole security package as this matter has obviously thrown up some glaring discrepancies. It should have been dealt with before, but until these things happen…'

'Yes, I can appreciate that, Harriet. I'm sure we'll sort it out. Like you, I am having trouble believing that Amy Watson might have been involved in all this, but we will find out, I'm sure. In any case I think Mark Grainger has a lot to answer for.'

'Please keep me informed, Simon, at anytime.'

As she left the room, he noted that her usual air of brisk efficiency was missing. This whole matter had obviously affected her badly. In her eyes she had been given a responsibility but had been found lacking. He sighed and turned back to where Jack was listening to the tape of the earlier call with Grainger.

After listening to it several times, Jack replayed one particular section. He looked up at Sinclair. 'Do you hear it? Another male voice in the background, but not Grainger's.'

Sinclair nodded. 'I thought I heard it too. Someone else? The driver of the SUV?'

Jack looked over at Simon. 'I suggest it's Reynolds' Colombian. Like I said, Simon, this thing is bigger than we think.'

'You don't seriously mean that de Santos is involved in this?'

'Could be, mate. Another layer of pressure on you just at the wrong time. I told you I thought the ransom amount was a little low. He's not interested in the money.'

'But it needs to be paid.' Grabbing his phone, Simon walked out of the study. 'I'm going somewhere quiet to make some phone calls. We don't have much time.'

*

Pacing up and down the lawn, Simon noticed it was now cold and dark. Looking back at the house, it blazed with light and appeared warm and comforting. Wherever these people were keeping Joanna, he hoped she was warm, dry, and not too frightened, but, of course, Amy was with her. Some inner sense still told him to trust her, despite Jack's misgivings. A stupid thought possibly, after what had happened that night. How might she actually be feeling about him now?

His phone began to ring. It would be Mannion again.

'Yes Stu…so only the two hundred and fifty grand leftover from the Mercier deal. We need to get another one and three quarter million from somewhere else.'

The voice on the other end sounded concerned. 'Everywhere's closed down now. They picked their time well, Simon. I can get on it first thing but nothing through by their deadline. We need someone with funds in place over there at the moment. What about your pal Orloff?'

The same thought had come into Simon's mind, but the man had already done him one favour recently; could he ask for another, based on friendship?

'I'll have to give it some thought, Stu. See if you can come up with any other ideas.'

'Sure thing, Simon. Charles and I will be staying in the office working on this. Keep in touch. If there's a way we can beat these bastards, we will.'

Trying to project an air of calmness about the situation, Simon just replied, 'Fine, thanks Stu.'

Without giving himself anymore time to think he found Orloff's number and listened to it ringing.

'Another late night, Simon? We must have it bred into us, eh? My excuse is making travel arrangements – what about you?'

Simon knew it was even later in the evening at Orloff's large house overlooking the Bosphorus, but Dimitri still sounded bright and full of energy. He cleared his throat. 'I find I have a problem, Dimitri.'

'Ah, that is indeed a shame. I have been keeping an eye on your circumstances of late – all nonsense of course – so do I assume that events are worsening? If so, I am glad you felt you could come to an old friend.'

To hear the sincerity in that deep voice overwhelmed Simon and for a moment he found it difficult to collect his thoughts. 'Dimitri, I need two million US dollars in a Swiss bank account by business opening tomorrow morning. I have a quarter of a million already there, but it's not enough.' He could hear his voice breaking, and he cursed under his breath. Dimitri would think he was cracking up.

There was a long silence at the other end, and, for a moment, Simon held his breath, then he heard the words, 'That should be no problem, Simon. I will email instructions overnight and my confirmatory written authorisation for movement of one and three quarter million will be delivered to my bank by special courier. He will be waiting on their doorstep when they open. You will give me the appropriate details, no doubt.'

Simon sighed with relief and replied, 'I'll email them directly, Dimitri, but I insist this is a loan. I suggest I offer my property here as guarantee, it could be worth all of that. I'll get my legal department to email documents about it to you first thing tomorrow.'

'There is only one thing I care about in this transaction of ours, Simon, and for friendship's sake I would appreciate the truth. What is wrong?'

Simon hesitated. He owed this man, and he had to answer honestly. 'Joanna has been kidnapped and my security expert suspects it is linked to all this other business. They want the money in place in a Swiss bank by first thing tomorrow for her release.'

He wasn't sure if he heard an explosive noise from the other end, but certainly something was going on. He heard raised voices and what appeared to be shouted instructions in a foreign language. Then silence. He began to wonder if the call connection had been broken but then Dimitri spoke, his voice sounding cool and efficient, and for the first time Simon thought he detected a slight trace of anger. This was something he had not encountered at any time in their past association. 'My apologies, Simon, I had to issue some changes to my travel arrangements and... certain other things. This is indeed sad news. Are your police assisting?'

'My security people don't want them involved for now. I'm not sure I agree with that and I'm going to tackle them again about it, but the money was my first thought.' He was now worried that he had asked this man for one favour too many. 'Dimitri, you know you don't have to do this if you have any reservations.'

'It is already done, Simon. The order has been given. Just think about your little girl. Do what you have to do, and my thoughts are with you, my friend. Keep me informed.'

The line went dead, and Simon stood in the darkness, feeling drained. The hand on his shoulder startled him. He turned to find Jack beside him.

'Your father's turned up. You'd better come in and see him. He's a bit hostile.'

Chapter Nineteen

Simon's initial reaction was to ask Jack to tell his father that he was busy. However, with a sigh he changed his mind and walked back into the house. He hesitated in the sittingroom just long enough to email Mannion instructions for him to send the relevant bank details to Orloff, immediately, and put Charles on notice about the loan on Woodhayes.

He found his father pacing up and down the hall under the watchful gaze of Andy Sinclair.

'What on earth are you doing here at this time of night? I didn't know you were coming.'

'It seems as if I've arrived in the middle of a madhouse. Your staff even had to vouch for my identity. Who are all these people? What's going on?'

Having to deal with his father's presence was the last thing Simon wanted, but there was no way out. He directed him over to the study, closed the door behind them and leant against it.

'Why are you here, Father?'

'Justine and I flew in this afternoon. Firstly, I've come out of courtesy to inform you that we intend to get married before the end of the year. She is anxious that both you and Joanna are involved in the formalities in some way. Initially, I thought it best if I broached the subject with you myself.'

With other thoughts still in his mind Simon attempted to brush over the matter. 'You must do as you please. It doesn't concern me.'

'So you still feel like that?' The words were laced with anger. 'You never understood the situation with Helene and Justine.'

'Father, I'm not interested in bringing all that up, especially now.' This was the last thing Simon wanted to discuss right now, but he sensed his father's determination.

'Well, perhaps it's time you did. You're always so wrapped up with your own life, you fail to stop and listen to others. You had the good sense to bring in people at your company as sounding boards, but you didn't allow the same in your personal life. Even as a child it was always difficult to discuss matters with you. That's why I took you on those camping trips, just the two of us, to see if we could get closer.' He gave his son a piercing glance. 'Is that how it happened with Olivia; you didn't listen to her? Perhaps she needed to talk to you about your marriage.' Ignoring Simon's protests, he turned away to sit on the Chesterfield. 'All I know is that, whether you like it or not, I am content in the knowledge that I have acted in the way your mother wanted regarding Justine. I'm not sure how I would have coped during those years without her genuine support. You never understood that. All you *thought* you saw was an affair going on behind your mother's back as she was dying. Now you're older I had hoped you might view it differently, but obviously not. However, I do think you should make some sort of effort, for Joanna's sake. To a young girl, a wedding, with all the dressing up involved, would be exciting, which brings me to my second reason for coming to see you, or more specifically, Joanna. I thought a visit might cheer her up at the beginning of a new school year. I wanted to touch base with you tonight to see what we might be able to arrange. I estimated Joanna would be in bed by now. If she's asleep, that is, with all this activity going on. What's all this about, by the way?'

Simon now knew there would be little chance he could avoid

an explanation, and the fallout was going to be bad. How bad he had no idea.

'We had a situation develop this afternoon. Joanna was kidnapped from her school. I've been asked to pay a ransom for her return.'

His father looked up at him, dumbstruck. 'Joanna kidnapped, and you call it 'a development'!'

Simon flung himself down into the chair behind his desk. 'Fletcher and his people are dealing with it and the money is there. It will all be over tomorrow.'

'You mean to say you haven't informed the police! What are you all thinking about; you know what happens with these people? You pay the money and get...' He looked incredulous, and anger was building. Simon could feel it, and it was coming his way. 'Please tell me this isn't connected with all the other rubbish I'm reading about in the international press. It sounds to me like a classic case of bad business partners and sore feelings when things go wrong.' He waited for an answer but received none. His gaze hardened. 'So, you've finally done it. You've been so mad keen to get involved in these mega deals that you end up mixing with unscrupulous people, making enemies all over the place, who are not only attempting to bring you down, but have now involved a young innocent child.' He looked away in disgust. 'You wanted to call yourself a father!'

'I told you, it's being sorted.'

Emile stood and came over to him. 'Well, it's a good job I'm here. Joanna will no doubt be traumatised by the whole thing. You might need to get Amy Watson involved as well. She was always so good with the child.'

Simon gave his father a level look. 'It seems likely that Amy is involved in the abduction. She's on CCTV collecting Joanna from the school and I've spoken with her during a phone call with the kidnappers.'

'That's the most stupid thing I've heard in years. There's no way she would be a party to anything like that.'

'I've just learnt she has some past connection with one of the people involved. She might…given enough provocation.'

Emile slammed his fist down on the desk. 'Provocation? Now what have you been up to? There's more to this than you're telling me. Did you make improper advances to her?'

Simon tried to work out in his mind how much to say by way of an explanation. 'She made some ill-informed and unjustified remarks about my dealings with Joanna. It annoyed me. I engineered a…situation to teach her a lesson. We had an argument, during which I told her the truth about Joanna. The exchange obviously upset her, and she left early the next morning, but…'

His father leaned in closer. 'But what, Simon?'

'Unfortunately, Joanna overheard us, and she now knows about me. She's taken it badly. I did my best to reassure her…and now this…'

Emile turned away, suddenly deflated. 'I wondered what might have happened to make Joanna attempt to get in touch with me by telephone, leaving a plaintive text message asking me to come. What a mess. That poor little girl; whatever must she be thinking.' He looked back at his son. 'You appreciate she's not mature enough to truly understand the circumstances between you and her mother? It will take time, whatever you say to her.' His grin was without mirth. 'God knows we both ought to relate to that.' He looked hard and long at his son. 'Did you ever feel Amy was trying to talk to you? I felt it. I had intended to speak to her on this visit, or at least ask you to do so. I sensed she had issues that were worrying her, but perhaps, once again, you failed to take the trouble to listen? Simon, it might have been about this predicament, and it could have been nipped in the bud.'

Simon just shrugged, his mind full of images both from the distant past and the not so distant. Had Amy wanted to tell him something? If it was that important, she would surely have pressed him.

His father was still standing in front of him.

'I'll just say one more thing. You wanted to act as Joanna's father and in the end I went along with it. I thought after this summer things had improved, but now with all that's happened I'm not sure you are fit to keep that role. Justine has said she is happy to help in any way she can with Joanna, so from now on I will keep even closer ties with that child even if, after this fiasco, I have to use the courts to do so.'

The door opened, and Simon looked up to find Jack Fletcher moving over to the desk. Neither man had heard the mobile phone ringing. After checking the phone display, he handed it to Simon.

'Could be Grainger back on again; if so, it's a different number to the one he used earlier.'

Simon answered the call. 'Grainger? I want to speak to my daughter. Now!'

'What about the money?' Grainger's voice came through clearly on speakerphone.

'It will be in my Swiss bank account first thing tomorrow morning, but your deadline does not account for any internal transfer.'

'Don't panic, you should know they're ahead of us on time. Here's the account number for the transfer.'

Simon took down the numbers and repeated them back. 'Let me speak to Joanna.'

'You can speak with her... chaperon.'

Grainger was obviously enjoying himself again. Simon gritted his teeth and waited; he then heard Amy's voice, sounding breathless. 'Joanna's fine. She has all her things—' The voice disappeared and there was the sound of a scuffle.

'Amy, what's going on?'

Simon sensed his father reaching out to take the phone, but Fletcher stopped him. Grainger came back on. 'I'll ring again at nine o'clock tomorrow morning after I check the arrival of the funds and then we can talk about collection.'

The line went dead.

Jack said, 'They're obviously using different low-grade phones when they call. For my money I maintain they're not too far away, taking the time differential between them leaving the school and their first phone call. They would have wanted to be out of sight as soon as possible.'

A thought began to form in Simon's brain. He looked at his father. 'You said Joanna rang you? She doesn't have a phone. When was this? What time?'

Fletcher looked from one to the other. 'What's this about?'

'Joanna must have tried to ring me when we were mid-flight. I found the text after we landed. I told you, she sounded worried.'

'She was at school then. I'm sure if she had asked to use a school phone, they would have contacted me somehow. Harriet would have known about it. What number did she ring from?'

Emile retrieved his phone and scrolled through the list. 'This is the one.'

Jack Fletcher took it from him and then looked across at Simon. 'You have a second phone here, don't you? I think this is the number. Could she have taken it?'

Simon opened the drawer in his desk. 'It's missing. She must have it, but she would never know how to use it on her own, let alone master a text.'

'She could have a school friend who showed her. If they haven't found it, she might still have it with her.'

Emile held up his hand. 'Wait a moment, in the call we heard just now, Amy said something about Joanna still having all her things.' He looked at the other two. 'Was that some sort of clue to say she knows about it?'

Jack prepared to leave the room. 'Well, unless they're being left unsupervised, they would be lucky to get out a call without being discovered. Anyway, we can't yet be sure where Amelia Watson fits in; it could be misleading us. At first light, I'm sending people out to have a look around in the general area radiating out from the school. We might just spot something.' He looked hard

201

at Simon. 'If the phone rings, call me, don't be a fool and do anything yourself.'

Emile looked at his son. 'I'm leaving too. Justine will wonder where I am.'

Simon cleared his throat. 'You can stay here if you like – both of you.'

The reply was cool. 'Thank you for the offer, but we're booked into a hotel in Windsor. Call me.'

Simon watched the two men leave. He was tired but he knew he wouldn't sleep. He lay back in his chair, closed his eyes and tried to clear his mind. All the blame was being heaped on him, it seemed, and no-one was considering how he was coping. He had tried to give the impression of someone in control, but that was far from how he felt. He knew the realities of kidnappings as well as anyone else and his stomach lurched at the possible outcome. He needed someone to share his fear and hurt. Someone who wouldn't judge him; a warm, caring touch, dark eyes full of understanding; but at the moment he had to cope alone, until… but he couldn't think that far ahead.

*

Amy felt the cold and damp coming up from the bare concrete beneath the sacking and it seemed to be seeping into every part of her. Joanna had earlier complained of the cold, so she had taken off her own jacket and wrapped it around the small body. However, left in just a short-sleeved blouse it wasn't long before she herself began to shiver. She wanted to stand and move around but they had been told to keep still, and now Joanna was half-asleep, curled against her, restricting any movement at all.

Before her mind, as well as her body, began to succumb to the cold and hunger she had to work out what, if anything, she could do about Joanna's secret hidden away in the satchel. She found it hard to believe that Joanna had been so despondent she had been forced to take the spare phone from the drawer in her father's study to try and contact her grandfather. Joanna had whispered to her that her school friend Sophie had shown her how to use the phone in an empty classroom during the lunch hour and had traced the number in France from the list of previous calls. When her grandfather didn't answer, Sophie had shown her how to send a text. What would Emile do when he found the message, Amy wondered. Would he contact Simon and then they would know about the missing phone? During the few words she was allowed to speak with Simon earlier she had tried to alert him. Miguel had been suspicious about what she had said and pulled her roughly away, and she thought for a moment he was going to strike her.

She considered the options. There was very little prospect of them actually being able to make a call, and Joanna had admitted that without her friend present she wasn't sure how to send another text. There must be some way they could use this opportunity. Amy tried to forget the tiredness and cold numbing her mind and racked her brains for her limited knowledge about state-of-the-art equipment. She had a vague idea that some sort of GPS signal pinpointed the whereabouts of a phone. If that was so, they could perhaps manage to switch it on and send out a signal, but this would only be of use if someone was looking for it.

A short while ago Miguel had disappeared, telling Mark he had to check on some last-minute arrangements. Amy had begun to form the impression that Mark was treating this whole matter as something of a game, unlike his companion. So, once more, she had tried to talk to him and persuade him to let them go, insisting that Simon Deveraux would probably reward him in some way. However, he became increasingly angry, and in the end, she was afraid to push him further.

She made up her mind. When there was enough light, she would take the risk of switching on the phone. It was worth a try, but she had to wait, and, without disturbing Joanna, she tried to make herself more comfortable.

Thousands of miles away Dimitri Orloff was also uncomfortable. He eased his considerable bulk to yet another position in the cramped seat. He was used to a more stylish mode of travel than this temporary arrangement in a Boeing cargo plane. Having sent his private secretary to Switzerland in his executive jet, his own altered travel plans had forced him to use his various airline contacts and talk his way onto the first available transport to Brazil; hence his current predicament. After a quick turnaround stop in West Africa, they would head out across the Atlantic. Thompson would be meeting him at Sao Paulo. Orloff still felt the anger buzzing through his system. For the first time in his life, he had doubted a friendship. It may only have been for a brief moment, but as a man of principle, as he saw it, this was something which disturbed him. A line had now been crossed and action had to be taken.

*

As the first glimmers of light penetrated the small window, Amy quietly moved the satchel closer and slid her hand inside. With her fingers she located the phone and, glancing over at Mark, saw that he was sitting on a work bench leaning against the wall with his eyes shut. He was paying no attention to her, so, commanding her ice-cold hand to retain its grip, she partially withdrew the phone. She knew how to switch it on from the time they had rung Emile. Joanna had whispered to her how the mute button worked, and with trepidation Amy glanced down and pressed the buttons. She quickly pushed the phone deeper into the satchel. Mark hadn't looked her way once, but her movements had now woken Joanna, who stirred, and he turned his head at the sound. Amy let out a thankful sigh that this hadn't happened a moment ago.

'We need to get up and walk around, Mark, it's cold on this floor,' she said.

'You'll just have to wait until Miguel comes back. Keep yourselves quiet until then.'

Amy sighed. Whether anything would come of her efforts she had no idea, but it was all they could try.

*

In an attempt to stay awake, Simon had gone up to his room to take a shower. He wanted to be ready for any phone call from Grainger and further instructions. Towelling himself dry, he thought he heard his phone – but it was too early, surely? Running through into his bedroom he picked it up. 'Deveraux.'

He heard the voice of Sir Arthur Dunne. 'Sorry to ring you so early, Simon, but I thought you might like to know that the Brazilian authorities have now decided to act, and they have de Santos in custody somewhere, under house arrest, pending further investigations. We can start to throw our weight around a bit now. Simon? Simon, are you there?'

Simon sank down on his bed. The sudden chill on his bare skin wasn't from the cool of the early morning, it was deep inside. 'No…no, they can't do that now.' His voice rose. 'Stop them, Arthur, you have to stop them!'

'Whatever is the matter, Simon? What do you mean?'

'He has her! He has my daughter!'

Chapter Twenty

Jack placed his coffee cup back on the table with a resigned sigh. 'Well, all I ask is they don't make a muck of it. Too many people involved now.'

Simon, dressed but still unshaven, had brought him up to date with the news from Sir Arthur and his predictable insistence that the appropriate authorities must be involved. He had said he would take it upon himself to inform Inspector Grant and also Reynolds, if there was the prospect of the Colombian being involved, as seemed likely. Grant would be arriving any minute.

Jack looked at Simon's phone on the dining room table. 'The best we could hope for is that someone switches on the other phone and we can get a GPS fix, but the prospect isn't likely.'

Just then Andy Sinclair put his head round the door. 'Jack, Inspector Grant has arrived, and I need to speak to you.'

'Let's hope he hasn't brought the cavalry with lights and sirens. There might be someone watching, although frankly I doubt it.'

As Inspector Grant entered the room Simon wasn't surprised to receive a stern look rather than a pleasant greeting.

'Mr Deveraux, as I have already said to Sir Arthur, it was a great pity that I was not officially informed of the whole situation surrounding you. I would have been inclined to bring Grainger into custody at a much earlier stage and this unfortunate escalation might have been averted.' He gave a small, resigned sigh. 'It seems to me that government officials and some of our brother law enforcement officers always tend to over-complicate matters. I have been making my own enquiries, and had come to the conclusion that your involvement was something of a smoke screen – although pretty costly to you, eh? In more ways than one, I'm sorry to hear. On my way over, after some quiet instructions to the local police, I understand Grainger's Renault has just been spotted parked up in Windsor, but empty. An unmarked car is keeping an eye on it. I gather the ransom payment is being dealt with abroad. When do you expect to hear news?'

Simon glanced over at Jack. He appeared to be in a low but animated conversation with Sinclair by the door. 'Grainger said he would ring this morning at nine o'clock, confirm receipt and arrange for Joanna's handover.' He looked at his wristwatch. 'About half an hour to go.'

*

Ignoring a whingeing Grainger, who demanded to know where he intended going, Hernandez, with some relief, headed the SUV down the track then drove about a mile to where, yesterday morning, he had left his black Audi just off the road in a clearing, out of sight. This would be the vehicle by which he would make his initial escape. After hiding the car, it had been a logistical nuisance to make his way on foot to a place where he could reasonably call for a taxi back to his temporary hotel accommodation and the SUV, but without a second person involved it had been necessary. He test-started the engine and confirmed a full tank of fuel. He then transferred his bag from the back of the SUV, checking that the various alternative sets of documents were in place. He would be using one set for the previously arranged private flight to France from a small airfield close to the south coast later that day.

Whilst he waited until he judged it was time to make the international call to confirm receipt of the money, he wiped over both vehicles, removing his fingerprints from any area he might have touched. He then made his call and confirmed, as expected, that the money was in place. Instructions had been given for this to be split up on receipt and dispersed into other accounts. He considered whether to call de Santos but thought better of it. He had been given leave to take certain steps and he would follow those orders. Part of him had never trusted the man, and the longer he waited to report the outcome the nearer he would be to the money. He smiled to himself as he pulled on a pair of close-fitting leather gloves. Once away and safely out of the country he might consider helping himself to some, if not all of it. He knew the relevant passwords and account numbers. Yes, that would be reward for all the messy little jobs he had done over the years, for what he considered a pittance.

He climbed back into the SUV and retraced his journey back down the lane toward the canal. He only saw one person; a motor cyclist turned out from a junction and followed behind. As Hernandez came near to the turning for the track, he signalled for the biker to overtake him. He watched as the rider acknowledged his signal with just a lazy wave, not even a glance, and carry on down the road out of sight. With a shrug he turned onto the track and drove down to the building. In a moment he would get Grainger to manoeuvre the vehicle until it faced back the way he had come.

Then all he had to do was make sure of the next few steps. It was nearly time for Grainger to make his final call. At that thought his mouth curved into a cold grin.

*

Simon tried to ignore the silent listeners as he made a note of Grainger's instructions.

'Why should I have to wait two hours to collect my daughter

when you have the money already? I want to collect her now, Grainger.'

'We have to get her there, don't we, and it will take us that long. Just a word of warning, there had better be no sign of you anywhere around beforehand, or anyone else, or it won't happen.'

'Joanna will be frightened and disorientated, left in a place like that on her own. I want Amy Watson to stay with her.'

'Sorry, she comes with me, Deveraux. Hard luck.'

'What if I gave you an incentive?' Simon ignored Grant's warning look and turned his head away. 'As a gesture of goodwill, I suggest you don't return to your car. The police have found it and are keeping a watch. They've just rung me to ask if I've seen you, to which you can guess my answer. Is that enough for you?'

Grant had turned away in exasperation, but Jack looked remarkably unmoved, and somehow...excited.

'All right, she'd probably be a nuisance anyway. We won't speak again, Deveraux.' Grainger's voice sounded excited. 'Nice doing business with you.'

Closing the call, Simon looked up at Grant. He was rubbing his chin, a puzzled look on his face. 'The Thames Path west of Reading? It's a strange place for this sort of thing. There could be any number of legitimate people about at that time of day. I'll organise for some plain clothes officers to be in the area.'

'Don't waste your time, Inspector. My guess is they won't be anywhere near.'

All eyes turned to Jack.

'Perhaps you know something I don't?' Grant sounded a little testy.

'I have a good idea where they might be. I've just been informed that one of my operatives scouting in the general area spotted a black SUV. It appeared to turn off down a small track. He thought it was worth a look, and found it parked near a disused building close to the canal. He's still there, keeping a covert watch. It could be a likely place. I think Grainger's talk about the time lag for the handover is a red herring. They intend to be off and gone before we suspect anything, probably leaving Joanna somewhere else completely.'

'We hope.' Grant made the remark without looking at Simon. 'Mr Fletcher, this is all a little sketchy, don't you think? If this is not what you think, we could be wasting time.'

'My gut feeling is that they're there, but they might now leave at any moment. We need to take them as they move out rather than chase them on the open road. I don't think Grainger was going to go back to his car, they'll use the SUV to leg it in the opposite direction, either back to London or south or west. They need a port or airport.'

Simon could tell Grant still wasn't impressed. As the discussion between the two men rambled on, he could feel the worry and frustration building inside him. All this talk was wasting time and Joanna was still in danger. He wanted to shout at them to remember that, and more out of desperation than hope he once more picked up his phone; then felt his heart leap. 'Jack, look at this!'

'They've done it?' Jack raced over and grabbed the phone from him and after one swift look he turned to Grant. 'The kidnappers have been using low-grade phones, but unknown to them Joanna Deveraux has with her the spare phone her father keeps in this house, which is exactly the same as this one. We've been hoping that somehow they would switch it on and send out a signal. As you can see, I told you they weren't far away; somewhere near the canal at Reading, and I'm pretty sure it's right where we already think.'

'It's still a risk, Fletcher. More importantly, we don't know if anyone is armed.'

'There's a possibility the Colombian is, but we don't want to start a shooting war. We need to secure him first.'

Grant thought for a moment, and then made a decision. 'OK. Find me a map, I need to see the area involved.' He looked at Simon. 'Mr Deveraux, you know Grainger. How do you view this?'

'He's in it for the money. He's banking on a new start somewhere. The other person involved may have his own instructions, unknown to us. That's more the concern for me, but as Jack says, if we can nip this in the bud before they suspect anything, I'd rather not wait around.'

'Mm…hm. We might get lucky with the surprise.' Grant spread out the map handed to him and Jack circled the area. 'I have one man with me. What numbers do you have, Fletcher?'

'Myself and five others. I have two fully licensed firearms with us. However, we're not set up for proper communication so we'll have to cobble something together, but I'm sure we can work with that.'

Grant looked at his watch. 'Right, as the man on the spot I will initiate matters. It would waste time to wait and co-ordinate with local assistance, but we need to appraise them and,' he cast a sideways glance at Simon, 'I suggest we'd better have some medical backup on call in case it all goes pear-shaped. Now, we need to sort ourselves out and get things moving.'

*

When Miguel returned Amy noticed a difference in him. He seemed cooler and even more focused than before. Mark began to question him about his absence, but he was told to be quiet and just do as he was instructed; first of which was to go outside and turn the SUV around. On his return Joanna asked Amy if she could use the toilet facilities, whereupon she, too, was spoken to sharply. As with Amy herself, the little girl was cold and hungry, and tears followed his harsh words. Feeling less than brave Amy clambered up from her position on the floor and took Joanna's hand. Staring at the two men she stumbled through to the outer room. It seemed even colder in this part of the building and shivers racked her body.

'When can we go home, Amy? I'm so cold and hungry.'

Trying to dry her numbed hands on the bottom of her skirt,

Amy managed a smile. 'I imagine it won't be long now. I think a nice bowl of soup would be just the thing to warm us up, don't you?'

Joanna came across to her and wrapped her arms around her waist. Amy could feel her shivers matching her own. 'I'm frightened, Amy. You won't leave me, will you?'

Amy held her close, tears very near. 'Of course not. You'll be home soon and think of the things you will have to tell Mr Floppy.' She took the small hand. 'We'd better go back now, or they might be angry.'

On entering the big room, she watched as Mark appeared to be gathering together the mobile phones he had used for his calls. She saw Miguel standing to one side, a strange anticipatory look on his face, and noticed a gloved hand slipping something into his coat pocket. In a moment of clarity her dulled mind knew what the article was. It was the gun. As in the Tate Gallery all those weeks ago, a feeling of impending horror settled on her, and she had to bite back a terrified cry.

'Go outside, Grainger, and throw the phones into the undergrowth and wait by the vehicle.'

'What are you going to do?' Mark turned, voicing his query.

The snarling reply came back, 'Just do as you are told,' which finally sent him outside, muttering under his breath.

Amy watched as Miguel turned and looked at them. She held Joanna close to her side.

'You will both wait here, and do not move. Understand?'

Amy could only nod and watch as he left the building. After what appeared to be only a moment, she thought she heard a sound followed by a cry. Something made her move over to the doorway. Her shocked eyes took in the sight of Mark lying face down on the ground near the SUV, totally still. Although she had never seen such a thing, she was certain that he was dead. As she began to understand, horror filled her being and she had to stifle a scream. She saw Miguel heading back towards the building, with the gun in his hand. Her numbed brain registered the danger, but what she feared surely couldn't be happening – could it?

When Miguel saw her, he grabbed her roughly and pushed her back inside. 'I told you to do as you were told, but no matter. I shall now carry out the rest of the plan. When anyone finds you, it will be thought that Grainger intended to leave on his own after killing the girl. He attempted to deal with you but, as an amateur, failed miserably, leaving you with just enough opportunity to turn the tables. Rather neat, don't you think?'

The dark face seemed on fire with anticipation of what was about to happen, and he moved further into the room towards Joanna. With strength she didn't know she possessed, Amy pushed him back, forcing him outside again. She called to Joanna, 'Run, Joanna, run away as fast as you can.'

Joanna emerged from the building, but, terrified by the sight of the two people struggling with a gun, she was too distressed to move and just screamed.

At that point Miguel managed to land a vicious blow against the side of Amy's head. With tears coursing down her face, she reeled back. There was nothing more she could do; she had no more energy. Then she vaguely heard what might have been a gun shot. Had he still managed to hurt Joanna, as had been his intention? Her heart failed her but then his remaining grip on her began to slacken and they both fell to the ground.

*

Simon's worry and frustration was mounting. He was standing beside Inspector Grant's car, parked close to the entrance to the track. Fletcher, Sinclair and Sgt Bowers had earlier disappeared into the surrounding undergrowth, intending to get as close to the building as they could. Carl, the motorbike rider, was still in place and keeping in touch with Jack by an open line on a mobile phone. Sgt Bowers was similarly in touch with Grant and had, so far, reported no sign of movement. Two of Jack's other operatives were spread out along the track itself, and a further person left at the wheel of a car parked down the road from Grant's vehicle.

Simon paced up and down, forbidden by Jack to go any nearer. He thought he heard a sound and turned back to look at Grant, who appeared to be talking into his phone. Then after a moment or two of silence, he heard an even worse sound, that of a young child screaming. Joanna! Ignoring instructions, he started to run up the track but then heard another sharp crack. Gunfire? He increased his pace. He had to do something to help.

Vaguely he heard other noises behind him out on the road and cast a look over his shoulder. Through the bushes he made out the silhouette of a police van. Just in time – he hoped.

As he came to the parked SUV, he saw figures moving around. A hand on his shoulder startled him. He turned, ready to strike a blow, but just in time recognised one of Jack's men.

'Just a moment, Mr Deveraux. Let me see how things are before you go any further.'

The man moved in front, but Simon followed on his heels. Rounding the back of the SUV his first sight was of a man lying on the ground. Grainger! He looked about the clearing and saw Andy Sinclair and Sgt Bowers restraining a man, who must be the Colombian. Jack stood near them with a small figure in his arms – Joanna! Simon rushed over to him, his heart pounding.

'Is she OK, Jack?'

'I thought I told you to stay away, Simon.' Looking down at the small figure sobbing quietly, he continued, 'I think she's all right physically but pretty shaken up.'

'Let me have her.' Simon reached out, wanting to give her the comfort of knowing he was there. Joanna turned her head and as soon as she saw him, she became hysterical. 'Go away. I hate you. These bad men have hurt Amy.' She struggled in Jack's arms. 'I want to be with her, I don't want you.' Her sobbing became louder.

Simon stood there, the initial feeling of relief and elation at finding her unharmed ebbing away. With her words his spirits dropped. He had hoped for a different response.

'Grainger came out, obviously to chuck the mobile phones

away. One actually hit me on the arm.' Jack shifted the weight of the small figure in his arms. 'Then the Colombian appeared and without warning shot Grainger in the back and started to return to the building. I have no doubt he wasn't done with his intended killing.' Simon's shocked gaze returned to Jack as he took in what he was hearing. 'I think he decided, or had been instructed, to make a clean getaway on his own. Amy Watson struggled with him, and I heard her shout for Joanna to run, but the poor little mite was so frightened she couldn't move. I knew it was a bad idea to break cover and rush him; he was too near to the girls and could have used either or both as a shield and we'd have been in an even worse hostage situation. Bowers obtained clearance from Grant to take appropriate action against the Colombian, and I got a chance to take him in the shoulder.' He hefted the child again, folding the edges of his coat around her. 'I told you the money wasn't the end game; in any case it's probably scattered down a convoluted chain of other accounts by now, most of them untraceable.' He looked again over the scene. 'We need some medical backup here.'

Simon's eyes moved over to the Colombian. He felt cold, unreasoning anger against the man, but knew that it was pointless to take it any further. 'Help is on the way, Jack. The police are here.' He turned again to look at Joanna and gave a deep sigh. 'Clear it with Grant but get her away from here. Take her to Carlisle's clinic and arrange for my father to meet you there. I'll stay and deal with Amy. I'll be in touch... and Jack, thank you.' With a heavy heart he watched the man walk away, cradling the still sobbing child. Trying to suppress his disappointment he looked around for Amy and finally spotted her lying in the doorway to the building with Jack's biker, Carl, bending over her.

With slow steps he moved over to the small, crumpled figure now covered in a couple of jackets.

Carl looked up at him. 'A bang on the head, but she's pretty much OK as far as I can see, except she's deathly cold. We need to get her some help.'

Simon knelt down, taking off his own jacket and wrapping it around the slender form. He noted the large bruise forming on the side of her face. She had risked her own life to save Joanna and they had all thought badly of her. Now it was his duty to do everything possible to make amends.

'She'll get all she needs,' he said quietly.

*

The hospital waiting room was crowded and noisy and Simon sat in a corner, attempting to concentrate on his own thoughts. Grant had sanctioned Joanna's removal but reminded Fletcher he would later be required to give a full statement of the events. Then he also left the scene, accompanying the Colombian in the first of the ambulances, which arrived within minutes. Sgt Bowers and Andy Sinclair stayed behind to liaise with the local police, who were starting to examine the whole scene. Sinclair said he had been instructed by Fletcher that Simon should either go to Woodhayes or London. If the local press became aware of what had happened, he was better out of the way under some sort of protection. To Sinclair's obvious irritation, Simon knew it was his responsibility to follow Amy to hospital. He fabricated enough of a story to allow him to ride with her in the second ambulance to the hospital in Reading. Sinclair detailed Carl to follow them so that he would be close by to watch for any problems.

Just moments ago, Simon had been relieved to receive a text from Jack to say Joanna was now at the clinic and his father had arrived. He didn't want to dwell too much on that situation at present but knew he could not altogether ignore it either.

He glanced again at his watch. It was now over an hour with no news of Amy. He'd given the staff as much information about her as he knew, which didn't amount to much, and then he'd been left. Looking around the room he saw Inspector Grant and another man come from the treatment area and move away outside. Had they been with the Colombian? He understood from Carl, who was waiting near the door, that he had been brought into the same hospital. Then Simon became angry. Surely the medical staff would not have allowed them to pester Amy for a statement before she was well enough. He rose to his feet and moved over to the reception desk. Just then a nurse headed towards him.

'Mr Deveraux? You can see Miss Watson for a few moments if you wish. Please follow me.'

As a curtain was pulled aside Simon saw Amy's small figure in the bed, connected to various pieces of apparatus. He moved over to her. His first thought was one of shock. She was paler than he had ever seen her, the livid bruise on the side of her face standing out in its darkness. Even her hair, drawn back from her face, seemed to have lost its fire. She opened her eyes as she heard someone move close. They, too, were clouded and dull, but there was also worry in their depths.

'Simon! Is Joanna safe? The policeman said she was.'

He eased onto a chair by her bed. So Grant *had* been speaking to her.

'She is, Amy, thanks to you. Have the police been a nuisance? The staff here shouldn't have allowed it.'

'They wanted to know about that man and... Mark.' She turned her head away. 'Uncle George will never know what happened.'

'Uncle George? Is this Grainger's father, the minister you lived with?'

She turned her head back to him. 'You know?'

He nodded. 'Harriet Freeman told us all about your life after we knew Grainger was involved.'

'I only met Mark again recently by accident in Windsor. He told me he was in a business deal with you but not to mention it. I never liked him, but after that... night,' she dropped her gaze away from him, and he knew her meaning, 'I asked him for a lift back to my lodgings but instead he took me to a hotel. I couldn't get away and he took my phone. I couldn't do anything to stop it, Simon. I didn't know whether to tell them the truth about – well –

217

you know.' She glanced at him. 'I wasn't sure if it would make any difference. I just knew I had to try and care for Joanna. The other man had a gun. He was there that day we were in the Tate. He looked right at me. He frightened me then, but I never thought it was going to end...' She broke off and closed her eyes. 'I'm sure Mark didn't either.' He watched as tears ran down her cheeks.

He took her small hand in his and was shocked at how cold she still seemed. He felt the trembling in her body and could only imagine the terror she must have experienced as the events unfolded. 'You did all the right things, Amy. There's nothing for you to worry about now. I'll contact Reverend Grainger and tell him everything.'

She turned her head restlessly from side to side on the pillow, her distress obvious. 'You don't understand. Mark said he's in a home and has dementia. No-one will be able to tell him about Mark or the truth about all the lies he told.'

Simon had to do something to calm her. 'I'll make sure someone has the information which they can pass on if possible.'

'It won't be the same... but thank you.'

He turned her head gently towards him. 'I'm the one who must thank *you*. You looked after Joanna both during this...mess, and before. Now we must make sure we get you better. As soon as you're fit to travel, we'll move you to Carlisle's clinic. Joanna's there now with my father.'

He heard a small sigh. 'With the pretty nurse.'

Her immediate connection startled him. 'Possibly, I don't know, but I'm sure she's in good hands.' He was eager to move the conversation on and not dwell on her remark.

'Simon, Joanna...she knows about you... about you not being her father. She told me.'

'I know. I was a fool that night... in so many ways and I shall never forgive myself. There is no way that I can tell you how truly sorry I am. For Joanna also; she's taken it badly. She wanted to be with you. I saw the CCTV when you collected her from the school. She looked so happy. I must admit I was envious.'

He felt her fingers tighten on his hand. 'You should be proud of her. She was so good through the whole horrible time. I tried to talk to her about you, but it must be difficult for her to understand, and with all that's happened… I'm sure it will be all right eventually, just give her time. I told her how lucky she was to have a family; so many don't – like me.'

'You do have a family, Amy, the Deveraux family. You are a part of us now, you belong to us and we'll take care of you.' He suddenly knew what he must say next, although part of him despaired at the thought, but he ruthlessly ignored it. He must do right by both this young woman and Joanna to the exclusion of everything else. 'I have been thinking that we could make sure you are family. We could get married. Joanna would be over the moon.'

He watched as she closed her eyes for a moment and a tiny smile curved her small mouth. Then she looked up at him, with the reproachful gaze he remembered. 'It wouldn't work, Simon.'

'Why not? I thought we got on quite well and in different circumstances…'

'It can't happen just to please Joanna.'

He sighed. He'd wanted it cut and dried, agreed upon now before he had a chance to think.

'We'll talk about it again when you're feeling stronger.'

'Yes, I do feel very tired. Perhaps I'll sleep.'

Just at that moment the curtain was drawn aside, and a young male doctor entered. Without a word he checked the various systems and cast a glance at the still figure. He looked at Simon. 'Could I have a word with you, Mr Deveraux?'

Simon stood. He placed a kiss on Amy's cool forehead. 'I'll see you again later. Get some rest now.'

There was a small sigh but no other reply.

He followed the doctor outside and they walked further along the corridor. Still consulting his chart, the man enquired, 'Do you know anything more about Miss Watson's medical history, Mr Deveraux?'

'Um, no, not really. No more than I've already provided, although both she and I had a check-up at a private clinic recently.'

The doctor looked up at him, surprise on his face. 'Really? Was there any outcome from that?'

Simon thought. 'Not that I'm aware of. She didn't say anything to me.'

Something stirred in his mind. In London after the visit to the clinic she'd seemed a little unsettled, but if there was something wrong, she would have told him surely, or Carlisle would have mentioned it?

'Do you have any objection to my contacting the medical person involved? I need some further information. I have to tell you, Mr Deveraux, we have detected some serious anomalies in Miss Watson's blood tests, and we are already taking proactive measures.'

Simon had difficulty understanding what he had just said. If there had been a problem, surely…his thoughts were interrupted by a nurse hurrying towards them. 'Could you come, Doctor, please.' He watched as they moved back along the corridor. He heard vague electrical alarms, and a strange unease settled on him.

Chapter Twenty-One

It was good to hear laughter again in the small bright room at the top of the clinic. It had recently been vacated by Ahmed, who, after his surgery and now with two good eyes, soon became a normal boisterous five-year-old. Even better, a family had been found who would care for him in the future.

For a moment Rose hesitated in the corridor. It seemed wrong to burst into a happy scene, bringing with her the threat of medical procedures. She turned away into the adjacent storeroom and leant against the shelving as she relived the last few days.

She remembered listening in horror as Uncle Henry had explained about the kidnapping. Her worry for the child was matched by thoughts of how Simon Deveraux must have felt during this time. When Joanna arrived at the clinic, she had been pale and distraught, and Rose recognised in her the bewildered shock she had seen so many times. The little girl was clinging to a well-built blonde man who carried her in, introducing himself as Jack Fletcher, Orion's security adviser.

After putting Joanna to bed and administering a light sedative, she and her uncle listened as he explained the details of the abduction and subsequent circumstances. Rose was curious that Joanna's father was nowhere to be seen. It was only later, after Emile Deveraux, the child's grandfather, had arrived, accompanied by a very stylish but warm and friendly Frenchwoman, that they learnt Joanna had found out the truth about her father. Mr Deveraux Senior said he had informed them of this, as he felt it necessary for the clinic to be in full possession of all the facts, in case it had any bearing on Joanna's treatment. Uncle Henry had acknowledged the news with a shake of his head, commenting that it was a lot for a child to suddenly absorb and comprehend, but went on to assure them that Sister McKenna was well versed in children suffering various trauma and Joanna would be well cared for.

She remembered being appraised by Simon's father and, returning his steady gaze, noticed his slight nod of acceptance. The likeness to his son was obvious and she felt again that strange fluttering of her senses. Where was he? How was *he* dealing with all this?

Then, the following day, the shocking news arrived that Amy Watson had died. Emile Deveraux seemed deeply moved and insisted that they immediately break the news to Joanna. He considered it better for her to hear and then recover from bad news all at once rather than drip-feed problems. Rose had marvelled at his caring and gentle manner with the child, explaining that Amy had been ill all along, and this would have happened anyway. There had been more tears, and a battered rabbit Rose understood to be called Mr Floppy was hugged, even in sleep. Emile Deveraux or Jack Fletcher took it in turns to stay with her all the time, as well as Madame Moreau, who seemed equally involved with the young girl. This support became even more necessary when two female police officers arrived to talk to her, and Rose had been astonished at how well Joanna dealt with it, although a rather disturbed night had followed.

Rose was aware that Simon Deveraux had been in daily contact by phone with his father, and one morning the night staff told her that he had in fact come to the clinic in person after Joanna was sure to be asleep and spent some time at her bedside. To her everlasting shame Rose found reasons to be in the clinic long after her duty ended the following night but saw nothing of him.

Shaking her head at her immature notions, she left the storeroom and entered Joanna's room, where a competitive game of snakes and ladders was in progress.

'Time for tea, Joanna. What would you like?'

'Could I have jam sandwiches please, Sister Rose?'

This was now Joanna's way of addressing her and she couldn't help but smile. 'What again! You had them yesterday. Are you sure you're not feeding them to Mr Floppy? He's looking a bit fat.'

Emile Deveraux shared a conspiratorial look with his granddaughter. 'I assure you, Sister Rose, any leftovers come my way.'

Still smiling, Rose left them together in peaceful harmony. It was so good to see, but she wished that Simon Deveraux could be sharing this too.

Then a few days later Rose was called to her uncle's office.

'I've just had a telephone conversation with Simon Deveraux, not a pleasant one either. He blames me for not disclosing Miss Watson's medical problems to him. He refuses to accept the fact that as she was an adult it was a private matter between us. It is unfortunate that she did not seek the immediate medical help I deemed necessary, as she assured me she would. She obviously said nothing to him, but Deveraux maintains that I should have informed him. He is now insisting that Joanna is removed from here and he will have no further connection with the clinic.' He shrugged. 'It's a decision for him to make, of course, but I feel he hasn't grasped the situation. As sad as I am at the outcome, there was very little I could have done; or anyone else come to that.'

'Perhaps he's just going through a very bad time at the moment, Uncle, with all this and his business problems as well. Joanna is calmer but I would like to have kept an eye on her for a few more days. There could still be insecurities buried under the surface.'

'I agree. I'm not sure what Emile Deveraux will say, but we'd better have a word, I suppose.'

In the end a decision was made for Joanna to accompany her grandfather back to Paris immediately. A new start in new surroundings was his view, and Rose felt it was a good decision. She would be sorry to see Joanna leave. As normality was returning, Rose considered that she was a nice little girl. It would be a shame if the situation with Simon Deveraux couldn't be resolved. During her conversations with Joanna, she had discovered that during the kidnapping Amy Watson had been speaking to Joanna about him, and Rose felt that she had to try and continue that dialogue.

'I've seen a lot of children who have had bad things happen to them. They are so lucky if there is someone who cares for them, whatever they are called. Amy was right to say you have been lucky in having someone you have called your Daddy to take care of you. He must have loved you to do that all these years. I am sure he will always go on looking after you. It doesn't matter what you call him; what does matter is that you show him you care about him too. He must be very unhappy at the moment. Try and think of that as well, Joanna. We must all help each other. I know you will, in time, because you are a nice little girl and I've liked being with you.'

She received a swift hug and a nod – perhaps as much as could be expected at that moment.

Later that day, with her father obviously sanctioning the move to France, Joanna left the clinic, accompanied by Jack Fletcher and Madame Moreau. Emile Deveraux made a point of speaking with her before they departed.

'I would like to thank you for your sensitive handling of Joanna. I've heard you talking to her about many things.'

'I'm sorry if you feel I have overstepped my position.'

'Not at all. As Dr Carlisle informed me, your experience in other crisis situations has given you a great insight and I personally am grateful for your caring assistance. I am sure Joanna has benefited. Once she is settled in, I will let her know that Madame Moreau and I intend to be married before Christmas. Hopefully she will find some excitement in the arrangements, and we will involve her as much as we can.'

Rose smiled at him. 'Please accept my congratulations, and I am sure Joanna will be delighted. Little girls love that sort of thing. I also hope matters improve between Joanna and... your son.'

She found blue eyes regarding her. 'That is also my wish. He too has been through a bad time. Perhaps he needs care and attention also.'

She couldn't help the feeling of warmth in her face under his steady gaze. 'Perhaps you're right.'

As once more she stripped out the little room, Rose wondered if she would ever hear of the Deveraux family again – and one member in particular.

*

In the darkness the old and rather battered car moved slowly along the rough road. Bonzo Thompson grimaced when he felt his passenger shifting uncomfortably in the seat next to him as they bounced through yet another unseen pothole. From that point of view, it was unfortunate that the lighting in this outlying part of Sao Paulo was intermittent – but tonight it could also prove rather useful.

Thompson had not met Dimitri Orloff in person until several days ago, although they had spoken by telephone many times over the last few years. Always impressed by the man's automatic assumption of instant results, he had found this reinforced by his striking appearance. At over six foot, with the build of a heavyweight lifter, he was a man to be noticed. He must be in his sixties, Thompson thought, but still appeared fit. His greying beard was neatly trimmed around a generous mouth, and the gaze from the dark eyes was shrewd and alert. At times, however, they also danced with amusement, and… more – which, as Thompson had witnessed for himself at a discreet distance in the hotel, ladies obviously found attractive. Nevertheless, he sensed that you needed to be wary of this man and not underestimate him, as had become even more obvious during their final discussions.

Another deep sigh came from the passenger seat. 'It seems this whole matter is causing me some uncomfortable travel arrangements.' There was silence again for a moment. 'Are you sure this is the right place?' The deep accented voice held a hint of scepticism. 'Why would they bring him out here? It would have been more convenient to keep him in the city with proper facilities.'

'I gather from my source they felt it better to remove him from any chance of communication with associates. There is only a local woman who cooks and cleans but she is gone by lunchtime each day.' Thompson peered at his watch. 'Ten o'clock. The guard should be changing about now. I'll pull off the road and wait for a while.'

He eased the car into a gap close to a barn-like structure and turned off the lights.

'Are you certain of these people, Thompson?'

'As certain as you can ever be. I have cultivated a certain rapport with one of them, and he now sees himself as someone important. The money being paid is more than generous. I have been at pains to explain how they should react with their story after we leave, assuming the anticipated outcome, of course, and, if played out correctly, there should be no comeback on them. If there is a different scenario, I think I can still handle them. I'm not anticipating a problem.'

After a few minutes of dark silence, they saw the lights of a vehicle in the distance. As it came past, Thompson shook his head. 'Not them.' Another set of headlights appeared, and a military-style jeep drove by with a driver and two others on board. 'That's it. We'll give them a minute or two to make sure they don't change their minds and return for something.'

Five minutes later the road remained empty. Thompson pulled out and headed in the opposite direction to the jeep's travel. After another cautious ten minutes on dimmed beam, a small one-storey building came into view, surrounded by a six-foot-high wall with a pair of solid metal gates.

'This is as far as we go by car, we'll do the rest on foot. It's better not to have any evidence of another vehicle nearer the property. The gates should have been left open for us. Make sure you have your gloves on at all times and stay back in the darkness.' He drew the vehicle off the road under a stunted tree. As they walked up to the house, he hoped Orloff would be careful; a sprained ankle now would be unwise. However, for such a large man he seemed to move with nimble grace. Once they reached the gates Thompson placed a cautious hand on the lever and pushed them open. A few steps down an overgrown drive, a figure materialised out of the darkness, and spoke in whispered Portuguese.

'You must be quick, senor. If anyone comes…'

The uniformed man seemed nervous, and Thompson reached out and laid a hand on his shoulder, replying in the same language, 'There will be no problem, Juan. It will all go as we agreed. You and your friend will be blameless… as long as you stick to the story.'

'Yes, and as long as you keep to our arrangement.' The voice was braver now.

Thompson took out a small key from his coat pocket. 'This is the key to the left luggage box at Sao Paulo train station. In it you will find the remainder of the monies promised which is to be divided between you and your friend.' He smiled slightly at the other man. 'Now, hide the key and we will proceed.'

They made their way round to the back of the building, where a light was showing from an open door. Thompson gestured for Orloff to remain out of sight whilst he and Juan entered the building. He returned alone a few minutes later.

'All clear. Juan and his colleague will keep watch at the gate. Follow me.'

He led the way into a room which was obviously a kitchen, and then into an internal hallway. With a warning finger he moved towards a door at the far end, under which a faint bar of light was showing. He opened the door quietly and they moved inside. A man in his early fifties was sitting at a desk in the far corner of the room. He was working by a small light, leaving the rest of the room in semi-darkness. He looked up, and after a moment sprang to his feet. Various expressions moved over the thin face, ranging from surprise to satisfaction and then the beginnings of fear, quickly masked as he called out, 'What is the meaning of this intrusion. Guards!'

'They are too far away to hear you, Senor de Santos,' Thompson replied quietly, again in Portuguese. 'I suggest for the ease of us all,' gesturing to Orloff standing in the shadows, 'that we speak English. I am aware you are fluent in that language.'

'I demand you tell me who you are and why you are here.' Now appearing back in control, de Santos replied in accented English and sat down again at the desk.

Thompson moved forward and took an envelope from his inside coat pocket and threw it down on the desk. 'My friend and I would be very grateful if you would copy out the contents of these papers and then sign the same, after which we will continue our discussion.'

Picking up the envelope, de Santos took out the two sheets of paper and started to read. After a minute or two he gave a laugh and threw them back on the desk. 'This matter of the Colombian deal is nothing to do with me, as my lawyers have informed the authorities; merely accusations by former employees with a grudge, and I will be proven innocent. All the rest,' he waved a hand at the papers on his desk, 'is utter nonsense and I will never sign such a statement. I fear you have had a wasted journey, and perhaps you will now leave. I shall see that the authorities hear about this intrusion.'

'Our discussion has, in fact, only just begun, and we will leave when we choose to do so. It is interesting to hear you speak of "grudges". This whole matter began because of a grudge you held against someone yourself. It might interest you to know that other parties have been very keen to allow this "grudge" to proceed until enough information was amassed, linking you in with the two companies involved. I might add they are now also being provided with evidence from a much stronger source.'

'Even if what you say is true,' de Santos gave a shrug, 'I still say it will be proved I know nothing.' He tore the pages into shreds and dropped them into a waste basket by his desk. Thompson bent and retrieved them. He wasn't worried, he knew that Orloff had at least two more copies on his person, but he wanted no traces left. He stepped a little closer. 'Then perhaps you will deny the fact that you know of a man by the name of Miguel Hernandez.' He noticed a slight reaction to this; a tensing of the jaw, but it was quickly concealed. Not unexpectedly de Santos would try and hold out for as long as he could with his denials. Thompson knew that they had a fair amount of time at their disposal but the sooner they were away the better. He took another step closer but felt a hand on his arm. Orloff moved into the circle of light by the desk and Thompson watched as de Santos sat up straighter in his chair, unnerved by the man's size and presence.

Orloff walked around the side of the desk and perched on one corner. 'I realise that at first you thought your friends had come to rescue you, but unfortunately, as you are now aware, this is not so. In fact, you might find your circle of friends diminishing as they contemplate the folly of being involved with your enterprises over the years.'

From the pool of light small dark eyes glared up at him. 'Who are you to speak to me in this manner?'

'It could be said that we are both businessmen, but you appear to play by a very different set of rules. As my friend has said, your latest venture has aroused a considerable amount of interest from many agencies. Because of this, the English broker's meetings with Hernandez and the approach to Orion were noted. Were you hoping that overtures for assistance from a fledgling brokerage firm would appeal to the basic generosity of an honourable man, who might otherwise have dismissed the deal as a non-starter? Did you also wonder why Deveraux chose to use his personal funds? I can tell you that he did so in the full knowledge that the deal was bogus, and his actions were in fact, being guided by others. Time was needed to amass information and he placed himself and his company in jeopardy to give others that time. I have no doubt that it has given you a certain amount of amusement to see how attitudes have changed towards him personally in financial circles, with a knock-on effect on his company. It was, after all, exactly what you were hoping for, was it not – to ruin him and his business?'

Watching de Santos, Thompson saw the semblance of a smile cross the face, but it was swiftly replaced by an air of innocence.

'Again, I have no idea to what you are referring.'

With a huge sigh, Orloff continued, 'In that case we have no option but to make you aware of certain hard facts. As we have said, your man Hernandez has been observed in all his movements; neutralising Orion's Rio contact to mitigate exposure of information to your detriment, then in London his choice of the broker, and no doubt, to break open the whole matter, the leaking of information to the press and regulatory authorities. In my estimation, the deliberate ruination of the character of an honest man is bad enough, but,' he leaned in closer, 'you have offended my own sense of honour by causing me to doubt a friendship. Even more than that, you then instituted the worst crime of all, which I cannot condone... the kidnapping of an innocent young girl with the full knowledge of her premeditated murder.' The deep voice had sunk down to a mere whisper.

For a moment de Santos shrank back in his chair but then he shouted, 'I know nothing of the girl. It is all lies or the fabrication of this... this Hernandez person.'

Giving him a sad smile, Orloff shook his head. 'I fear Hernandez even now might be telling a different story to the British authorities. They caught him in the act. The child is safe, but two other victims are not. I think this time there might be too much evidence for even you to overcome.'

As the bluster drained away Thompson thought de Santos now appeared smaller and older. Having overheard part of a long telephone conversation between Orloff and Deveraux he knew just how damning the evidence would turn out to be. To save his own neck, Hernandez was revealing information from not only the present but also the past; some of which was hitherto unknown to the authorities. He listened as Orloff calmly told de Santos just how much information Hernandez was supplying, even down to his own admission that he had been considering helping himself to some, if not all, of the ransom money. In that moment Thompson saw the expression change to one of pure hatred as de Santos realised how totally he had been betrayed. Then he sat upright in his chair again, an element of bluff remaining.

'There is money available. I can tell you how to find it if you help me out of here. There are only the two guards.'

As he reached into an inside pocket, Orloff's voice was hard and cold. 'We have no need of money, especially from you, so we will not accept your offer. Now I would suggest you begin writing out the statement, or we might have to initiate a less...friendly conversation. After all, consider this, such an admission might even assist in your defence, and save you the humiliation of a public trial.'

Thompson stood beside de Santos, who looked at them both and then slowly began to write, finally signing his name and adding the date. Perusing the papers Thompson picked them up and placed them in his inside pocket.

Moving off the desk to stand beside it, rather like a dark avenging angel, Thompson thought, Orloff commented, 'This statement will now be put in the hands of your guards, who will tell their superiors they intervened in your attempt to destroy it. They have been paid well to keep to their account. I imagine your lawyers would have a hard time denying its contents, written in your own hand. However, even if this statement did afford you some negotiation, you will go to prison for a long time, my friend, of that you can be certain. I imagine it could be an uncomfortable time for you there. Think about it. Those who, in the past, have been incarcerated because of your dealings will be with you, and you will be one of them, so they will not fear you. I wonder if it will appear strange to your warders how you come to have so many accidents. It is remarkable how stairs and showers can always be dangerous places for the unwary.'

'You cannot frighten me with threats of that nature.' The man glared at them, but his hands were clutching tight to the edge of the desk.

'I merely state a likely probability. So, we offer you another suggestion for you to avoid all this nastiness.' Orloff turned his head and nodded.

Thompson took a small bottle from his coat pocket and laid it on the desk. Glancing up he first took in the cold implacable gaze of Dimitri Orloff and then looked down into the shocked stare of the seated man.

Picking up the bottle of tablets, de Santos gasped, 'You... you can't mean...'

'You must admit it would be, even for you, a clean and honourable ending.'

Looking at each of them in turn de Santos muttered, 'I cannot.'

Orloff walked over towards the door and looked back over his shoulder. 'After all the misery you have caused in your life, you have been given a choice, something, no doubt, you denied many others. I know which action I myself would choose, but the decision is now in your hands.'

Leaving the building they walked back to the gate, where Juan and his companion were waiting.

After first crumpling the papers slightly Thompson handed them to Juan. 'Here is the document which you will contact your superiors to say you found. Stick to your story despite any denials.

Now or later there might be further developments, about which you know nothing. I repeat, stay calm, no blame can be attached to either of you.'

The two men exchanged a nervous glance.

Thompson continued, 'Remember, be careful how you deal with the money. Don't appear to have come into sudden wealth or questions could be asked.'

Now receiving definite nods, he and Orloff stepped through the gates and heard the lock closing behind them. Neither spoke until they were once more at the car.

'So, it's done? He wrote it out correctly?'

'Yes, I made sure of that. If those two keep their heads there should be no problem. Even if they don't, there is no proof. No-one saw us leave the hotel and no-one will see us arrive back. The management is already aware you are checking out early tomorrow to catch your flight to Geneva. Tonight, after dropping you off, I will park the car where it will soon be looted. Tomorrow I too may decide to leave the country on business, in say – Florida.' He cast a glance at his companion. 'You know, sir, I expected de Santos to make more effort to use us to extricate himself from his situation. Yes, he tried to bribe us, fair enough, but he wasn't very persuasive.'

Orloff tried to settle himself better in his seat. 'I must admit to a certain surprise at the lack of effort myself; the news of his betrayal must have shaken him. He might now gamble that his written admission will secure some leniency. However, I suggest to you that at some time the fear he instilled in others for so long will come back to haunt him. He can't fail to see that what we suggested might happen to him is likely to come true. I feel at some point he will make his choice. As with so many of his kind, they are brave when they are in power and can issue orders, but in the end they are often just small men. Nevertheless, however worthwhile it will be to have rid the world of a person such as that, this is not the sort of night's work I would want to repeat.' He gave his companion a glance. 'You have done well, Thompson.

If Florida palls, perhaps the lure of Istanbul might interest you.'

Thompson took his eyes off the road for a moment. 'It might do, sir.' Then he added, 'Things at least should go better for Deveraux now.'

Orloff's reply seemed a long time coming and, unseen in the darkness, his face took on a worried look. 'It might at least speed matters up as far as legal wrangling is concerned. From how Deveraux sounded when I last spoke to him, he is nearing his limit. He needs help, and I hope he finds the right person to provide it.'

Chapter Twenty-Two

This ceiling looked just the same as the one in the previous hotel, Simon thought. He'd stared at both over the last two nights. Lying on the hard bed, fully clothed and wide awake, he knew he needed rest, but his mind was too full of thoughts: thoughts about the past, the last few weeks, and the future.

After Amy had slipped peacefully away and he had finally released his grasp on her cold hand he had been left with an overwhelming sense of anger that this had been allowed to happen. Standing out in the corridor, cursing both himself and everyone else involved, it was only when Carl appeared at his shoulder that he realised he had been shouting out loud. The young man guided him to a quiet area until he could begin to bring his emotions under control. He continued to stay with him during the completion of necessary paperwork, and then organised a taxi for them both back to Woodhayes. Stumbling upstairs to his room Simon knew nothing more until the following day.

Almost mechanically, he had endured a succession of interviews with Grant's people and the local police. Sir Arthur rang to inform him that various factions were all squabbling about who had jurisdiction over Hernandez. Simon wasn't really concerned, as long as the man paid for his crimes. It might be better if the matter *was* dealt with in another country, or the whole kidnapping saga would be revealed with the consequent press interest. There had only been a brief mention of some sort of incident near the canal in the local paper and Simon was thankful he had been spared any intrusive questioning.

Over the following days he had attempted to push all this to the back of his mind and focus on the concluding FCA investigation. He would have their decision soon, but it was not helping the situation re the viability of Orion. There had been endless meetings with Charles, Stuart, and other key members of staff, all of whom were still his staunch supporters and he was grateful for this. The haemorrhage of clients now appeared to have stopped, and he even sensed a different attitude in various press articles, particularly led by Tony Broadbent; however, prognosis for the future was still pivotal. He wanted to make changes to assist with this, but he was beginning to find it difficult to think coherently, and he wasn't sure how best to implement these anyway. His waste baskets became full of torn-up paper. Ideas floated through his mind, but they were gone before he had grasped them.

When the authorities finally agreed the release of the two bodies, he had felt it necessary to take on full responsibility for arrangements. With the help of McDonald and Fletcher's contacts they had managed to trace George Grainger, only to establish that his health was such that there was no prospect of him comprehending, let alone dealing with, the situation. Simon was certain that, despite everything, Amy would have wanted Mark Grainger's affairs dealt with properly and so this had been done.

He found he had more of a dilemma with arrangements for Amy herself. What would she have wanted? In the end he discussed the matter with Harriet Freeman, and they came to an agreement for a simple cremation. The Carlton House chaplain officiated during the short service, at which Simon had thought only himself, Harriet, and a tearful Anne Francis had attended. However, he was surprised, but also pleased to find later that

Pamela Dunne had also been present. The coffin had been topped by a single spray of bronze chrysanthemums, which reminded Simon of the first time he had seen Amy at Carlton House, with her hair shining in the sunlight. He had experienced a surprising depth of emotion during the proceedings, feeling weighed down with a sense of loss and guilt. Those feelings had remained with him since, day and night – particularly at night.

He had moved out of Woodhayes, leaving the Gilmores as caretakers. McDonald had told him that he would press for the repatriation of the ransom monies and Simon intended to arrange with Dimitri that his loan against the property should be converted into a sale. His personal belongings had been sent to the London flat or into store.

During regular, but brief telephone conversations with his father it seemed Joanna was settling in well, and he had even spoken to her himself on a couple of occasions, albeit in a rather stilted fashion. Simon now regretted his blistering argument with Henry Carlisle. On reflection, he could see the man's dilemma and it had led to Joanna being removed to France. Since she had left, he felt in a vacuum. She seemed further away from him than ever, now also in a geographical sense. However, it was good to know that, so far, she was showing no sign of stress, mental or physical, and perhaps the total change was for the best, but he missed her. Her bright chatter had in the past sometimes irritated him after a long day, but it had also made him smile. He had to find a way to begin rebuilding the relationship between them, but he was at a loss to know how to start. She might find him a continuing reminder of what had happened and blame him accordingly.

Was he to blame, particularly about Amy? Why hadn't the girl spoken to him about her problems, for God's sake? Did she try, and somehow the moment passed as other events took over? Had that happened before with other people? All his thoughts seemed to be just a continuous circle with no end. Worry about important details to keep Orion afloat, jumbled together with images from childhood with his mother, morphing into time spent with Amy; then stark memories of two different hospital rooms, each time holding cold hands in his, and feeling the emptiness.

The London flat had not been the answer; he had to get completely away. After another day he had packed a bag, switched off his phone and left. There would be some consternation when it was found he was out of contact, but he needed to find some peace. After wandering around he had walked into a small hotel and paid for a room in cash. It might keep Fletcher's bloodhounds at bay! But after yet another sleepless night he moved on again – only tonight to have the same thing repeated. Even with the aid of a bottle of cheap whisky, sleep was still eluding him. He was now so tired the circles in his mind seemed to be spinning faster and faster. Perhaps he was having a breakdown! All the pressure for so many years was finally having its effect.

He swore to himself, rolled off the bed, collected his belongings together and walked out. It was a cold November day, with sleety rain in the air. He hefted his bag and started wandering through the streets. After stopping off in a steamy café for a hot drink he started walking again, in no particular direction – or was he?

He knew deep down the person who could help him calm his jumbled thoughts, but he was afraid what might happen to him if she turned him away. They hardly knew each other and yet there was something between them… something important. He felt on the edge of a precipice – one wrong move and he would topple into the void – but he had to try and cling on to some sort of hope. His hope was her.

*

Rose entered the reception area, having finished her last shift at the clinic for the next seven days. She had agreed an open-ended contract with Uncle Henry but he wanted her to convert this to a permanent one. He and Aunt Moira were away for a much needed three-week break and she had agreed to wait for their return before making up her mind. At her request, their family relationship was not common knowledge at the clinic in case it caused feelings of animosity amongst other members of staff. However, Uncle Henry had insisted that she stay in the flat on the other side of the road, usually reserved for visitors who required accommodation.

She sensed the colder air as she exited the lift into the foyer and was grateful that, on a night like this, she only had to cross the road.

'Just leaving, Sister?'

Rose turned with a smile. Michael was a new night porter, but she always found him pleasant and courteous.

'Yes, that's right. It doesn't sound too nice outside.'

'No indeed. Er... Sister, I just wanted to mention that a man was asking after you earlier, wanting to know if you were around. He looked a bit rough and dishevelled, and I was pretty noncommittal. I thought I saw someone moving about outside a little while ago, so I just needed you to be aware.'

Rose thought for a moment. She couldn't think of anyone who might be asking after her. Then her senses were on alert. Could it be...? No, of course not, she was just being ridiculous, and he wouldn't behave in that fashion; nor by any stretch of the imagination could he be classed as 'dishevelled'. 'Well, thanks Michael, for the warning, but I'm sure there's no problem. Goodnight.'

She stepped outside into the cold. As she was about to cross the road a voice spoke out of the darkness.

'Sister McKenna?'

Whirling around, Rose saw the shadow of a man. He must have been leaning against the iron railings. For a moment she was afraid and then something about the height and build of this person seemed familiar.

'Don't be afraid. It's Simon Deveraux.'

The figure moved closer to her into the light of a streetlamp and she could now recognise him. 'What... what are you doing out here in this weather?'

'Waiting for you; I need help, Rose – your help.'

'If you're ill you need to see a doctor, Mr Deveraux.' She ignored his informal way of addressing her.

'All I need is you – to talk to. Please, Rose.'

Was it her imagination or did she detect some sort of raw emotion in his words, nothing like the cool, controlled person she had thought him to be? He also seemed unsteady on his feet. She almost called out for Michael to come and help him inside, but after a second or two she made up her mind.

'You'd better come over to the flat. At least it will be warm and dry.' She watched him turn and pick up a bag, then follow her.

Opening the front door, she was met by a welcoming blast of warm air. She switched on the lights and then turned to look at her guest. She was shocked by what she saw. Gone was the suave, immaculately groomed wealthy businessman. Michael had been correct. He was certainly dishevelled. His clothes looked as if they had been slept in, and he was unshaven, but it was his eyes which caught her attention. They were dull and flat, red-rimmed by lack of sleep, drained of all the vitality she had noticed in him before. He appeared as someone almost at the end of their resources. Her training took over, cancelling any other more conflicting thoughts.

'I think you had better get out of those wet clothes.' She took his overcoat and suit jacket from him and hung them next to a radiator. 'Sit down. I'll make you a warm drink.' When she returned, he was leaning back on the sofa with his eyes closed. She wondered if he was asleep, but he straightened up as she came over to him.

'You should be at home, not wandering around in this weather.' As he took a sip of the drink, warm milk and honey with a few drops of brandy, he grimaced at the taste. She studied him again. 'It might be better if you didn't drive. You need to ring for someone to collect you or call for a taxi.'

To her surprise he gave a harsh laugh. 'I've nowhere to go and no money.'

'That's ridiculous, of course you have.'

He put down the mug and leant his elbows on his knees, bending his head. 'I've used all my cash. I don't want my minders tracing me, dragging me back. Back to where? I've moved out of Woodhayes – too many memories; even the flat in town is the same. I keep remembering when we were all there that weekend…before it all went wrong; but the memories keep following me, everywhere I go, and I can't sleep.' He raised his head and looked at her, his eyes bleak. 'All these years I've tried so hard, Rose, tried to do the best… for everyone. Then, thinking I was so important, I behaved like a crusading knight trying to rid the world of wrongdoing, putting my company and employees in jeopardy, and worse… endangering Joanna. Now everything's falling apart, and people have suffered, and it's my fault. What am I going to do, Rose? Please help me.'

He had that lost look about him, in common with so many others she had seen when their lives had been decimated, and the despair in his voice cut into her. He had sought her out when he was obviously in trouble, and she couldn't turn him away. 'You just need to rest for a while.' Taking his arm like a child she led him through to the spare bedroom. 'Undress, lie down, and try to relax and sleep.'

She left and returned with his hardly tasted drink. He was lying under the duvet, his clothes a crumpled heap on the floor. 'You'd better drink the rest of this while it's still warm. It will do you good.'

He sat up, revealing a bare torso. Although she had seen many male bodies, she felt her breath quicken at the sight of him. He took a few mouthfuls of the drink and then lay back down. 'I told you. I can't sleep, that's the trouble. The thoughts won't go away and I…I'm frightened. Stay with me, Rose.'

'I'll just go and sort out these wet clothes and then I'll be back. Close your eyes.'

Minutes later she tiptoed back into the room, hoping to find he was asleep, but he turned his head towards her. 'Don't leave me. Stay with me.'

She opened her mouth to give an immediate denial to his request, but she knew inside she would not do so. She turned off the light, picked up a spare blanket from a nearby chair and lay on top of the duvet, still fully clothed. 'Close your eyes and go to sleep. I'm here.' Instinctively she reached over to smooth some hair from his forehead and heard him give a small sigh. He reached for her hand and held onto it. She heard him murmur, 'So soft and warm.' In a moment or two she could tell he was asleep.

*

After a disturbed night, acutely aware of the proximity of the man lying next to her and his restless turning, Rose sat alone in the kitchen. Now showered and dressed in a loose blouse and jeans, she was trying to wake herself up with a cup of coffee. What should she do about Simon? Someone needed to know where he was. If they started looking for him the police could be involved, and, inevitably, the press. She had been scouring the papers for weeks but had seen no reports of the kidnapping incident. It had seemed strange, but there must be some reason. Perhaps it was a blessing, because the newspapers would have had a field day with a story like that, putting more pressure on the man still sleeping in the other room. For the first time in her life, she had taken an interest in the financial section of the papers, trying to ignore the fact that she was only doing so because she wanted to know what they were saying about him. The attitudes were mixed but one journalist appeared to have been consistently on his side. Today's paper had been delivered and she turned to the appropriate section. A headline immediately caught her eye stating that a Brazilian businessman, who had been under house arrest for possible financial irregularities, appeared to have taken his own life. It was rumoured that a signed statement had been left, but so far the authorities had made no formal announcement. The journalist, Anthony Broadbent, went on to indicate that from his local sources it was likely that this man was involved in the Colombian mine deal and perhaps any further revelations would help clear up the financial investigations surrounding Orion Investments.

Rose closed the paper and placed it in a drawer. Was this something Simon should know about? Would other people be trying to inform him? Would it be good news or bad? She just didn't know. After last night she was sure about one thing – he couldn't take much more before he broke down completely. If Uncle Henry had been here, she would have spoken to him; but now it was her decision. She had to let someone know who would make the right choices. After considering the matter for some while she slowly decided who she would contact.

*

It was after midday before she heard movement. Walking through into the bedroom she found him sitting on the side of the bed, rubbing his hands over his face. He looked up as she entered.

'I… er… I must have slept after all.'

'I'm sorting out your clothes. If you have any more with you, I think you will feel better if you have a shower. Meanwhile I'll make you something to eat.' She received a polite, 'Thank you,' in response. As she turned to leave, he stood, dressed only in close-fitting jersey boxer shorts. It was ridiculous, but the sight of him nearly naked was doing strange things to her. She knew from his medical records that he was fit and healthy and it was apparent he worked to keep it that way; his body was lean and muscular, with a dusting of dark hair on his chest arrowing down lower… She mumbled, 'Er, the bathroom's just across the hall,' and fled into the kitchen before she made a fool of herself. What was it about this man that attracted her so?

He appeared some twenty minutes later looking more as she expected, dressed in casual woollen jumper and cords. However, when she studied his face, although now clean shaven, she could see that he was still pale, and his dark blue eyes were clouded.

'Come and sit down.' She indicated the breakfast bar. 'I'm making some eggs and toast. The coffee should still be hot, so help yourself.'

'Thank you, you're very kind. I'm being a nuisance.'

As she put the plate of food in front of him, she sensed a brittle politeness in his manner. He was either now regretting his decision to contact her, or his real feelings were being ruthlessly kept at bay. She felt, and hoped, that it was the latter, but if so, she had to somehow encourage him to remain with her until he was fully in control.

'Am I keeping you from work?'

He had eaten a little of his food, which was something, and she was making fresh coffee for them both. 'I'm on a few days' holiday.' That was as much as she was prepared to say; he had, after all, fallen out with Uncle Henry.

'I'm glad you're still here.'

The words were said in a quiet voice, but she sensed he meant them, and this pleased her. So, he didn't regret anything.

'Is it possible for us to dispense with formality... Rose? After all, we have spent a night together.'

She stared at him, expecting to see some humour or amusement in him after such a remark, but there was none. His expression showed only a simple request, almost pleading. She bit back her sharp retort and just said, 'If that's what you want, I don't mind.'

'I want a great many things, Rose, but I don't know how to start. I'm afraid to even try.' He rubbed his hands through his hair. 'I don't know what's happening to me; I never used to be like this. I could always make instant decisions, but just lately...'

'Perhaps you're trying too hard, and there are too many decisions. Choose just one thing at a time.' Rose saw him nod his head. 'Take your coffee into the other room. I'll be through in a minute and we can have a talk – that's if you want to.'

As he left the kitchen, he turned back to her, his face serious. 'I do want to talk, Rose, and only to you.'

Ten minutes later she walked into the sittingroom. He was standing near the sideboard, holding something in his hands. He turned towards her, and she was horrified to see the expression on his face; desperation and... fear?

Chapter Twenty-Three

Hurrying over to him, Rose now saw he was holding the handmade card which Joanna had sent as a thankyou for taking care of her. It had been accompanied by a letter from Emile Deveraux, once again expressing his own thanks.

'Dear God, even here I can't get away from the memories. I thought with you… but I…' He crumpled up the card and in an angry gesture threw it across the room, then made for the door.

'Simon, wait. You can't go like this.' Rose ran after him and caught his arm. It felt hard and tense under her hand. 'Please stay. If you go, I'll only worry about you.'

He turned and looked down at her. Then he pulled her roughly into his arms. She could feel his body shaking and heard him whisper into her hair, 'Will you worry, Rose?' She drew back and ran a hand down his cheek; she could only tell the truth. 'Yes, Simon, I would worry.'

As she drew him down on the sofa beside her, it seemed so natural for him to put his arm across her shoulders. After a long silence she felt him sigh, and some of the tenseness left his body. Should she try and open the conversation, or would he be able to speak first?

'There seems so much to say, Rose. At times I just want to blank the whole thing out, but I know you will say that's wrong, so I suppose I should begin with the obvious.' He looked down at her. 'Do you really want me to do this?' As she nodded, he looked away again and cleared his throat. 'You must be aware from the medical records that Joanna is not my biological child, and she has now found this out?' There was a resigned note in his voice.

'Yes, my…er… Dr Carlisle pointed it out to me.'

'I was waiting until Joanna was older before I explained things to her. I thought she might be able to understand better. My father thought I was a fool for taking the course of action I did and warned me there might be trouble. Perhaps he's been proved right after all.' He sighed again. 'Another black mark against me.'

'Your father seems to genuinely think a lot of Joanna, and despite any misgivings, I'm sure he's proud of how you've brought her up.'

'I'm not so sure, Rose. My father and I already have other issues between us, and this is likely to have made it worse.'

'Neither your father nor anyone else can deny that you haven't done your best for Joanna. I think she is growing up into a nice little girl.'

'That's half the problem; she is growing up. When she was a baby, mine, as I thought, I wanted to help and be hands-on with her care. Her nanny supervised my attempts at this. Even after I… knew… I still felt it important to have a personal involvement but then I began to realise that if I became too close and personal with her, and the truth ever came out, I might find myself in trouble. So, I started to back off, and once on that course it was difficult to do anything else until… until Amy arrived, and then it seemed easier – a link between us. I think, because of her own experiences of being brought up in care, she must have found some sort of empathy with Joanna, and it helped… helped us all; only for me to behave badly towards her. My actions upset and embarrassed her. Thankfully, I was able to apologise, admit that I had been at fault and let her know how much she meant to our family.' He paused. 'I asked her to marry me.'

The words he had just said repeated themselves over and over in her brain as, on the lame pretext of checking out the laundry, Rose hurriedly left the room. They also connected somewhere even deeper inside her. Had he fallen in love with Amy? Was the thought that in some way he had contributed to her death the reason for his anguish?

She now had to admit to herself the extent of the impact which this man had had on her life in such a short time. Even before she had met him, Uncle Henry's comments and obvious regard for him had raised her curiosity and interest, and she had even attempted to find out more about him, but there was surprisingly little of a personal nature. Never had she encountered a man with whom she found such an instant connection, and who had afterwards stayed in her thoughts. Of course, he was handsome and rich, but there was something more to him than that. He cared – just like her – but they had shown it in different ways. His generosity had enabled disadvantaged people to be treated at the clinic; the same sort of people she had also helped around the world.

Now *he* needed help, but could she continue to give it after hearing those words? It mattered. Why it did so, she didn't dare to explore, and despised herself for it. No, she must think of Joanna. The little girl needed her world to be safe and secure and that included having her "Daddy" back. This would only happen if she could convince Simon to try and bridge that gap. It would be difficult, but he had to be encouraged to try.

She returned to the sitting room and busied herself with closing the curtains on the growing dusk.

'What did I say to upset you, Rose?'

Unaware he had come to stand behind her, she turned and found herself in his arms. His hands moved up to her shoulders and he looked down into her face, his blue eyes intense. She tried to brush the remark away. 'Nothing at all. Why do you say that?'

'You left the room so abruptly a moment ago, and you seem different now, distracted. Tell me what's wrong, Rose. It's important.'

She knew she would have to answer. 'Did you love Amy?'

He rested his forehead on her hair. 'I wondered if it was something to do with that. Did I love her?' She felt him sigh. 'Not perhaps the way you mean. I felt all sorts of things about her; but at the end of the day, I should have recognised how young and inexperienced she was and acted accordingly. In my stupidity I didn't, and I regret that more than I can say.'

He turned away and picked up the crumpled piece of card, attempting to straighten it out.

'Joanna made it for me as a thank you. Your father sent it to me.'

He turned, and watched her, his face tight. 'I'm sorry, I shouldn't have done that. Joanna made me a birthday card this year, and a cake. I thought it was wonderful. I know I'll never have another one from her.' His voice almost broke. 'I miss her so, Rose.'

Seeing his emotion, she felt overwhelmed herself, but she must stay strong for him. 'Come and sit down again and tell me more.'

He joined her on the sofa. 'When I first met Amy, at a school event, she had the temerity to reproach me for what she saw as shortcomings in my dealings with Joanna. The criticism angered me, and I wanted to punish her in some way. I tricked her into an embarrassing situation which, unintentionally, pushed her into the hands of the kidnappers. Her treatment by them might have contributed to... what happened.

'We also had a divergence of views on certain aspects of my lifestyle, especially when she became aware of my ownership of works of art. In her view I was profiting at the expense of the artist. It rankled with me because I was only attempting to act as a... custodian... and anyway, some of those pieces formed the basis of a fund I had set up for Joanna when she was a baby. I wanted to make sure she was financially independent – whatever might happen to me.' He gave a short laugh. 'Just as well in the circumstances.'

He was quiet for a moment, but Rose knew there was more to come. 'At other times she was kind and caring, and taught Joanna a lot by example... and perhaps me too.' He glanced at her. 'Yes, I also found her attractive. You saw her; she was pretty, and her youthful innocence was enticing, which might easily have led to...' he paused. 'Then I would watch her interacting with Joanna and she was like her older sister, and we all had fun together. That's what I miss most: the sense of family. I think she felt that too. I'm sure her past was not ideal. That's why I wanted to give her the chance to be part of our family, especially after what she had done for Joanna.' He looked down at her again. 'She turned me down, Rose. She guessed I was making the gesture more for Joanna than myself. I intended to try and talk to her about it again, but I never had another chance. Maybe it was just as well; had things been different she deserved the opportunity to make her own future, not be tied down with obligations. We would always have been there for her, and we will certainly never forget her.'

He stood, crossed over to the window, then turned and stared at her for a moment. He closed his eyes and said, 'What else do you want to know, Rose?'

Did she dare ask the other question she had in her mind? It was none of her business after all. She took a deep breath. 'What happened to your wife?'

He opened his eyes again and looked at her, his face and whole body now taut and stiff. 'My wife died on a holiday in Italy in a senseless speedboat accident, no doubt after one of the boozy parties she still seemed to enjoy. A young man died with her. A kind "friend" afterwards informed me they had been together for some while. I have no doubt he was her lover, and in all probability Joanna's father. They were going away together.'

The cold, matter of fact statements horrified Rose. 'How do you know she was leaving you?'

'Amongst Olivia's belongings returned by the police was a letter addressed to me, but not posted, in which she explained what she was planning.'

'But…but if it was not posted, perhaps she had changed her mind.'

'I doubt it. I found out she had already sent a letter to a firm of solicitors asking them to start divorce proceedings. It was a shock to find out that way, but I think we were both past any form of dialogue by then. Several months later Joanna came down with a persistent virus and Carlisle started to make some checks. You know what the results showed. Anger didn't cover my feelings; I felt… violated. The child I had loved and cared for as mine was nothing of the sort, and Olivia had kept the lie. She didn't have the courage to admit the true circumstances. No wonder she wanted a termination… and I managed to talk her out of it!'

Rose watched as he started pacing around the room.

'After the birth she made it clear she wanted nothing more to do with Joanna and she made no mention of any arrangements in her letter. I suspect she thought nothing would be discovered and I would agree to custody.'

'Didn't you try and contact any of her family or of this man?'

He rounded on her and she recoiled at the anger in him.

'Don't you think I tried? I knew Olivia only had an elderly maiden aunt living somewhere in South America, so it was out of the question to contact her. The man involved came from a well-connected Spanish family. I wrote to them and then visited personally, outlining the circumstances, suggesting some biological tests to determine true paternity. They categorically denied any possible involvement in that way as the man, so they said, was already engaged to the daughter of a family friend with a wedding imminent. I could have taken the matter to court, but it would have made things worse. Not only might it have become public but if I had proved my case Joanna could have become an embarrassment to them and quite likely have been unloved and unwanted. I considered making corrections to her birth certificate, but somehow, I didn't want to do that; in my mind she was still my child. I made a decision then, and I must stand by it. For God's sake, she had no-one else!' He ran a distracted hand through his dark hair. 'I was so angry at the time, I disposed of all Olivia's belongings; everything. Now perhaps I think that was wrong. Joanna has nothing relating to her mother. I have a file of papers for her to look through when she's older, and I'll see she has independent advice so she can then decide what she wants to do, if anything.' Again, he ran a hand through his hair, frustration evident. 'First, I have to somehow find a way to make things right with her.'

On impulse Rose stood and placed her hands on his arms. 'I'm sure it will all work out, and I'll help you all I can; that's if you wish me to.'

He drew her to him and lowered his head until his mouth was a whisper away from her own. 'You know that's what I want, Rose.' His kiss was gentle and sweet at first, then more urgent. He picked her up in his arms and carried her through to the room he had occupied and laid her on the bed. 'I need you Rose… in every way.'

*

It was still dark as she woke, and the memories came back to her. Despite his obvious need for her he had taken time to explore her body, arousing her as no-one ever before, but he seemed to want assurance that she was happy to take matters further. She had thought herself an experienced woman but had never felt so desired and needed, and her answer was easy to give. They had finally fallen asleep wrapped close around each other.

Still drowsy she reached out a hand wanting again to feel his presence – but all she encountered was coldness. She sat up, now fully awake. He was nowhere to be seen. For one dreadful moment she thought he had left without a word. Was that all he had wanted, a few hours of sympathy and female company?

Her stomach lurched at the thought. Then she heard some faint sounds, and in the half-light spotted his bag and clothes from the night before, and a sigh of relief escaped her. Climbing out of bed she found her blouse lying on the floor and, wrapping this around her, moved through into the sittingroom. It was still in darkness, but she saw a faint light from the kitchen and pushed open the door. He was sitting at the breakfast bar, dressed in a bathrobe, part of the facilities provided with the flat. He turned his head as she approached, and his glance swept her body.

'Go back to bed, Rose, you'll catch cold.'

She walked over to him. 'I missed you. I thought… I thought you had left.'

He looked at her in astonishment. 'Left!' His expression changed. 'You thought I was capable of something like that?'

She felt his censure and wanted to make amends. 'I'm sorry, I was still half-asleep. I expected to find you there.'

He picked up the mug in front of him. 'I needed a drink, and then I began thinking.'

'Come back to bed with me and let's talk. It's not good to think alone.'

He gave a short laugh. 'You know what will happen if I come back to bed with you.'

She leant against him. 'Well, we can do a bit of both… can't we?' She tugged at his arm, and he followed her through to the bedroom.

Once in bed she tried to keep as far away from him as she could. He was lying back with his arms folded behind his head. His expression was neutral, but she caught a glimmer of amusement in his eyes as he murmured, 'We'll see who weakens first.'

'So, what were you thinking about?' Part of her wondered if this was such a good idea after all. She was convinced, however, that he still needed to talk.

'I was thinking about why I feel so angry. I shouldn't have been so stupid with Amy. Her thoughts about Joanna were valid enough to her, and I ought to have recognised that she was genuinely trying to help. I could, and should, have just brushed it off, but then if I had it would have altered subsequent events; her involvement with us as a family and her beneficial presence when Joanna was in danger. What happened to her at the end was tragic, but I hope that knowing she was valued and wanted as part of our family gave her some sort of pleasure and peace.' He sighed. 'I think my father was right when he suggested there was something she wanted to talk about, but I didn't make the time to listen. I should have done, I know that now, and it's something I regret.' He turned his head and looked at her. 'He thinks I make impetuous decisions. He told me he'd been glad to see that I had put some checks and balances in place in my company to prevent any disaster,' he closed his eyes, 'but that still didn't stop me.' He moved restlessly and their bare thighs touched. He glanced down at her again. 'I'm not sure this is very conducive to a confessional.'

Rose slid farther away from him. He was talking and he mustn't be distracted.

'You said you and your father had some sort of issues. I'm sure he cares about you.'

'Something happened in the past which still affects our relationship today, perhaps more than I think. Maybe a psychologist would say it was some sort of trauma and the start of the anger.' He shifted his position again, and she waited. 'I thought my father was having an affair with Justine Moreau whilst my mother was dying.'

Rose listened in stunned silence as he recounted the time of his mother's illness when he was young and what he thought he had observed. He described his silent slow-burning anger, and yet the inability to speak out about it to his father, and how the situation led to a rift between them. Even now, despite his father's recent explanation of the circumstances, he still had lingering doubts. 'It might have been better if he had told me about my mother's illness earlier, and I could have spent more time with her; time I will never have back and perhaps to adjust to the whole situation.

I made the decision not to go into the family law firm in part due to my feelings toward him. I changed career direction to business studies and eventually started my own company. It became my focus; all-consuming. Looking back, I suppose it would have been better to have had a frank and honest discussion with him. I think he was hurt when I went my own way, but at the time I didn't care.'

On hearing his words, for a moment Rose became worried about the steps she had taken after Simon had first come to her. However, knowing the response she had received, something told her he must be mistaken in his views.

'Simon, I'm sure you're wrong. I cannot begin to believe that your father is the type of man who would behave in the callous way you have suggested; nor do I believe it of Madame Moreau. She was so caring of Joanna. Remember, they are both shouldering a great deal of responsibility for her, but I think this also shows a great regard for you. I understand they are to be married shortly. How will you deal with that, for Joanna as well? So far, she doesn't appear to have made the connection that if you are not her real father, then she also doesn't have grandparents.'

He sat up and stared down at her. 'God, I'd not thought of that! If she should work it out… but I won't let that happen. I'll work as hard as I can to keep the connection, whatever it costs.' He swore under his breath. 'I can't cope with much more of this soul searching.'

She felt his fingertips brushing aside the strands of long dark hair curling around her breasts, and then his lips were on her skin. As daylight began to flood into the room, she wrapped herself around him, welcoming his advance.

Chapter Twenty-Four

Over the next few days, they found mutual pleasure in just being together and time ceased to matter.

Rose began to feel that some of Simon's tension was easing, and there was no longer the lost, uncertain look in his eyes. At other times, however, he was quiet, and she guessed his thoughts were still distracted. Should she ask more questions, or was she now prying just for her own sake?

They were sitting on the stools at the breakfast bar, still in bathrobes, having eaten an impromptu meal, when she found the courage to try.

'Simon, have you any idea what went wrong between you and Olivia?' He would either answer her, she thought, or brush the query aside.

He turned to face her. 'I've wondered myself. After we started living together it somehow seemed sensible to marry. I was pushing to build my business and things like dinner parties were socially advantageous contact points, particularly with a good hostess. Olivia was in no way domesticated so they were for the most part professionally organised, but very…discreet, things like a chartered yacht at Monaco and a New Year's weekend in Scotland. I should perhaps have seen her lack of domesticity as a warning. Olivia loved her fashion work and was often away;

far too much. Then again, perhaps so was I. Her reaction to the pregnancy confused me. Not only that it had happened at all, but also I couldn't understand her genuine horror. For the last weeks before the birth she booked herself into a private hospital, and I was actually in the States when Joanna was born. She was a week old when I first saw her. I think it was then I finally accepted we had become totally incompatible. She obviously wanted her career and not a family; something we should have sorted out from the beginning, I suppose. I just assumed and assumed wrongly. Her lack of any affection or interest in Joanna was incomprehensible to me at the time, and perhaps I over-compensated. That was why Carlisle's discovery was so shocking to me. However, I was determined that even if I had been taken for a fool, Joanna would not be the one to pay.'

He studied her for a moment, and Rose couldn't read his expression. 'Perhaps that's why professional women have such a dilemma – marriage; job; children. Which do they choose, or can they have it all? What about you, Rose? I can vouch for the fact that you're an excellent cook, and you seem to enjoy the process.'

'Yes, I do. At home I became aware that if I wanted to eat regularly, I would have to learn how to cook.'

He raised an eyebrow in question. 'Did you not...'

'Oh, don't get me wrong, my mother is wonderful, but a cook she is not. Once she's outside in her garden, mealtimes are rarely on the agenda.' She knew she would have to explain. 'My parents agreed many years ago to follow separate lives, but they are still fond of each other.'

'I see. Rather unconventional, but perhaps for some it works. You're a beautiful woman; hasn't any man made you desire another kind of lifestyle?'

What sort of answer did he want? She could make a shallow throw-away comment, but he had been so open about his own inner thoughts that Rose considered she owed him honesty in her own. She now found herself struggling to remember the details of her other relationships. Each one had seemed so important at the time, but since meeting Simon they now seemed distant memories, such had been his impact on her, especially during these last few days. Then a feeling of cold dread crept over her. Was she the sort of woman always moving from one affair to the next? She wouldn't deny she had enjoyed her career and its challenges, but deep inside she wanted to be with a man she cared for, build a proper relationship with and yes, she wanted a home and the extra closeness that children would bring. She then acknowledged to herself that she wanted these simple pleasures with this man, getting to know all the small things on a daily basis, trying to understand him, something she had never even considered with the other men in her life. From the beginning it was as if she had found a part of her that had somehow been missing, a deep connection, and she was certain that this feeling would grow.

He had been quiet, watching her, but again she couldn't read his expression. It worried her, as she felt it was important. However, with enormous effort she began to tell him about Paulo and the problem with his rigid Italian family connections, indicating that because of this she could understand Simon's own Spanish difficulties. Then as she told him about Max, she realised that although there had been tears on both occasions it was more her pride which had been hurt. There had been no pining for either man; no "what might have been" and now they seemed insubstantial, something in the past. It was a form of release to have spoken about them. Feeling gentle fingers on her cheek she looked up into Simon's anxious face. She had no idea she had shed tears.

'Don't cry, Rose. I knew from the beginning someone had hurt you. From what you've just told me neither man was worth any of your tears; but I believe you also know that yourself now. I think you do want more out of a relationship.'

She nodded; glad now that she had told him the truth.

He stood and glanced out of the window. 'It looks a reasonable day out there. Shall we go for a walk? I think we could do with some fresh air.' He smiled at her, for the first time a proper genuine smile, full of pleasure and warmth.

Later, as hand in hand they left the flat, a young man further up the road on the opposite pavement followed them, reaching for his phone.

*

Charles McDonald placed the file he had been reading back on his desk and shifted the phone to his other ear.

'That's good to hear, Emile. Not before time, though, we really need him back here now. Everything's coming together and we must get it all signed off. The press is clamouring for some answers, as well.'

The voice at the other end sounded sharp. 'I don't care what anybody wants. If we drag him back too soon, he could go under again. Fletcher says all his reports are that this is the first time he's been seen out. It's a start, but I'd like him to make the first move. He'll do it when he's ready. He's obviously not keeping up with any news yet.'

'What about contacting Miss McKenna and asking her opinion?'

'I promised her we would handle everything and not involve her. If Simon found she had been in contact with me behind his back it would destroy any confidence he might now have in her. I gave my word and I'll stick by it. Let's give it a few more days.'

'OK, Emile, until the end of the week, but I may have to move after that. I'd like to be able to resurrect something from this mess. How's Joanna?'

'She seems to be all right, one or two tantrums, but no nightmares or flashbacks. She knows about the wedding and Justine is involving her as much as possible. We both talk about Simon in her presence. Yesterday she asked if he was coming to the wedding. She didn't appear to have any adverse reaction when we told her that of course he was. I think it would be good for him to be with her again and start getting back to normal.'

'Amen to that, Emile. I'll keep things quiet, as much as I can, and perhaps we can talk again early next week.'

'That's fine, Charles. I'm sure Simon will be grateful for all the help you and Stuart have given to sort this out.'

McDonald gave a laugh. 'Perhaps we're just looking out for our jobs. Bye Emile.'

*

In the darkness Rose lay in the warm bed, listening to the sleet pattering against the window. Simon was curled up against her with his head on her shoulder, still fast asleep.

Over these last few days, she had observed a change in him which was causing her some apprehension. She was seeing flashes of the incisive businessman returning. Of course, she was happy about this, but it might also mean that his need for her was not so great. Having said that, there had also been changes in other ways; his more ready smile, and warm looks, and in bed there was still passion but now it was also tinged with a delicious sweetness, as if he really cared. She told herself not to read too much into this, but it was difficult.

Yesterday he had spent a lot of time making notes on paper she had provided for him, and for the first time he had used his phone; not to make a call but obviously finding information. Since being with her he had not been interested in any news bulletins, and she had managed to stop the daily newspaper delivery, but his mind was obviously refocusing itself on something. She wondered whether to contact Emile Deveraux but decided against it; knowing her decision was made for selfish reasons.

As her eyes had now adjusted to the early morning light she looked down at the dark head and lightly touched his cheek. He sighed and nuzzled into the soft skin of her breast. She stroked the hair at his temple and noticed one or two silver strands. He had already accomplished so much in his life and appeared to have tried his best but, in some ways, fate had not been kind to him. She wanted to wrap him in a warm cocoon and keep him from any further hurt; but it wasn't her life to live and with an ache inside she knew she might have to let him go.

At that moment the sleet rattled at the window again as if something was trying to force its way in to take him from her.

*

The next morning, he seemed quiet, and she sensed he wanted to say something to her and found the waiting unbearable. She had washed her hair and was trying to brush out the tangles when he came back into the bedroom. He smoothed the hair away and kissed the nape of her neck.

'Do you mind if I make some phone calls today, Rose?'

She looked back at him through the mirror. Knowing this would have to come, she tried not to show her unease. 'Mind, why should I mind? I need to go for some groceries later, so you can have some peace.' She didn't admit that she found the prospect of listening to him pick up his life again was painful.

He sat on the side of the bed. 'There are some unfinished things I want to do for Amy, and I feel perhaps I ought to do the decent thing and contact the office.'

'You might also think about ringing your father and speaking to Joanna.' She hadn't meant the words to sound as a criticism, but he must have picked up on her tone. In the mirror she saw him glance up at her.

'I'm aware of that, Rose, and it was also my intention to do so.'

She heard disapproval in his voice and knew she would have to be careful not to show her real feelings. 'I'd better dry my hair and then I can be off.'

As he left the room she was nearly in tears. This was the first time there had been any unpleasant exchange between them and she longed to run after him and explain, but she knew that would leave her open to all sorts of further pain.

261

She tried to stay away shopping for as long as she could, but eventually she let herself back into the flat. He came to greet her. She could see how energised he seemed, his eyes bright and alive. He took her into his arms.

'You've been gone a long time. I was getting worried about you.' He kissed her. 'I've missed you.'

His words warmed her heart, but she would have to steel herself for what he might tell her in response to his telephone calls.

'Oh, by the way there's some mail for you.' He pointed to the breakfast bar. 'One from Australia by the looks of it.'

She knew who it would be from, but something made her hesitate to tell him.

Over lunch he said that he had spoken to his father. There had been no reference made to his absence, just a query about his general welfare. Joanna, it appeared, was out with Justine – wedding preparations. Since arriving in France, she had been fascinated by Madame Moreau's fashion shop and workroom, and was now a favourite with the seamstresses there, and known as the 'Petite Madame'. His father had said he would be sure to tell her that Simon had rung to speak with her. They were looking forward to him coming out to France. He said that Joanna knew he would be coming and hadn't raised any queries.

Rose considered that a good sign and told him so. He didn't say anything further about any other calls he had made, and it was later in the day before he said he wanted to speak to her. Trying to keep calm she went with him into the sitting room.

'I want to do something useful as a permanent reminder of Amy; the problem is I'm not sure if the idea is feasible. I have spoken to Harriet Freeman, the headmistress at Carlton House, and we have agreed to look into the possibility of setting up some sort of foundation to assist young people with practical help on how to further a career in music. It isn't intended for music tuition itself, but information on how to obtain funding, if required, and the various ways to access this type of career; help which Amy herself would have benefitted from. I have friends I'm going to approach to see if they wish to be part of the idea. What do you think?'

Rose knew instinctively that his personal money would be involved. He was still trying to make amends for the guilt he felt about Amy. She smiled up at him. 'I think it's a wonderful idea. However much talent a person might have, it needs to be channelled in the right way, or setbacks and rejection can lead to disillusionment. I hope it's a success for you.'

He planted a kiss on her forehead. 'Thank you, Rose. I spoke about it to my legal head, Charles McDonald, and he's getting someone he knows to look into how we go about setting it up. Quite honestly, I was surprised that, like my father, he appeared to take my absence so calmly. I had expected to be hauled over the coals for disappearing like that.'

Rose was relieved that so far everyone had kept their word in not mentioning her involvement. She had no idea how Simon might view her interference in his affairs, although it had been intended for the best of reasons.

'From what Charles said it looks, for the most part, as if matters with Orion have pretty much been sorted out. I'd like to explain everything to you, but other authorities are involved, and it's not supposed to be common knowledge. I have a feeling though, it won't be too long before someone in the press breaks the story. Charles wants me in the office tomorrow, some things need signing. I'll have to go.'

Rose felt compelled to make a remark. 'Don't let them keep you too long. It might—'

His mouth covered hers, stopping any further comment. 'I know. Thank you for worrying. It shouldn't take long. When I get back, we'll go out to lunch. Would you like that?'

Happy with anything which kept him by her side, Rose just nodded, but a small voice warned her that he might find it all too easy to pick up his world again.

*

Dressed and ready to leave for their lunch, by two o'clock there was still no sign of Simon. Rose knew that she must make a decision. This was what she had feared the most; he was himself again and no longer needed her, but had it ever been more than a temporary loss of confidence on his part? She remembered moments of incredible intimacy and the tender feelings between them, the sense of belonging and mutual caring. Could it have all been one-sided, in her own imagination? He was an experienced man, and had given her more pleasure than she had ever known, but were those acts she took for tenderness nothing of the kind? She found it hard to believe; he had seemed as caught up in the swirl of emotion as she had been.

What would happen now? Would they stay lovers for a while and then drift apart, as with Paulo? This time it would be so different. The pain inside her at the thought was more than she could bear. There was no way she could deal with it, not this time. Simon would notice and there would be embarrassment, even recriminations. After all, he had made no promises to her. There was also the possibility that what had happened with Amy would always be there in his mind, like another constant presence. No, this time she must save herself, whatever the cost.

She was packed, the note written, a taxi ordered – everything done in a haze of misery, when she heard a car draw up outside. It was too soon for her taxi and she moved to the window – in time to see Simon climbing out of a red sports car. Her heart missed a beat. She had hoped to be gone before he arrived. She had lent him her key and as she heard the door open her legs turned to jelly.

He burst into the sitting room, but she kept her back turned, not wanting to face him yet.

'Rose, I'm so sorry. I never intended to be...'

She finally turned and saw him looking at the luggage, confusion on his face. She had to get this over with. 'The letter from Australia was from a... friend. I'd been waiting to hear about an opportunity. I've decided to take advantage of it. I've a flight booked, and a taxi is on its way.' She pointed to the coffee table. 'I had left you a note, explaining. You're welcome to stay here. Just put the key back through the letterbox when you leave. There's food in the fridge.' She could hear herself babbling, and knew the tears were near. Then a car horn sounded outside – her taxi. She bent to pick up her cases and chanced a look up at him. His face appeared calm and still with no expression, but his eyes held some strange emotion. Her own were beginning to swim with tears. She must go now, or she never would.

'Goodbye, Simon. I hope everything works out well for you. Say hello to your father and Joanna for me.'

She somehow made it out of the flat and down to the waiting taxi before the tears started to flow.

'It's the airport, miss, isn't it?'

'Er, yes… no. Could you just drive around for a while, please.'

Thoughts ran around in her head. Perhaps she ought to have stayed instead of running away. Maybe she could have made it work. Why hadn't he said something; attempted to stop her leaving.

Trying to staunch her tears, ignoring the concerned looks of the driver, she needed time to think. She knew she would end up at her usual bolt-hole, but she would take the long way home. By then she would have herself in some sort of order before she arrived.

'Could you take me to Euston Station, please?'

In her head she spoke to her friend. I did find a rich, sexy man, Gwenny, but I ended up breaking my own heart.

*

Jack Fletcher coasted his car further down the road and, in the gathering darkness of late afternoon, saw Andy near the corner, stamping his feet. He grinned to himself. Carl had been given some time off 'to see his girlfriend before he forgot what she looked like' and Andy had volunteered. With the weather as it was today, Jack considered he would have to treat him to a pint or something stronger. He drew up beside him, leant over and opened the passenger door.

'Hop in, mate. Our lad's on top form again, so we can wrap this up from now on. I'll treat you to a drop of something to warm you.' He noticed Andy looking back up the road and then following the passage of a taxi as it came past. 'Come on, boy, get in. It's perishing cold.'

As Andy sank into the passenger seat, he was looking puzzled. 'You just brought Deveraux back, didn't you? The girl's just left, on her own, in that taxi. She had luggage with her. Seems a bit odd; did he say anything about it?'

'Not to me. I offered him a lift, only to wait for the last hour, parked outside a jeweller's like a damn getaway car. I got the impression he was after something for her. You're right though, it does seem a little odd. We'd better take a look.'

He carefully reversed down the length of the road and parked opposite the flat. In the darkness, with the curtains still open they could see into the lighted room.

'He's standing there with his coat on, just staring. I don't like it, Jack.'

'Oh hell!'

Chapter Twenty-Five

The small parking area was empty as Simon coasted the Mercedes to a stop. It was nearly too dark to see down to the stream, but this suited his purpose. Without giving himself any time to think he retrieved the small box from the back seat and moved off down the path. How different it looked tonight from the hot summer day when they had enjoyed their picnic. He shivered in the cold wind and increased his pace.

Having performed his duty, he retraced his steps to the car. Once again in the comparative warmth of the vehicle, he leant back in the driver's seat and closed his eyes. He felt weary beyond belief. These last few days had been manic in his workload, but he knew the reason he needed to keep busy, and he must not think about it now – but in this quiet spot his mind refused to obey him.

He could still remember seeing the luggage, and then her face, pale and racked with some deep emotion. He had found it impossible to process what she was telling him, apart from one stark fact – she was leaving! The blow was so tremendous he was incapable of speech, and worse, he could feel the chasm opening up under his feet again. He needed her – but she was going – and then she was gone, leaving only the faint aroma of her perfume to taunt him. Why had it happened so suddenly? He'd thought she was happy, as he had been, as happy as he had ever imagined he could be.

Then he had heard the doorbell. Had she come back after all? Dare he move, without falling down into the blackness – a blackness which this time would surely swallow him? The bell rang again, and he turned round and stumbled to the door. He vaguely registered Jack Fletcher standing there with Andy Sinclair behind him. He heard them speaking to him but didn't understand the words. He watched as if at a distance as they spoke together, concern on their faces, and he only began to react when later he found himself back at the company flat, with Jack telling him in no uncertain terms to accept the proffered drink.

Somehow that night he had slept, although he had been aware of Jack's hovering presence. The next day he had woken and known that to save himself he had to accept what had happened and move his life on, as hard as that had seemed. So he had showered, dressed, and, adopting the attitude of a man in control, presented himself at the office, with Jack in close company. Some warning had obviously preceded his arrival, as first Susan and then Charles had treated him as if he was a sick child. Their solicitous attitude might have been funny if he had felt like laughing, but he didn't feel... anything.

During an initial discussion with Charles, he was taken through the formal reports on the surprising events which had taken place in Brazil but, somehow, they now seemed unimportant. Of more concern was the final result of the FCA investigation. One or two suggestions had been made, none of which surprised him. He had already made plans for some changes which would take account of their comments. It became obvious that Charles, Stuart and their respective senior staff had handled the matter impeccably and all he was required to do was sign a formal letter accepting the report. He then called in Stuart Mannion and went on to explain to both of them his thoughts about the future of Orion. He outlined his intention to cease any foreign exposure and concentrate on a UK- only standalone company. In order to achieve this, he told them, over a period of time he intended to withdraw his own personal funding in Orion and also relinquish control of its day-to-day running. He saw the exchange of looks and went on to explain that he was, in essence, handing the company over to them, only retaining a role as an independent paid consultant if they so required. He also assured them that any financial withdrawal would be done at a rate whereby it could easily be recouped by them. This revelation caused even more reaction, but he could see from their facial expressions that they were already starting to think about future possibilities.

Typically, it was Charles who made the first comment. 'That sounds fine for us, but what about you? You're a little young to go into retirement, boy, or are you thinking of starting up something else and possibly trying to compete?'

'I'm going to give myself some thinking time, see what I want to do. The new foundation will take up a lot of my time, and I still have connections with Orloff. When all the South American monies are sorted out and handed back, I'll resurrect the Azerbaijan deal with him. I've also spoken with Jack Fletcher, and I've agreed to finance the setting up of a proper security firm with him and his people. He's going back to Australia for a week or two, but we'll get together again in the New Year. Who knows, I might even suggest to Tony Broadbent we jointly compile a book on how not to run a business.' No-one else seemed to think the remark funny, and in truth neither did he, but there was maybe something in the idea. 'I don't want to get myself tied down with managing a big operation again, Charles. It doesn't leave time for anything else, and I have Joanna to think about.' He sensed they understood his meaning. He went on to impress upon them how indebted he was for their support and hard work both before and during these last months and hoped the proposed changes would serve as some recompense. He said he would draft an appropriate memo to all staff and arrange a full meeting with key members. Clients still with the firm would also be advised of the changes.

He had made time to speak with Sir Arthur, who confirmed

that the Brazilian authorities were about to make public their stance on the whole de Santos matter. They were preparing to take action against those seen to have covered up or profited from his illegal dealings, past and present. The two dummy companies had already been wound up, and Simon's deposit would soon be made available. Likewise, Hernandez was assisting the authorities in facilitating the return of the ransom monies with his knowledge of its onward movement. Brazil would be applying for his extradition, as might Colombia. It would be up to a court to decide if this could be granted or if his activities in the UK meant he had to stand trial here. Simon hoped that the man would be extradited. He would no doubt receive a custodial sentence somewhere in South America, and as far as he was concerned, that would serve just as well as punishment for his activities in this country.

Sir Arthur also said that a brief joint statement had now been agreed by all parties involved and would shortly be released to the press, which would infer invaluable financial expertise in bringing the matter to a head. This, Sir Arthur felt, when people worked out what was actually being said between the lines, would go some way to clearing up both his and Orion's position. Simon agreed that this was very welcome as far as Orion was concerned. The financial mauling the company had received over the last few months had been more than he had anticipated. Sir Arthur then told him that in this regard Orion might soon find itself the recipient of various business approaches. From somewhere deep inside Simon found anger welling up. There was no way he was going to profit from all the pain this whole matter had caused.

'Arthur, whether it offends you or not, if I suspect that any of these are linked, I'm not prepared to deal with them.'

'I think you are making a grave mistake, Simon. This could help repair some of the damage and recoup losses.'

'I don't want to discuss it any further, Arthur. Orion will operate by itself, not with handouts from grateful nations.'

When he had informed Susan of the up-coming changes to

the firm, she immediately made it clear that she would not wish to stay on once he had left. This was something he was glad to hear, and gave him an opportunity to put forward his proposal.

'Actually, this is something I was hoping you might say, as I wondered if you would feel able to accept a role in a new foundation I hope to start. It is intended to be run from an office being set up within Carlton House. There will be accommodation provided. I would very much welcome your expertise in assisting me in such a new venture.'

He could see that she appeared interested and flattered by his request. She promised him an early decision, and he had the feeling that she would accept.

Leaving London this afternoon he had called on the Angelous, and informed them of his foundation idea, wondering if Julia would be prepared to offer her assistance. They both seemed enthusiastic about being involved and Julia said she would speak with others who might also be interested. They had asked him to stay for the night, but he knew he had one more duty to perform.

So now, this also was complete. His last for Amy; and he hoped she would have approved. He remembered how much she had enjoyed their day here. For some strange reason he found himself reluctant to just drive away and leave her in the cold and dark on her own. Glancing at his watch he confirmed there was time to spare. He reached out and turned on the radio, then leaned back in the seat, closing his eyes. Music filled the interior, and as he listened the sounds flowed through him, evoking delicate images, almost ethereal, as if from another world, and the more he listened the more he was sure that Amy was now happy and at peace. He shook his head at such thoughts and looked down at the display on the dashboard. What was it he was listening to? Elgar's "Symphony No. 1", third movement. The words meant nothing to him, but he also knew that he would not forget it. He sat up and started the car. As he drove away, he knew he would not be coming back to this spot again.

He was staying in Dover tonight and catching the early

morning ferry to France. He now had to concentrate on important matters there – but after that? There was something he had to do; he had to be sure.

*

It was just after twelve noon on Christmas Eve and Simon stood watching the wedding guests milling around the buffet. The civil ceremony had taken place an hour ago in a private suite at the same hotel where he was staying. Although being offered accommodation with his father and Justine, he had considered it prudent not to accept, rather than risk any problems arising to spoil their occasion. So far Joanna had been polite to him but quieter than he remembered. He himself had made an enormous effort to treat her no differently than before and not make a special fuss.

He knew for certain that today he had been immensely proud of her. She had been given the role of sole bridesmaid and, in his view, had handled this to perfection, taking the bride's small bouquet when required and even being given responsibility for a tiny box containing the two rings. The bride looked stylish, dressed in a lavender suit and feather-trimmed hat. Joanna was wearing a frothy white dress with a wide cummerbund and large bow in matching lavender. To his untutored eye she looked the picture of every young girl's dream.

The small number of guests were mostly unknown to him, friends of the bride, but he vaguely remembered an elderly couple who had flown over from Montreal. They had spoken to him earlier and he began to recall them visiting his parents' house when he was young. While speaking to them the wife had made a telling remark, which had resonated with him.

'I'm sure Helene is resting easier, knowing that Justine and Emile are looking after each other so well. I know she was worried about how he would cope, with you also being away. Justine was such a good friend of your mother; I'm sure they have both needed comfort from each other. This is the ideal outcome, don't you think?'

Looking across at his smiling father circulating through their friends with his hand tucked into the arm of his new wife, Simon could do nothing but agree.

He felt a tug at his coat sleeve and found Joanna beside him.

'Grandma Justine said that as I had been so good, I could have an icecream.' She wrinkled her nose. 'I don't like some of the other things to eat.'

The chocolate confection in the small bowl was rapidly melting in the warm room as she waved a spoon towards her new grandmother. 'Did you know that I helped design the hat? I drew some pictures and the sewing ladies put all the feathers on just as I wanted.' The spoon came back towards her mouth for another lick, but its contents slid off and fell on her black patent shoes, and also the carpet. Simon reached for a pile of napkins and bent down to clean up the mess. Looking up, he encountered an anxious gaze; she was obviously waiting for him to be angry with her. It was on the tip of his tongue to do just that; she ought to have been more careful, it could have spilled down her dress, and there were still photographs to come, but he heard *her* quiet voice from only a week or so ago making the suggestion that, if he felt angry, he should take a split second to think before he said or did anything. He smiled up at the child as he rubbed at the carpet, and saw her expression change to relief. He felt good; after all, it was no big deal. Wiping her hands with some more napkins, he felt a hand on his shoulder.

'Having a good time?' His father looked from one to the other. 'I'm afraid I'm going to take my bridesmaid back; we have to take some photographs.' He regarded Simon for a moment and then added, 'By the way, I'm sure it would be much more convenient if you were staying with us instead of the hotel.' He gazed down at Joanna. 'Do you think that would be a good idea?'

She looked up at Simon and then said, 'Yes, I can show you all my new things.'

Without giving Simon a chance to comment, his father went on, 'After the first photographs, why don't you go down and organise things with the hotel and get your belongings packed, and you can follow us back when we leave.'

After enduring an obligatory photograph or two Simon went down to the main foyer to speak to the concierge about his luggage and bill. He heard a male voice that he thought he recognised, and turned, trying to locate the person. A man of about his own age was standing a few yards away with a small party. Just as Simon located him the man in question turned and spotted him also.

'Good God! Simon, of all people.'

Simon moved over to him and held out his hand. 'Gerry, nice to see you again.' Gerald Bristow had been in his class at business college. He came from a well-connected English family, but Simon remembered him as a down-to-earth, sensible young man, perhaps slightly bookish, although the need for glasses accentuated that impression. He had proved to have an outstanding grasp on economics and, Simon thought, with his connections had probably ended up in the Civil Service. During their time at college, they had socialised together on many occasions and Simon's lasting impression was of a pleasant colleague.

'Are you staying here, Simon, or just passing through? Perhaps trying to keep away from the UK press? I read all that rubbish about you. A bit more truth is coming out now, I believe.' Behind the thick lenses the eyes were shrewd. 'Someone approached me about my thoughts on possibly pulling out of Orion. I told them not to be so daft, you were solid.'

Simon smiled. 'Thanks for that, Gerry. It wasn't pleasant, but maybe we're over the worst now. I'm actually in France for the holiday. My father was married for the second time here this morning. We're just about to leave.'

Gerry turned his head and indicated his own party, standing to one side. 'My in-laws have a special anniversary, so I thought

I'd push the boat out. Got to keep them happy! I'm settled in France now. Look, why don't we get together.' He pulled out a small card from the inside pocket of his jacket and handed it over. 'Give me a call after Christmas and we'll fix something up.' He looked over Simon's shoulder. 'Looks like your folks are coming. Sweet little girl. Yours?'

Simon just nodded. 'I'll be in touch, Gerry. Thanks. Have a good holiday.'

*

Although the newlyweds were not intending to take a break until the spring, they had decided that they would like to attend midnight mass that evening. There were household staff; a housekeeper-cook and a young maid who could keep an eye on Joanna in her grandparents' absence, but Simon said he felt happier to remain at the house. Out of Joanna's hearing, his father pointed out to him where presents had been secreted and suggested that he could play Father Christmas and place them round the tree when Joanna was safely asleep.

After joining everyone for a light dinner, Joanna said she would show him her room. There was evidence of storage boxes in one corner, which Simon noticed immediately. It was obvious she was preparing her things for the move with her grandparents to another property in the New Year. Simon tried to hide any disappointment he felt at this, knowing he must think long-term. After all, he had sanctioned that in the New Year Joanna would attend an international school in the city. It had excellent reports and Simon agreed with his father that it might benefit Joanna to mix with a wider selection of other children. Since her move to France, she had been receiving long-distance tuition from Carlton House, and the evidence of this he saw strewn around the room. He had to bite back a comment about tidying up the mess and watched as, having now changed out of her special dress, she sat on the floor, showing him how she did her work.

'I like drawing and colouring best. When I'm older I am going to design dresses. Grandma Justine likes a lot of things I've drawn. Her sewing ladies like them too and I watch them when they make clothes.'

'You need to try hard at other subjects as well, you know.' Simon was aware that her present enthusiasm might not last, and that she would also need to concentrate in other areas. 'After all, your grandmother has to know where countries are in the world so she can buy materials and contact clients. She also has to be good at arithmetic so she can work out what to charge and do her accounts at the shop. There are a lot of things you have to be good at if you run a business.'

'Yes… I suppose so. I'll speak to Mr Floppy about it.' In an obvious effort to change the subject, which amused him slightly, she commented, 'Did you know I already have a present from Father Christmas? It's under the tree. Come and see it.'

He followed her back downstairs. The tree was in the large entrance hall, its lights now switched on and creating a sea of colour. Joanna rummaged at the bottom and pulled out a large box.

'A big man with a grey beard and a fur hat brought it the other day. He said he was helping Father Christmas because he had so much to do.'

Simon was a little disturbed at the idea of a strange delivery for her and inspected the parcel with care.

'Grandpa was here when it arrived, and he and the man talked together. The man had nice smiley eyes, but he spoke in a funny way.'

Simon began to have an inkling of who the man might have been and relaxed slightly. After all, his father would not have accepted an unknown delivery in the house had he not been sure of its authenticity.

'Do you think he really was helping Father Christmas? I thought he had elves for that, and anyway, how did he know that I now live here?'

Simon looked up at the star on the tree and remembered the evening in the London flat. *Don't spoil illusions.* 'Well, I'm sure Father Christmas needs all the help he can get. Even with the elves it must still be a very big task to reach all the children. I also think he's used to people changing addresses and has some sort of system to work it out. Let's put the parcel back for now.' He wanted it out of sight in case curiosity about its contents was too much for the child. 'This tree looks splendid. Did you help with the decoration?'

'Yes, but Grandpa fixed up the star. I like it better than a fairy.'

Without thinking Simon said, 'Amy made a wish on a star when we were in London.'

'What did she wish for?'

He shouldn't have said anything, but it was too late now. 'I don't know, Joanna. If you make a wish it has to be kept secret.'

'I miss her.'

The words were quiet, but he felt every one of them. 'So do I, Joanna. When I was with her in the hospital, I told her how much we all thought of her. She said you had been very brave, and I felt so proud of you, just as I did today. It's such a shame she didn't know she was poorly until Uncle Henry found out, but by then the doctors couldn't help her. We must make sure we never forget her.'

He felt a small hand creep into his own. 'Shall we call the star 'Amy's Star' and then we will remember every Christmas.'

He squeezed her hand. 'I think that would be a very nice idea.'

'When we were with those bad men, she was angry with me when I told her about you... well, you know. She said I was naughty because you had taken such good care of me all these years. I've been thinking and talking to Mr Floppy. If you're not my daddy, then Grandpa isn't my real grandpa either, and that makes me sad.'

Simon's heart sank. So she *had* worked it out. What could he say? 'Joanna, it doesn't matter what anybody is called, what matters is that they love you and care for you. I love you and I always will. When you were a baby, I gave you your name. I hope you like it. Your Grandpa loves you and now you have Grandma Justine who loves you as well. We could all be happy together, and I'm sure Amy would like that.'

She let go of his hand and looked up at him for a moment. 'I'll talk to Mr Floppy about it again. It's so difficult to understand.' She then turned and walked back upstairs.

Simon felt drained. He heard voices from another part of the house but needed to be by himself. He, too, walked back upstairs to his room. He sat on his bed and pulled out a long thin box from his briefcase. He let the bright contents slide through his fingers. Never had he felt quite so alone.

Chapter Twenty-Six

Unsure how much time had elapsed as he sat and gazed at the shifting pool of light in his hand, Simon heard a light knock on his door. He went to open it and found his new step-mother outside, now wearing a warm winter coat, obviously ready to leave for church.

'Am I interrupting you? I just wanted to say that we will be leaving shortly. Joanna is in bed and half-asleep already. Jeanette said that she will be available until we arrive back if you need anything.' She appeared to hesitate. 'Would you mind if I spoke with you for a moment?'

'No, of course not.' He stood aside and she moved past him. He pulled out a small chair for her and sat back on the bed.

'I know there have been difficulties between us, but for Emile's sake I want to put this at an end.'

Simon was about to make a remark, but she held up a hand to stop him.

'I care deeply for your father. He is a good man and deserves to be happy. I want him to be happy with his son and his granddaughter, and I will do all I can to bring that about. To this end I need to make you understand what happened all those years ago. I know he has tried but I am still not sure you believe.' She hurried on before he could make any comment. 'As you know, Helene and I were friends at school and then college. My childhood was... unhappy, and she was my confidante and rock. I was so pleased when she and Emile married, I could see they were right for each other. I was already working in the retail fashion world when I met my husband at a trade show in Toronto. He was based in France, so I moved there with him, but as a foursome we all tried to keep in touch. I didn't know about Helene's illness until Emile wrote to me. I immediately returned to see her and was shocked at what I found. She was worried about you knowing quite how ill she was, because of your education, and she begged Emile not to tell you until it became necessary. I could see how it was affecting him, too. I wanted to stay but I knew I had responsibilities of my own. I never imagined that a few weeks later I, myself, would be a widow. The Paris traffic is always bad, but because of a drunk driver, an innocent man paid the price. Even with Helene's circumstances, Emile did what he could to help me, and I will always be grateful to him for that. I put my business on hold because I knew I wanted to be with Helene for the end. She had done so much for me all those years before; I needed to repay that somehow. She confided in me that she was worried how Emile and her 'wonderful' son would cope. She made it quite plain that she would be happy if – how did she put it – as I was free again, we might be able to become close and look after each other. I later understood that she said much the same to Emile. He loved his wife, as I had loved my husband, but at times like this, as I had already experienced, we all need mutual comfort. I think you must have witnessed something of this and drew your own conclusions. Simon, I swear to you, nothing improper took place between us at that time, nor did we even think of it. Emile couldn't understand your change of attitude, and over the years we have spoken about it often. He repeated over and over how much he cared for you and how proud he was of your success, built up on your own, not inherited from him. As time went by, we found being so far apart on two continents was strengthening our feelings of affection; it was only at that time we began any closer association. On a visit a year ago, Emile made the suggestion of his moving to France. I had no say in the matter. I felt he had already made the decision. He said he hoped that this way, not only would we be able to be closer together, but he might also see more of you and Joanna. I swear all I have just told you is the truth. I like to think that Helene is happy that her wish has been fulfilled.'

Simon gave a deep sigh. Something of what she had said echoed inside him; the loneliness of being apart. He looked up and smiled at her. 'I do understand, finally. Perhaps it was grief clouding my judgment at the time. However, I want you to know that I have always been grateful to my father for his interest in Joanna, considering the circumstances, even more so just lately.'

'Simon, we have tried to help because not only do we care for Joanna; we also care for you. You have needed help, and we were glad to be there. I'm sure, despite what you might think, you would have helped if we had required assistance. It's what families should do, and I know Emile and I would both like us all to be a family.'

Simon looked into her earnest face. 'I would be very happy if that were possible. Will you forgive my previous attitude and permit me to call you Justine?'

She reached out her hand and touched his knee. 'I would be delighted.' She glanced at the clock on his beside cabinet. 'I must go now, or we'll be late.'

As she stood, Simon also moved off the bed and the box by his side fell to the floor. The bracelet spilled out onto the carpet, casting flashes of light around the room. Justine bent and picked it up. She looked up at him. 'This is beautiful, so delicate. The flowers – roses, I think – are exquisite. A little too old for Joanna, and somehow I don't think it was purchased for me... but a special Christmas present for someone you care for?'

Simon took it from her and placed it back in its box. 'I'm sure... but the other party... I'm not so sure, Justine.'

She turned to leave but, in the doorway, hesitated and looked back at him for a long moment. 'I thought she was rather a lovely girl. Make sure Simon, don't just leave it. Our grasp on life can be so tenuous at times.'

As the door closed behind her, he sat back down on the bed, thinking again about the nagging doubt that had never left him.

*

Mercifully, Joanna woke at a reasonable hour, so the household was already prepared for the day ahead. After a sketchy breakfast, the presents were methodically dealt with, until only two remained. One was a slim A4-sized brown envelope, and the other the mystery parcel. Joanna decided to open the envelope first and appeared puzzled when she found inside two photographs and a typewritten letter, but as she read it a delighted smile began to form on her face.

'A dog! For me! Look, he's sent me a letter.' She looked again at the two photographs of a curly scrap of chocolate brown sitting in a basket.

'Joanna, this is not a present from Father Christmas,' Simon told her. 'This is just from Grandpa and Grandma Justine and me, as something extra for being such a good girl. An early birthday present, even. He's too small to leave his mother just yet, so you might have to wait a little longer. The new house has a big garden, and Grandpa and Grandma Justine don't mind him coming to live there, but,' Simon gave her a stern look, 'it's only fair you make sure that you look after him properly. Will you promise to do that?'

'Oh, yes, I will. I promise. Can I give him a name now?'

Her grandfather took the papers from her and looked at them. He was already prepared for the impending tornado as Simon had sought his views on the gift. 'One chewed chair leg, young lady, and he'll be outside in a kennel. So I'm relying on you to keep him under control.'

'Oh, I will, Grandpa. I will.'

'Hmm, we'll see. Perhaps you had better deal with this last item, it's nearly lunchtime.'

Joanna drew the box towards her and began to unwrap it. As she discovered the contents she sat very still. Simon became concerned and started to move towards her, but his father laid a hand on his arm. He watched as she slowly drew out a soft toy rabbit with long floppy ears, clothed in a blue flowered dress and a large bow. 'Mrs Floppy!' Her voice was a mere whisper. 'Oh, I've always wanted someone for him to talk to when I'm not here.' She stumbled to her feet and raced out of the room.

*

When lunch was announced a short while later, the three grownups found a painting by each of their place settings. They were handcrafted Christmas cards from Joanna, each one different and obviously created with painstaking care. Simon looked at his and noted what appeared to be a recent addition. The new words said, 'To Daddy'.

Somehow, his emotions in shreds, he worked his way through the splendid meal, but as soon as he could, he excused himself and went back up to his room. He picked up his phone and found the number he required. After a while it was answered.

'Jack? Happy Christmas to you as well…Yes, she's fine, so she should be with all her presents. She was pleased with yours. You'll find a thank you note waiting for you when you get back. Are your folks well? Good, I'm sure they've been pleased to see you again. Erm… look Jack, I wondered, if you had a moment, could you do something for me?'

*

Ireland – March 2011

The Irish countryside south of Monaghan blossomed green and

lush, but Simon's mind was on other things as he drove the rented saloon down the narrow lanes.

Since the beginning of the year, he had been frustrated that he still had commitments to deal with. At times he had found it necessary to impose an iron discipline over his wishes and thoughts.

His father's move to the villa on a leafy street in the Paris suburbs, convenient to Justine's business and Joanna's new school, had gone well. Joanna was delighted with her new room, and Justine, within reason, had left her to decide how she wanted to organise her things. One piece of serious advice was that, with the impending canine invasion, it might be better to have Mr and Mrs Floppy kept in a safe place. No-one in the house could imagine the ramifications if this treasured pair were mangled by sharp teeth. A carpenter was called in who built a mock house-like shelter on a wide shelf where the pair could reside in safety.

The new school was proving a hit, with grudging feedback on teachers but obvious excitement at the opportunity of, once again, mixing with other children.

One week after the arrival of Alphonse – nobody could dissuade Joanna from calling the poor scrap by a better name – Emile and Justine decided to leave for a two-week holiday and left Simon in sole charge. He had been assured that if he was worried about anything they would return immediately, but he had been determined that this would not happen. In fact, he found the time quite pleasant, more so than in the past at Woodhayes. He felt there was now a better rapport between himself and Joanna. On weekdays he would take her to school, before returning to the house to deal with work and then picking her up again in the afternoon. At weekends they went out into the surrounding countryside for long walks – Alphonse never seeming to tire, unlike the human companions. After a difficult session with a disgruntled gardener about the state of the flower border, it was agreed that some dog training classes would be a good idea and so it had proved. Joanna was thrilled to display to her grandparents on their return that Alphonse could already "sit" and "stay"– although her grandfather considered that this was only achieved if the animal decided there was no other course left open to it!

Simon had come to appreciate how relaxed he now felt in the family atmosphere. He was, however, keeping in touch with London and had made a couple of lightning visits back when required. His meeting with Gerald Bristow had proved useful, and interesting. Gerry had indeed gone into the Civil Service after college but had not felt at home. He met and married the daughter of a Swiss banking family but disliked the idea of becoming involved in yet another "dynasty" situation by going to work for his in-laws. He'd had enough with his own immediate family, he commented to Simon. So, with the backing of his new wife, he had started a business school in Paris, teaching mainly postgraduates. It was doing well after only two years, so much so that he was now looking to expand. On hearing how Simon was restructuring his life the proposition was put to him that he might like to take on a part-time lecturing role. Simon found the idea appealing, but left the option open for the time being. He wanted to discuss the proposed changes in his life with another person – and he couldn't wait to do so.

Still deep in thought, he nearly missed the turning onto the track leading towards an extended two-storey whitewashed stone cottage surrounded by a large garden displaying colour everywhere. His palms felt damp on the wheel as he parked next to a blue Mini. What happened next was going to be the most important event in his world right now. He would see *her* again! Taking a deep breath, he walked towards the front gate. He could feel his heart pounding.

*

Rose looked at her watch. She would have to hurry and get changed: her shift at the nursing home started soon. Clearing away the dinner things she removed a batch of scones from the oven, intended for tonight's meeting of helpers for her mother's first garden Open Day of the year on Sunday. Even her mother ought to be able to deal with something as simple as this for her guests, she thought! She went to the front door and stood on the top step of the porch, surveying the colour already clothing the garden, even this early in the year.

She called out, 'I'm just going to change, Mother. The scones are out of the oven, cooling; I'll leave you to put them in the container until tonight.' She heard a vague reply from somewhere close, but it was the sound of the front gate which caught her attention. She looked towards the sound – and her heart stopped. *He* was coming up the path towards her.

Over all of these months she had made a show of life being normal, but deep underneath was a well of emotion; pain and regret, and such loneliness as she had never experienced. Although in her dreams she had pictured, and hoped, for this moment, now it was happening she didn't know how to cope.

He stood in front of her at the bottom of the steps, casually dressed but looking… so wonderful. She wanted to fling herself into his arms, but that would betray her. What was he doing here? Perhaps he was only in Ireland on business, something to do with the dire economic situation in the country – but how had he known where to find her? She voiced the question out loud.

'What are you doing here?'

'Hello, Rose. You're a long way from Australia.'

There was an edge to his voice, and she sensed hurt, but it was probably her imagination.

'We need to talk.' He began to climb the steps towards her.

She wasn't prepared for his sudden appearance, and she had to buy some time. 'I can't stop now; I'm just leaving for work.' She turned and ran upstairs to her room. She must get away as soon as she could. With trembling hands, she removed her blouse and was stepping out of her skirt when she sensed movement behind her. He was there, standing in her bedroom doorway. She had left the door open in her haste. 'How dare you follow me! Please leave, can't you see I'm changing?' She felt vulnerable standing before him in her underwear. She reached for her uniform dress.

'You forget, I've seen you in considerably less.'

She turned to glare at him, fastening the belt around her slim waist, and reaching for her navy cardigan. 'That's hardly the point, and not the remark of a gentleman.'

He smiled slightly. 'Sweetheart, I've had many ungentlemanly thoughts about you.'

Grabbing her bag, she brushed past him and ran back down the stairs. She was aware of him following. As she left the house, she heard him call, 'Rose, wait.' Ignoring the plea, she started the Mini, pulled out past a small red saloon, and drove away down the lane.

Simon stopped at the gate and watched her disappear. In frustration he banged his fist down on the gatepost. From behind him he heard a voice say, 'Young man, would you care to come inside?'

Chapter Twenty-Seven

All afternoon Rose had tried to concentrate on her work, but at times it had become impossible. She kept remembering that awful journey from London on the train to Liverpool and then the ferry across to Dublin, before she rang her mother asking to be collected. Even her mother's obvious pleasure at her unexpected arrival only partially warmed her chilled body. Chilled not from the long and arduous journey, but from the knowledge of once having something precious, but now lost. She had to work hard to keep her emotions from spilling over; the journey had not, after all, been long enough to forget. She admitted to herself that she probably never would. Over the following weeks her mother had given her concerned glances but hadn't asked questions.

The clock remorselessly ticked round to six and she knew she would have to return home. At least her mother would be too busy tonight for any questions, but she would have to be prepared for tomorrow.

Arriving back at the house she was surprised not to see any other vehicles parked outside. She walked up the path and saw someone sitting on the top step. Her heart leapt into her mouth. He was still here! He stood as she approached, looking tall and almost menacing.

'Hello, Rose. Please don't run again. You know we must talk.'

She walked past him into the hall. Everywhere was quiet. She called out, 'Mother?'

'She's not here, Rose.'

She turned round on him. 'She must be: she had a meeting tonight.'

'I gather it's being held elsewhere.'

He was so close. She studied his face. He looked strained, thinner than she remembered, but the look in his eyes made her pulse beat fast and hard. She wanted to touch him, feel his warmth, but how could it happen, and not be hurt all over again. Tears started to threaten, and she closed her eyes. The light touch of his fingers on her cheek was more than she could bear, and she was in his arms, where she had wanted to be for so long. He stroked her hair, murmuring soft sweet words. After a moment or two he held her away from him, the blue eyes scanning her face. 'Your mother has left you some supper. Come and eat it, you look tired.'

Wiping her face with a trembling hand she shook her head. 'In a moment; I need to get out of this uniform.' She turned to go upstairs then looked back. She needed a moment or two of space, on her own.

As if understanding, he said, 'I'll wait in the kitchen, but please don't decide to run again.'

After a quick shower, she made her way downstairs again. True to his word he was sitting at the large wooden kitchen table, leafing through one of her mother's gardening catalogues. The incongruity of this made her smile and she felt the tension easing. She set the kettle to boil and turned to him. 'Are you taking up horticulture?'

He looked at her, also with a smile, 'No, but any information I can glean would be welcome to my parents. A new canine introduction to the family is playing havoc with their garden.'

She made them both coffee and came and sat down. She kept the width of the table between them, and saw that although he had noticed her action, he made no comment.

'How is everyone? Did you have a good Christmas?'

'Polite conversation won't help, Rose. We have issues much deeper than that, but I'll try to be patient. Eat your meal while I continue to broaden my knowledge.'

They were both quiet, and she tried to eat, but found it difficult to swallow. After a while, he closed the book, walked around the table and, taking her arm, moved with her into the conservatory. It was still light enough to see the profusion of early growth in the garden – spring in all its glory, and Rose was somehow uplifted by the sight. He was here with her, and appeared to want to stay, and there was hope inside her.

He sat beside her on a comfy seat and took her hand. 'Why did you lie to me? You never did intend to go to Australia. The letter was from your father.'

She was amazed. 'How do you know that?'

He smiled gently. 'Because I've been looking for you. I felt there was something wrong with the way you left, the level of your emotion, and I had to be sure. Unfortunately, I had other commitments to discharge first before I could concentrate on finding you. It turned out to be ridiculously simple in the end. Jack Fletcher had gone back to Australia to see his family for Christmas, so I asked him to help. His people, coincidentally, live north of Perth and I asked him to make enquiries about the partial return address in the city that I remembered from the back of the envelope. He found the place and the McKenna name. He paid an initial visit and then I took over by phone.'

Rose turned her head away, biting her lip.

'It was quite an interesting telephone conversation with your father. He told me a lot of things about you. Things you should have told me, like Henry Carlisle being your uncle, for a start.'

She had to maintain some dignity, so she turned back to him with a bold stare. 'Our family association was not known at the clinic for professional reasons, and you had just had an argument with him anyway—'

'And,' he interrupted her, 'you thought because of that I might not like you either? Rose, it wouldn't have made any difference, and in case you're still worried, I've spoken to Henry and made it up with him. I understand now that he was in an awkward position, and although he would have liked to help, he doubted that very little would have changed in the outcome anyway.' He began rubbing his thumb against the palm of her hand, and she found it hard to concentrate. 'I also understand that you contacted my father about my disappearance and the reasons why. No wonder my reception was so cordial. Did you realise that Jack and his cohorts were keeping watch outside; just in case I decided to go walkabout again?'

The look on her face must have given him the answer. 'Thank God they did. Jack was around to pick up the pieces when you walked out on *me*. Rose, I nearly broke apart again. I couldn't understand how or why it happened. I thought…it was so good. Mentally I managed to claw my way back, but I know I'll bear the scars for the rest of my life. Now, I need some answers – truthful ones.'

She saw the determined look on his face and knew she had to tell him. 'You needed time and space to get your control back again, that's why I didn't want a full-scale search for you. I rang your father to explain, so he could contact your office and judge if your presence was necessary. He promised me he would keep them away from you for as long as he could. Over those following days I watched you changing, coming alive again. I knew you were picking up your life once more, and you would move on.'

He let go of her hand and stood up, looking out of the window. 'It never occurred to you to do something like talk to me about it. Why? You had me talking enough about *my* problems.'

What could she say? She still didn't know his true feelings. 'I suppose I didn't want to embarrass you by being around; making you feel that you owed me something. I didn't want to be just a part-time lover, when you felt the need, so all I could do was leave.'

He turned to face her, his expression neutral. 'What makes you think I want you as a part-time lover?'

She felt mortified. Perhaps he didn't want her, or anyone at all, but if he didn't why was he still here? She now regretted her choice of words.

'You seem to have a bad opinion of me, Rose. First you think that I would run out on you without a word after a one-nightstand, and now you think I would use you casually as and when I felt the need. Then again, perhaps it's my fault for reading too much into our brief association. Was I doing that, Rose, or did I see the truth – a truth that neither of us can deny? If you want me to speak first, then I will.' He stepped closer to her. 'After what happened with Olivia, I became wary of emotional entanglements, not wanting to make promises or commitments. However, since knowing and being with you, I've found an emotion so deep and all-consuming that I can't begin to describe the enormity of the loss I felt when you left that night. A loss that has stayed with me, until now... now I'm here with you once more. I love you, Rose, and I want you with me always. I want to marry you.'

She felt the tears running down her cheeks. All these weeks when they could have been together, and all this misery – if only she'd been brave enough to stay and not run. She catapulted herself into his arms. 'I love you too, Simon. I've missed you so. It broke my heart to leave you. Why didn't you try and stop me?'

He stroked the dark hair back from her face. 'I told you. I was in too much of a daze; everything around me was collapsing again. What I thought we had found between us seemed so incredible; it gave me no warning. Before I could gather my thoughts, you were gone, but I remembered the look on your face; it was the same as I felt inside. I knew there was something wrong and I had to be sure. As badly as I wanted to chase after you, I couldn't escape from my other responsibilities. Tell me again, Rose, do you really love me?'

She took his face in her hands and kissed him. 'I love you,

Simon, and I always will. I've found a part of me I didn't know was missing until you came into my life. I want to be with you… but…'

He moved her away from him, his face now desperate. 'But what, Rose? Tell me; don't keep silent. I must know what you're thinking. We've lost so much time already through not talking.' He drew her down beside him on the seat.

Rose knew she had to be brave enough to voice her inner worries. 'I do love you, and I want to be with you; to share your life, but that's the point. You're the successful businessman again; travelling, meetings and social commitments. You say you don't want a part-time lover, well, I wouldn't want to be a part-time wife, waiting for you to arrive home for a few days before you went off again, or trying to fit in at functions making small talk to impress people.' He was about to comment but she put a finger on his lips. 'I also worry I would find myself with a moral dilemma about your wealth and lifestyle. I've had first-hand experience of how some people live in miserable conditions around the world. I know you have been incredibly generous to others less fortunate, but I'm nervous about living with double standards. I so want to be with you, to make a home and even a family, but we must be happy, or it will all fall apart.' The tears started to fall as she contemplated losing him again. 'I'm sorry, I don't know what else to say.'

He held her close. 'I understand your feelings and values, Rose, and I love you all the more because of them. It again shows me the kind of person I had come to admire, and… love. There are things I need to tell you which, I think, will answer your questions, and allay any fears. However, they might best be discussed in a less emotional atmosphere.'

Rose looked at her watch. 'Mother will be home soon as well. Where are you staying? I didn't see your car.'

He looked at her for a moment, then appeared to make a decision. 'Your mother is staying elsewhere tonight, and I loaned her my car.' He said nothing more.

Finally, the truth hit her. 'You…she… you are staying here tonight, and she is aware of this?' He just nodded. 'You talked about me, and she made the excuse to leave?' He nodded again. She didn't know what to say, whether to be angry or not.

'She loves you too, Rose; she knows you have been unhappy, but this time she felt it was different and she should not pry into your life. She understands how I feel, and I promised not to hurt you. We agreed she should take my car instead of her own. If you had seen mine still here as you arrived… well, you might have disappeared again. It's now up to you, Rose. I have a room booked in Monaghan, which your mother will use tonight, or you can drive me there and bring your mother back; but I would like to stay.'

What did she want? Rose knew all too well what it was; but if she took the step there was no way she would be able to give him up again, and there was so much left unsaid. She looked at him, taking in all the planes and hollows of the face she had come to know so well, and thought she might not see again. No, there was no way she would get through her life without him near, whatever allowances she might have to make. She saw something in the deep blue eyes; pain, anxiety, longing, and she wanted to change that to happiness and hope. Surely, they both deserved that. She reached out her hand for his. 'Yes, Simon, I would like you to stay.'

He took her in his arms and, without saying a word, just held her. He then moved her away a little. 'I could do with a drink, Rose, before…' She knew his meaning and smiled. He seemed embarrassed, which she found endearing. 'I'd like to tell you about what happened in France. I think you'll be pleased.'

Once more sitting at the kitchen table, but this time side by side, he explained to her about his father's wedding, the talk with Joanna on Christmas Eve and how lonely he had felt afterwards. She could feel the pain in him again and took his hand. He went on to detail the conversation with Justine and how he had revised his opinion of the events of all those years ago. It was, however, his description of the Christmas card which gave her an insight into the depth of his feelings, and she was so happy for him at the outcome.

'I kept hoping something like that would happen. It must have been so confusing for Joanna over these last months, but she is now confident that her safe world is still there, with you part of it. What will she make of me, Simon?' Some of her anxiety returned. There was no way she could now spoil this precious reunion.

He stroked her face and kissed her softly. 'She will love you as much as I do.' He drew her to her feet. 'Let me show you just how much.' He kissed her again and held her close to him. 'God, I need you, Rose; it's been so long.'

*

It seemed as if they had hardly slept all night, and Rose felt drained when she woke to find Simon wrapped round her. She had revelled in the feel of him again, his comforting strength and warmth. She didn't want to break the spell, but, embarrassed that her mother might suddenly come home, she wanted to be ready, washed and dressed. She moved slightly and with a groan Simon opened his eyes, and then planted a kiss on her lips.

'What's the time, sweetheart? Still early, I hope?'

His meaning was quite plain, but Rose was determined. 'If I don't get up now, I'll never be awake enough to go to work later.' She hadn't even given work a thought, but he wouldn't know that. As she left the room she looked back and saw him sitting up, staring at her with a bemused expression.

Now showered and dressed, they were once again sitting at the kitchen table. For some reason neither had eaten much at breakfast, and Simon seemed quiet.

Rose glanced at him. 'You said you wanted to talk to me today. Don't forget I have to be at work after dinner.'

For a moment she saw a shadow pass over his face, then he

turned his head and looked out at the garden. 'Perhaps we could sit outside?'

'I'll tidy up in here and then I'll join you.' She knew she was putting off the moment, for just a while longer, but couldn't help herself. She finally made some fresh coffee and took mugs out to where he was sitting on a garden bench, in the early morning sun. As she sat down, he slid an arm round her shoulders, and she smiled up at him.

'I'm ready now. It all sounds very mysterious.'

He took a deep breath. 'When I was at the flat with you, I worked on ideas I had been planning, but not then finalised. I need to explain them to you now, because they affect us.' He held her closer. 'Rose, I'm giving up Orion, or almost.' She tried to turn and look at him in amazement, but he held her still. 'Listen until I've finished. I decided I didn't want the pressure of running a large company any longer. I realised that this had been part of my problem with Joanna. I spent too little quality time with her. Amy was right. Also, being effectively a one-parent family didn't help. I only had Margaret Horton and the Gilmores to fall back on, but they all did a brilliant job for me, and I've made them aware of my gratitude. Anyway, I'm pulling my private money out of Orion and my current legal and financial senior managers will take over the day-to-day running. I have agreed to act as an independent paid consultant, should they need me. I'm not intending to set up another company; I'm just going to play around with private deals. I have a very good and trusted associate in this respect, and we already have several ideas.

The new foundation is taking off in a big way. We've decided to call it the Carlton House Music Foundation. I'll be putting most of my time into its first year, but after that I intend to just have my name as the patron. The people already in place can run it well enough without me. There have already been a lot of enquiries from the musical world wanting to set out what they have to offer in every genre, from orchestras, music schools, summer workshops, small clubs, theatres, you name it. They can see the benefit in having their details made available from one central source to anyone who might have an interest. From initial canvassing we have started to receive interest from students and other connected parties. We're even considering organising open days or weekends at Carlton House through the summer holidays for face-to-face meetings. I think it's going to turn into something quite important.'

Rose could hear the pleasure in his voice, and she was happy for him. Perhaps its success would go some way towards easing the guilt she sensed he still felt surrounding the tragic events which had brought it about. There was something, however, that she must ask him.

'Simon, I'm not quite sure how to put this, but I know you've told me what Amy meant to you, and I'm sure none of us will ever forget her but…'

He turned her face to him. 'You're quite correct that she will not be forgotten,' he watched as the dark eyes closed, 'but I do not retain any feelings towards her that could come between us now, or at any time in the future. I'm just sad that a life of promise was not fulfilled, but I'm sure you have seen even more painful examples of this. Life has to be dealt with, good or bad. We now have a chance of something spectacularly good and we must cherish every day.'

He held her close and kissed her. When he let her go, he could see the relief in her eyes, but he needed to continue reinforcing how he intended his life to change.

'I've toyed with the idea of doing some writing about economics, either by myself or with a financial journalist I know quite well. It might not happen, but it's something else to consider. Also, in a strange coincidence, over the holiday I met up with an old college associate who now lives in France. He runs a business school in Paris, and he put an idea to me which I could be interested in. He suggested that I might like to act as a lecturer, not full-time, unless I wanted to.' He picked up her hand and played absentmindedly with her fingers. 'There are lots of uncertainties and they need evaluating, but it's work which would keep me at home.' He paused. 'I now need to ask you something, Rose.'

The tone of his voice, hesitant, unsure, surprised her. 'Of course.'

'Would it be hard for you to give up your career? You seem to enjoy it.'

Rose knew her answer was important. 'I needed employment to earn money, as we all do, and yes, I do enjoy nursing, that's why I chose to do it. I'm working through a maternity leave contract which will finish at the end of this month. I've been offered a further contract but…I'm not sure what I want to do yet.' She had thought she might take up her father's offer of a visit to him and possibly working in Australia for a while, but now was not the time to voice that idea.

'I wondered if you might still wish to become involved in your humanitarian work.'

'Not any longer; after Haiti I decided I had perhaps done enough.'

'Yet you seemed keen to focus your day on work earlier this morning. You might find it hard to leave behind.'

The voice was quiet, and he didn't look at her. So this was the reason for his preoccupation. Reaching out for his hand, she said in a soft voice, '*You* are the only thing that matters to me now.'

He turned her face up to his. 'Rose, will you marry me and come to France, so that we can be near to Joanna, and help me with her future? As I've said, I don't need to strive any longer to build another business. I've seen where that can lead. I want to concentrate on family; that's why I intend to do as much of my work from home as I can. If I did need to be away, you can come with me. We will be near enough for you to visit your mother, and she can come to us at any time. We could always go and see your father, too, and spend some time there. Rose, I want us to be a family and enjoy our life together. I want a proper home with a wife I adore and, if you are willing, a place to nurture our children.

You are now the centre of my world, but I want to know that you would be happy. That is the most important thing. You're an intelligent woman and I don't want to stifle that. I'm sure there will be many other things which would be of interest to you, and I will encourage you in anything you want to do.' He took her face between his hands. 'I love you, and I just need you with me, Rose. I know I'll never be whole again without you by my side.'

She looked into his deep blue eyes and knew there was only one answer. 'Simon, I love you, and I want to take care of you, and I would like to be part of your world, if you will have me.' She placed her mouth over his to seal the bargain.

When he let her go, he reached into the pocket of his jacket and drew out the bracelet. 'You remember on that dreadful day when I was late, this was the reason. I spent ages trying to find the right gift for you. I was going to ask you to come to France with me for Christmas and I intended giving this to you on Christmas morning.' He took her wrist and placed the bracelet around it.

The morning sun glinted on the stones, and Rose traced them with one finger and then looked up at him. 'It looks very expensive. This is what I mean, Simon, about…about your lifestyle. These must be rubies.' She watched as he raised his eyes heavenward.

'I've already said I know all about your views, my love, and you will no doubt be pleased to know they are not rubies. If you want to be particular, they are rhodolite garnet set in rose gold. Just be a good girl and enjoy them. They are given with love and a great deal of pleasure.' He placed a finger under her chin and turned her face up to him. 'Please.'

She sensed how much he cared that she should like his gift, and in truth she had never had such a beautiful one, but it was the giver who mattered, and always would. 'Thank you, Simon. I will wear it with pride and love.'

He gave her his first smile of the day and wagged a finger at her. 'You know, I think, earlier on, you were just worried about your mother coming home and finding us still in bed.'

'Don't be silly. I'm over thirty.' She couldn't, however, stop the heat staining her cheeks, which, of course, he noticed.

'Why, Sister McKenna, I do believe you're embarrassed at the idea.' He stroked her arm. 'It was rather good, wasn't it?'

His eyes were now alive with mischief, and she thought how marvellous it was to see; and he was right, it had been wonderful, both of them grateful to be together again. Then a thought struck her. 'If we're going to have all these children you mentioned, we will have to start pretty quick. My clock is ticking.'

He laughed out loud. 'There's no problem with that, my pet, we can start as soon as you like.'

Rose felt her insides melting at the look in his eyes; then she heard the sound of an approaching car. 'It looks as if Mother has stayed away from her garden as long as she could.' She pulled Simon up from the seat. 'Let's go and tell her the news.'

Chapter Twenty-Eight

Paris, June 2011

Simon stood just inside the sitting room at his father's villa, looking out over the terrace to the garden where the wedding guests were still mingling, some sitting in garden furniture, others under the gazebo consuming the last of the refreshments.

He was glad of these few quiet moments; it helped him put in place the various high points of the last few busy weeks. After breaking the good news to a delighted Maureen McKenna, and in a phone call to Patrick, he had suggested to a crestfallen Rose that it might be best if he returned to London, then Paris, to deal with his commitments, leaving her to work out the rest of her contract without distractions. She could then join him, and they would be able to enjoy free time together. He also wanted to speak to his father and Justine about his plans and discuss with them how best to broach the new developments with Joanna.

After being back in France for nearly a week, he finally made his decision and suggested Joanna might like to take a trip to the countryside with Alphonse and maybe take a walk and find somewhere to eat. Resting for a moment on a broken tree stump, he attempted to turn the conversation round to how she was enjoying life in France.

'Grandpa tells me you really like the new house, and I think you seem to like the new school. Are you happy, Joanna? Do you like living here?'

She took a moment or two to answer, rubbing one hand against the dog's curly head as he sat beside her. 'It's better than it used to be. I like being with Grandpa and Grandma and I also have Alphonse, which is super. You have been here as well.' She looked up at him. 'Will you be going away as much as before?'

'No, I won't, Joanna. In fact, I'm thinking of coming to live in France, too.'

She turned to him with a bright smile. 'Will you? Are you going to live with us?'

'No, but in fact there's something I want to tell you and I hope you will like it.' He took a deep breath. 'I have been seeing a very nice lady, and I would like her to come and live with me. We would get married and she would then be your new mummy. Would you like that?' He watched her closely, trying to gauge any reaction.

'Is she a really nice lady?'

The small face was curious, but he sensed a slight anxiety in the tone of voice, so he smiled at her and said, 'Oh yes, very nice; you know her already. Do you remember Sister Rose?'

Before he could say any more, Joanna leapt up and danced around. Alphonse, sensing her excitement, started barking. 'Sister Rose will be my new mummy! Do you mean it?'

He just nodded, and then without warning she wrapped her arms around his neck. 'Oh, that would be just perfect! Will you have babies? I would love that!'

He tried hard not to laugh and wondered how he would describe this conversation later to Rose. 'Well, we must think about that, but maybe. So, you would be happy if she became part of our family?'

'Oh, yes please. When is she coming? Will there be another wedding? What will she wear?'

The questions went on for days. The idea of having a new

mother, and it being Sister Rose, was only made more exciting by the realisation that she would have yet more grandparents. This threw the child into such a frenzy of delight that she was difficult to control. Her bedroom floor became littered with sketches of wedding dresses, and he guessed there might have to be some diplomatic discussion as to whose views would prevail.

When, two weeks later, Rose was due to arrive at the airport, his private emotional welcome was hijacked by the whole family wanting to be there to greet her. He was warmed by the fact that, whatever her own personal desires, she accepted the unexpected boisterous welcome with good-natured amusement, desperately trying to disentangle herself from Joanna's suffocating hugs in order to allow him the briefest brush of her lips. He was sure his eyes must have held the same look of rueful suffering; the longing to be alone together unavoidably held at bay for the moment.

It was decided that they would occupy a suite at Simon's usual hotel rather than stay with Justine and Emile. This would leave them time to be alone and free to make plans and arrangements. As soon as the wedding date of the first weekend in June was fixed, Justine tentatively suggested the Rose Garden at the Rodin Museum as a possible venue for the civil ceremony. After viewing the area neither Simon nor Rose herself could envisage a more perfect location. It was difficult to believe that there was such an oasis of calm and quiet so close to the bustle of the city.

The next main consideration was where they would make their home. Even though his father's district of the city was pleasant enough, Simon preferred, if possible, to live completely out of Paris altogether. It was considered likely that Joanna would stay with her grandparents during the school week but transfer to them at weekends and holidays, although there would no doubt evolve a permanent reshuffle of accommodation. After many hours of discussion, he had managed to convince Rose that his requirement for a sizeable property was not being ostentatious. He listed practical requirements of a place for him to work, a possible private room for Rose herself, and enough bedrooms for Joanna, guests and children. At this point he had roared with laughter at her expression, and any further discussion had been interrupted for some while. His most difficult problem was to convince her that staff would be required, ideally living on the premises. After what he knew, to her, must have been a lot of soul-searching, she had finally agreed that it made sense. Remarkably it was Rose who found the ideal property, fifteen or so miles south of the city. It was a large farmhouse, recently extended and renovated, standing in its own extensive grounds, with various outbuildings which they decided might be used for further accommodation or other uses. After spending a day being shown round by the agent, they both agreed it would be ideal; and all the hard work to bring it up to modern requirements having already been done was a bonus. Simon could tell that Rose was relieved that the thought of living in such a large property was offset by the fact that it still managed to retain its homely atmosphere. Once purchased, they had decided on one or two further alterations, which were now complete, and had spent many hours visiting antique fairs and markets to fill the spaces with suitable furniture over and above the various items taken out of storage in England. Jack had insisted on visiting the property and, with a pointed look at Simon, demanded various security features be installed. At Rose's suggestion her mother was asked to come to France to assist with ideas to renovate the grounds.

Patrick had by then arrived from Australia and joined Maureen in a suite at the hotel. The rest of the accommodation began to slowly fill with other wedding guests as the day approached, culminating last night in a splendid dinner for all. Simon had initially invited Dimitri Orloff but, on further discussion between them, they acknowledged that awkward questions surrounding the Christmas visit to Joanna were possible, and regretfully it was thought better for him not to attend. During their various conversations, both business and personal, Simon had observed that although Dimitri seemed pleased to hear about Joanna, Rose and wedding plans, in a strange way he had rather brushed aside Simon's latest updates on the outcome of the whole difficult period for Orion. An open-ended invitation was issued for them all to visit Istanbul whenever it was possible.

Today the weather had been warm and pleasant, perfect for the ceremony. Simon knew he would always remember it as a day that had given him more pleasure than he could ever remember. Rose had been insistent that only the two sets of parents attend the actual ceremony, and in this he thought she had been perfectly correct. It created a more personal and intimate atmosphere. Indeed, throughout the formalities all that could be heard were the sounds of bees and other insects amongst the floral magnificence all around them, and the perfume was heady in the light breeze.

In deference to the colourful surroundings, the ladies had obviously decided not to try and compete, as both Justine and Maureen had chosen to wear pastel colours. Rose looked breathtakingly elegant in a sleeveless calf-length cream silk dress, worn under a fine lace jacket, her dark hair piled into curls threaded through with pearls, a wedding present from her parents. She carried a small posy of cream rosebuds, and at times her solitaire diamond engagement ring caught the sunlight and sparkled with its own fire. Joanna had decided to reprise her white dress, but this time trimmed with cream silk, and she wore a circle of cream rosebuds in her hair. Now aged seven, he could see the growing maturity in her as she performed the same duties as she had for her grandparents.

After the ceremony they drove back to the villa, where Emile formally welcomed the waiting guests and asked them to congratulate the happy couple with a champagne toast. Even Alphonse was there, sporting a silk bow around his neck – although the life of its pristine condition was likely to be limited.

Simon let his eyes wander around the garden. Gerry Bristow and his wife Zena were talking with Charles and Stuart and their respective wives. When Simon had broken the news to him,

Gerry had immediately issued a dinner invitation for him and Rose. Simon had been puzzled at Rose's apparent nervousness at the coming meeting. Finally, he understood. She had heard a lot of talk about college education and business schools, but, as Patrick McKenna had told him, Rose had made the decision to forego university and start nursing training immediately after 'A' levels. He could see that she somehow considered herself inferior in some way, having opted for vocational training, and worried that others would be less than impressed and that it might reflect on him. Knowing her well enough by now he knew it would be no use trying to convince her that she was his wife, he loved her and didn't care what anyone else thought. In any case, her own studies had probably been far more onerous, and arguably more important. She just needed to build her confidence, and so it had proved. Although Zena Bristow was younger, both women had initially appeared slightly in awe of each other, but as the evening progressed Simon was pleased to see them relax as they chatted together. He was glad he had kept his silence and not risked embarrassing her by speaking out on the matter.

His gaze moved on to where Jack Fletcher was talking with Rose's friend Gwenny Thomas. He had been amused to see that the two had paired off almost at once and he had a suspicion that Jack was quite smitten. He himself had liked her immediately; blonde, bouncy and outgoing, a complete foil for Rose. He had, however, been slightly intrigued by her obvious scrutiny of him at first, but then it seemed as if she had reached a decision and he had passed some sort of test. Gwenny mentioned that she had just started a nursing recruitment agency in Cardiff, and he was aware that she and Rose had been discussing the possibility of enlarging on the idea. He knew he would honour his promise to help Rose with anything she might wish to involve herself with outside the marriage, but, somewhat selfishly, he hoped it might not take up too much of her time.

Under the gazebo both sets of parents were sitting with Uncle

Henry and Aunt Moira. The likeness between the twin sisters was obvious now, but Simon felt that Rose perhaps took more after her father, both in looks and temperament. It must take a certain amount of calm authority to command ocean-going vessels, and this calmness was apparent in his daughter. Since her arrival in France, it had been noticeable how Joanna was less excitable, and responded to Rose's quiet presence. Simon remembered his own experience during those days with her in London. He had been so sure then that she was the only one he needed beside him, and he would do everything in his power to keep it so.

He had admitted to himself that over this last year he had changed, particularly these last few months. He no longer felt the compulsive drive which, although it had enabled him to create his business, had also kept him a prisoner of his own success, always striving for more. He now understood the pressure he had lived with for so long. Amy had shown him that relaxation was possible for him, and he could have time with family. He now wanted to begin enjoying that in his life with Rose.

He looked over at her now, as she moved from group to group, with Joanna swinging from her hand, and Alphonse trotting sedately behind. He pushed back the sleeve of his dark suit and glanced at his watch; time to go. They were driving down to the farmhouse, to finally settle into their new home and he couldn't wait to be there. Joanna had at first demanded to accompany them, but some quiet persuasion from both sets of grandparents had saved the day. On the spur of the moment Simon had suggested that perhaps a house-warming party for the family could take place the following weekend. He knew that Rose would understand.

As if sensing his gaze, she looked up at him, and leaving Joanna with her grandparents, moved towards him. His beautiful wife, and how he loved her, now more than ever. He would take the best care of her he could, especially after the wonderful news she had given him this morning.

'Is it time to go?'

'Yes, I think so. I must admit I'll be glad to relax and get out of all this finery.' He tugged at his grey silk waistcoat, a concession to one of Joanna's sartorial ideas.

Rose smiled at him. 'I feel the same. I'll just go upstairs and fetch my jacket and bag.'

He grasped her arm. 'Ask Jeanette to run up there, Rose. It's been a long day for you.'

She looked at him and stroked his face. 'I'm not an invalid. Having a baby is perfectly natural, you know.'

'It may be, but I'm not taking any chances.' He wrapped an arm around her still slim waist. 'You're too important to me... both of you. I happen to love my beautiful wife, Madame Rose Deveraux, and I can't wait to be with you in our new home, together.' He watched the emotion in the dark eyes and again felt it flow through him, as on that first occasion. He kissed her, and didn't care who saw them, then let her go. He could see he would have this tussle with her for a while yet. If all went well, he would soon hold their child in his arms, and something he had always hoped for would finally be complete.

*

It was actually well over an hour before they finally left. Everyone, it seemed, was having such an enjoyable time that no-one wanted to bring the festivities to a conclusion.

After yet again promising Joanna there would be another party at the weekend, Simon eventually drove the Mercedes out of the Paris suburbs, and onto the country roads. It was only a few miles now to the farmhouse.

He gave a chuckle. 'I'm glad we didn't take up Justine's offer of staying over for the night. You know what would have happened, it would have been lunchtime tomorrow before we left. I'm looking forward to a quiet hour or two and treating myself to a drink. Only one glass of champagne on my wedding day doesn't seem quite right.'

He heard an answering laugh from Rose. 'You should be so lucky. I only had a couple of sips, just to keep up the pretence.'

'Mm…I never thought of that. Perhaps I should abstain for the next few months to keep you company.' His voice then became serious. 'Rose, I'm sorry, I didn't mean to involve us in any entertaining just yet, but I had to…'

He sensed the dark head turn his way and knew the look in her eyes would be sympathetic.

'I realised why, Simon. You were afraid that Joanna might feel she was being left out, now I was here. Just give her time and she'll become more comfortable with all these changes.'

He reached for her hand and kissed her fingers. 'I knew you would understand. I love you, Rose.' Looking through the windscreen at the curving road bordered by hedgerows, he said, 'Not long now…*what the hell!*'

'Simon, that van…!'

*

Smiling to himself at the prospect of ever seeing his contented guests depart, Emile went inside to take the call.

Standing in the hallway, he heard the voice speaking on the other end of the telephone but could not believe what he was hearing. He suddenly found himself shaking and had to lean against the wall for support.

'You are sure? There is no doubt? Both? Oh God!' The voice continued but he was almost past understanding. 'I see… yes, yes, of course I'll… I'll see them when they come.'

As he dropped the receiver on the hall table his eyes caught the reflection in the mirror above. He didn't recognise the face looking back at him. It was the face of an old man, sorrow etched in every line. How much more pain could he endure?

At the sound of pattering feet, he turned. A small form, surrounded by clouds of frothy white, raced towards him from the sunlight.

'Grandma Justine says you need to come. Uncle Jack has to leave now.'

Emile felt his legs give way and he fell to his knees, almost in supplication. How could he ever find the courage to tell her; he would never have the words. She came to a halt in front of him.

'Grandpa, why are you crying?'

Chapter Twenty-Nine

La Ferme Etoilée, south of Paris –January 2021

The elderly man and young woman stood just inside the small stand of trees on the top of the rise above the farmhouse.

'Thank you for not laughing, or being angry, Grandpa. Robert wanted to come with me, but I said I needed to talk to you first, alone.'

Emile pulled the scarf tighter around his neck and put his hands in his overcoat pockets. The wind was cold, and he'd left his hat in the house. He'd been too preoccupied with trying to work out the reasons for this suggested stroll. He'd had the vague notion it was all arranged for a purpose; but he'd never imagined this!

'Perhaps you thought you could twist an old man around your fingers better on your own.'

Joanna grasped his arm. 'No, Grandpa, I would never do that about something… so important. I love and respect you too much.'

'So you love and respect me, eh, but you're still prepared to give me a shock like this, and why come up here?'

He turned to look at this girl who meant so much to him. Nearly seventeen now, in his eyes she was becoming prettier each day, her dark hair standing out against the cream fur-lined parka. From the start, he'd wondered if his need for a close interaction with her had been born out of the sense that she was the daughter he'd never had. The stillborn girl delivered to Helene all those years ago had been a sadness neither had wanted to speak about, to anyone, but Simon's arrival had mellowed that loss. As a daughter-in-law there had never been much personal contact with Olivia. To him she had always seemed a rather brittle person, with no warmth, and he hadn't been surprised at the eventual outcome. The difference with Rose had been so apparent. He'd known from the start she would be good for Simon, Joanna – and the whole family – but it wasn't to be. Even now after all these years, he made sure he kept the lingering sadness he still felt, well hidden, or thought he did. Yet, with that special closeness to Joanna, he had sensed that she understood, but would never intrude on his inner dark places.

'I love it here, Grandpa. I always feel happy when I'm here. Daddy loved it too, as soon as he knew the name. He called it Star Farmhouse and told me he would take me out at night and show me all the constellations – just as you did.'

Emile had felt that sense of déja vu as he had sat in the garden with her all those years ago, remembering when he and Simon had done the same on their camping trips. Now there were three stars on the tree each Christmas as reminders.

Joanna gazed around her. 'Do you remember that week when everybody came back, and we all planted these trees? It was so much fun and look how they've grown.'

He had always marvelled at the extraordinary bond that still seemed to exist between all those who had been at the villa that dreadful day. Everyone had remained in touch with each other over all these years – like some sort of private club.

How they had made it through that first night he would never know. The aura of shock had been like a solid weight settling over everyone. Jack Fletcher had immediately abandoned his plans for returning to London and had taken control. He and Patrick dealt with all the officials who arrived at the house in those first hours, and then the avalanche of press. Jack had demanded to be taken to the accident site – as he said later, he needed to be sure that nothing suspicious or untoward was involved, although he considered it unlikely. He and Patrick had also taken it upon themselves to identify the bodies. Emile had felt unable to do so; in fact, he had ceased to function at all for several days. It was good fortune that Henry Carlisle and Gwenny Thomas were still with them, as their medical care was called upon in any number of ways for several days.

Joanna had swayed between bouts of uncontrollable tears and pale-faced silence for about a week, and then suddenly she seemed to gather herself, and acted as a comfort to others, including himself. This had continued over the years, even until today, and he had been amazed at her store of resilience and inner strength. She had lost so much, so quickly; childhood innocence and dreams shattered in a moment, like the slamming of a door.

The autopsies and inquests had later been endured. The van driver, himself injured, was judged to have been at fault, admitting he was late for a delivery and consulting paperwork strewn around his cab rather than concentrating on his driving. He had hit the Mercedes broadside at speed, despite Simon appearing to have attempted to swerve out of his way, but there had been nowhere to go on that narrow road. The car was forced into the ditch – and stumps of previously felled trees and remains of old metal posts from a former road sign did the damage – but it was thought to have been instantaneous. If a group of cyclists out for a ride on that fine summer evening hadn't come upon the scene it might not have been discovered so quickly.

There had been a joint funeral, private and for the family only. However, so many people made it clear they wanted to express their condolences, a reception was later arranged with, at Emile's wish, the request that those attending make a donation to designated charities, amongst them the Carlton House Music

Foundation and MSF. The amount eventually raised had been staggering, and also humbling.

Sir Arthur Dunne had attended, not only with his wife, but also his grandson, Robert, and Emile had been pleased that for once Joanna would have some companionship of her own age. Since the terrible events, he had become concerned that, apart from school, she was growing up in a home environment populated by older people. Justine's young maid, Jeanette, had been assigned to act almost as a companion – rather like Amy Watson – and he had been relieved to see this worked well.

During that first visit Joanna and Robert had appeared inseparable and he was aware that they had kept in touch thereafter. Perhaps it was about then that he had started to notice the gradual change in her, not only as she became older in years but also matured in other ways. Her schoolwork commitment was exemplary, and she was rewarded by frequent trips to London to stay either with Jack Fletcher, now married to Gwenny, with two young children of their own, or the Carlisles. As an extended family there were annual trips to see Patrick in Australia and also Maureen, in Ireland, who actually spent a good part of the year in France, tending the now magnificent garden at the farmhouse. When not required by the family, the property was sometimes rented out as a high-end summer holiday let. Emile had blocked any sale, and he sensed Joanna felt happy at this. As a couple, they often spent time here; the journey along the country road now eased as nature reclaimed and softened the scars of the accident site.

'Grandpa, you're so quiet. Please talk to me.'

'What do you want me to say? You know already what any sensible response from an adult would be. You're both too young to consider engagement, let alone marriage, and neither of you have completed your studies or formulated a career. You might feel differently, as the years go by, and could meet someone else. You should know this already.'

'Yes, Grandpa, we do, and we have thought about it. After I

came to France to live and Robert found out, he wrote to me and we have kept in touch ever since; you and Daddy knew about it. You were thoughtful enough to invite him to come with us on our last trip to see Grandpa Patrick. From the start we both found it was good to share thoughts with someone of our own age. I had Mr Floppy to talk to, but it never gave me any real answers. Robert was unhappy about what was happening with his parents and their talk of a divorce. After his mother left, he said his father was too tied up in his work to understand that he and his brother needed to have time with him, and they felt lonely. I could relate to that and I think he knew I understood. It's why we've become so close; we needed each other.'

Emile heard these words with regret. How easy it was for adults to leave children wandering alone in their own wilderness. 'Joanna, you know your father loved you and always did the best for you, and things would have improved even more had…'

'Yes, I know, Grandpa. Thinking about all the things that Amy and Mummy Rose told me, I realised how unhappy I must have made him, but despite that, he still loved me. I wanted to show him how much he meant to me and try to be the best I could for him…and I still do. After you and Uncle Charles explained all the arrangements made for me, although I didn't always understand everything, I knew nothing mattered other than Daddy had always been just that, and always would, and how much I loved him. When you told me how he had taken care to provide for my future, I felt even more ashamed of the way I had behaved. I now want to get top grades so I can do my fashion design course and work with Grandma Justine. I will do the very best I can to make him proud of me.' She turned to him, and he saw tears in the dark eyes. 'I'm so pleased you and Grandma have temporarily closed the villa and decided to live out here, letting everyone, including Robert, come as well. I want to keep you all safe. I have my other grandparents, and so many wonderful uncles and aunts, but you are extra special. This horrible virus frightens me sometimes. I couldn't bear to lose you too.'

He patted her arm and attempted a smile. 'I'll try and stick around a little longer, but you realise that this pandemic problem will somewhat affect the plans you've made?'

'Yes, I know. Robert was fortunate to be able to begin his university electronics course over here in Paris, but it's awkward and nothing's certain at the moment. He's finally persuaded his grandfather to allow his brother Andy to come and join my school, but I don't know when this will happen now. Robert says that when he's qualified, he wants to start his own business. Uncle Dimitri said he might be prepared to help with this.'

'What! You've spoken about it with *him*?'

'No, not all of it. In one of our video calls, he asked us about our careers and when Robert mentioned his idea, he said he might be prepared to help. He's an absolute sweetie.'

Emile considered that if Orloff became involved with any scheme, Robert might find him less of a 'sweetie' and more a strict demanding partner. When Orloff had been informed of the tragedy he had immediately appeared in Paris and ran a temporary office from the city for nearly two months. During this time there were many meetings between them, but also with McDonald, Mannion and Gerry Bristow. Orloff had intimated he would be prepared to place business with Orion and act as a backstop for any shortfalls whilst the intended changes were made, but he drove a hard, although fair, bargain.

It had also been necessary to sort out more personal and painful problems. Although, after Olivia's death, at Charles' insistence, Simon had made a simple will, benefitting Joanna and appointing guardians, this had not yet been amended in respect of Rose or any decision as to the permanency of their move to France. The full implications were, therefore, complicated and time-consuming, with both English and French lawyers involved. Patrick and Maureen had been kept fully involved in all the negotiations, and in view of this Emile considered it only right that, in a private meeting, he made them aware of the true circumstances surrounding Joanna. It transpired that Rose had already told them and they had taken the view that Joanna was their granddaughter, no matter what, and would act accordingly. He then found the courage to make them aware of the notation in Rose's autopsy report which had been pointed out to him by Henry Carlisle. He could see that they felt the same level of sadness, and for a while Maureen had to seek consolation from her husband.

'I appreciate you making us aware of all this, Emile,' Patrick turned to him, his arm still around his wife's shoulders. 'It gives us comfort to be able to share, just for a moment, in their planned future.'

Emile then decided to also show them the handwritten list he had found amongst Simon's papers. It contained half a dozen Christian names, two of which were circled; 'Henri Patrice' and 'Amelie Rose'. He noted from their faces that they, like him, wondered which one it might have been. A few days later he gladly agreed to Maureen's wish for some permanent remembrance at the farmhouse, known only to the three of them.

As the financial meetings had progressed and it became obvious that Joanna would be well provided for, it had begun to worry Emile. In assuming the role of her official guardian, he knew that there might come a time when this would attract the wrong sort of men into her life. He would have to keep an alert and watchful eye on any situation - and was this now the beginning?

As if suspecting his thoughts, Joanna went on, 'We thought it might be better for Robert to have independent financing, rather than you thinking he was trying to make use of me. As you've explained, I have to wait until I'm much older before I can use any monies, and I wouldn't do so without your guidance anyway. No doubt if he asked, Robert's own grandfather would be able to help. You've told me that the farmhouse will belong to me one day and Robert and I know this is where we would like to live; to make it the family home Mummy Rose and Daddy always intended. There is already accommodation provided for the staff, but the other outbuildings could be converted into an office for Robert and a workshop for me.'

He felt her watching him. 'Mummy Rose and Daddy are here, aren't they, Grandpa?'

She deserved to know the truth. 'Yes, I came one evening and scattered their ashes in the garden. This was where they were going to start their life together, so I just completed the journey for them. That's why I never wanted it sold.'

Coming close to him, she held his arm. 'It never will be, Grandpa.' She kissed him on the cheek. 'I would like to carry on that journey with Robert, but with your blessing.'

He sighed. 'An informal engagement when you're seventeen I will approve, but anything else… well, that might take longer than you think.' He felt her snuggle into his arms and relished the warmth and vitality she brought to him.

'JoJo?' The voice held a trace of diffidence and anxiety.

They both turned and Joanna held up her hand. 'It's all right, Rob. I'm fine.'

Emile regarded the young man standing a few feet away, the strong wind ruffling his blonde hair. He had obviously been worried about her and felt it necessary to disobey his orders. As their eyes met, he saw determination in the face – not arrogance or defiance – but just a certainty of doing the right thing. Yes, this boy might well do.

He looked down at Joanna, still clinging onto his arm. 'As your legs are younger than ours, why don't you go back to the house and tell Grandma we're on our way in for lunch? Your old dog had the right idea, keeping out of the cold and staying close to the kitchen range.'

She placed kisses on both male cheeks and raced off down through the moon gate arch in the garden wall, disappearing into the garden itself, already showing signs of spring foliage.

Emile took Robert's arm and began walking down the slope. 'Well, young man, as you seem keen to take my granddaughter away from me, suppose you start trying to convince me why you think it would be such a good idea.'

 **Matador**

For exclusive discounts on Matador titles,
sign up to our occasional newsletter at
troubador.co.uk/bookshop